The Surplus Girls' Orphans

Polly Heron has worked as a librarian specialising in work with schools and children, an infant teacher, a carer and a cook. She lives in Llandudno in North Wales with her husband and two rescue cats, but her writing is inspired by her Mancunian roots. She enjoys reading, gardening, needlework and cooking and she loves living by the sea.

Also by Polly Heron

The Surplus Girls

POLLY HERON

The Surplus Girls' Orphans

CORVUS

Published in paperback in Great Britain in 2021 by Corvus,
an imprint of Atlantic Books Ltd.

10 9 8 7 6 5 4 3 2 1

A CIP catalogue record for this book is available from the British Library.

Paperback ISBN: 978 1 78649 969 1
E-book ISBN: 978 1 78649 970 7

Printed and bound by CPI Group (UK) Ltd, Croydon, CR0 4YY

Corvus
An imprint of Atlantic Books Ltd
Ormond House
26–27 Boswell Street
London
WC1N 3JZ

www.corvus-books.co.uk

To Vivienne,
wherever you are

Chapter One

MOLLY FOLDED OVER the tops of the cone-shaped white paper bags, gathering them in front of her on the counter. 'That's tuppence ha'penny, please, Mrs Preston.'

'There you go, love.'

Taking the proffered tanner, Molly opened the till, dropping the coin into the little wooden compartment with the other silver sixpences and sliding the change up the smooth sides of other boxes into her palm before counting it into Mrs Preston's hand.

'Your Nora's children are lucky to have a generous grandma like you.'

She wasn't buttering Mrs Preston up, even though she intended to ask for a donation. It was the simple truth. Mrs Preston's grandchildren were presented with a quarter of dolly mixtures each – each! – every Saturday afternoon.

'Aye, well, you can't take it with you,' said Mrs Preston.

Molly beamed. She couldn't have hoped for a better opening. 'Then I wonder—'

'What's this box for?' Mrs Preston prodded one of the collecting-boxes.

'Upton's is collecting for the orphans.'

'At St Anthony's? Why's that, then? No one from your family works there, do they?'

'No, but we're all used to seeing the children round and about in their grey uniforms, aren't we? Someone told me they're doing maypole dancing in the orphanage playground on Monday, so I asked to see Mrs Rostron – she's the superintendent – and asked if Upton's could provide sweets – you know, to make the occasion a little more festive.'

'Why have you drawn a barber's pole on't box?'

Molly laughed. 'That's not a barber's pole. It's meant to be a maypole. So much for my artistic skills! I'm asking folk if they wouldn't mind popping in a farthing or a ha'penny if they can spare it, to buy sweets for the maypole dancers.'

'As a reward.'

'That's right; and the other box is for sweets for the rest of the orphans.'

'That's a kind thought of yours, Molly, and I'm sure it was your thought, not Mr Upton's. Here's a penny.'

'A whole penny? I don't want you to think I'm being cheeky.'

'Take it, love, and I'll leave it to you to decide which box it goes in or whether you split it between the two.'

'Thank you. I appreciate it – and so will the children.'

'Well, if you can't help your fellow man…' Mrs Preston slipped her bags of dolly mixtures into her wicker basket and left the shop, setting the brass bell jingling above the door.

Molly considered, then dropped the penny into the plain box. Folk seemed readier to donate a bit of copper into the maypole box and, yes, it would be nice to reward the young dancers for their efforts, but it didn't feel right to leave out the others, which, let's face it, was most of them. It was Mr Upton who had decreed there must be two boxes – well, no, what he had said was that the money should be just for the dancers, but Molly had got round that by adding the second box.

It might be the tail-end of April, but it was as hot as the height of June. Would it stay like this for the maypole dancing on Monday afternoon? She pulled down the blind on the side-window, where sunshine glared through, putting the bootlaces and broken chunks of inferior chocolate on the far-thing tray in danger of gluing themselves together. The sugar mice already had a sheen on them. The shop's twin smells of wood and sugar thickened the hot air.

With a lull between customers, Molly quickly assembled a couple of dozen paper bags. Fold, fold, twist, flatten. She could do it in her sleep. She had been doing it in her sleep since she left school. She had thought, while she was away down south during the war, that when she returned home, she wouldn't be happy in Upton's any more, would need work that was more stimulating; but that had been before her life had changed for ever. When she finally came home, it had been a relief to be invited back to Upton's. It was somewhere safe, familiar, undemanding; a place where she could, with no effort, behave normally on the outside even while she was reeling with shock and despair on the inside.

It was nigh on three and a half years since peace had been declared. Her unhappiness had subsided into a lingering ache tucked away in a corner of her heart. Sometimes she searched the faces of people in the street, looking for a sign, a clue, a flicker of something in their eyes, a brief twist of sorrow about their lips. Pretty well everybody had suffered at least one loss, thanks to the Great War, but were there other people who kept a special corner of their hearts for a grief they could never share with the world? She couldn't be the only one – could she?

The bell danced as the door opened. Dora came in, her hated curls bubbling out from beneath her cloche hat. Her face was all smiles as she clung to Harry's arm. He was beaming his head off too.

'I know we're not meant to barge in on you while you're at work,' said Dora, 'but I couldn't wait. Look!' She let go of Harry. 'Harry's bought me a ring.'

She thrust out her hand. With a delighted exclamation, Molly caught her fingers and drank in the sight of three dark red stones in a line.

'They're only garnets,' said Harry.

'Don't say "only",' Molly chided. 'It's beautiful. It suits you, Dora. Did you choose it or did Harry surprise you?'

Dora gazed at it lovingly, cradling her left hand in her right. 'We chose it together. Well, I chose it, really, but Harry agreed.'

'I took her to Millington's.' Harry puffed out his chest.

'They were ever so discreet,' said Dora. 'The man took Harry to one side to ask about prices and then he sat us beside the counter while he brought out a tray covered in velvet.' She pouted. 'I'd intended to spend all afternoon trying on every single ring, but I saw this straight away and—'

'Goodbye to playing with all the other rings.' Lifting the counter-flap, Molly came through and hugged her cousin. 'You got engaged on Valentine's Day – and now you've got your ring. It's one excitement after another.'

'We're not like you and Norris,' said Dora, 'being sensible, saving every penny. We both wanted a party when we got engaged and we both wanted me to have a ring.'

Molly would have liked a ring too, but it was way too late to say so. Besides, what girl wanted to ask for a ring? It wouldn't have felt dignified. It wouldn't have felt romantic.

'We're older than you,' she said. 'It's not as exciting when you're older.'

'Blimey, Molly, you make yourself sound ancient.' Dora giggled. 'You're twenty-seven, not ninety-seven.'

'Oy, you.' Molly pretended to slap her. 'Stop yelling my age from the rooftops.'

'There's only us here,' said Dora, 'and Harry's family now, as good as.'

The door opened and they all looked round.

'Here's another member of the family,' said Harry.

Norris walked in, looking dapper in his sharp turn-ups and banded trilby, his brown eyes rather striking against his fair skin. His jacket sat well on him, adding a touch of breadth to his shoulders, though Molly thought he looked his best in cricket whites. She brightened. She might not have an engagement ring, but she had a fiancé with a decent job and good prospects. Good-looking too – and better-looking since she had persuaded him to shave off his moustache. She didn't like moustaches. Prickly things.

Her footsteps tapped on the floorboards as she went to draw Norris in.

'Look. Harry has bought Dora an engagement ring. Isn't it a beauty?'

Cheeks flushing prettily, Dora offered her hand.

'It's second-hand,' said Harry, 'but that meant I could afford a better ring.'

'Very dainty,' said Norris.

'Has Auntie Faith seen it yet?' Molly asked.

'We're on our way home now,' said Dora, 'but Upton's is on our way, so we couldn't resist popping in. I was going to burst if I didn't show somebody.'

'I'm honoured to be first.' Molly gave her another hug.

'While we're here,' said Harry, looking across the counter, 'let's get something to help the celebrations along. A box of Milk Tray or how about some Sharp's Super-Kreems?'

'I don't think Auntie Faith and Uncle Paul will need any help to celebrate,' said Molly. 'As for Gran, she'll dance a jig on the kitchen table when she sees Dora's ring.'

Dora laughed and sneaked another look at her garnets. Molly's heart warmed. She wanted her cousin to treasure every moment of this special day.

'I want to,' said Harry. 'Back behind the counter, wench, and get serving.'

Molly slid through the gap and let down the counter-flap. Moving past the shelves of glass jars of acid drops and pear drops, lavender lozenges and sugared almonds, she stopped by the display of tins of toffees and boxes of chocolates that most customers gazed at before purchasing a quarter of raspberry shapes or a Fry's Turkish Delight.

'Super-Kreems, please,' decided Harry.

Auntie Faith would have preferred Milk Tray to toffee, but Molly didn't say so. She picked up one of the red tubs with its picture of the bowler-hatted, monocled chap with the improbably large head, placing it on the counter.

'What are these boxes for, our Molly?' Dora had wrenched her gaze away from her ring for long enough to spot the collecting-boxes.

'I'm collecting for the orphans to have sweets on May Day and before you ask, that's a maypole, not a barber's pole.'

'Oh aye,' said Harry, 'they're doing their display on Monday after school, aren't they?'

'The maypole box is for sweets for the dancers and the plain one is for the rest of the children.'

'I can see why you'd want to reward the children dancing in the display,' said Norris, 'but the others won't have done anything to deserve it.'

'It's not a question of deserving,' said Dora. 'It's a question of our Molly being kind.'

'I've got a heap of change in my pocket.' Harry spread it on the counter, slapping down a couple of coins that threatened to roll away. 'Take what you need for the toffees and let's put a tanner in each of the boxes. Here, Dora, you put them in.'

'Harry, that's very generous,' said Molly. 'Are you sure? It's a lot of money.'

'It's not every day a fellow buys his girl a ring from Millington's.'

Dora nudged him. 'Less of the "girl", if you don't mind. I'm your fiancée.'

Sliding one arm round her, he gave her a quick squeeze. 'Best word in the English language, that.'

'You daft ha'porth.' But there was no disguising Dora's pleasure. She dropped a sixpence into each box. There was a tiny chinking sound as each one landed on top of the coins already inside.

Harry turned to Norris. Harry had such a cheerful, open face. 'How about you, Norris? Have you got any change burning a hole in your pocket?'

Norris smiled, but it was a tight smile. Perhaps he hadn't yet got used to his clean-shaven upper lip.

'The things I do to please you,' he had said after he shaved off his moustache, his tone indulgent, as if he spent half his time giving in to her whims.

'The things I do to please your Molly,' he'd said to Mum when she admired his hairless upper lip.

'Aye, she's a lucky lass,' said Mum. 'There's no denying it.'

Norris removed his change-purse from his jacket pocket. It was made of dark leather, a flat semi-oval in shape. Norris opened it. Now it was an oval, one half with a leather cover beneath which were the contents, the opened half with a lip round the edge so that when the change was tipped out of the covered end, it was held safely. You could tip it as heartily as you pleased and the change wouldn't fall out.

Norris jiggled it slightly. Beneath the brim of his trilby, a frown fluttered across his brow. Please let him be generous.

'What have we got here, then? A family reunion?' Mr Upton came through from the back, where he had been having his afternoon tea-break with his invalid wife. She had survived the influenza after the war, but hadn't been the same since, poor lady.

'Our Dora came to show me her engagement ring,' Molly explained, whereupon Dora waggled her hand at Mr Upton.

'Very nice, I'm sure,' he said. 'Congratulations.'

'And her fiancé has bought toffees to take home to celebrate.'

'Super-Kreems: a good choice. I hope everyone enjoys them.'

The door opened and three little girls bounced in.

'I'll see to these young ladies,' said Mr Upton, making the children giggle, 'while you see your visitors out, Miss Watson.'

'Yes, Mr Upton.'

'We haven't got you into trouble, have we?' Dora whispered, bustling to the door with Harry in tow.

'Course not. He's a good old stick, Mr Upton.'

'Are you coming to the dance tonight?'

'We'll see you there.'

Dora gave her a quick peck on the cheek, then looped her arm through Harry's and carted him off for her garnet ring's next appearance in the spotlight.

Norris appeared by Molly's shoulder. 'When you're ready,' he murmured.

He had come for his weekly packet of mints. When they got married, he was going to buy her a bar of Cadbury's Dairy Milk every Saturday.

'Eh, he's going to spoil you rotten, lass,' Gran was fond of saying.

'She's a lucky girl, especially at her age,' Mum would agree. 'There are plenty of girls left on't shelf these days.'

Aye, there were. Surplus girls, they were called. Molly had read about them in Mum's *Vera's Voice*, which had published a series of articles earlier this year. They hadn't been woe-is-me articles, but cheerful, encouraging pieces about how surplus girls should plan for the future and get themselves trained up to do the most highly qualified work they were capable of, to give themselves a chance of a reasonable salary in a world where women earned less than men simply because they were women. The most interesting of the articles had centred around a new business school here in Chorlton. Fancy sleepy little Chorlton having something as modern as that! Not that

Molly needed any such thing, of course. Her future had been all mapped out by Norris – by Norris? *With* Norris. Her future was mapped out with Norris.

She went back behind the counter, where Mr Upton was waiting for the girls to make their choice from the selection on the farthing tray. He was always patient with children.

'They'll be grown-up customers one day,' Mrs Upton had told Molly on her very first morning, the day after she left school.

'It's one of the pleasures of running a sweet shop, watching your customers growing up and having little customers of their own,' Mr Upton had added.

Molly had gone home from her first day at work and repeated what the Uptons had said.

'Customers having little customers?' said Mum. 'It's not as though you'll be there to see it, our Molly. You'll be wed with little customers of your own long before then. Me and Auntie Faith both married at nineteen. You'll do the same. Just you wait.'

But when Molly was nineteen, the war started. She and Norris were walking out by then.

'Don't you fret about him marching off to war, Molly love,' said Gran. 'It'll all be over by Christmas.'

Except that it wasn't. It dragged on and on. Molly knitted socks and mufflers and hemmed dozens of bandages; but after Passchendaele, in a blaze of patriotism, she took herself off to London to engage in what she hoped would feel like real war work. She was taught to drive and was attached to an office, her work a mixture of clerical routines and driving army officers to meetings.

Afterwards, after everything, she came home and stepped back into her old life behind the counter at Upton's, spending her day weighing a quarter of aniseed balls, a quarter of marzipan marvels, replenishing the farthing and ha'penny trays, breaking the dark slab of treacle toffee with the little silver hammer, and assembling gross upon gross of white, cone-shaped paper bags. Fold, fold, twist, flatten.

Norris came home as well and, after some discussion, they got engaged. It seemed the right thing to do – it was the right thing to do. Molly knew that. It was part of stepping back into her old life. She was lucky to have her old life still there, waiting for her, ready to enfold her and make her safe.

Some girls were racing up the aisle, those that were lucky enough still to have someone to marry them, but that wasn't Norris's way.

'I reckon a five-year engagement should do it,' he told Mum and Dad. 'We'll save our nest egg first and I must work towards my promotion. That way, I'll be in a position to provide Molly with the best of everything. I'll rent a new house, with electricity. You'd like Molly to have electricity, wouldn't you, Mr Watson, and indoor plumbing? Do you think she'd like a vacuum cleaner, Mrs Watson? I can't have my wife beating the rugs, not in this day and age.'

'Our Molly's lucky to have found such a generous man,' beamed Mum.

'And don't forget the bar of Dairy Milk you'll get her every Saturday,' Gran added.

'As if I would.' Norris beamed at Gran as if she had uttered a wonderful witticism.

'Eh, our Molly's a lucky lass,' said Gran.

That was what everyone said. Norris was good-looking and well-mannered and his generosity was a local legend.

'Well, now, isn't that generous?' said Mr Upton. 'These young ladies have a penny between them. They have each chosen a treat from the farthing tray and they want to give the other farthing to the orphans. Isn't that kind?'

Molly smiled at the children. 'Which box would you like to put it in? The box for the children who aren't dancing has less money and it's for more children.'

Mr Upton bristled. 'Don't influence them, Miss Watson. They probably want to give their farthing to the dancers – don't you, girls? Don't you like the thought of the children dancing round the maypole?'

Yes, of course they did, the same as most people. At this rate, the other orphans would have to make do with low-quality chocolate chunks broken into tiny morsels and a bag of sherbet they could all stick one wet finger in.

Norris turned to watch as the little girls skipped out of the shop, the brass bell tinkling merrily in their wake.

'What about you, Norris?' Molly asked. 'Would you care to make a donation?'

His smile changed. No, it didn't. Not a muscle had moved in the vicinity of his mouth, the corners of which were still upturned, lips slightly parted, showing a glimpse of teeth.

'I've already given,' he said, 'when Dora and Harry were here.'

'No, you didn't.' Molly's smile didn't falter either. Except that it did – but only inwardly. 'You were about to, then Mr Upton came in.'

'Put you off your stride, did I?' joked Mr Upton.

Norris produced his change-purse once more. He opened it with a gentle shake, easing a few coins from one end to the other, where he could examine them.

'Harry gave a whole shilling.' Molly turned to Mr Upton to show she was addressing her remark to him, but really she was reminding Norris. 'Sixpence for each box.'

'Gracious, he is pushing the boat out today, isn't he?' said Mr Upton.

'You wouldn't think he was saving up to support a wife and family.' Norris pawed at the coins in his change-purse. 'Thruppence, I think.'

'Thruppence for each box?' asked Molly. It was worth a try.

'For the dancers. Here. You put it in.'

'Thruppence, eh?' Mr Upton nodded complacently. 'Very open-handed of you, if I may say so. Most folk have given a farthing or a ha'penny.'

'Generosity should be tempered by common sense.' Norris lapped up the approval. 'You shouldn't throw your money around – as Harry Turnbull would do well to learn. He spends like there's no tomorrow.' It was the darkest criticism Norris could level at anyone. He waggled an indulgent finger at Molly. 'I know you were hoping for more than thruppence, but my first responsibility is towards you personally, towards your happiness and our future. Look after the pennies and the pounds will take care of themselves, that's my motto. You appreciate my point of view, don't you, Mr Upton?'

'I do indeed, Mr Hartley. Be grateful for the thruppence, Miss Watson.' Mr Upton made it sound as if she had been angling for half a crown.

'Here's tuppence for the mints, Molly,' said Norris.

'Thank you. And do you happen to feel like splashing out on a bar of Dairy Milk for your fiancée?'

Norris's head gave a little jerk, then he chuckled. 'You are a card, Molly. Isn't she a card, Mr Upton? Wait until she's Mrs Norris Hartley. Then she'll have a bar of chocolate every Saturday without fail. Now I must cut along. I'll pick you up later as usual, Molly. Good day, Mr Upton.'

'Good day to you, Mr Hartley.' Mr Upton watched Norris leave the premises before turning to Molly. 'Now there's a generous fellow, if ever there was one. You're a lucky girl, Miss Watson, and Mrs Upton thinks so too.'

Chapter Two

SITTING ON HER bed, with its faded patchwork quilt made donkey's years ago by Grandma Watson when she was a bride, Molly flexed her stockinged toes, enjoying the pleasantly achy sensation after a day spent on her feet, before reaching to pick up her good shoes from the bedside mat. Beside her on the quilt lay the two discreet cuffs, each adorned with a silver buckle, which she had made to tart up her shoes for dancing.

The first time she had worn her stylishly buckled shoes, she had pointed one foot for Norris to inspect, saying jokingly, 'Look at my smart new shoes,' fully expecting his admiration.

Norris had paled before saying jovially, 'The things ladies spend their money on! Fancy shoes that can only be worn on the dance-floor.' He had turned to Mum. 'I trust you're going to give your Molly some lessons in managing the housekeeping before we get married, Mrs Watson,' and everyone had laughed as if he had made a great joke – well, everyone but Tom.

Then Molly had explained how the cuffs slipped onto her shoes, nestling in the instep underneath with the buckle showing on the top of her shoe, and how the buckles had cost a few coppers on the market (that was a lie: they had been a shilling each from Elizabeth's, the wool and haberdashery shop on Wilbraham Road), whereupon Norris had laughed heartily and sworn she was a card for teasing him.

'You're a card, Molly. Isn't she a card, Mrs Watson?'

Folding the cuff around the T-bar of one of her shoes, Molly fastened the hooks and eyes on the side and jiggled the buckle into position in the centre. Shoes on, she stood and straightened her clothes before going onto the landing and leaning over the polished banister rail to call down the stairs.

'Mum! May I use your looking-glass?'

Mum and Dad's room was at the front of the house, as befitted the master bedroom. The Watsons lived in a pre-war semi-detached house in a quiet close off Cavendish Road, not far from the premises of the family's thriving building company of Perkins and Watson, itself a stone's throw from Chorlton Station. Grandad Watson, who had started the firm with his friend, had worked like a Trojan, ploughing every penny back into the business and never thinking to move his family out of the two-up two-down they then occupied. Dad, however, a few years after his marriage when the children started coming along, had taken the view that a builder's home should reflect his abilities, and he had moved the family to this house, with its indoor plumbing, two double bedrooms and a box-room big enough to take a single bed. With the landlord's agreement, Dad had taken on responsibility for the house's repairs and maintenance and the landlord had been so impressed with the quality of Dad's work that he had employed Perkins and Watson to maintain his other properties.

Molly blinked as she entered the bedroom, even though Mum's snowy nets softened the light coming in. Her own room had no windows, something she hated, though she never said so. Growing up, she, Tilda and Christabel had shared the big back bedroom, leaving Tom, the lone boy, with the box-room. When she and Tom came home from the war, and with Tilda and Chrissie married, she and Tom had swapped rooms. There hadn't been any discussion. It had just been the

14

accepted thing that, with a son and a daughter at home, the son got the better room.

Positioning herself in front of Mum's dressing-table, Molly checked her appearance in the large circular mirror. She was wearing a jumper knitted in lightweight leaf-green wool, with a cross-over front with a sash that she had tied in a saucy bow at the side, teamed with her ivory skirt patterned with violets. It was an attractive ensemble and of good quality. The Watsons weren't rolling in money, but the building business kept their heads well above water.

'You look nice, love,' said Mum when she went downstairs. Mum could be relied on for a mild compliment. 'Norris will be proud.'

She hadn't dressed for Norris. Well, she had, obviously. It was right to look your best for the person you were with, especially if that person happened to be your fiancé. But Molly had dressed for herself too, for the pleasure and pride of looking her best. Still, she might sound big-headed if she said so.

'She looks better than nice, Mum.' With a rustle, Tom peered round the *Manchester Evening News* to give her the once-over from the armchair. 'She's a corker, is our Molly.'

Warmth spread through her chest. 'Thank you, kind sir.' She ruffled his hair. Her dear brother had gone to war brown-haired and come back with a thatch of silver. 'Ah, but with limbs and lungs intact,' he said over and over when he first came back and was subjected to the same surprised comments time and again. Limbs and lungs intact, and that was something to be grateful for; but what horrors had he witnessed, what actions had he been obliged to commit, that had turned his hair white?

'Will you be warm enough in short sleeves?' Mum asked. 'It's only April.'

'Never mind the date,' said Dad. 'Go by the temperature.'

'It's always warm in the church hall once the dancing gets under way,' said Molly, 'and it'll be warmer still tonight.'

A cheery rat-tat at the front door heralded Norris's arrival. Molly let him in.

He gave her a peck on the cheek. 'Are you ready?'

'Don't I look ready?'

'Oho, what's this? Fishing for compliments? You look very fetching as always, Molly.'

'Thanks. Come and say good evening while I get my things.'

Norris disappeared into the parlour while she pulled on her jacket and put on her hat in front of the age-spotted mirror in the hall-stand. The deep upturned brim did a sterling job of concealing much of her hair, which suited her just fine. The less strawberry-blonde mass on show, the better.

Her hair was thick and inclined to be coarse, which made it bushy, and the instant hair fashion had changed, she was one of the first to have hers chopped, much to Mum's dismay. Her bob rested at chin-length. The fashion was to have it clubbed all the way round, but on Molly's hair this had simply released its natural volume, causing it to spring outwards as if she was wearing a bizarre lampshade on her head, until the clever stylist had cut layers into her hair to tame it into the flattering shape that came naturally to everyone else.

Picking up her handbag, she clicked it open to scan the contents. Other girls had smaller bags for evening, but it wasn't worth her while to have one of those, because of always needing to carry her purse.

'All set?' asked Norris as she presented herself in the parlour doorway.

She kissed her parents and Tom goodbye. The evening was turning to dusk, but the unseasonable warmth lingered, muting the fresh green scents of the privet hedges and the tang of new growth in the compact front gardens.

'Who would have thought it would still be so warm at this time?' Norris remarked. 'Are you certain you fancy being shut inside a stuffy hall? All those people, all that dancing, the crush.'

'We always go, and Dora's expecting us. It's her special day.'

'Dora has a sight too many special days, if you ask me. Getting engaged, then having an engagement party, now this.'

Molly squeezed his arm. 'Spoilsport.'

'No I'm not. I'm concerned that by the time her wedding comes round, it'll feel like just another of Dora's events.'

'Don't be daft. Weddings are always special.'

'Some more so than others. Ours will be, because of the foresight and saving up that has gone into preparing for our life together afterwards.'

'Whereas Dora's will be just another roaring old knees-up,' said Molly. Which would she prefer? Couldn't you have both? Commitment as well as fun?

'Anyway, Dora's special evening, as you call it, will be steaming hot and crowded. Wouldn't you rather be out here in the fresh air?'

'I promised Dora.'

'You didn't actually promise.'

'Even so.'

He didn't answer.

Molly caught her lip beneath her teeth. 'I – I don't mind paying for us, since it's my idea.'

It wouldn't be the first time. When they went to see amateur theatricals or to listen to a concert that wasn't to Norris's taste, she always slipped him the entrance money plus extra for refreshments before they went in. And it wasn't lying, was it, to tell the world and his wife, 'Norris is taking me to see *The Pirates of Penzance*,' because he was taking her: he was escorting her, opening doors and walking on the road-side of the pavement.

'It isn't a question of paying,' said Norris. 'It's the temperature. You can't tell me anyone relishes being squashed on a dance-floor in this unexpected heat. You look so pretty. You don't want to get crumpled. Anyway, we'll undoubtedly see

Dora and Harry before too long, as I bet you anything they'll leave early.'

'Well...'

'You wait. Everyone will leave early. They'll be gasping for air like grounded fish.'

Was it really worth arguing over? It wasn't as though she would be leaving Dora high and dry. Dora and Harry would be surrounded by friends.

'All right,' said Molly.

'You don't mind, do you?' Norris murmured.

'Of course not.'

She lifted her face with a smile. Yes, of course she would have preferred to attend the dance, but she wasn't going to be moody about it.

'Good girl.' Norris reached across with his free hand to give an approving pat to the fingers looped inside his opposite elbow. 'Giving in gracefully is good practice for when we're married.'

How complacent he sounded, but then, he had every right to. Most folk would agree with him that it was the man's job to make the choices. But did he have to decide absolutely everything? Dad wasn't like that. Neither were Tilda's and Christabel's husbands. Sometimes she wondered what she had let herself in for.

'Dora's ring was pretty, wasn't it?' she remarked as they strolled on their way.

'Pretty enough, I daresay.'

'You said it was dainty.'

'Cripes, yes. Talking about saving the day. I was halfway to saying "How tiny" when I realised what a gaffe that would be and changed it to "dainty". Wait until I choose your wedding ring, my girl. You'll get more carats than anybody else at the church social. That's what comes of watching your money.'

'All that matters is that the ring is given with love – like Dora's.'

Norris laughed. He would make a good missionary, chuckling benevolently at the innocent foibles of the natives. 'You say that now, but what would you think if I fobbed you off with a second-hand trinket, eh?'

They strolled about, chatting, for a good hour or so. As the evening cooled, Molly drew Norris determinedly towards the church hall.

'There's still time for a dance.'

'It's not worth paying to get in this late.'

As she dragged him along the road, Dora, Harry and others could be seen outside the hall.

'Told you,' said Norris. 'Look how flushed they all are.'

It was true. They were – but not crotchety, fed-up flushed. They were happy, smiling flushed.

Dora ran to meet them, her sweet-pea-pink dress streaming behind her, then settling into floaty folds when she stopped.

'I thought you were coming, Moll.'

'We changed our minds.' Vexation pinched her spine, but she uttered the half-truth with a smile. 'It's such a lovely evening for a walk.'

'You missed a lot of fun.'

'It must have been hot in there,' said Norris.

'Boiling,' Dora agreed cheerfully. 'To start with, they opened all the windows, then we took the dancing outside and passers-by joined in.'

'Without paying?'

Molly bit down on a pang of disappointment for the missed pleasure. 'I'm glad you enjoyed it.'

'Oh, we did. When I showed off my ring, the gang clubbed together and the Page twins went to the florist's and banged on the door until they opened up and made me a bouquet. Harry wasn't allowed to buy a single drink all night! Folk are so kind.'

'You deserve it,' said Molly.

'You missed our announcement. Me and Harry are getting wed in September. Mum and Dad say we can live with them, so there's nowt to wait for.'

'Goodness, that's quick.'

'Keep your voice down,' Dora hissed. 'You'll have folk thinking I'm...y'know.'

Harry joined them, sleeves rolled up, jacket slung over his shoulder, held in place by a crooked finger. 'Evening, Molly. Evening, Norris.' He thrust out a comradely hand to shake Norris's.

Others clustered round as well. They were breathless and pleasantly dishevelled. Molly felt uncomfortably prim.

'Come on,' said Bernie Oldfield. 'We're taking the happy couple for a fish supper. We're all treating Harry and his good lady.'

'You can't pay for us,' said Harry. 'You've already bought Dora flowers and kept us in drinks all evening.'

'Oh, aye, the vicar's wife's best fruit cordial,' said Bernie. 'That set us back...ooh, coppers, wasn't it, lads? We're all mucking in to pay for your supper, and no arguments; only this time, there's a port and lemon in it for you, Dora.'

'I don't mind if I do,' said Dora.

'You'll come, won't you?' Bernie turned to Molly and Norris. 'You missed the dance, so you can't miss giving the soon-to-be newly-weds a spot of nosh and something to drink their health with.'

'Fish and chip shops don't sell alcohol,' Norris pointed out.

'If we go to Rafferty's, they have tables in the back and they'll let us bring drinks in from the pub.'

'Molly and I won't join you for the meal, if you don't mind,' said Norris.

'Norris!' Molly protested, but she pretended to laugh, not wanting to spoil the happy atmosphere.

'It's a bit late in the evening for me.' Norris patted his stomach, indicating some unspecified reason why late-night eating wasn't desirable. 'But we'll walk with you and see you settled.'

Molly didn't object. She had learned the hard way that one feature of a prolonged engagement was that the smallest suggestion of a public tiff led to hoots of masculine laughter and jokes about already being hen-pecked.

As they set off, Dora linked arms with her.

'There's going to be a big day trip to Southport. We'll catch the early train and arrive mid-morning in time for a talk in one of the hotels about the archaeological digs going on in Egypt; then a posh three-course meal in the hotel; followed by a walk down Lord Street to see the shops; and the rest of the afternoon at the Pleasure Beach; then back to the hotel for a late tea before catching the train home.'

'It sounds splendid.'

'You'll come, won't you? And Norris. I've put your names down. Harry says me and him can go, but it's to be our final fling, then we have to save everything for being married.'

The group arrived at Rafferty's in a jumble of laughter and good humour.

Bernie nudged Norris. 'Let's go and get the drinks. What's everyone having?'

'You start putting the order in,' said Norris. 'I'll be with you in a minute, after I've seen to the tables in here.'

He led the way into the chippy, with its busy, crackling sound of frying and its warm, vinegar-laden atmosphere. Mr Rafferty shook the frying-baskets and doled out chips into newspaper, deftly flicking all the crispy bits into a separate pile to be given at closing time to a half-starving family with the dad out of work.

Bypassing the queue, Norris marched into the dining area at the back. He pushed the tables together, sat Dora and Harry in pride of place, and prevailed upon Mrs Rafferty to fetch her best tablecloth from her sideboard and the candlesticks off her mantelpiece. Satisfaction stretched Molly's smile. It was good to see Norris making an occasion out of it for the happy couple. When Bernie walked in, gingerly carrying a tray crammed with glasses, Norris came to the rescue, doling out the drinks. He even called for silence and made a toast.

'Here's to you, Dora and Harry. Molly and I are sorry we can't stay, but we wish you all the best for your future happiness. Dora and Harry!'

'Dora and Harry,' everyone chorused, raising their glasses.

Mrs Rafferty appeared, brandishing a notepad. 'Fish and chips all round, is it? Are you paying separately?'

'Tot it up and give the bill to me,' said Bernie. 'We're all mucking in to treat Dora and Harry.'

'We'd best be on our way.' Norris took Molly's arm. 'Have a wonderful time, all of you, especially you, Dora and Harry, and many congratulations.' He shook hands warmly all round, then came to Dora. 'May I kiss the bride?'

'Oh, Norris, you are a one,' trilled Dora as he leaned down and brushed a kiss on her cheek.

Molly's smile was still in place, but something inside her had gone cold. She hugged Dora and kissed her. Smile, smile. Say all the right things. Smile, smile. As they eased their way out, cries of 'Thanks, Norris' and 'Cheers, Norris' filled her ears. Smile, smile.

'Well, that was most pleasant.' If Norris exuded any more goodwill, he would glow in the dark.

Molly's smile dropped. 'I'm sure everyone will remember you as the life and soul of the party.'

'Think so? That'd be champion.' Norris chuckled. 'I like the thought of all the chaps and chapesses looking back in years to come and reminiscing about how old Norris got the party off to a spanking start.'

She tried again. 'You didn't put your hand in your pocket, Norris, not once.'

He gave her a startled glance. 'I didn't hear anybody complaining.'

'Of course not. They were all too chuffed with how you got the supper-table set up. But you were meant to go to the pub and help Bernie with the drinks.'

'He managed all right. They lent him a tray.'

'You should have gone with him and paid half.'

'You said yourself I was busy getting the meal set up,' Norris pointed out. 'I even charmed Mrs Rafferty into putting her own candlesticks on the table. That was a special touch. A fish supper with candlesticks and Irish linen. Very posh.'

Molly chewed the inside of her cheek. He had an answer for everything.

'I did Harry and Dora proud, though I do say so myself.' Norris was all complacency. 'I'd have expected you to be happy about it. You're supposed to be so fond of Dora.' He stopped walking and turned her to face him. 'Shall I tell you what I think this is? I think Miss Molly Watson is succumbing to a bout of the sulks.'

She was utterly taken aback. 'I'm not sulking.'

Norris waggled a finger at her. 'That "surprised" voice tells me otherwise. Dora's exciting day has put your nose out of joint, hasn't it? A long engagement can be hard on the female of the species when she's got her sights set on her gran's veil and being carried over the threshold. But you'll thank me for it one day, when we've got our substantial nest egg and Dora and Harry are still shacked up with your Auntie Faith.'

'I'm not jealous of Dora.'

'Good, because you've no need to be. If anything, she should be jealous of you. In all probability, she will be one day.'

'How did we get onto this?' Molly asked. 'I only said I wished you'd spent a bit of money.'

'Oh aye? And would anyone else have thought to prevail upon Mrs Rafferty to decorate the table?' Tucking her arm firmly in his, Norris started walking again. 'You saw how delighted everyone was. You can't put a price on that, Molly, and I'm surprised at you for thinking money is more important.'

'I never said that.'

'Don't fret. I know you didn't mean any harm. I know you're in a bit of a tizz.' Norris's voice was warm. 'It's a good job you've got me to take care of you.'

Molly felt the need to stand up for herself, but she was careful to speak lightly. She mustn't reinforce the silly notion that she was in a tizz. 'Really, Norris, you make me sound incapable of taking care of myself. I was clever enough to learn to drive, clever enough to learn to change a wheel; clever enough to leave home under my own steam.'

'Yes, Molly,' Norris said sombrely, 'and look how that turned out. Everyone knows you set off for London, intending to win the war single-handed, and I daresay your parents were proud of you, and quite right too. But you and I both know you made a hash of things down south.'

It was hard to breathe. Her heartbeat slowed down, as if it might stop at any moment.

'I'm not saying this to hurt you,' Norris assured her in his kindest voice. 'It's a gentle reminder, that's all. Sometimes you need to be reminded, for your own good. But that's our little secret, isn't it?'

Chapter Three

THE LAD WAS hanging about on the pavement when Molly left the shop with Mrs Upton's wicker basket on her arm. He was just a youngster, maybe nine or ten, his pale, freckled face beneath a cloth cap that swamped his head. Molly smiled inwardly: he must have a mum like hers. 'You'll grow into it,' Mum had said repeatedly when her four were nippers, thereby getting the most wear possible out of their clothes.

Wait a minute: he didn't have a mum. He was in the grey uniform of the orphanage. What was he doing here? This wasn't St Anthony's patch. It was a fifteen- if not twenty-minute walk from there to here. And anyway...

'Why aren't you at school?' she called.

The boy looked away as if he hadn't heard, but she knew he had. When she had opened the shop door, they had looked straight at one another. The boy had a narrow, oval face with a dent in his pointy chin. It was a cheerful, eager face, or would have been but for a look of...was that wariness? Well, no wonder, if he was bunking off school.

'Morning, Molly.'

'Morning, Mrs Livesey.'

Molly smiled at her mum's friend and when she glanced back, the boy had gone.

She walked briskly round the shops, buying some veg from the greengrocer, a couple of cutlets from the butcher and a box of Shredded Wheat at the grocer's. The weekend's temperatures had subsided back to normal and May Day was mild and fine. It was easy to stride out in this weather, but Molly always put on a smart pace, even when it was as hot as Hades. She wouldn't take advantage of Mrs Upton's invalid state by dawdling when she was sent on errands.

Returning to the shop, she walked through to the back to put away her purchases. Mrs Upton lay on the bed, propped up against a pile of pillows and cushions. She hadn't been upstairs since 1919, poor love. She got dressed every day and usually sat in the armchair, but sometimes, like today, she lay on the bed. Without a word, Molly put the kettle on and tipped a couple of drops of eucalyptus oil into a bowl, adding boiling water. The pungent, cleansing aroma flooded every corner of the room. Making space on the bedside table, Molly slipped a crocheted doily onto the surface and placed the bowl on top.

Mrs Upton took a series of small sniffs, like an animal scenting danger. Then she breathed a sigh and relaxed, her thin frame spreading as her muscles unclenched. 'Thanks, love.' The influenza had left her with a raspy voice, as if she was permanently on the brink of a stinking cold, though she swore she felt fine, just weak.

Molly smiled to hide her concern. 'I'd best get back behind the counter.' Mr Upton didn't like her to spend too much time in the back.

In a gap between customers, Mr Upton said, 'Hand me the collecting-boxes and I'll count the money.'

'I was going to leave the boxes out until three.'

'Squeezing the last farthing out of folk?'

'The whole point is to raise as much as possible.'

A few more farthings and ha'pennies made their way into the boxes, mostly into the maypole box, as the usual Monday crowd came in for their weekly quarter of Maynard's Wine Gums or Pontefract cakes. Shortly after twelve-thirty, a handful of children from the elementary school clattered in. These were the half-timers, who, once they turned twelve, were allowed to have jobs in the afternoon. This lot had got into the habit of popping in for gobstoppers and Black Jacks every Monday before starting work at one.

'I'll see to them,' said Molly, leaving Mr Upton to serve old Mrs Lofts.

Glancing over the children's heads, she noticed the lad from earlier, hovering at the back. He was older than he looked if he was a half-timer, but then, it was often difficult to gauge people's ages. So many children were undersized through being underfed and it was common for working-class women to age well before their time. The Watsons were lucky that their family firm had always ticked over nicely.

Molly was kept busy doling out bootlaces and packets of Rowntree's Pastilles, accepting payments, giving change and making sure no one slipped a fruity chew into their pocket. She didn't serve the boy with the orphanage uniform, but that made sense. Orphans wouldn't receive pocket money. She took the final payment and the children bustled towards the door, the orphan in the lead. He opened the door, looking back as he did so. His eyes met hers. His were blue – and scared? Anxious? He tore his gaze away and ran outside. The gaggle of youngsters followed, bursting out into the sunshine, chattering and messing about, stopping just this side of rowdy, the brass bell jangling wildly as the door was hauled shut. The bell quietened and the usual calm atmosphere crept out from behind the sweet-jars.

'Thank goodness they've gone,' said Mrs Lofts. 'They shouldn't be allowed in, if you ask me.'

'It's just high spirits,' said Molly.

Would it be cheeky to ask a customer she hadn't served to pop in a coin for the orphans?

Her glance went to the boxes. She froze, tiny chills making the hairs stand up along her arms. One of the boxes was missing.

Her breath caught. The orphanage boy – the way he had turned and look at her. Had he swiped the collecting box?

With a heavy block of disappointment wedged tightly inside her chest, Molly crossed the orphanage's tarmacadamed playground and mounted the stone steps to tug on the old bell-pull beside the door. She felt foolish as well as disappointed. Last time she had come here, she had run up the stairs to Mrs Rostron's office, bubbling over with her happy plan to treat the children on May Day. She had known then that Upton's would get just one chance at this. There were other sweet shops nearer to St Anthony's and, after the resounding success that her plan was undoubtedly going to be, they would be fighting one another to be allowed to do it next year; except that Molly's plan wasn't going to be a resounding success after all, not now that one of the boxes had been stolen.

Had that orphan-boy taken it?

Along the passage from the superintendent's office was a gas-lit alcove where Miss Allan had a desk with her clunky old typewriter. A cupboard squeezed in on one side, a battered filing cabinet on the other. Miss Allan had worked here since the 1880s – here, in this alcove off a dingy landing that smelled of beeswax and boiled vegetables. She must be on the verge of frostbite every winter and gasping for air every summer.

'I'm sorry,' said Miss Allan, sounding anything but. 'Mrs Rostron is busy. Can you call back later?'

'I'm on my dinner-hour and I have to get back.'

'You're attending the maypole dancing display, aren't you? If you come early, you might be able to see Mrs Rostron then.'

At the end of the corridor, the door opened and Mrs Rostron appeared. 'Miss Allan, do you have— oh.' Mrs Rostron had the kind of eyes that missed nothing. Could she tell that Molly's wonderful scheme had fallen apart? 'Miss Watson, what are you doing here?'

Good manners be blowed. Molly hurried to the office, slipping inside.

'I apologise for barging in, but this is urgent— oh. You have a visitor.'

'Indeed I do, as I imagine Miss Allan informed you.'

Exuding displeasure, the superintendent closed the door and sat behind her desk, which was so tidy that it wasn't until you looked carefully that you realised quite how many papers and files were on it.

On the other side of the desk sat a lady of Molly's mum's age or thereabouts, superbly dressed in a mouth-wateringly expensive costume of royal blue dress with a matching long-line jacket that encased her plump figure. She wore a fox-fur around her neck; the glassy-eyed head lay along one shoulder; and the front of her hat was adorned with a mass of tiny flowers that made her hat appear as pudgy as her face. Who was she? A patron?

'I'm sorry to interrupt you.' Molly gave Mrs Rostron's visitor her most winning smile.

The lady, however, wasn't won over. She turned her head away with a telling huff of breath, but not before she had run narrowed eyes over Molly in a way that made her feel thoroughly dishevelled.

'This is Miss Watson from the sweet shop,' Mrs Rostron informed her visitor, though she didn't favour Molly with the lady's name. Neither did she offer Molly a seat, even though her office contained two chairs for visitors.

'I'm here concerning the money for this afternoon's sweets,' Molly began.

'And you know my opinion of that,' the visitor said to Mrs Rostron as though Molly weren't present. She was well-spoken, as befitted her expensive appearance, but was her refinement a little too 'refained'? 'Giving the orphans sweets for dancing sets a bad precedent. They might always expect to get something for nothing.'

'It isn't something for nothing,' Molly exclaimed. 'It's a reward—'

'It's an advertisement for your shop.'

'It's a thank-you from the locals for the dancing display.'

'Exactly: something for nothing. They shouldn't receive payment for their dancing. And what of those who aren't involved? I believe you intend to shower sweets on them also. How do you justify that?'

'I wasn't aware that I needed to.' Molly's spine was getting stiffer by the moment. 'It's simple fairness.'

'Fairness, you call it? Now I've heard everything. It's bad enough you want to indulge the dancers, when the privilege of performing should be enough, but to indulge the rest of the children for no reason whatsoever...' With a glance at Mrs Rostron, who was listening impassively, she drew in her chin and her chubby throat bulged sideways. 'I'll say no more.'

Molly glared at her, then thought better of it. Whoever she was, she was important.

'If you would kindly come to the point, Miss Watson,' said Mrs Rostron.

'One of the collecting-boxes has vanished. There are two, one for the dancers and one for the rest of the children. That's the one that's gone missing.'

'Do you mean it's been stolen?' demanded the posh lady.

'I'm afraid so. I can't prove it, but it might have been a boy from here who took it.'

Mrs Rostron snapped to attention in her seat, her gaze locked on Molly's. 'Describe him.'

'As I say, I have no proof—'

'Describe him.'

Oh, crikey, what if she was wrong? 'Nine or ten, thin face, freckles. Blue eyes.' She lifted a finger to her chin. 'A little cleft here. He was wearing a man's cap.'

'Daniel Cropper,' said Mrs Rostron. She sat back, shaking her head. She wore her hair in what looked like a loose bun, but there must be a couple of dozen pins secreted inside it, because it never lost so much as a strand.

The mass of silk flowers on the front of the visitor's hat quivered as she leaned forwards. '*Now* will you find that boy a place in Southport? I said no good would come of having him here. He's nothing but trouble.'

'He's just a lad—' Molly began.

'He's a runaway,' said Mrs Rostron. 'We get them sometimes, children who keep trying to go back where they came from. Not that Daniel is from Southport, but he's desperate to get there.'

'Do you think he's on his way there now?' A cold feeling uncurled in the pit of Molly's stomach. She had been vexed at the boy for stealing, had even wanted to get him into trouble, but now that felt petty. All that mattered was his safety.

'I'll ask Miss Allan to telephone the police.'

'Quite right too.' The visitor tilted her head in unconcealed satisfaction. 'That boy isn't just a runaway. We now know he's an out-and-out thief. The sooner we see the back of him, the better.'

Aaron jumped off the tram and headed for Victoria Station at a sprint, dodging a handsome shire dray-horse and a motor-van as he zigzagged across the road. The middle of Manchester smelled of smoke and old buildings. Petrol fumes, too. Some folk swore you couldn't smell the motorised vehicles, but he could, maybe because after four years of inhaling the thick stink of mud, the sour smell of gun-smoke and the overpowering rotten-egg stench of entrails, he now spent as much time as he could outdoors in air far purer than that here in town. A day or two walking in the Peak District was an occasional treat, but mainly tramping across the meadows that stretched alongside the banks of the Mersey had become a necessary and deeply appreciated feature of his life.

He strode into the station, passing the vast bronze memorial tablet that had been unveiled earlier this year, with its long lists of the names of the men of the Lancashire and Yorkshire Railway who had given their lives for King and country in the Great War. In other circumstances, he would have paused to pay his respects, but this situation was urgent. He came to a halt, scanning his surroundings.

A couple of bobbies were already in the booking hall. Would they be here anyway or were they on the look-out for a young runaway? They headed for a ticket-office window, excusing themselves to the queue as they made for the hatch. Aaron sidled closer to listen.

'Have you sold a Southport ticket to a young boy this afternoon?'

He didn't wait for more. He marched towards the platform gates.

'Southport?' he asked a porter pushing a sack-trolley loaded with brown suitcases with labels glued on.

The porter jerked his chin. 'Over there. Best get a move on.'

Aaron shoved a ha'penny in the slot and took a platform ticket, then dived through the gates and hurried alongside the train. The sharp-sweet aromas of coal and steam filled his senses, awakening an answering spark in himself. He had always loved travelling by train.

It wasn't a corridor-train. Good. Each door opened straight into a compartment, which meant that that pesky young feller-me-lad wouldn't be able to leg it down the length of the train when Aaron found him. At the top end, where the massive black engine was building up steam ready to haul its load from the station, the peak-capped guard started walking towards him, slamming doors as he went. Aaron looked into another compartment, then glanced back the way he had come. The coppers were on the platform, accompanied by a fellow in the round-brimmed cap and longer jacket of a senior railway guard. Aaron bounced on the balls of his feet, wanting to hurry but needing not to draw attention.

In the next compartment, a small figure sat in the far corner, back straight, chin up. You had to hand it to him: he had spirit. He was good-looking too, which came as a surprise. Aaron had seen Daniel Cropper's face pinched with worry, taut with frustration, cold with anger, blank with heartache; but never before with this open, hopeful expression. He looked relaxed and determined at the same time. Vulnerable, too, when you knew the reason behind it.

He opened the door and climbed in, pulling the door to behind him without slamming it shut. Daniel looked at him, then slumped in the seat, his chest caving in, shoulders curling round them; but only for a moment. He lifted his chin, slanting Aaron a sideways glance through narrowed eyes. Aaron could practically see the cogs turning as the boy calculated his chances.

'Don't, lad,' he advised. He kept his voice quiet, gentle: there was an answering flicker of surprise. The boy had been braced for him to come down hard. 'It's time to come home.'

'That's not my home.'

Aaron sat down at the other end of the opposite bench-seat. He had to keep the situation calm if they were to evade the boys in blue. The upholstery dipped, the springs shifting to accommodate him.

'Either you come back or you let the police take you back.'

'The police?'

'Two coppers are searching the train. Things will go a lot easier if you come with me. I'll keep you out of trouble, if I can.'

'I'm already in trouble.' The voice of experience.

'Not if I can help it. But you need to come right now, son.'

'I'm not your son.'

'This afternoon you are.' Rising, he peeled off his jacket. 'Put this on and roll up the sleeves.'

'It's miles too big.'

'That's the idea. It'll hide your uniform. Fold your cap and stick it in the pocket.'

Daniel's mouth bunched mutinously. 'I always wear this cap.'

'Your dad's, is it? The police are looking for a young lad in orphanage grey with a man's cap. We can't take any chances.'

The boy blew a sharp breath. It sounded sulky, but his blue eyes were over-bright. He shoved his arms into the jacket sleeves and – no time to waste – Aaron rolled them up. Daniel removed his dad's cap, revealing sandy hair whose colour made his freckles more noticeable, and pushed it into a pocket.

'We're going to walk over to that trolley of luggage, then we'll cross to the other side of the platform and head back to the barrier. If anyone asks, your name is Roy and you're nine years old.'

'I'm eleven…almost.'

But his scrawny body would pass for nine. A spell at St Anthony's would do him a power of good, would put some meat on his bones and probably see him shoot up an inch or two.

'I'll get out first,' said Aaron. 'Don't look at the policemen. They're nothing to Roy and Roy's dad.'

He jumped down, then turned and, before Daniel could object, lifted him out, hoping to create the impression of a younger child. As they made their way back to the booking hall, he kept one hand lightly on Daniel's thin shoulder. Who could say if he might take it into his head to bolt?

Beside the war memorial, Aaron stopped.

'Now then, Daniel Cropper.' The boys at the orphanage were called by their surnames; he added Daniel's first name to sound less stern. 'Before we set foot outside, hand over the money you've got left.'

The boy jabbed at the ground with the toe of one shoe. 'My name's not Daniel. It's Danny.'

'Oh aye?' Most adults would have given him a thick ear for the backchat...only it wasn't backchat, was it? There was no defiance in the lad's demeanour, only misery. 'All right then, Danny Cropper. The money, please. I know you pinched it.' He held out his hand.

The lad dug deep in his pockets, bringing out two handfuls of small change, which he tipped into Aaron's palm. Then he delved in his pockets again.

'Crikey,' said Aaron. 'You had all this left over after buying your ticket? That collecting-box must have contained loads.'

'No, it didn't,' Danny muttered. 'There wasn't nearly enough. I asked for my train ticket, but when the man finished counting my money, it wasn't enough. He was annoyed because it was all farthings and ha'pennies and it took him ages. He told me to hop it.'

'But you still got on the train.'

Danny shrugged, pushing out his lower lip in a don't-care way. 'Platform ticket.'

Aaron pretended not to watch as the lad struggled with himself, obviously dying to ask but also desperate not to.

'How do you know about the collecting-box?' Danny asked at last.

'I could ask you the same question,' Aaron countered.

'Everyone knows. Mrs Rostron told Mrs Atwood and she told the monitors. Mrs Wardle doesn't agree with it.'

'Did Mrs Rostron say that?' He couldn't imagine the orphanage superintendent being so indiscreet.

'No, but we all know. Mrs Wardle doesn't agree with anything apart from early bed and cold water. So how did you know I swiped the collecting-box?' Danny persisted.

'I overheard Miss Allan on the telephone to the police station.'

'You mean Mrs Rostron got her to snitch on me?'

'I'm sure Mrs Rostron simply asked Miss Allan to provide the police with all the information available, so they would understand the situation, including your need to get to Southport.'

'That's it, then. If Mrs Rostron knows about the money-box, I'm for the chop.'

'Maybe,' Aaron agreed. 'Then again, maybe not.'

Chapter Four

'WELL, I DID tell you to stop collecting money this morning,' said Mr Upton, as if Molly should have foreseen the theft. His I-told-you-so air was hard to take, but you didn't answer back to your boss. She felt like answering back, though. No, she didn't. She was too sick at heart. She had looked forward to giving the orphans a treat and now half the money had disappeared – no, not half. It was the other children's box that had been taken. The dancers' box was still here, containing more money even though it was for considerably fewer children.

'Perhaps we could use the dancers' money for all the children...' she dared to suggest, but Mr Upton was having none of it.

'That's for the dancers. I said all along we should be collecting only for them.'

We? What had he done to help? He hadn't asked a single customer for a donation, though he had been happy to take the glory when anyone praised the idea.

'Excuse me a minute.'

She went into the back and took her purse from her handbag. She didn't have much on her, but it was a start. Back behind the counter, she examined the contents of the farthing and ha'penny trays.

Mr Upton glanced up from behind a display he was constructing of chocolate boxes and Walnut Whips. 'Do the trays need topping up, Miss Watson?'

'No.' Molly slid her money onto the counter, eyeing it in the hope that it was somehow more than it had been inside her purse. 'If I buy dolly mixtures, I wonder how many each child would get.'

'If they get just one each, it would be one more than they have any right to expect.'

Molly looked Mr Upton straight in the eye. 'Will you let me have an advance on my week's wages? I want to treat the children. Half a crown should do it.'

'Two and sixpence!' Mr Upton froze. A Walnut Whip fell from his lifeless fingers. 'My dear Miss Watson, you forget yourself. What would Mr Hartley say if I let you fritter your hard-earned money in such a manner?'

'This is nothing to do with Norris.'

'Of course it is. He's your fiancé and you know how careful he is with his money.' He ducked his head behind the display once more.

'Exactly: with his money. This isn't his, it's mine.'

'Actually,' Mr Upton corrected her, his face bobbing up briefly, 'it's mine at present.'

'Which I'm in the process of earning.' Oops: that sounded tart. She switched on a smile, injecting all the warmth she could into her voice since Mr Upton was concentrating on his display again. 'I want to do the right thing. I'm concerned about letting Upton's down, as well as the children.'

'Upton's?' Mr Upton popped up like a jack-in-the-box.

'Now that the collecting has gone wrong, I feel responsible. Please let me put it right.'

It was the right thing to say. Mr Upton gave her half a crown, which she spent on bootlaces, which she cut into pieces, and midget gems. It looked like a decent haul if you didn't think closely about the hundred or so children for whom it was destined. Meanwhile Mr Upton, having finished his display, prepared the sweets for the dancers, each of whom was going to receive a paper bag of goodies from the ha'penny and penny trays, lucky beggars.

Shortly before four o'clock, Molly went through to the back. Removing her white apron, she put on her jacket and hat, slipped her handbag over her arm and picked up the cardboard box containing all the sweets.

'The display is at half past for about twenty minutes. After that Mrs Rostron will say a few words and then I'll give out the sweets. I'll be back before half-five,' she added quickly before Mr Upton could demand her earlier return.

When she reached the orphanage, the playground had undergone a transformation. Bunting hung from the trees that grew around the edge, in gaps that had been left when the tarmacadam was laid. A line of grey-clad boys carried wooden chairs, which they put down in rows under the direction of a girl in the uniform of the orphanage's staff, a dark-blue dress which was mostly hidden beneath a long, plain white apron with a bib with wide shoulder-bands. She wore a crisp white collar and cuffs and a starched white cap. Behind the boys with chairs came bigger boys with long wooden forms, the sort that were used for sitting on or for PT, one lad at either end of the form. Girls in grey dresses beneath white pinafores hovered with cards in their hands, presumably name-cards to reserve seats for the most important guests. As if girls weren't capable of carrying chairs!

In the centre of the square formed by the seating, the maypole rose, its red and blue ribbons tethered by a leather strap.

'I wondered how they would erect the maypole with no hole in the ground for it,' said a friendly voice beside Molly. A good-looking young woman had appeared beside her. She was smartly dressed in a fawn edge-to-edge coat, its demure colour livened up by fancy top-stitching on the collar and cuffs. Her eyes were a soft blue-grey colour, her hair light brown and fashionably bobbed beneath a hat that looked like a too-big beret. 'But I see Mr Abrams has worked his magic as usual.'

The maypole had been erected on a square base with short wooden struts angled to hold it securely upright.

'Mr Abrams?' said Molly.

'The caretaker and general handyman. He was a carpenter before the war. And you must be from the sweet shop.' The stranger smiled and nodded at the cardboard box. It didn't have a lid and the paper-bagged contents were on show.

'Molly Watson, from Upton's near the station.'

'Vivienne Atwood, from the Board of Health.'

Her face was heart-shaped with clear, frank features, the faint lines under her eyes and at the sides of her mouth suggesting she was a few years older than Molly.

'The Board of Health? I haven't heard of that.'

'Not many people have. It's new.'

A pair of girls, hair tightly plaited, approached them.

'Excuse us,' said one. 'Mrs Atwood, Mrs Rostron says please will you come to her office now?'

'Are you the lady from Upton's?' asked the other. 'You're to bring the sweets inside, please.'

Molly followed her young guide up the stone steps and through the open front door. On the left was an opening without a door, with a couple of steps leading down into a big cloakroom, while on the right was a closed door through which excited young voices could be heard.

'They're getting changed for the dancing in there,' said her guide in a tone of undisguised envy. 'The girls are going to wear coloured dresses.'

Then came the corridor on the right which led to the staircase up which was Mrs Rostron's office. Straight ahead, down a few steps, was the dining room with rows of wooden tables, with long forms to sit on. How uncomfortable, having nowhere to rest your back as you ate. Presumably, the powers-that-be would say that if you were sitting up straight, you didn't need a back-rest. A woman with a white apron over her dress and an old-fashioned mob-cap covering her hair appeared through a door at the far end. She had a tray in one hand, which she waggled briefly before setting it on a table and disappearing back through the door.

The girl fetched the tray and brought it to Molly. 'This is for the sweets to go on. You can leave it here until after the dancing display. No one will pinch anything, not after the trouble there's been today. Do you need me any more?'

'No, thank you.'

Molly arranged the dancers' sweet-bags on the tray. There wasn't room for the other sweets as well. It was rather a relief. The sight of them made her cheeks tingle with shame.

She went back outside. The seats were filling up.

'Neighbours, mostly.' Mrs Atwood appeared at her side. 'One or two parents, of course.'

'Parents?'

'Not all orphanage children are orphans. Sometimes a child, or a family of children, is sent here because the mother has died and the father has no female relative who can step in. Recently, Mrs Rostron took in a pair of brothers whose family lost everything in a fire and the mother couldn't provide a new home for them because the father had absconded.'

'I hadn't realised orphanages did that,' said Molly. 'What brings you here? Does the orphanage have a health problem?'

'We're concerned with health in the most general sense. We aren't doctors or nurses. One of our jobs is to assume the responsibilities previously held by the Boards of Guardians now that the last of the workhouses are being closed down. There's a link between orphanages and workhouses – an unfortunate one, of course, all to do with children in dire need. Still, the main thing is the children are cared for. My hope is that the care will become kinder under the new Boards of Health.'

'That sounds worthwhile.' Molly smiled. 'It makes my job feel very ordinary, but when I came back from the war, I found it a comfort to go back to it.'

'I can appreciate that. What war work did you do?'

'Clerical work and driving army bigwigs about, down in London.'

'When the war ended,' said Mrs Atwood, 'I thought the world would become a better place – fairer, you know – but in many ways it's slipped back to the way it always was.'

'That's true. It's not exactly a land fit for heroes.'

'There's a lot to be done, plenty to be modernised. The new Boards of Health have a lot of work ahead of them and some aren't fully staffed yet. Personally, I have a special interest in orphanages.'

'Did you grow up in one?'

'No. I was adopted when I was a baby, so you could say I was one of the lucky ones.'

'And now you want to make things better for other children in need of care.'

'It all comes down to attitude. That's my opinion, anyway. It's not just a matter of having the money or the will. You have to have a good heart. Take this place, for instance. Why do you suppose it's called St Anthony's?'

'Lots of schools are named after saints, so why not an orphanage?'

'But why St Anthony in particular? Do you know what he's the patron saint of? Lost things. Not even lost children, just lost things. That tells you a lot about the prevailing attitude when this place was set up.'

'That was years ago.'

'And there are still plenty of people with the same attitude, but I have the impression you're not one of them. Look, I mentioned that some Boards of Health are still recruiting and that goes for the division I'm in. There are a couple of posts available. It's paid work, not voluntary. You might want to give it a go.'

'Me?'

'I assume there's no Mr Watson in the picture or you wouldn't be out at work; and – no offence – but a girl who's got what it takes to head to London to do her bit for the war isn't the type to have no choice other than shop work.'

Molly opened her mouth to say 'I'm engaged', but what came out was: 'I haven't got the right experience.'

Mrs Atwood shrugged. 'Personally, I think attitude is more what it's about. Not that I would have any say in whether you got a job, you understand. You mentioned clerical work; that's important. You have to be able to keep records and so forth; and if your skills need brushing up, there's a business school right here in Chorlton. Forgive my bluntness, but I assume you're a surplus girl. This business school is particularly for surplus girls.'

'I read about it in *Vera's Voice*.'

Mrs Atwood smiled. 'So did I. I was working in London at the time. I applied for the position at the Board of Health here, but my office skills were very basic, so I wrote to the Miss Heskeths' school and got taken on.'

'What about...? I mean, are you a widow?'

'A war widow, yes. Like so many.'

'I'm sorry to hear that.'

'Thank you.' Mrs Atwood spoke in a calm, almost flat voice, as if she had said it a hundred times before but had never got used to it. 'The business school isn't far from here, actually. It's in Wilton Close – do you know it? It's on the far side of the recreation ground.'

'I know where the rec is. How do you attend the business school if you're working?'

'The ladies run it as a night-school. Oh, look, here's the hot-potato man.'

Molly looked round. 'It's Bunny.' She watched him using the wooden handles to manoeuvre the cart with the boiler on top. Once it was in position, he lowered the handles and the legs touched the ground.

'Bunny?'

'I can tell you're not from round here.' Molly smiled. 'Everyone knows Bunny. He's always out and about.'

'He's offered to give every child a hot potato,' said Mrs Atwood.

'How kind.' Molly kept her smile in position even though it nearly killed her. A delicious salty potato for every child – what a treat. If only her own treat could have lived up to expectations.

'The children are about to be led out,' said Mrs Atwood. 'Are you going to take a seat?'

'No, I'll stand at the back. I need to be able to go inside to fetch the sweets.'

'I'll go and park myself. I enjoyed meeting you, Miss Watson. Maybe we'll bump into one another again.'

It was most unlikely…unless Molly applied for one of the jobs Mrs Atwood had mentioned. And why would she do that?

Mrs Rostron came outside and took her seat on the front row. Then the children filed out in silence, a long line in grey, starting with the oldest. They all sat cross-legged in rows on the ground. The smallest children were led out by a nursemaid in a blue dress with a white apron and a second nursemaid helped her chivvy them into position. When everyone was settled, Mrs Rostron nodded and a fiddle-player stepped forward and started to play a lively jig. The dancers marched out, the boys in white shirts instead of grey and the girls – oh, the girls! No wonder Molly's little helper had been envious. There were six girls, each in a dress of a different colour, light

44

blue, pale green, soft yellow, shell-pink, lilac and cream. After their regulation grey dresses with white pinafores, they must feel like princesses; and judging by the round eyes of the children watching them, they looked like princesses too.

The children took their places around the maypole. One of the boys had the job of unfastening the ribbons and walking from dancer to dancer, handing them out. Then there was a pause in the music. From somewhere came the count of 'One, two, three' and the dance commenced, boys skipping in one direction, girls in the other, winding in and out, changing direction, the ribbons going up and over, down and through, as the children made the intricate shapes of the dance, until in the end the ribbons were wound close to the maypole and, with a final flourish by the fiddler, the display ended.

Hurrying indoors, Molly picked up the tray with the treats for the dancers. Warmth radiated through her. The children more than deserved their reward. She took the tray outside, standing back while Mrs Rostron made a speech thanking the audience and the dancers.

'...and Miss Watson is here with a special treat from Upton's to thank the dancers for their hard work. The rest of the children were supposed also to receive some sweets, but unfortunately—'

'Oh, but—' Molly began before the brief glare she received from the superintendent silenced her.

As Mrs Rostron continued and the children cast glum looks at one another, Molly handed the tray to one of the nursemaids and hurried back inside. If she came back with the rest of the sweets, Mrs Rostron would be able to correct her error and the children would cheer up.

As she headed for the dining room, she almost bumped into a man coming round the corner. She jumped back.

'I'm sorry,' she began – then stopped. Stopped moving, stopped speaking. Her throat constricted.

The man was carrying a tray; and not just any old tray, not the kind of tray you had in a dining room to put plates on, but a tray from a sweet shop. A penny tray, no less – a full penny tray, with white mice and chocolate-covered nuts and fruit jellies encrusted with sugar, mint balls and marzipan hearts and violet delights, gobstoppers and strawberry dreams and packets of aniseed balls. He must be a sweet shop-owner who had heard about the theft from Upton's and had decided to step in where Upton's had failed. Yes, she was glad the children would have such a wonderful of selection of sweets to share, of course she was. And, yes, that was more important than anything else, but even so... Compared to the splendour of this fellow's penny tray, her measly bits of cut-up bootlaces and midget gems would make Upton's would look mean and ridiculous. Molly's heart shrivelled under the disappointment.

'Stand aside, please.' She was taken aback by how cold she sounded, but she couldn't help it. If she stayed here another minute, she might shed tears for all the good intentions that had been flattened by the day's events. 'Just...just stay put while I share out these sweets. Then you can be as flashy as you like.'

Chapter Five

THE SAVOURY SMELL of bacon lingered in the air as the front door shut behind Dad and Tom. Mum always sent them off with a hearty breakfast sticking to their ribs, while toast and marmalade was good enough for her and Molly. Dead on quarter past seven, Dad and Tom set off, Mum seeing them on their way from the front door.

'Another couple of years, our Molly,' she said, coming back into the kitchen, 'and you'll be seeing Norris off to work with a good breakfast inside him.'

'Do you think he needs it? He's a clerk, not a builder.' Molly put the butter dish and milk jug on the larder shelf. 'I don't imagine he requires bacon and black pudding to set him up for the day.'

'I didn't mean that.' Mum stacked the plates, cutlery on the top. 'I meant two years isn't long to wait.'

Molly shook the tablecloth outside the back door. 'I suppose not, when we've already waited three.'

Mum paused in the scullery doorway and turned round. 'What I *really* meant...'

About to fold the tablecloth, Molly paused. 'What?'

'I hope our Dora's plan to get wed in September hasn't put your nose out of joint.'

'Why would it? I always knew I was going to be engaged a long time.'

Mum deposited the plates beside the sink. 'There's ten bob on the mantelpiece for you.'

'What for? My birthday was weeks ago.'

'It's a contribution towards this day out to Southport. It's not going to be cheap and I thought a bit extra would help.'

Molly crossed the kitchen and positioned herself in the scullery doorway. 'Are you trying to make me feel better after the fiasco of the sweets yesterday?'

Mum shooed her aside so she could get back into the kitchen and collect the frying pan and the egg-coddler from the stove. 'Can't I treat my daughter if I feel like it? You know I slip Tilda and Chrissie a little summat now and then for the grandchildren. It's only fair to give you a few bob an' all.'

Molly slid an arm round her and kissed her cheek. 'Thanks. You're a love.' She popped the folded tablecloth in the drawer, then picked up the teapot and swilled the dregs round. 'Mum, what if I was interested in an office job?'

'Well, I was surprised when you went back to Upton's after the war.'

The teapot stilled. 'You never said.'

Mum shrugged. 'You're old enough to know your own mind. You're clever and I'm sure you'd have been capable of more, if you'd wanted it, but you didn't.'

No, she hadn't. Not then. She hadn't felt brave enough or strong enough to try anything new.

Did she now?

She threw the red day-cloth over the table-felt that protected the table's wooden surface. It ballooned and settled.

Mum put down the frying pan. 'Are you thinking of it now? It's not like you need to. You're not one of these surplus girls you read about. You've got Norris to look after you. Eh, I remember how pleased we all were when you got engaged.'

Molly laughed. 'Do you remember Gran saying "I can rest

easy now", as if it was all she'd been hanging on for before she popped her clogs?'

'It's what you want for your daughters and your grand-daughters: marriage to a good provider. It was a weight off all our minds.'

It had been a weight off Molly's mind too – or not so much off her mind as off her heart. Norris was a safe harbour and she was lucky he wanted her. What a relief it had been to have this opportunity to build a happy and prosperous new life. She had gladly gone along with everything he suggested. Did that mean it was her fault he now expected her compliance? As time had passed and she had felt better, stronger, in herself, she had lost the instinct to fall in with his every wish. Norris had taken to softening her up through small, persistent remarks against which it felt churlish to hold out.

At what point had softening her up transformed into wearing her down? And as for what he had said to her on Saturday night...

'But then,' said Mum, 'if you do want to try office work, why not?'

'Really?' She hadn't expected that.

'Aye. Better to do it while you're engaged than spend your married life wondering.'

'Oh.' Something inside her seemed to shrink.

'You sound disappointed.'

'It's not exactly a ringing endorsement of my capabilities.'

'Is that what you wanted?'

What did she want? Was she considering changing her job? Going to the business school?

'If you want to know what I really think,' said Mum, 'I'll tell you. I think we all lost summat in the war. All of us: soldiers, civilians, the world over. All those poor lads who came home without an arm, without a leg, with bad nerves, with night-mares. Our Tom came home with silver hair.'

49

'Oh, Mum.'

'I'd give ten years of my life if I could set him free from whatever it was that did that to him. Everyone came home with or without something.'

She looked at Molly, an intent look that caused something to flutter in the pit of Molly's stomach, followed by a feeling of emptiness.

'What about you, our Molly? What did you come home with or without?'

He had better put a collar on – and a tie. Heck, it was like dressing for church. Aaron picked up the small drawstring bag into which he had tipped the money Danny had swiped, and slipped it into his jacket pocket, where it formed a heavy lump. He stepped outside into the cool morning air and set off for St Anthony's. He liked this time of the morning, even in the depths of winter. Not too many people about.

He lived in a cottage a stone's throw from Chorlton Green. It wasn't the most convenient address for the orphanage's caretaker, but while there was accommodation in the building for the female staff, there was nowhere suitable – namely, separate – for a man; so here he was in Soapsuds Cottage, so called because its first tenant had run the laundry up the road. The road was called Soapsuds Lane – well, not really. The Ordnance Survey people would be surprised to hear it. They and the Royal Mail and the folk who ran the census didn't know it as Soapsuds Lane, but then they weren't residents of Chorlton Green and its environs.

Soapsuds Cottage had been a ramshackle little place when he moved in, but one of the advantages of being a carpenter was doing your own repairs; and not just repairs but improvements. He still experienced a swell of pleasure each time he used the narrow spiral staircase he had lovingly constructed and installed to replace the old ladder that used to give access to upstairs. He had rehung the doors, replaced rotten floor-boards and made good the furniture.

To the amazement of the neighbours, he had built a piece of trellis which he had attached to his south-facing back wall beside the scullery window; and up this he grew sweet peas and black-eyed Susans each summer. With the left-over wood, he built a piece of trellis for frail old Mrs Mulvey in the adjoin-ing house and planted sweet peas for her. She swore that trellis was the only thing that kept her cottage standing.

Approaching St Anthony's, Aaron walked past a length of the orphanage's ivy-encrusted brick wall. Getting rid of that ivy was on his list of jobs for this year. Bunny had offered to lend a hand and Aaron wanted to get the children involved.

Letting himself in, he made a tour of the building, as he always did first thing. It wasn't one of his duties to do so, but he toured the place last thing before he left and immediately he arrived to ensure all was well.

From the outside, the orphanage was a severe-looking build-ing shaped like a back-to-front capital F, with ground-floor windows set too high in the walls for anyone to see out of. Inside, it was a rambling place, with steps up into this room and down into that one, rooms that led into other rooms, and no such thing as a long corridor: there were corners everywhere. It was as if, after designing the stark exterior, the architect had got royally drunk before he made a start on the floor-plans.

Breakfast was in full swing, the dining room bright with young voices as the kids tucked into their porridge followed by bread and marge. The food here was plain grub, but no one went hungry and in that respect these orphans were luckier than some of the local children who lived with their families.

'You're looking posh today, sir,' piped up Mikey Layton.

In the orphanage, he was Layton One and his younger brother was Layton Two. Aaron called them Michael Layton and Jacob Layton, much to Mrs Wardle's disgust, telling her to her face that, as caretaker, his duty was to the building, not for the care of the children and he had no intention of being hidebound by heartless Victorian rules. Mrs Wardle had marched straight to Mrs Rostron, demanding to have him sacked, but Mrs Rostron had backed him up, though afterwards she had told him privately not to push his luck.

'It's not Sunday, is it?' quipped Mikey.

'It can't be,' retorted Aaron, 'or you, Michael Layton, would have washed behind your ears.'

He proceeded on his way, leaving a ripple of delight behind him. Where was the harm in having a joke with the children? But there were some adults, mentioning no names, who couldn't tell the difference between banter and backchat.

Mikey and Jacob Layton were new here, having arrived in tragic circumstances. When their father had abandoned his responsibilities and left his wife and children, the family had resorted to doing a moonlight flit to escape the bailiffs, but the cottage in which they had taken refuge had burned to the ground and the Laytons had been lucky to escape with their lives. The fire had left them with nothing. Mrs Layton was now a live-in maid in a house in Wilton Close and the two boys had been accepted here.

In view of all that, if a spot of light-heartedness helped them feel more at home, then why not?

Michael – or Mikey, as the other kids called him – was settling in well. A sensible lad, he seemed determined to make the best of things, which was admirable, but at the same time tugged at Aaron's heart. Mikey Layton was a schoolboy. He should be mucking about and having fun. Instead he had lost his home and his family had been scattered.

But it was the smaller Layton brother who caused Aaron more concern – young Jacob. There was something vulnerable about him. But Aaron knew he had to be careful. Since taking up his post here after the war, he had interested himself in the daily life of St Anthony's above and beyond his duty as caretaker, something that hadn't gone unnoticed by Mrs Rostron.

'It's one thing to take a group of children to the rec for a game of rounders, Mr Abrams,' she had cautioned him, 'quite another to take a personal interest. Children are quick to perceive – and resent – any suggestion of favouritism. For a member of staff, personal involvement in a child's life is not appropriate and I will not permit it.'

A couple of times since then, he had had to pull himself back from getting involved in a tragic case. Mrs Rostron wouldn't thank him for overstepping the mark – or, more likely, her 'thanks' would take the form of dismissing him.

But it didn't hurt to chat to the kids, did it, as long as he didn't single out one in particular. He often exchanged a few words with one child or another, or with a group of them, as they were clattering about after breakfast, getting ready to set off for school. The Laytons set off earlier than everyone else, because, while all the other St Anthony's children went to school in Chorlton, Mikey and Jacob had previously lived in Stretford and Mrs Rostron had elected to leave them at their old school until the end of the school year, which was just a few weeks away.

Finding Jacob Layton – yes, all right, having gone looking for Jacob Layton, Aaron spotted him, cap on, ready for school, hovering by a door that was open onto the playground. Cool air streamed in, summoning up a tingle in Aaron's bloodstream. He much preferred being outdoors to inside.

'Waiting for your brother?' he asked.

'Yes, sir.'

'Settling in here? Making friends?'

'Yes, sir.'

Yes, sir; no, sir; three bags full, sir. Well, what answer had he expected to such a bland question? 'Are you any good at cricket? I have a bit of a knock-about sometimes of an evening with the boys.'

'I'm not much good. I can't catch.'

'It just takes practice. I take a group to the rec now and then. You might like it. Sometimes I organise rounders and the girls come too.'

'*Girls?*'

'Aye, and they've been known to slaughter the boys. I know it's tough moving into a new place, but you'll soon be part of the furniture...if you make an effort.'

That got the boy's attention. He jammed his elbows into his sides, as if to make himself as small as possible. 'I'm trying, sir, just like Mrs Rostron said.'

'I didn't mean that,' Aaron said gently. 'I only meant that settling in properly is partly a matter of attitude.' But here was a chance to refer to Jacob's wider situation and he took it. 'I know about your other brother, the one who was sent to the reformatory, and I know you're under orders to mend your ways or else Mrs Rostron will send you there too. A piece of advice. You want to follow a big brother's lead? Follow Mikey's – Michael's. He's a good sort.'

'Yes, sir.'

The lad started to roll his eyes, then thought better of it. His face closed up. He had probably heard that particular piece of advice a hundred times recently, from his mum and his oldest siblings, who were out at work and fending for themselves, probably from his teacher and headmaster as well. Most impressive of all, he would have heard it from Mrs Rostron.

Mikey Layton came running downstairs, face cheerful beneath his school cap.

'Here comes trouble,' said Aaron with a grin. 'Off you go, lads.'

Watching them hurry away, Aaron couldn't help linking Jacob Layton to Danny Cropper. Two troubled boys. Should he encourage a friendship between them? Or might that lead to more problems? Wouldn't he do better to leave well alone? Mrs Rostron would warn him off, and quite rightly.

But nothing would stop him wanting the best for every child or looking for ways to achieve it. That was how he coped with the war, with what he had seen, what he had done – what he had been obliged to do. He had experienced the world at its worst and the only thing that could possibly make sense of what he and hundreds of thousands of ordinary men like him had seen and done was to make the world a kinder place for the children growing up in it.

He could have returned to his old job as a carpenter, and done well from it, but that was no longer enough. Some might see his role as caretaker of St Anthony's as a step backwards for a skilled craftsman, but he didn't view it like that. To his mind, it was a way to contribute to the well-being of the next generation, especially here, in this environment, where the children had already lost so much.

What could be more important than finding ways to make these children's lives a little easier?

Dressed as he was, Aaron couldn't knuckle down to work properly, but there was some measuring he needed to do and he got on with that until it was time to set off for Upton's and return the money. Then Danny's misdemeanour could be forgotten. The lad deserved another chance. He was another one going through a tough time.

The shop-bell jingled above Aaron's head as he walked into the shop. Sweetness smacked him in the face. He caught the succulent aromas of butterscotch, boiled sweets, treacle toffee and fudge, together with a waft of mint and aniseed, beneath which lurked the darker scent of liquorice. Behind the counter, the girl from yesterday was up a wooden stepladder, examining the quantities of sweets in the row of glass jars on the top shelf, while an older man with thin, oiled hair and a grey moustache, presumably Mr Upton, jotted in a notebook.

They both turned to look at him. The girl's hair swung at chin-length, an unusual colour, not fair, not red. Her eyes were an unusual colour too. They were hazel, but not the usual brown-hazel, more of a greeny-hazel, and her skin was creamy-smooth. She was still young enough to be referred to as a girl, though a chap of the same age would flatten you for calling him a boy. That bibbed white apron was unflatteringly bulky, but it nipped in where it was tied, showing how trim her waist was. Aaron's heart bumped.

'Good morning,' said Mr Upton. 'What may I get you?'

'Actually, I've come with an apology.' He looked up at the girl. He had an odd hollow feeling in his chest.

Her eyes widened in surprise – and then narrowed accusingly. 'It's you.' With a toss of her chin, she directed her gaze on Mr Upton. 'This is the man I told you about from the other sweet shop.' She clattered down the stepladder.

Mr Upton frowned. 'I don't recognise you, sir.'

Aaron addressed the girl. 'So that's why you were upset yesterday.' He smiled at her. This was going to make the explanation easier, friendlier. He wanted her to feel friendly towards him. 'I don't have a sweet shop. My name's Abrams. I'm the caretaker at St Anthony's.'

'But you had that penny tray.'

'I'd just been up the road and bought it.'

'The entire tray?'

'I knew one of the collecting-boxes had gone astray—'

'Been stolen,' said Mr Upton.

'I didn't want the children to miss out, so I bought a penny tray. When you bumped into me, I was taking it to the kitchen for the children to have later. It wasn't my intention to upstage you.'

'I see.' Discomfort stained her face, highlighting her fine cheekbones. 'Then I'm the one who ought to apologise.'

'Not at all. An easy mistake to make.'

'I hope Miss Watson didn't speak out of turn to you,' said Mr Upton.

Aaron didn't deign to reply to that. Fancy talking about her as if she weren't present. 'I've brought this for you.' He took the drawstring bag from his pocket, holding it out to her. 'It's the money from the collecting-box.'

Mr Upton's hand snaked across and grabbed the bag, leaving Aaron's hand and Miss Watson's reaching towards one another. The shopkeeper scrabbled at the drawstring fastening and upended the bag. Coins tumbled out, clashing and bouncing on the counter.

'Is it all here?' he demanded.

'All of it.' Including the coppers Aaron had put in to cover what Danny had used to get himself to town. That seemed to be all Upton cared about.

'Did you get it back off Daniel Cropper?' asked Miss Watson.

Aaron looked her straight in the eye. 'Danny isn't your thief.'

Yesterday he had taken Danny from Victoria Station straight to school, telling the headmaster the same tale he later told Mrs Rostron; that on his way to the ironmonger's, he had come across the Cropper lad playing truant. 'He's worried about his dad. You might cut him some slack.' But of course neither of them had. Mr Bertram had caned Danny and Mrs Rostron had given him the strap. He would probably get a clip round the ear from the local bobby as well, for wasting police time.

'But...' Miss Watson looked a little dazed. 'He was here in the shop. A group of children comes in every Monday. They lark about, but there's no harm in them. Daniel Cropper was here at the same time. After they'd all left, the collecting-box had gone.'

'Why blame him?' He hated to mislead her, but he had to protect Danny.

'Well...' She rubbed her chin. 'He didn't spend anything.'

'The orphans aren't given pocket money.'

'And he was hanging about outside when we opened.'

Aaron shrugged. 'Playing truant.'

Miss Watson pressed the flat of her hand to the snowy bib of her apron. 'I was so sure. I described him to Mrs Rostron and she said he was a runaway.'

'Aye, a runaway. That doesn't make him a thief.'

He edged towards the shop door. Hell, this was vile. He hadn't expected it to be this hard. After telling all these lies on Danny's behalf, he was in danger of believing them himself.

'I hope you've learned a lesson from this, Miss Watson.' Behind the counter, Mr Upton moved about fussily. 'You've been wrong about everything. You've wrongly accused a boy of theft and wrongly assumed this gentleman was a rival shop-keeper out to do us down. The next time you have one of your clever ideas to help someone in need, kindly keep it to yourself.'

Chapter Six

MOLLY LOVED WALKING on the meadows that ran alongside the River Mersey, Lancashire this side, Cheshire over yon, and now that the evenings were drawing out, Norris was happy to oblige. Had he brought her here to please her – or because it wouldn't cost him anything? Or, since she was happy to do it, didn't that matter? She had asked herself this question many times, as well as that other question, the disloyal question, the one no loving fiancée should ask. Was she the only one to notice that he never willingly stumped up for anything?

Other questions had arisen too. After the war, she had been deeply grateful to Norris for his kindness and understanding, but she accepted now that at times his kindness weighed her down – and sometimes it didn't feel entirely kind. What he had said to her after they had left Dora and Harry's fish supper hadn't been kind. Oh, on the surface it had. On the surface, it had been a well-intentioned reminder of his reliability and devotion. It was a reminder he had delivered once or twice during their engagement and previously it had made her gratitude surge up with such force that it left her muscles weak and trembly.

But it hadn't had that effect last Saturday night. It had made her feel – trapped. That was a strong word and it had taken her a few days to face up to it. What had, those previous times, felt like a reaffirmation of love and security had seemed last Saturday to hold the hint of – of a threat.

It was a lot to take in and she had questioned her own judgement, her own instincts, more than once. She needed time to think things through. For now, it was best to carry on as normal.

As she and Norris walked across the meadows, the piquant tang of earth and greenery did Molly good. Her shoulders relaxed. Here and there were tall lady's smocks with their flowers of palest lilac, and pretty clumps of cowslips with their clusters of drooping yellow blooms.

She told Norris about Mr Abrams from the orphanage buying an entire penny tray so the children wouldn't be disappointed. It felt important to talk about money. She had to prove she wouldn't be silenced.

'He must have money to burn,' said Norris. 'Who is he, anyway?'

'The caretaker.'

Norris issued a snort of laughter. 'I hope he takes better care of that building than he does of his bank account.'

Unhooking himself from the hand Molly had looped through his arm, he stooped to pick a stem of speedwell, its tiny flowers the bluest of blues. He reached towards her, smiling, and tilted her hat. Molly grabbed it and pulled it straight.

'What are you doing?'

'Putting this behind your ear.'

She took it from him. 'I'll look tipsy if my hat is skew-whiff.'

She slipped her left hand through his arm, which bent to receive it. He looked smart in his blazer. 'It must be spring,' she had teased when he turned up at her house wearing it instead of his faithful tweed jacket. As they continued walking, nodding to an old boy and his dog, she breathed in the fresh green scents.

'Anyway,' said Norris, 'that sort of fellow probably doesn't have a bank account. He probably keeps his money under the mattress or stuffed in an old sock.'

'That's an unkind thing to say.'

'What's unkind about it? He's a caretaker, for pity's sake. We're not talking about the intellectual elite.'

'Well, I think it was generous of him,' said Molly.

'Oh, undoubtedly. The man has a good heart, I'll give him that. But what do you suppose his wife said when he went home and told her? I wonder how she's feeding her family this week.' Norris's left hand reached across his body to press the hand he held in the crook of his elbow. 'I'll never do anything like that to you, you may be sure. I'll never fritter my money away.'

'Our money,' she said mildly.

'What?'

'Our money. "With all my worldly goods I thee endow." So it'll be our money.'

His arm moved and her hand fell away.

'You are a tease, Molly Watson. Haven't I said it before? You are a tease.'

He caught her hand and swung it between them as they walked, as if she had made a grand joke and her light-hearted mood had infected him. Molly didn't exactly stop him swinging, but she put the brakes on, so the swing became less ebullient and gradually stilled.

'Seriously, Norris, it will be our money, won't it? You shall view it that way, shan't you?'

'What a strange question. It'll be my duty to provide for you – and my pleasure. You're going to have a vacuum cleaner and a woman to do the rough; and you won't have to battle with one of those vast old kitchen ranges with a mind of its own. You can look forward to one of those modern contrivances and a tin of Kleennoff.'

'Don't forget the bar of Dairy Milk every Saturday.'

Norris laughed. 'By Jove, you aren't going to let me forget that, are you? Very well. I did promise and I always keep my promises. A bar of Dairy Milk every Saturday it will be, my girl.'

'You haven't answered my question. Shall you regard your wages as ours?'

'Everything I earn will be used for the good of our household. What's brought this on? You don't usually give me such a grilling. You're normally too busy looking forward to all the domestic advantages marriage with me is going to bring.'

Strictly speaking, it was Mum and Gran and Auntie Faith and Mrs Upton, and all the women they gossiped with, who were eagerly anticipating Molly's gas cooker and her piano and her stair carpet. Molly had looked forward to them as well, to start with. At what point had she realised that, for all his fancy talk about future domestic wonders, Norris was deeply reluctant to put his hand in his pocket in the here and now? She had once said something along these lines, but he had countered by telling her how hard he was saving for their future, how seriously he took his responsibilities; how, in years to come, when other women's husbands were drinking half their wages and buying on hire purchase, she would be grateful to have such a reliable husband. Which had made her question seem mealy-mouthed and selfish.

There was a golden glow around the clouds. The evening sky had deepened from blue to violet, edged with pink.

'Red sky at night,' said Norris. 'It's time I took you home.'

He started to turn round, but Molly stopped.

'Let's walk via Chorlton Green and Beech Road.'

'It's longer that way.'

'I'd like to.'

Was it daft to want to walk near the orphanage? To imagine going there in an official capacity, like Mrs Atwood? It wasn't as though they would pass the building. All they would do was cross over Church Road at one end, and St Anthony's was at the far end. Definitely daft.

'What would you say if I got myself a new job?'

'But you've been at Upton's since you were a lass.'

'Maybe it's time for a change.'

'You'll have enough of a change when we get married. There's no need for my wife to go out to work. You'll be the queen of our little household. I'll always take care of you, Molly.'

'Don't you want a clever wife?'

'Of course I do. A wife who knows precisely how I like my eggs boiled and who knows not to put marzipan on the Christmas cake.'

'And who'll manage the housekeeping efficiently.'

Norris beamed. 'Goes without saying. I'll furnish you with a proper little accounts book and you can have different pages for the butcher and the grocer and incidentals.' He chuckled. 'Not too many of those, if you please. Not too many incidentals.'

He stopped and turned to her, his face shining with love. He did love her, she knew he did.

'Does that mean you'll hand over your wage-packet to me every Friday?' she asked.

The smile dropped from Norris's face. She practically heard the splat as it landed on the pavement. Then he chuckled.

'How quaint, Molly. What a quaint idea. So old fashioned and, frankly, working class. It's best to have one person in charge of the funds and you're aware of how I excel at that. After the way I've saved up and been careful all this time, you can trust me. You know you can.'

'I can't think of anybody better qualified than you to be careful with money.'

Couldn't he hear the dry note in her voice? Norris sighed softly, as if she had just made her wedding vows.

They walked past the hedge that bordered the recreation ground. The rec had started life on the other side of the road, but there were red-brick houses over there now. Molly wasn't old enough to remember this change happening, but Dad knew when everything had been built, even if he hadn't built it himself. In the cooling twilight, the privet hedge threw a long trail of crispness into the air and the earth added a tang of promise. The vast beech tree that overhung the road spilled a canopy of bright young leaves.

'Norris, when we go on the day trip to Southport, I want to take part in everything. The lecture, the hotel meals, everything. I don't want to go for a walk while everyone else goes on the Pleasure Beach.'

'I can't think of anything better than a stroll in the sea air.'

'I mean it, Norris. I – I'm happy to pay my way if I have to.'

'There's no need for that.' He said that sometimes, but it never stopped him accepting her contribution when the time came.

'Mum gave me money towards it. Ten bob. Wasn't that good of her? I'll put it in the kitty for both of us.'

'That's champion of her, I must say. Ten whole shillings. As a matter of fact – and this will make you laugh – my mother gave me money too. Here I am, in my thirties, and she still sees me as her little lad.'

'I think it's sweet. How much did she give you?'

'Fifteen shillings.'

'Fifteen!' Molly squeezed his arm. 'Aren't we lucky in our mothers?'

'Indeed we are. So we'll both put ten shillings in the kitty.'

'You're putting in ten?'

'Then we'll both have put in the same. I can't say fairer than that.'

'Can't you?' Molly stopped walking. 'I can.'

Norris's eyes widened. 'Molly!'

'My ten bob is more than yours.'

'Now you're being daft, love.' Norris wagged his finger at her in mock telling-off; Molly felt like biting it. 'You'll have to shape up if I'm going to trust you with the household accounts book.'

'Didn't you do fractions at school, Norris? I did. My ten bob is all I was given. Yours is two-thirds of what you were given. So, no, both of us putting in ten shillings is not the same.'

Heat flushed through her. Honestly, she had had enough of being treated this way. Enough? Too much, more like. In that instant, her whole world shifted. The doubts and questions about her engagement that had been building up, and which she had only in the past few days started to articulate to herself, shuddered into a crisp new focus.

She inhaled sharply. The air was pungent with the scent of new growth. Very fitting. In that instant, she knew she was about to enter a phase of new growth herself.

Her stomach turned a somersault. 'I'm sorry, Norris, but I'm – I'm breaking off our engagement.'

'*What?* You can't. I never heard anything more ridiculous. Here we are, having a pleasant evening together and now, all of a sudden, this. What's got into you?'

'I'm sorry to let you down, but—'

'But what?' He scrubbed his face with his hands, knocking his trilby at an angle. 'I shaved off my moustache for you.'

'I know.'

'What have I done wrong? Don't you believe I'm going to provide you with the modern cooker and everything else we've planned to have?'

'Of course I believe it. It's your unwillingness to spend money in other ways. Small ways.'

'This can't possibly be because of keeping five shillings out of what Mother gave me.'

'It's not just that.' How petty she sounded. 'There were other times, too.'

'Such as?'

'Such as, the donation you made towards sweets for the orphans.'

'I seem to remember Mr Upton complimenting me on my generosity. Are you suggesting I should have been foolishly generous, like Harry, throwing his money around like there's no tomorrow? I've been saving carefully to give you the best possible start to married life and now it turns out...' Norris swallowed hard, pressing his lips together and blinking rapidly. 'Well, you've certainly given me something to think about.' He stood up straighter, pushing his shoulders back. 'I suppose it's better to get it out in the open than to let it build up.'

'It's been building up for some time.'

That was true, even if she hadn't altogether realised it was building up, but it was the wrong thing to say, because he immediately countered with, 'Then why didn't you say something sooner? You shouldn't have let it go this far. If you'd spoken up earlier...I love you, Molly. You know I do.'

Guilt tightened her chest. Was she supposed to remain engaged to Norris to spare his feelings at the expense of her own? She couldn't do that. She had to break it off. People would call her a jilt and would whisper behind her back, and her family would curl up in shame, but she couldn't continue with her engagement.

'This business with the money from our mothers was the last straw. I'm sorry, Norris.'

'This is very hurtful, Molly.' His brown eyes were dark with reproach. 'Everything I've done these past three years, everything I've worked for, has been for you, for our future. And now you want to call it off because of five bob. Do you imagine I intended to drink it down the pub?'

'Of course not.'

'Then what do you think I was going to do with it?'

'That isn't the point. The point is, you didn't put all the money towards our kitty.'

How trifling it sounded. It sounded like she was the mean one. But it had built up over three years of watching Norris's penny-pinching and small, needless economies; three years of watching him carefully shunting coins from one end of his change-purse to the other and scrutinising them while he worked out how few of them he could get away with parting with on this particular occasion.

Three years of being patronised. Three years of that chummy voice sounding so kind and indulgent when really he was talking down to her. Three years of being kept in her place. A future of ending up cowed and browbeaten, with everyone else thinking how lucky she was.

But she couldn't say any of that. If she tried, he would turn it all around and make it her fault. He was good at that.

'Norris, I'm sorry. I'm going to do something else with my life.'

Norris's head snapped back as if she had struck him. A flush sharpened his cheeks. 'What? What are you talking about?'

'I want to try for another job. I'm interested in the new Board of Health.'

'You don't need a new job. You're engaged to me.'

Hadn't he heard her the first time? 'I don't want to be engaged any more.'

'You can't snap your fingers and declare it over. It has to be a joint decision – like getting engaged was a joint decision, and agreeing to wait five years. You can't just call it off. Look, you're upset. We're both upset. We'll discuss this on another occasion.'

'No, Norris. I'm going to see if I can get a new job and—'

'And live at home with your parents for ever, because you can't afford to leave? You won't earn enough to support yourself in any comfort. Women don't. Everything in life is geared towards the female of the species being looked after by her menfolk, first by her father, then by her husband. That's the way it's meant to be. It's why women don't earn much – because it would be unnatural if they did. How can you imagine that life on your own will be better than life with me? Life on your own will be a damn sight harder – pardon my French.'

'It's what I want to do. I met someone at the orphanage, who told me a little about her work, and there was an article about the new Boards of Health a while back in *Vera's Voice*.'

'So you're basing this on a chance meeting and a piece in a story-paper.'

'I'm basing it on the fact that I'm capable of doing more than working in a sweet shop. I'm basing it on a wish to do some good in the world.'

Norris screwed up his mouth thoughtfully, then huffed out a breath. 'Yes, I will say it. Need I remind you of what transpired the last time you struck out on your own in the world?'

Molly's throat bobbed and her hands fell to her sides. It was all she could do not to cup her hands over her mouth as remorse washed through her.

'I have your best interests at heart. I know you think you can cope in the big wide world, but you can't. Experience has shown that you can't. And you want to help other people?' Norris laughed softly, a sad sound.

Doubt assailed her. Her insides felt heavy and numb. Yes, she had come home from the war and sought refuge in her old life behind the counter in Upton's, but she was stronger now. She had recovered from past mistakes and no longer needed to hide herself away. The more she had dwelt on her conversation with Mrs Atwood, the more drawn she felt to this new way of opening up her life. Yes, opening it up. She was ready for more. She was ready for something new.

A quiet resolve steadied her. She tightened her fists and then relaxed them. 'I do want to help others, Norris. What's more, I think I'll be good at it.'

'Oh, really?' Was that a sneer? 'What makes you think that?'

She lifted her chin. 'Because I understand, from my own experience, that life doesn't always turn out the way you expect.'

'Well, I suggest you don't say that in your letter of application,' scoffed Norris, 'or they won't look twice at you. They'll want an upright, respectable person, who can set a good example.'

The hairs on Molly's arms bristled. 'Do I take it from that, that I'm not suitable wife material?'

Norris backed down immediately. 'Of course not. I meant no such thing, as you well know. You're exactly the right sort of wife, Molly, but you have to understand your limitations. You're my best girl. Haven't I looked after you all this time, eh? Done everything in my power to prepare for our future? Our secure, prosperous future. You can't want to put that in jeopardy.'

But she could. As bizarre as it sounded in a world where prospective husbands were thin on the ground and spinsters were ten a penny, and where she was not merely a spinster but an old maid whose thirtieth birthday was a lot closer than she would like – as bizarre as it sounded, she wanted to take a chance. A new life beckoned – a new future. The want, the need of a worthwhile job, of wider horizons and personal fulfilment, was so intense that her heart squeezed.

'I might not be offered a post.'

She had to say it. She had to face the possibility, had to bring herself down to earth. She didn't say it for Norris's benefit, but he nodded.

'Very well then. I suppose there's something to be said for letting you try.'

'For *letting* me?'

'And if you don't get a job, I won't hold this conversation against you. We'll simply carry on as though nothing has happened. And if you do get a job, well, I'll say "Good for you," and cheer you along. I can't say fairer than that.'

'Stop it. You're talking as if we're still engaged.'

'We are, as far as I'm concerned; and I'm sure your family will agree.'

She sucked in a breath. 'Then you'll all be wrong, won't you?'

'Are you mad?' Gran's faded blue eyes were wide with shock. 'Norris is a good catch. You won't find a better one, not at your age.'

'I'm not looking for a better one.'

It was an effort to hold her voice steady. Did she sound defiant? Realising that tension had hauled her shoulders practically up to her ears, Molly forced them down again. The upset she had caused in her family was simply frightful – but what had she expected? She surely hadn't been daft enough to imagine that anyone would take her side – had she? Everyone was shocked and hurt and dreadfully frightened that she would be mad enough to cast aside her secure future.

When she went to bed, her heartbeats slow with misery at having hurt her family, Mum came and sat on the mattress, like she used to do in the days of bedtime stories.

'Molly, is this my fault? D'you remember saying about an office job and "what if"? And I said, "Better to get one while you're engaged than spend your married life wondering." Is this because of that?'

Molly reached for her hand. Crikey, Mum was trembling.

Molly held her hand tightly. She wanted to kiss Mum's knuckles.

'This isn't anyone's fault, and certainly not yours, Mum. This is something I want to do. I want to find out what I'm capable of.'

'What you're capable of is being a sound wife and mother. As for being capable of something else, why would you want to? What's the point? You need to get married. That's what women do. That's where we get our security and our status. You're a lovely girl. You're bright and friendly and you've got a good heart and, up until today, I'd have said a sensible head. In a different world, you'd have had your pick of half a dozen fellows, but not these days.'

'Do you mean I should marry Norris even if he isn't the right man for me?'

'Isn't he? He has been for the past three years. I've never heard you say a word against him. He's decent and hard-working. He'll keep a roof over your head and there'll always be food on the table and a fire in the grate. That's what life is about, Molly.' Mum blew out a breath of pure exasperation. 'I shouldn't have to say these things to you. You're aren't a silly girl of sixteen with her head in the clouds. You're the best part of thirty.'

'Thanks for reminding me.'

'You might never get another chance. Don't throw this one away.'

So much for wanting to kiss Mum's knuckles.

It was the same with everyone.

Auntie Faith said, 'Norris is a good catch. You'll not find a better one, especially not at your age.'

Dora said, 'What's got into you, our Molly? You and Norris have been together for years.'

'Eh, Molly Watson, is it true?' asked the neighbours when Mum sent Molly to the butcher.

'Have you really called it off with that nice Norris Hartley? And him promising you a gas cooker an' all. There'll be plenty ready to step in and take your place, if you don't watch out.'

Returning home with the shopping, Molly hesitated outside the open back door, hearing voices in the kitchen.

'It isn't just the shock of our Molly doing something so out of character,' Gran was saying – and did she sound tearful? Molly's heart clenched inside her chest. 'It's the humiliation to the whole family. It's not something you can explain away. The girl's making the worst mistake of her life and it reflects badly on us all. It makes her look feckless and it makes us look as if we haven't fetched her up proper.'

Dad, bless him, tried his best with a practical suggestion.

'If you want an office job, love, I'll give you a go in Perkins and Watson. It wouldn't be the first time we've had a lady clerk.'

'Thanks, Dad, but the job I'm interested in isn't simply an office job. It's to do with helping people in the community.' Molly hugged him. 'But thanks for offering.'

She chose not to ask whether her acceptance would have been conditional upon 'seeing sense' and getting back together with Norris.

And that was another thing: Norris...

'Don't be too hard on her,' said Norris.

Just how had he ended up in their sitting room, talking it over with the family?

'She's having a touch of the collywobbles,' he went on. 'It's the long engagement. Now that your Dora is rushing up the aisle, it's put the wind up Molly, what with her being so much older. It's the equivalent of when women take too much exercise and their insides go all deranged. Molly...well, I won't court trouble by suggesting her brain is deranged, but her feelings are. It's her kind heart, you see. Haven't I always said she's got a kind heart? She's taken it into her head to have a bash at this Board of Health malarkey and I suppose I'll have to go along with it.' He chuckled. 'I blame those orphans and their maypole dancing. That's what put it into her head. It shows what a kind heart she's got, wanting to help poor mites like that.'

Molly stood up and left the room before her deranged feelings got the better of her and she seized the ornamental tankard from the mantelpiece and bashed Norris over the head.

What if she failed to get taken on by the Board of Health? Would everyone expect her to go back to him?

The only one who seemed to be on her side was Tom. He enfolded her in a hug that smelled of wood shavings, brick dust and soap.

'Do what's right for you.' His words were warm against her hair. 'Word of advice?'

'As long as you don't suggest asking Norris to take me back.'

'Wouldn't dream of it. Get Dora to cross your name off the list for going on the jolly to Southport. Better all round if you don't go.'

She suppressed a shiver. 'Much better.'

Molly wrote and rewrote her letter of application until she was sure she couldn't improve it any further, her tummy fluttering as she dropped it into the pillar-box. After that, as she waited for a reply, it became increasingly difficult not to be rattled by the remarks of her nearest and dearest. Shouldn't they support her instead of criticising and worrying?

And what if they were right? It was impossible not to feel quivery on the inside when she considered the enormity of what she was doing. Was the possibility of this job and a fresh future really worth casting aside what might well be her one and only chance of a settled life? But she couldn't express her anxiety in case her family marched her straight to Norris's house for a reconciliation.

In any case, the flutters she felt weren't just the anxiety stirred up by the shock and distress of her family and friends. There was a healthy dose of anticipation in there as well. She badly wanted this opportunity. Would Mrs Atwood's colleagues at the Board of Health consider her suitable?

Chapter Seven

JACOB RAN AS fast as he could, his heart pounding so hard it felt as if his chest might burst apart. This would never have happened had Thad still been here. But Thad wasn't here, was he? He had been packed off to the reformatory, leaving Jacob alone and unprotected, running for his life from a crowd of boys whom Thad had bullied mercilessly and who were now bent on giving Jacob the hammering of his life for having been Thad's faithful crony.

From behind, a hand snatched at his shoulder but failed to cling on. Jacob flung himself onwards but had no more speed in him. The boy behind was so close that his harsh breathing got mixed up in Jacob's ears with the sound of his own ragged breaths. Then all the air was knocked out of him by an almighty thump on his back and he and the other lad tumbled to the ground, arms and legs in a tangle, his pursuer's weight squeezing the air from Jacob's lungs. As the other boy hauled himself to his feet, all Jacob wanted was to stay where he was until the stunned feeling subsided, but he couldn't afford that luxury. The palms of his hands smarted where the skin had scraped off and his knees were red-hot, but he scrambled up before the angry mob could drag him up.

In spite of his exhaustion, his muscles tightened instinctively, ready for flight, as they encircled him, these lads whom

Thad had slapped around. Thad had clobbered each and every one of them to the ground – aye, more than once – prodding them with the toe of his boot as they lay curled in the dirt, dreading the rib-cracking kick.

Jacob gulped. These boys were going to kill him. The bugger of it was that he had been as scared of Thad as any of them. Oh yes, he had hero-worshipped his big brother, had been proud to run in his wake. It had been exciting to pinch stuff off the market and leg it at top speed. Being with Thad had made him feel bigger and stronger. Everyone was wary of Thad, even the teachers – when he could be bothered to attend school. He had started chucking his weight around at home an' all and something that was half-horror and half-delight had sent tingles down Jacob's backbone when Thad cheeked Mum or Dad. Sometimes Dad had given him a clip round the ear, but Thad didn't care. Thad didn't care about anything.

Oh aye, he had hero-worshipped Thad.

He had been shit-scared of him too. Shit-flaming-scared. Thad was a bully and a thug. He'd belt you one as soon as look at you. Being Thad's faithful sidekick had kept Jacob safe from Thad's fists and from his sneers and taunts – well, usually. Hell's bells, he had seen other kids wet themselves in fear enough times to ensure he wanted to be on Thad's good side, in so far as Thad had a good side.

And now he had been left to face the consequences of everything Thad had done.

He was surrounded. His attackers were closing in, squeezing the air out of the situation. His throat closed. His bowels slackened. He was as good as dead.

'Oy! What's going on?'

Mikey! Thad had loathed Mikey, ragging and taunting him and generally making his life a misery; and because Thad had done it, Jacob had an' all.

Now here was Mikey, pushing his way through the group, and he was going to make the other boys stand aside so he could land the first blow.

Except that what came out of Mikey's mouth was, 'Leave my brother alone. You were all too scared to stand up to Thad. Now he's gone, you want to take it out on Jacob. Very brave, I must say. Well, I'm not having it. If any of you...' Mikey turned in a slow circle, staring into the eyes of every single boy. '...If any of you lays a finger on my little brother, you'll have me to deal with. I have plenty of mates, not just in my class but in the top class an' all. So if you want to get clobbered, go ahead and beat up my brother. Otherwise clear off.'

Jacob could barely believe his ears. Mikey had as much reason as anyone to maul him to pieces. Instead he was standing up for him.

'Why?' he asked after Mikey had out-stared the other boys and they had slunk away, muttering.

'You're a pain in the neck, Jacob, but you're my brother.'

With a shrug, Mikey stuck his hands in his pockets and sauntered away, leaving Jacob gawping after him, relief thundering through him at the thought of what Mikey had saved him from...and a sort of wonder as well. After Mrs Rostron had shipped Thad off to the reformatory, she had told Jacob in no uncertain terms that he must pull his socks up or else run the risk of following Thad, the prospect of which made the sound of his pulse thrash inside Jacob's ears. Imagine being stuck in a place full of Thads.

'Follow Michael's lead,' Mrs Rostron had advised – ordered.

'Copy Mikey,' urged his family. Even his oldest sister's fiancé, who barely knew them, had told him to follow in Mikey's footsteps.

And after what Mikey had just done for him, Jacob was more than happy to do so.

Mikey had a half-time job, which meant he bolted down his school dinner dead on midday, then legged it to Brown's, the stationer on Beech Road in Chorlton, just a hop and a skip from the orphanage. He had got the job there when they still lived in Stretford. All the other half-timers were able to get local jobs, but not Thad Layton's brother. He had had to go further afield because of Thad's reputation.

All of which meant that, come the end of the school day, Jacob trailed home alone. Home? The orphanage? That was a laugh. No, it wasn't. Funny was the last thing it was. Their old home might have been two scabby rooms in an over-crowded house, but at least it had been their own place. At least he had lived with his family. Now they were scattered to the four winds.

As he dawdled along, a figure stepped out in front of him. Thad! His guts churned. Then his eyes adjusted and the dread subsided, leaving a sour taste in his mouth.

It wasn't Thad, but it might as well have been. A big brute of a boy – and he was a boy, still in the short trousers lads wore until they left school. Big shoulders and sticky-out elbows that were ready to shove you aside. Shrewd eyes and a sneering mouth. Taller than Thad – perhaps in the top class, desperate for July so he could jack in school. No, not desperate. Lads like him weren't desperate to leave. It was their poor mums who were desperate not to have to hide from the truancy bloke.

'I know you,' said the boy.

'I don't think so.' Jacob's every instinct screamed at him to scuttle to safety. Was this how it had felt for all those kids who had cringed when Thad came striding into view? 'You're not at my school.'

'Are you Thad Layton's brother?'

'No.'

The boy threw out his chest and laughed as if he hadn't heard such a good joke since Christmas. 'You're one of the brothers. There's you and the po-faced one. I've seen you from a distance. Your Thad pointed you out.'

Oh heck. This didn't bode well. 'Nice to meet you. I must...' He attempted to step around the boy.

A hand caught his arm – not hard, not with an iron grip. He could have wrenched free, but if he did, next news he would be flat on his back on the pavement, winded and helpless. He knew, because that was what Thad would have done.

'That's not very friendly,' said the boy. 'Here's me, stopping to say how do. A pipsqueak like you should be grateful.'

'I am.' I'm not, I'm not.

'That's better. What's your name?'

He gulped. 'Jacob.'

'I'm Shirl.'

'I've never heard that name before. It sounds like—'

Shirl thrust his face into Jacob's. He smelled of unwashed flesh and aniseed balls. His nose was peppered with blackheads.

'Sounds like what, pipsqueak?' He bullied forwards a few steps, forcing Jacob to retreat.

'Nowt, nowt.'

'Me full name's Shirley. You wanna make summat of it?'

'Me? Never.'

'I'll have you know Shirley were a boy's name long before it was a girl's name. What's your name?'

'I told you. Jacob.'

'No, it in't. It's Jemima. What's your name?'

He swallowed. His Adam's apple was as big as a golf ball. 'Jacob.'

'Sorry, I didn't catch that. What's your name?'

'Jacob.' He had to hold his nerve. Giving in, showing weakness, was a sure way to earn a kick up the arse.

Shirl laughed. 'You're a joker, aren't you? I like a good joke.'

Before Jacob knew what was happening, Shirl shoved him and he staggered backwards, pushing out a huff of breath as he banged into the wall. Looking down into his eyes, Shirl casually planted a hand round his throat and squeezed. Jacob gagged – tried to gasp – couldn't. Panic swept through him. Black dots swarmed before his eyes, or were they Shirl's blackheads?

Shirl's voice spoke into his ear. He couldn't make out the words, but he didn't need to. He knew what they were. Opening his mouth, he tried to drag in a breath. A tiny rasp of air crept in, but couldn't get down his throat. His heart had doubled in size. It was going to explode.

Shirl let go. Jacob doubled over, gasping, eyes streaming, hot liquid sloshing in his bowels. Even though he was bent over, Shirl's face was in front of his. He lurched upwards, but Shirl's face was still there, right in front of him. Even when he tried to turn away, Shirl's face was there.

'Sorry, pipsqueak, I thought you wanted to answer my question. Am I wrong? Only, if I am...' Shirl's hand moved towards Jacob's neck.

'Jemima,' Jacob whispered.

'Louder.'

His throat was hot and tight. He coughed to clear it. 'Jemima.'

'Once more for luck.'

'Jemima.' His eyes were wet. Shame sent tremors through him. He wanted to spit in Shirl's face. Was this the way Thad's victims had felt?

Shirl clapped him on the shoulder. 'Good for you. I knew you'd see sense. You had a paper-round, didn't you?'

He blinked at the change of subject, the change of mood. 'Just for a few days. My sister got me the job, but then...we had to move. We're not allowed to have paper-rounds at the orphanage.'

'Yeah. Shame, that. It could have been useful.' Shirl looked at him, his eyes demanding a response.

'Useful?' His mouth was bone-dry, his tongue swollen.

'Aye. It were your Thad's idea.'

'What was?'

'Never mind that. It'll never happen now. Time for you to get home to the orphanage, is it?'

'Aye.' Relief coursed through him. He wanted to sag against the wall, but had to hold himself upright, had to try to look strong. He started to back away.

'Hold your horses, pipsqueak. You haven't finished yet. You haven't asked me what job you've got to do.'

'Wha...what?'

'Your Thad worked for me and he still owes me a job.'

'He's gone to the reformatory.'

'I know. Heaven help the reformatory. The thing is, he isn't here to fulfil his commitments, so you'll have to do it for him. I wouldn't ask your Mikey to help out, but I can trust you, can't I?'

'I...' How did you say you didn't want to, to Shirl?

'Thad did a job for me reg'lar and I haven't time to find someone else, so it falls to you as his brother to do it for him. Just this one time, while I look for someone else.'

Hell's bells and burnt toast. His heart beat so hard it hurt. 'One job? One time?'

'Aye. Just take this little packet to Chorlton and hand it to a boy with red hair, who'll be waiting on the corner by St Clement's church. Easiest job ever. It's on your way home from school, so you won't even have to go out of your way.'

Anxious to get it over with, already feeling relieved because in a few short minutes he would be free of it, Jacob started off along Edge Lane, only for Shirl's meaty hand to clamp down instantly on his shoulder.

'Don't hurry,' Shirl ordered. 'Don't draw attention.'

Jacob forced himself to walk. Coming to the fork in the road, he veered into High Lane. You could almost spit from here to St Clement's. It was practically over and done with.

A couple of youths sauntered towards him, hands in pockets. He crossed over so he was on the same side of the road as the church. Another youth stepped out from between the stone pillars of a gateway in front of him and they did that side-stepping thing, where you try to get round each other, but both of you step the same way. That was all it was; but in a dark, squirmy place deep inside, Jacob knew he was kidding himself. He was in trouble, but he side-stepped again just in case he was wrong.

Then the two youths over the road crossed to this side and he couldn't pretend any more. One of them slid an arm round his shoulders as if they were best mates, urging him through the gateway. He tried to resist, but it was no use. The nerve of these lads was staggering. To force him inside someone's front garden – or did they know the house was empty?

Fear was meant to feel cold, wasn't it? But his fear wasn't cold. His was hot and sharp, piercing his belly.

'Give it here, kid.'

'Give what here?' He tried to sound jokey, as if it was all a big mistake, as if they would slap him on the back and say, 'Wrong person. No harm done.'

There was no answer, just laughter as they stood round him, shoving him from one to another. Of all the ridiculous things to think, he realised it was the first time he had ever been on a garden lawn. It was like having a posh green carpet in front of your house. Thad had always nicked stuff that he could flog to someone else, but in his secret heart, Jacob had cherished the mad idea that what he wanted to steal was a small square of lawn that he could keep for himself and sometimes touch as a treat, a sort of promise for the future, a consolation for the crummy, overcrowded, feud-filled life they had led in Cromwell Street.

With a jolly 'Heave-ho, me hearties,' the boys turned him upside down and shook him good and hard, laughing all the while. His piece of Plasticine got dislodged and tumbled from his pocket, followed by the screwed-up man's handkerchief with D on it in blue embroidery. D for Denby, D for Dad. He would never ever forgive Dad for walking out on them, but Dad's snot-rag had been in Jacob's pyjama pocket the night of the fire and was now all he had left of his old life, the life he hadn't cared for at the time, but which he now longed for with all his heart.

The world whooped and he was back on his feet with a thud that jarred him all the way from his ankles through his knees to his hips. There were hands all over him. Were they about to strip him naked? No, they delved in his pockets – and out came – please, not Shirl's packet – oh shit. A blow to the small of his back shunted him forwards into another thump in the bread-basket. His body doubled over, only to be hauled upright to receive more blows. Then, with a suddenness that almost toppled him, they whirled away and were gone, leaving him on his own in the front garden of a house with steps up to a covered porch and a grand bay window to either side, standing on a lawn, a real lawn, not the grass in the rec or on the meadows, but a real lawn. It wasn't meant to have been like this. His first time of standing on a lawn shouldn't have been like this.

As he stumbled along the road to the church, someone crossed the road, aiming straight for him. Jacob nearly wet himself, then he realised it was Bunny. He had left his hot-potato barrow over on the other side. Coming from Stretford, Jacob hadn't known Bunny before he was sent to St Anthony's. Bunny looked a bit of a mess in his mismatched jacket and trousers, but his heart was in the right place, so everyone said.

'You all right, son? You don't look quite the ticket.'

'I'm all right,' Jacob mumbled – or perhaps he just thought the words without saying them.

He rushed on, leaving Bunny behind. As he rounded the corner, there was the red-haired boy, not even as big as himself. To his everlasting shame, tears burst forth and poured down his face. The red-haired boy hurried to him, hissing, 'Shut up. Don't make a show of yourself,' looking over his shoulder as if PC Plod might pop out from behind a tree.

Jacob explained, or tried to, but all that came out of his mouth was a muffled howl. Red Head grasped what had happened and, grabbing Jacob's arm in sharp fingers, marched him straight back down Edge Lane. Once they were past Longford Park, there was Shirl, lounging on the corner, not smoking but looking like the kind of hardened schoolkid who could smoke if he felt like it.

After battling so hard to quell his distress, Jacob got hiccups. Abrupt explosions of breath punctuated his attempts at explaining. He felt like the snotty kid in the babies' class, made to stand in the corner after peeing himself.

'He says he had it nicked off him,' said Red Head, as if Jacob needed an interpreter. Maybe he did. Maybe he was babbling. Other kids had babbled after Thad had finished with them. Now he was one of those kids.

'He does, does he?' Didn't Shirl believe him?

'It's true... They d-dragged me into a garden and...' A violent hiccup wrenched the words away.

'Suppose it's true.' Shirl addressed Red Head. 'Suppose he really was jumped on.'

'I was, I was.' His flesh was clammy. 'Cross my heart and hope to die.'

Cross my heart and hope to die? Lads didn't say that. Thad Layton's brother didn't say that. But he wasn't Thad Layton's brother any more, was he? He was Jacob, alone, unprotected, vulnerable, easy pickings. Jemima.

'In that case...' Shirl took him by the shoulder, thrusting his face at Jacob's. At the side of his nose, in the crease where it joined his face, the blackheads had developed into a cluster of yellow-tipped pimples. 'In that case, you have to pay back for what you lost and the only way to do that is to do more jobs.'

More jobs?

Hell's bells.

Chapter Eight

MOLLY ALIGHTED FROM the tram into a mist of drizzle so fine it left a sheen of damp on her face. Would her bob survive intact? There needed to be only the merest sniff of rain in the air and all those clever layers put in by the hairdresser surrendered and her hair sprang out all over the place. She wanted to look her best this morning.

She drew her shoulders back as she walked into Albert Square, where the Town Hall looked older than it was, having been built when the Victorians had smothered everything in pointed arches and ornate buttresses, its grand clock-tower sweeping majestically towards the sky. It looked more like the setting for a Gothic novel than the centre of administration for the city and its suburbs.

Inside was all dark wood and tiled floors. Introducing herself at the reception counter, Molly was directed to the second floor. As she left the staircase and walked through the doors onto the landing, a corridor stretched ahead of her, most of its doors closed. Halfway along, a line of four wooden chairs stood against the wall, two of which were occupied, one by a middle-aged woman with a colossal handbag on her lap, the other by a thin man with an air of gravity, who wouldn't have looked out of place answering the door in a stately home.

Molly walked along the corridor, conscious of her heels tap-tapping on the floor. She was wearing her good shoes, but would the cutaway bits to either side of the T-bars count against her? Gran said that cutaways, while acceptable for dancing in the evenings, looked tarty in the daytime. But the only other shoes she possessed were her work shoes, which were flat and clumpy and didn't make her feel the way she wanted to feel today.

As she arrived alongside the chairs and the people who were presumably also here to be interviewed, a figure emerged from the room opposite – Mrs Atwood, dressed in a calf-length, olive-green dress with a sash of bottle-green buckled at her hip. The effect was well-groomed and tasteful while remaining plain enough to appear professional. Her eyes were true hazel, her hair light brown, but not mousy; rather it was a rich sepia colour. She wore it in a flattering chin-length bob, which fell smoothly, not just because it was nicely cut, but because it was the sort of obedient hair Molly would have killed for.

'Please come in for a moment,' said Mrs Atwood.

It was a large room – and it needed to be, with five desks in it, one at the front facing the other four, which stood in two rows of two, like a miniature classroom. Rays of May sunshine spilled through the windows, illuminating one of the desks – showing her the desk that would be hers? Don't be daft.

'I'm glad you applied,' Mrs Atwood said softly before adding in a louder voice, 'Let me tick you off the list. Now, if you'll join Mrs Bracegirdle and Mr Stebbins in the corridor, we're just waiting for Miss Oliver to arrive. You'll be interviewed by Mr Taylor, who's in charge of the local Board of Health.'

'And by me,' rang out another voice. 'Kindly give out the correct information, Mrs Atwood.'

It was the posh lady from Mrs Rostron's office. Today her glassy-eyed fox-fur bared its teeth on the shoulder of a cream wool costume of loose collarless jacket over a matching dress with a wide lacy collar that did her plump neck no favours. The tiny silk lily-of-the-valley adorning her hat quivered in indignation.

'I beg your pardon.' Mrs Atwood's voice was composed, but her smile slipped. 'I was unaware that you'd be joining Mr Taylor in the interviews.'

'You're aware now, so kindly inform the candidates that Mrs Wardle will interview them.'

She went to the desk at the top of the room, plucked a pen from the groove and bustled importantly from the room.

'Perhaps I should inform Mr Taylor as well,' Mrs Atwood murmured. She glanced at Molly. 'You didn't hear me say that.'

Goodness, what was going on here? Molly looked at the front desk, picturing Mrs Wardle behind it, in charge. It was all too easy to imagine Mrs Wardle very much in charge. And what of Mr Taylor?

She sat in the corridor, awaiting her interview. Another young woman arrived, was greeted by Mrs Atwood and sat down. The door beside the chairs opened and an older gentleman emerged. He had waves of white hair around the sides of his head and a closely trimmed beard over a jutting chin. Bright-blue eyes and a gentle curve to his cheeks – a kind face was Molly's first impression; but there was a droop at the corners of his eyes and a crinkle in the line of his mouth that suggested frayed nerves.

'Mrs Bracegirdle, please.'

He waved the first candidate into the office. Molly shifted in her seat, trying unsuccessfully to get comfortable. She had a considerable wait in front of her: the curse of being at the end of the alphabet. Mrs Atwood had left the door to the big office open and Molly had a clear view of the wall-clock, its pendulum and weights hanging solemnly below the silvered dial with Roman numerals, so she knew exactly how long Mrs Bracegirdle's interview lasted: twenty minutes. When Miss

Oliver's turn came, she was also in there for twenty minutes, as was Mr Stebbins.

At last it was Molly's turn. She was shown into a smaller office, containing a single desk, though there were two chairs crowded behind it, one of which was occupied by Mrs Wardle.

'Please take a seat, Miss Watson,' the man invited her.

'There's no need.' Mrs Wardle looked Molly up and down. 'I have encountered this person on a previous occasion and I regret to say she failed to create a favourable impression.' She flicked her hand dismissively at the same time as looking down at a sheet of paper in front of her. 'You may depart.'

'Mrs Wardle!' exclaimed the man. 'Miss Watson's application was sound and she deserves to be interviewed.'

'That's a matter of opinion. And if you had permitted me to scrutinise the applications, as I wished, we needn't be in this position now.'

'Of course, if you have met Miss Watson before, you ought to excuse yourself from these proceedings to ensure impartiality.'

'Certainly not.' Mrs Wardle cast her eyes heavenwards, setting her lily-of-the-valley bobbing. 'Oh, very well. Sit down, if you must.'

Molly sat, wiping her face clean of all expression. The man took his place behind the desk.

'I am Mr Taylor and I'm newly in charge of the Board of Health for the area to the south of the city centre, and this lady—'

'I am Emmeline Wardle. My extensive knowledge of the difficulties faced by, and in many cases caused by, the dregs of society, has been gleaned from years of supporting my husband in his charitable works and it will be of enormous value to the Board of Health as it takes over the responsibilities of the various Boards of Guardians. The person appointed today will be answerable to me.'

'Not exactly,' said Mr Taylor.

Mrs Wardle ignored him. 'Perhaps you would like to start, Miss Watson, by explaining what you imagine a sweet shop worker has to offer.'

'I'm used to dealing with people of all ages in a polite, pleasant manner.'

Mrs Wardle made a sound that, if she hadn't been a lady, might have been called a snort. 'You think that's all there is to it?'

'The Board of Health will have a lot of work to tackle. New ways must be found to assist those in need – more compassionate ways.'

'Compassionate? You evidently don't grasp the nature of the people involved, the feckless, the lazy, incompetent with money, requiring guidance in all aspects of their lives.'

Molly lifted her chin. 'Not everyone in need is like that. I'm sure most are decent folk down on their luck; war widows, soldiers whose lungs were destroyed by mustard gas, honest people who hate to be dependent but who currently have no choice.'

Mr Taylor leaned forward. 'You said more compassionate ways are needed.'

'I believe so. Going to the workhouse used to be a source of terrible shame. Wouldn't it be preferable to support people through their darkest times in their own homes, so they can maintain their daily routines and keep their self-respect intact?'

'Self-respect?' said Mrs Wardle. 'Gratitude and a proper humility would serve them better.'

Molly fought against a feeling of disillusionment. Was this the attitude of the Board of Health?

'You mentioned self-respect,' said Mr Taylor. 'Do you see this as important?'

'Yes, sir. I don't mean in a big-headed way,' Molly said quickly before Mrs Wardle could cut in. 'I think that the proper sort of pride can bolster people through difficult times. I believe that one feature of providing assistance has always been the shame attached to it. A person in need who is treated with courtesy and understanding might be persuaded to see, not the shame, but the rightness of being helped; the rightness of the community helping them get back on their feet.'

Mrs Wardle sniffed – well, that was to be expected. As for Mr Taylor, it was impossible to tell what he was thinking, but he wouldn't look her in the eye.

'I see no need for further questions,' announced Mrs Wardle. 'Do you, Mr Taylor?'

Mr Taylor mumbled something and rose to his feet to show Molly out. 'Thank you for attending,' he said as he opened the door.

Molly glanced at the wall-clock in the office opposite. Her interview had lasted half as long as those of the other candidates. That said it all, didn't it? She might as well leave. The sooner she returned to Upton's, the sooner she could start earning some money today. Mr Upton wasn't pleased about this interview. Well, he would be pleased enough when he heard she had fallen flat on her face.

She ran downstairs and was almost at the bottom when a voice called her.

'Miss Watson! Wait!' Mrs Atwood came hurrying after her. 'Didn't you realise you were meant to hang on? Please come back. Mr Taylor wants to speak to you.'

'Really?' Molly started up the stairs. 'He barely said a word during the interview.'

'That's his way, I'm afraid. He's no match for Mrs Wardle. You'd never think he's in charge. He has to do things behind her back.'

Mr Taylor's door was shut. Molly knocked and went in. Mr Taylor was alone. She caught a hunted look on his face before he relaxed and smiled.

'Take a seat. I'm glad Mrs Atwood caught up with you.'

'Did you want to ask more questions?'

'No. You wrote a very good letter of application and acquitted yourself well in this interview. You've obviously considered what this position could involve. You're – well, you're not old fashioned in your outlook. I believe you to be the sort of person the Board of Health needs and I'd like to offer you the post.'

Surprise rippled across Molly's skin.

'Will you accept it?' Mr Taylor leaned forward encouragingly.

'Well – yes, but...'

'Good. That's settled.'

Behind Molly, there was a cursory knock and the door opened.

'I'm ready to discuss the candidates, Mr Taylor,' said Mrs Wardle. 'What's she doing here?'

Mr Taylor shot to his feet. 'Ah – Mrs Wardle, ladies, would you excuse me for a minute? I just have to... Miss Watson, while I'm gone, would you care to give Mrs Wardle your good news?'

Jacob and Mikey had to set off for school before anyone else at St Anthony's, because of walking to Stretford. To begin with, Jacob had groaned at the early start, but ever since Mikey had rescued him from that mob, he had relished the chance for the two of them to be together. Mikey was a decent sort. Why had he never seen it before? He knew the answer to that: Thad.

Walking beside Mikey along Edge Lane, Jacob tried to keep in step, but Mikey was taller and he had to lengthen his stride. Suddenly, Mikey did a quick double-step that took him unawares; then Mikey pushed Jacob's cap forwards and ruffled his hair. Jacob made a grab for his cap before it could fall off. If Thad had done that to him, it would have been a form of bullying, but coming from Mikey, it was fun.

'You all right, squirt?' Mikey said 'squirt' in a cheerful voice, not like when Shirl said 'Jemima'.

'Why wouldn't I be?'

'No one bothering you at school?'

'Not since you stopped them.' Jacob lifted his chin. He was proud of his brother.

'Everything all right at St Anthony's?'

'What's this about?' asked Jacob.

'Just making sure you're all right. You seem a bit worried sometimes.'

Jacob felt a chill at the back of his neck. 'I'm fine.'

But he wasn't. He didn't think he would ever be fine again.

Would today be a delivery day? That was what it was called, delivering, which sounded ordinary and casual, helpful even.

And it wasn't so bad. Yes, it was. No, it wasn't. It was dead easy. You took a small parcel, more of a packet, really, small enough to fit in your pocket, from Stretford to Chorlton. Given that the school was in the part of Stretford closest to Chorlton, and the orphanage was at the end of Chorlton nearest to Stretford, that wasn't far, not when you thought about it. He had been paid too, which had come as a surprise.

'Here's the parcel. Put it straight in your pocket,' Shirl had instructed him the first time after that horrendous occasion after he had been knocked about and robbed. 'Take it to Chorlton Green and sit on a bench. A bloke with a blue neckerchief will come and sit there too. He'll have a newspaper to read. Slide the packet onto the bench in between you without looking at it. That's all there is to it, pipsqueak. Think you can manage that? The bloke will fiddle around with the paper and a packet of fags, then he'll go; and if he happens to leave a tanner behind on the bench, well, don't go chasing after him to give it back.'

'You mean...?' Jacob had known what it meant, but what if he was wrong?

'What d'you think I mean, pipsqueak? God, you're thick, aren't you? In fact, you're worse than thick. You're Jemima.'

Everything had happened as Shirl had said, including the appearance on the bench of the sixpence. Jacob had shuffled towards it, closing his hand over it and shifting it casually to his pocket. Sixpence! It was the first money he had had since his world went to the devil in a dog-cart. The children at St Anthony's weren't allowed to have money, even if they earned it like Mikey. He had to hand it over to Mrs Rostron and it would be given back to him – or to Mum – when he left.

Where could he hide his sixpence? The only place that was even vaguely private was the small cupboard beside his bed, but that was regularly inspected to make sure it was tidy. Eventually he had settled upon using a tiny crevice in the wall that ran round the orphanage grounds. The wall was smothered in ivy, but underneath that was solid brick. By squeezing his hand between the thick stems, he had discovered a crack in the brickwork that was as good a hiding place as any. Mr Abrams was going to clear the ivy, but that would take ages and, anyroad, he was going to start on Church Road and Jacob's hidey-hole was round the corner on High Lane.

There was two and six in there now. Two and six! He had never known riches like it. Anyone who imagined he had benefited financially from being Thad Layton's loyal follower was sadly mistaken. Whatever money they had gathered through one means or another had ended up in Thad's pocket, apart from the odd copper, which Thad would chuck his way in an off-hand manner that was positively insulting, but which Jacob had had to pretend to take as a joke.

But now – now he had money of his own stashed away. But instead of planning what to get for himself, all he could think about was how much he wanted his mum. When she had dumped him and Mikey in the orphanage, he had hated her, but inside he had known it wasn't her fault. It was Dad's for scarpering and leaving his family high and dry.

Mum was a servant now, living in a smart semi-detached house, doing the cleaning and the shopping. Her big ambition was to take on the cooking an' all. Soon after he had moved into St Anthony's, Jacob had gone round there and banged on the back door and begged her to let him live with her. Blimey, he'd have kipped in the garden shed, if only he could be near her. She had gone all weepy and had refused – well, she'd had to, he had known that, but it hadn't stopped him feeling all churned up, which had somehow come out as defiance, which made Mum go all narky. He had turned to march away, only to hurtle back at top speed, chuck himself into her arms and sob his heart out. When he calmed down, Mum had taken him into the scullery to wash his face. Neither of them wanted him to return to St Anthony's looking like a tear-stained sissy.

Now he had the chance to buy summat for Mum, and never mind the catapult and the comic he should be coveting for himself. Who would have thought that a bar of chocolate or a box of Rowntree's Fruit Pastilles for Mum would take precedence? Only – what would Mikey say? Mum would be bound to tell him if Jacob gave her a present, and the orphans didn't get pocket money. Mikey would ask all sorts of questions that Jacob couldn't possibly answer.

Just like 'You all right, squirt?' was impossible to answer truthfully.

Would he see Shirl today? He never knew when a delivery would be required. He would be on his way home from school as normal – normal! What was normal about your stomach being so cramped with nerves that you could barely put one foot in front of the other? Would Shirl appear? Was he lurking around that corner? Behind that pillar-box? In that shop doorway?

As he headed to St Anthony's at the end of the day, Jacob told himself over and over that maybe today wouldn't be a delivery day. Hell's bells and burnt toast, how had he got himself into this mess? At least it would be half-term next week and he would be safe from Shirl's demands. Maybe Shirl would forget about him when the schools were off. Maybe he would never see Shirl again.

Oh aye, and maybe Thad had been an angel sent straight from heaven to act at all times out of the goodness of his heart.

A meaty arm swung round his shoulders. Jacob flinched, then tried his hardest to unflinch by pushing his shoulders back, but Shirl wasn't fooled.

'Cor, you're a real Jemima, aren't you?' Shirl gave him a shake that flooded Jacob with recognition. Thad used to do things like that. A quick shake that looked like nothing to anyone watching, but if you were on the receiving end, it was a warning, a threat, a put-down. It made you feel two inches tall.

'If I am,' said Jacob, 'why bother with me?' Did he really imagine Shirl would say, 'Good point,' and send him on his way?

'That's what I like about you, pipsqueak. You've got a sense of humour.'

'Actually, I'm glad to see you, Shirl. I – I reckon I've paid you back for losing the parcel that time.'

'Losing it? Having it nicked off you, you mean.'

'I don't want to do it no more. You can clobber me if you want, but I've had enough.'

'Ooh, who'd have thought it? Jemima's got teeth.'

Suddenly the arm wasn't round his shoulder any more. It was round his neck. Jacob's eyes popped.

'Just one problem, Jemima. You've accepted payment. That's makes you one of us.'

Chapter Nine

STRANGE TO THINK it was for the final time. Strange and exciting, and there was a little voice inside her head asking why she had taken so long to make this change. At six o'clock, Mr Upton locked and bolted the shop door, drawing the blind down over the glass pane, and Molly fetched the broom to sweep the floor for the final time. Then she laid the fly-nets over the farthing and ha'penny trays and took the trays of milk and plain chocolates into the back, where she placed them on the cool marble slab in the larder.

After that it was time to polish the counters before removing the glass jars of boiled sweets from the bottom shelf. Every day for years she had cleaned one shelf during her half hour's tidying before she went home. Yesterday she had cleaned the top shelf, so today she was starting again at the bottom – except she wasn't starting again. She was finishing for ever.

She wet-dusted the shelf, dry-dusting each jar before she returned it, making sure every label was front and centre. In the time that remained – and there had to be time remaining or Mr Upton would want to know the reason why – she constructed white paper bags. Fold, fold, twist, flatten.

'All done.' Having counted the day's takings and carried them through to wherever he hid them, Mr Upton reappeared, smiling. 'Leave that, Miss Watson. Mrs Upton and I would like to invite you to raise a glass with us.'

Molly took off her apron and he waved her through. Mrs Upton was seated in her armchair. On the table beside her was a bottle of Harvey's Bristol Cream and four dainty glasses – four?

'Excuse me a minute.' Mr Upton disappeared back into the shop, returning a few moments later with Norris. 'Look who I found passing by.'

Molly smoothed what threatened to be a grimace. Norris had no business being here and the Uptons had no business inviting him. She pinned on a smile as she took a seat close to Mrs Upton and accepted a glass of sherry.

'Mrs Upton and I always knew this day would come, but we weren't expecting it for another two years. Miss Watson, you've taken us all by surprise, but we wish you well in your new endeavour. New endeavours!'

He raised his glass. Norris and Mrs Upton followed suit, echoing the toast. Norris smiled bravely.

'Make sure you come back and tell us how you're getting on,' said Mrs Upton.

'I will,' Molly promised. Dear Mrs Upton was going to miss her. Mr Upton was going to take on a fifteen-year-old, which was all well and good in the shop, but what about all the little ways in which Molly helped Mrs Upton? You wouldn't want a youngster helping you straighten your stockings. It wouldn't be dignified. Because the Board of Health wanted her to start work on a Monday, Molly had given a week and a half's notice, so it wasn't as though Mr Upton hadn't had time to look about.

Afterwards, Norris escorted her home. She didn't want him to, but could hardly refuse. He didn't offer his arm, just maintained a flow of unchallenging conversation and hung back when they reached her gate.

'I'll leave you here if you don't mind,' he said. 'I wish you all the best.'

'Thank you, Norris.' She couldn't help softening.

'All I've ever wanted is your happiness. I realise I've fallen out of favour for now, but you'll always be my girl.'

'Norris—' She was rapidly hardening again.

'I know, I know. I don't want to put my foot in it, but I must tell you I haven't given up. I'll do my utmost to win you back. I'd be a pretty poor sort of fellow, wouldn't I, if I didn't try?'

Eagerness bubbled inside Molly as she crossed Albert Square, heading for the Town Hall. As of today, she worked here. Around her, men in pinstripes and bowler hats, and women in neat coats and hats and tappy heels, headed in the same direction. Did she look like them? Did the world realise at a glance that Molly Watson was now a bona fide Corporation employee? Was she overdressed in her maroon dress with the cream collar and cuffs? Mrs Atwood had looked smart in that olive-green on the day of the interviews. Molly wanted to be smart as well – but was she too smart?

'You can't wear that.' Mum had twisted her mouth dubiously. 'It's your Sunday dress.'

Well, she couldn't wear her blue because it had daisies on it, while her green had pink pinstripes. That had left the maroon. Smart. Sober. Professional.

'You could wear your shop clothes,' Mum had suggested. 'Black skirt, white blouse, very appropriate. You can't go wrong with a black skirt and a white blouse.'

Molly had stuck to her decision. Now, inside the building, spotting several women in dark skirts with white or cream blouses, she felt an uncomfortable flutter. Don't be daft. It didn't matter what she looked like – well, it did, of course, but it didn't matter as much as how well she did her job.

As she entered the office, Mrs Atwood rose from her desk. Her dove-grey dress was straight up-and-down, its elbow-length sleeves ending in flicked-back ivory cuffs with pearly buttons. A smart dress. Phew! Molly exhaled softly. What a twit she was, getting hot and bothered about clothes.

'There's a coat-stand behind the door,' said Mrs Atwood, 'and this is your desk.'

Molly couldn't help glancing at the 'teacher's' desk at the front.

'I know.' Mrs Atwood pulled a face. 'There used to be just these four desks in here. We came in one morning to find that Mrs Wardle had moved herself in, though of course the porters had done the donkey work, and this is where she's been ever since, facing the rest of us as if she's in charge.'

'And isn't she?'

'Yes and no. Mrs Wardle failed repeatedly to wangle her way onto the Deserving Poor Committee before the war. There were lots of upper-class charitable committees in those days. Some of them are still around, but they don't have the clout they used to. They were run by the local upper crust: hence Mrs Wardle's ambition.'

'But she was never accepted.'

'No, but she's making up for it now. This business with the Boards of Guardians giving way to the Boards of Health is perfect for her. She's been connected to a couple of Boards of Guardians for years, so that's given her a foothold in the new system. She's sticking her fingers in as many pies as she can and dear Mr Taylor is far too fuzzy to do a thing about it. Let me show you the office diary. You'll be working with me until you find your feet.'

'Good morning, Mrs Atwood.' Mrs Wardle bustled in, making straight for her desk in its position of importance. 'Miss Watson, welcome. I have my doubts about your suitability, so I'll be observing you closely. I deem it best if you work alongside Mrs Atwood while you learn the ropes.'

'I've already explained that,' said Mrs Atwood.

'Good morning, ladies.' Mr Taylor appeared. He looked like he was going to walk right in, but then he saw Mrs Wardle and came to a halt. 'Good morning, Miss Watson. Settling in, I see. Good, good. I've asked Mrs Atwood if—'

'Thank you, Mr Taylor,' said Mrs Wardle. 'I've already given Mrs Atwood and Miss Watson their instructions.' The silk rosebuds on her hat swayed and bobbed as she made a show of leaning over to examine papers on her desk.

'Um, yes, quite so.' Mr Taylor retreated.

Mrs Wardle looked up. Before she could speak, Mrs Atwood turned to Molly.

'I'll start by showing you the offices whose whereabouts you'll need to know, and where the ladies' WC is. This way.'

As they walked along the corridor, a bespectacled young girl came towards them pushing a trolley with two large wire trays, the top one filled with bundles of letters, the bottom one holding just a few. She steered the trolley to the side for them to get past.

'Thank you, Miss Platt.' Mrs Atwood stopped. 'Miss Watson, this is Miss Platt, the junior from the post-room. Miss Platt, this is my new colleague, Miss Watson. Miss Platt delivers and collects our post six times a day.'

Molly nodded at Miss Platt, who was all of fifteen years old. Her mousy hair was tied back and she wore a black skirt with a white blouse.

'Are you going to the Board of Health office?' Mrs Atwood asked. 'Might I see the post, please?'

Miss Platt rifled through a section of bundles in the top tray and handed one to Mrs Atwood, who flipped the band off it and flicked through the envelopes, removing two or three and fastening the remainder together before handing them back. Then she set off again with Molly in tow.

'Poor kid,' Mrs Atwood murmured. 'She came in last week wearing a summer dress. Nothing fancy, just a simple cream thing with a modest neckline and long sleeves, but she was sent home to change back into her black and white.'

'Is my dress suitable?' Molly whispered.

'Oh yes. It's the done thing for the female office workers to wear black or navy with white, but it's different for the likes of you and me. We get out and about and we have to look the part. It sounds frightfully snobby to say it, but we need to look smart and prosperous so that the people we deal with will look up to us.'

Molly frowned. It did sound snobbish. On the other hand, if it meant people in need accepted their assistance...

'Why did you take some of the letters?'

'So that our esteemed Mrs Wardle doesn't see them, of course. I know it seems an iffy way to behave, but needs must, especially with Mr Taylor not being up to it.' Mrs Atwood gave her a cheeky smile. 'You'll get the hang of it.'

'We're going to see a Mrs Fletcher,' said Mrs Atwood as they passed a row of tired-looking houses. 'She was once a lady's maid, as she'll undoubtedly tell you, but she didn't choose wisely when she married. She told me she was too much in love to listen when her family warned her against Albert Fletcher. I thought she meant her relatives, but she meant the family she worked for. Here we are. I warn you, it's pretty grim.'

The house was a tall, thin terrace, considerably more than a two-up two-down, so surely the Fletcher family couldn't be that badly off. Instead of knocking, Mrs Atwood turned the handle; the door was unlocked. A sour smell hit Molly in the face: mould, cabbage and cat pee. Her stomach rolled. What sort of job was this? Imagine going home with her maroon dress, her Sunday dress, smelling of this. Mum would throw a fit.

Mrs Atwood was halfway up the stairs. Molly hurried after her.

'Take your time,' advised Mrs Atwood. 'Watch the treads. Some are wonky.'

Mrs Atwood stopped on the landing. Catching up, Molly felt bile burn its way up her throat as she beheld the black pools of mould that coated the walls – the ceiling too. If some mould dropped off and fell on her – don't be daft. Mould clung; it didn't fall off. Even so, the thought of invisible wisps of the stuff floating in the air made her hold her breath. That was daft too. She couldn't avoid breathing for the entire visit.

'I know it's shocking, but please try not to let it show,' Mrs Atwood advised before she knocked on a door, waiting a moment before opening it.

At first glance, it was a decent-sized room until Molly looked more closely and realised it provided one family's entire living quarters. There was a big bed, a table with mismatched chairs, a gas-ring smelling too strongly of gas, and a shabby cupboard on which stood a bowl and a couple of saucepans stacked inside one another. Judging by the width of the chimney breast, the fireplace must be pretty big, though it was impossible to tell as it was hidden behind washing draped over two wobbly clothes horses, with more washing dripping from the pulley-airer near the ceiling. Bluebottles buzzed round the cupboard and yellowed newspaper did duty as a tablecloth. Why was there a banana crate in the corner? Good lord, it served as a cot for not one but two babies.

Black mould bubbled where the walls met the ceiling. Below the picture rail, pale oblongs in the greying whitewash showed where pictures had once hung. There were no ornaments, no trinkets, nothing pretty. The sole decoration was provided by a framed photograph of a stern-faced woman in a crinoline, with a lace widow's cap over her hair and an oval cameo brooch pinned to her upright collar.

'Good morning, Mrs Atwood.' Mrs Fletcher was a thin creature with a lined face. Blue eyes regarded Molly with open suspicion. 'Who's this?'

'My colleague, Miss Watson.'

'She's not from the Panel, then?'

Mrs Atwood turned to Molly. 'Mrs Fletcher has an appointment coming up to see the Panel.' She made it sound almost like a social occasion, something Mrs Fletcher had a choice about. 'So you can understand she's feeling nervous.'

'It's all very well, you saying the Boards of Guardians are being done away with,' said Mrs Fletcher, 'but their Panels are still up and running, aren't they? And they still have power.'

'Yes, but the Boards of Health are involved too,' Mrs Atwood reassured her.

'For all the good that'll do,' muttered Mrs Fletcher. 'You know what the Panel's like. If you've so much as a glass bead to your name, they make you sell it to prove you've done all you can to support yourself and you aren't scrounging.'

'Personally, I'd like to see the Panels disbanded,' said Mrs Atwood. 'They have such a fearsome reputation. But,' she added to Mrs Fletcher, 'they do have a duty to ensure that public funds aren't wasted.'

'I'm not seeking charity.' Mrs Fletcher jutted out her chin. 'Things are hard, but my family isn't a charity case. God forbid we should sink that low. If I have to sell anything, I will – I already have.' Her glance fell on the empty spaces on the walls. 'But it would break my heart if I had to part with my brooch.'

'Your brooch?' asked Molly.

Mrs Fletcher hesitated, then delved into the back of the cupboard and brought out an old Green's Custard tin. Prising off the lid, she produced a hanky, which she unwrapped to reveal a cameo brooch. 'I've never pawned it, not once, no matter how much Albert went on at me.'

'Let me help you write a letter to the Panel,' said Mrs Atwood. 'That's allowed these days. Of course, whether they pay any attention to the letter is another matter. It will depend on the balance of the Panel – how many Guardians, how many Board of Health.'

'Surely it should be the same number from either side,' said Molly, 'with an extra person from the Board of Health to have the casting vote.' How else was the system ever to change?

'Ideally,' agreed Mrs Atwood, 'but there are still many more Guardians than Board of Health people. Still, we can but try.'

Molly looked at the photograph. 'Who is this?'

'The mother of the lady I worked for. Madam gave it to me as a present when I left service.'

'I've spoken on Mrs Fletcher's behalf to the Panel,' said Mrs Atwood, 'and she's been granted permission to keep the photograph, as it's of no interest to anyone else, though she'll probably have to sell the frame.' She sighed. 'Being allowed to keep the photograph reduces the chances of keeping the brooch, I'm afraid.'

Molly looked at the brooch. 'Isn't it the cameo from the photograph?'

'Yes. Madam gave it to me.'

'When you left her service,' Molly finished for her. She turned to Mrs Atwood, unable to suppress a smile. 'That's what you should say in your letter: that the brooch was a gift from Mrs Fletcher's former employer – and you can prove it, if necessary, by referring to the photograph. If the Guardians on the Panel are as old fashioned and set in their ways as you've implied, then a gift from an employer, and a lady of means at that, is something they should regard with sympathy.'

'You may well be right,' said Mrs Atwood. 'That's a good idea.'

Mrs Fletcher's tired face brightened. 'Thank you, miss,' she said and Molly felt she had been accepted.

Later, as they left, Mrs Atwood said, 'Well done for spotting the brooch in the photograph. We must get back to the office now. This afternoon we need to call on a family that has suffered a bereavement. They lost their young son.'

'How sad. What was wrong with him?'

'He wasn't ill. It was an accident. He was hit by a tram, poor child. You live in Chorlton, don't you? Do you know Limits Lane? It's on the border of Chorlton and Stretford.'

'I'm from the other end of Chorlton, near the railway station,' said Molly. 'What assistance are we going to offer?'

'None, unfortunately. This is a family that, however hard up, has never sought help. I only know of this tragedy because it was reported in the *Manchester Evening News*.'

'So we're simply going there to offer our condolences?'

'It's better than nothing.'

They returned to the Town Hall, where Mrs Atwood took Molly to the canteen. Afterwards Molly popped out to find a grocer's and purchased a quarter of tea. Back in the office, she sat at her desk with her handbag on her lap, rearranging its contents to make room for the tea, which was sitting on her blotter.

Mrs Wardle came in, rosebuds bobbing on her hat. 'Really, Miss Watson, is this why you wished to work in town? To make it easier to do your shopping? Groceries scattered all over the desk – I don't know.'

'I...' Molly began.

Mrs Wardle took something from one of her drawers and bustled to the door.

'Make the most of your time here, Miss Watson. I don't imagine it will last long.'

*

Limits Lane was a poor-looking little road, more of a glorified track, really, with grand, leafy Edge Lane at one end and a bumpy slope down to the meadows at the other. On one side was a spread-out row of shabby cottages, each inside its own tiny privet-hedged garden. At the far end was the ruined remains of a cottage.

Molly perked up. 'Limits Lane: I knew it rang a bell. My dad is a builder. That end cottage burned down in April and the owner wants Dad's company to clear the remains.'

'Small world,' Mrs Atwood commented as she opened a gate which gave a prolonged squeal. 'Here we are. The boy's mother is Mrs King.'

The door was opened by a school-age girl with red-rimmed eyes. Mrs Atwood introduced them and the girl opened the door wider to let them in. Even though Molly had witnessed severely cramped conditions and rampant mould today, it still came as a shock that the cottage's floor was nothing more than compacted earth.

Mrs King, eyes bleak and not quite focused, sat hunched in a tatty armchair, with her children hanging about her. A couple more women perched on wooden chairs while another busied herself with the kettle. There was barely room for anyone else.

Mrs Atwood edged towards the bereaved mother. 'Mrs King, I'm Mrs Atwood from the Board of Health and this is my colleague, Miss Watson. We've come to offer you our deepest condolences on the loss of your son.'

'That means they're sorry our Len got squashed,' one of the children whispered to a smaller one.

'Thank you,' said Mrs King. Her chin puckered. 'It's good of you to come.'

'What's the Board of Health when it's at home?' demanded another of the women.

'We've taken over from the Boards of Guardians,' Mrs Atwood began.

Indignation rustled round the cramped space.

One of Mrs King's daughters twined her arms around her mother's neck. 'They've not come to tek us away, have they, Mam?'

'Of course not,' Mrs Atwood said gently. 'I hope you'll find the Board of Health more sympathetic and more useful to you than your Board of Guardians would have been.'

'Is there still the Panel?' asked one of Mrs King's visitors.

'Mrs Shelton, please,' murmured Mrs King.

'That's all right,' said Mrs Atwood. 'Yes, the Panel is still in operation.'

'And the means test?'

'Well, yes.'

'That don't sound very sympathetic to me. Does it to you?' Mrs Shelton nudged the woman beside her.

Mrs King lifted her head. 'What brings you here?'

'As I said, we've come to offer our condolences.'

'That's reet kind of you. Thank you.'

'And are you here to be useful?' Mrs Shelton enquired. 'Sympathetic and useful, you said – so you can offer to pay for the funeral.'

'I'm afraid I can't do that.'

Mrs Shelton lurched upright in her seat, pursing her lips in triumph.

'Perhaps it's time for us to go,' murmured Mrs Atwood.

'Aye, p'raps it is,' Mrs Shelton agreed.

Molly fumbled in her bag for the packet of tea, then pressed her way into the group. 'Mrs King, I'm sure lots of folk must be dropping in at the moment, so here's a little extra tea to help tide you over. You don't want to run out.'

She held her breath. Would her gesture be accepted – or hurled back in her face? Something shifted inside the room and the atmosphere mellowed.

'That's proper neighbourly of you, miss.' The woman at the

range reached across and took the packet. 'Will you stay for a cup?'

'If it's no trouble,' said Molly. 'Thank you.' She looked at Mrs Atwood. 'We'd like to hear about Len, wouldn't we?'

Chapter Ten

'M RS ATWOOD SAID it was a good idea to take the tea and she's going to do it herself if she finds herself in that situation again.'

Was she boasting? Molly glanced round the table as they ate their evening meal of pork chops with apple sauce. Mum always had a hearty meal ready at the end of the day, because Dad and Tom came home hungry as hunters. Gran was here too, having invited herself specially.

'Fancy,' said Gran, 'and on your first day an' all, but then you've always been a kind girl. That's one thing Norris has always appreciated about you.'

Molly subsided. She didn't want to talk about Norris, but her family seemed to have other ideas. Tilda turned up with the children and engaged in a loud conversation with Mum about the benefits of a happy marriage. Molly ground her teeth. Mum had sent her on an errand to Christabel's yesterday evening and Chrissie had told her to her face that she and Tilda were under strict orders to lay it on with a trowel how wonderful marriage was, whenever they saw her.

Later, Auntie Faith and Dora popped round to hear about her first day.

Dora dragged her aside. 'This job of yours, is it my fault?'

'Your fault?'

'Aye. Because of me and Harry setting a date.'

Molly blinked. 'You think I changed jobs because you set a date?'

'It must have been hard for you to see us getting engaged and then organising our wedding so soon after, when you've been waiting for Norris since Adam was a lad.'

'I haven't been waiting for Norris. A long engagement was what we settled on at the outset.'

Dora put on her sympathetic face. 'You don't have to pretend with me, love. We all know it were Norris's idea.'

'What if it was? I agreed to it. Norris wanted to save up.'

'Well, you had to agree, didn't you? It were that or nothing for you, especially at your age.'

Molly's astonished intake of breath hit the back of her throat, rendering speech impossible. Not that it mattered. She was stumped for words. Was that what others thought of her? That she had been obliged to fall in with the five-year engagement because it was her only chance? Ruddy heck. Didn't it occur to anyone that she had been happy to agree to the long engagement? And just why had she gone along with it? She had never asked herself that before. Could it be that, deep down, she had been reluctant even then to tie herself to Norris?

It was high time she joined the local business school for surplus girls. She had meant to do it anyway, but now she felt fired up. Would Mrs Atwood mind? She had mentioned being a pupil there the first time they met.

'I wouldn't want you to feel I'm muscling in on your patch,' Molly explained the next day.

'I think it's an excellent idea,' was the encouraging reply. 'If you take my advice, you'll sign up for everything they can teach you. Even if you don't use it in this job, you never know how it might benefit you in the future.'

The future. That was what this was about. Choices. Opportunities. Self-sufficiency. She wouldn't earn as much as a man, which was jolly unfair these days with all the war widows and surplus girls having to fend for themselves, but at least her money would be her own to dispose of as she saw fit, rather than living her life beholden to a tight-fisted husband, who would watch like a hawk the way she managed the house-keeping, while expecting her to be eternally grateful for her vacuum cleaner.

Before she applied to the business school, she had to tell her parents about it. It would be difficult to go ahead without their support – but, given that they were as baffled as anyone by her rejection of Norris, what would they say? It was exasperating to be on the receiving end of everyone's confusion, the niggling comments and the tactics to make matrimony appear wonderful. Explaining Norris's failings might bring her family firmly onto her side, but she had to keep her lips firmly shut on that subject or there was no knowing what Norris might say in retaliation.

'You've only just started a new job and now you want to go to business school,' said Dad. 'What's going on, Molly?'

'That's a lot of change all in one go,' Mum added.

'I know you're worried about her,' said Tom, 'but she's determined to do this, so we need to help her. I think attending the business school follows on naturally from having the new job. Come on, Dad. Learning secretarial skills will improve Molly's prospects no end. She might even end up in our office!'

Molly had been all set to talk Mum and Dad round, but Tom had done it for her. He was the best brother in the world. They ended up talking about the fees. Dad wanted to pay, but Molly insisted the money must come out of her own salary.

'Assuming I get a place,' she added.

'Of course you shall,' said Mum, 'a bright girl like you.'

Molly penned a careful letter of application to Miss Hesketh and Miss Patience Hesketh at the business school.

'It's only Miss Hesketh you need to address it to, really,' said Mrs Atwood when Molly gave it to her to look over. 'Miss Patience is an absolute lamb and you'll love her, but Miss Hesketh is very much in charge.'

Molly nodded politely, but didn't commit herself to making the alteration. If Miss Hesketh was in charge, Miss Patience would probably appreciate the courtesy of being included. Molly had recently been on the receiving end of enough astonishment and anxiety about her own apparently incomprehensible decision to feel determined to offer every possible civility and support to every female she came across.

She was invited for an early evening interview the following week. She wore her lucky knickers, which she had been wearing the evening she and Tilda won the beat-the-clock crossword competition at the church social and the day the hairdresser put the clever layers into her bob. She damped down her hair to make it as smooth as possible and went downstairs.

'Are you ready, love?' Mum's cheery voice set alarm bells ringing. 'Look who's going to take you.'

Molly bit back a retort. It might, after all, be Tom. But, as she entered the front room, Norris sprang to his feet, beaming.

'You look smart, Molly. Doesn't she look smart, Mrs Watson? May I have the honour of escorting you to your appointment?'

'How do you know about it?' She would clobber them.

'Your gran told me. Dear old soul, she was worried I'd take it amiss, so I said I'd deliver you to your interview myself and that made her feel much better.'

She felt like gnashing her teeth. 'I don't need to be delivered, thank you. I'm not a parcel.'

Norris chuckled. 'You are a card, Molly. Haven't I always said your Molly's a card, Mrs Watson?'

'You may have mentioned it,' Tom murmured. He put down the paper and stood up. 'I've already offered to walk Molly there, so your services aren't required, old bean.'

Norris looked crestfallen, but only for a moment. 'We'll both escort her. Is that acceptable, Molly? Being escorted instead of delivered? And by two gentlemen – won't you look important? Quite right too.'

Oh, the temptation to tell him to sling his hook, but she couldn't, not in front of her family, who had accepted him into their midst as their future son- and brother-in-law. It wouldn't be respectful.

Outside, she linked arms with Tom, giving him a secret squeeze, which he returned.

'May I have your other arm?'

Norris crooked an elbow enticingly in her direction and she couldn't decline, could she, not when she was already hanging onto Tom. So they walked across Chorlton three abreast through evening sunshine edged with gold. But when they reached the corner of Wilton Close, she stopped.

'I'll see myself to the house.'

'No need,' said Norris. 'If they see you arriving in our company, they'll understand how precious you are.'

Tom unlinked from her. 'Leave her be, Norris. Our Molly's perfectly capable of walking up the road on her own.'

Tom made a move as if to kiss her cheek. The Watsons always kissed or shook hands in greeting and farewell and to say goodnight. But Molly quickly stepped away. If Tom kissed her, Norris might also swoop in for a peck and she couldn't have that.

Saying a swift goodbye, she entered Wilton Close, a quiet cul-de-sac with two pairs of large semi-detached houses on either side and another at the top. Peering over the garden walls to check the numbers on the front doors, she opened the gate to number 4 and walked up the path to the porch. The front garden had a neat lawn, with shallow flowerbeds next to the walls adjoining next door and the pavement. Forget-me-nots and grannies' bonnets mingled with the sparkling white of honesty and the wispy petals of cornflowers.

She rang the bell. The door was opened by a thin middle-aged lady whose dress fell past mid-calf length, as befitted her years in these days of ever-shortening hemlines. Pale-blue eyes and fair skin suggested her hair had once been blonde, but now it was grey. Not white like Tom's, but grey. She wore it in an old-fashioned bun, again as befitted her age. She ought to have been drab, but she wasn't. There was a kindness about her, a gentleness that was instantly appealing. Molly warmed to her, at the same time hiding a smile. This had to be Miss Patience, the 'absolute lamb'. Never in a million years could it be the Miss Hesketh who was in charge of everything. The most Miss Patience would be in charge of was the tea-tray.

'Miss Patience Hesketh?' she asked.

'And you must be Miss Watson. Do come in. Let me show you into the sitting room.'

Molly entered a high-ceilinged room with a gracious bay window. The furniture and curtains spoke of quality, but also of age. The Miss Heskeths must be what Dad would call middle class without the money.

'This is my sister, Miss Hesketh,' said Miss Patience, 'and this is Miss Watson.'

'How do you do?' Miss Hesketh offered a firm, bony hand. Firm and bony summed her up pretty accurately. She was all angles. She had the same colouring as her sister, but hers was set in a sharp face with penetrating eyes and a no-nonsense mouth that looked as if it considered smiling to be nonsensical.

Molly quelled a flutter of panic. She had come here assuming this interview was a formality. Now she wasn't so sure.

'How do you do?' She shook hands firmly, fearful of being damned instantly and for ever in Miss Hesketh's piercing eyes if there was a suggestion of a wet lettuce handshake.

'Please sit down.' Miss Hesketh barely gave Miss Patience time to usher Molly to the sofa before continuing, 'You submitted a very good letter of application. Tell us about your new position.'

Molly described the sort of work she had been doing.

'None of it sounds like office work as such,' said Miss Hesketh. 'What makes you wish to attend our business school?'

'I know you teach surplus girls, so you'll understand that, as a surplus girl, I want to have as much training as I can, so that I keep my options open for the future. I – I haven't been a surplus girl for long. I was engaged until recently.'

'You poor dear,' murmured Miss Patience.

'Your personal life is none of our business,' stated Miss Hesketh.

Heat rose in Molly's cheeks. 'I only meant that I'm aware of the responsibility I've taken on. It's up to me to do the best I can for myself.'

Miss Hesketh nodded. Approval?

'I had intended to apply here anyway and sign up for everything you offer, but a colleague whose opinion I respect also said it would be a good idea.'

'That would be our dear Mrs Atwood.' Miss Patience smiled. Our? Dear?

'When we received your letter,' said Miss Hesketh, 'Mrs Atwood told us you're a hard worker and you've made a good start in your new post.'

Warmth filled Molly's chest. She must thank Mrs Atwood for the impromptu character reference.

There was a soft tap on the door and Mrs Atwood – Mrs Atwood! – popped her head round. 'Have you finished? May I join you?'

'I think we've finished, haven't we, Prudence?' Miss Patience looked at her sister. 'Come in, dear. Poor Miss Watson, you appear surprised.'

'She doesn't know I live here.' Mrs Atwood sat at the other end of the sofa. 'The Miss Heskeths' other pupils just attend the night school, but I'm fortunate enough to be a pupil-lodger. You were worried about treading on my toes by applying, so I thought I'd best keep quiet about being in digs here—'

'Being a paying guest,' Miss Hesketh corrected flatly.

'—being a p.g., in case I frightened you off entirely.'

Paying guests. Pupil-lodgers.

Molly sat up straighter as a new idea unfolded.

Norris popping up in Mum's front room. Norris pumping Gran for information. Norris generously supporting her in her new endeavour.

If she lived here, she would be well away from him.

Tilda and Chrissie singing the praises of their happy marriages. Dora, convinced her top-speed race up the aisle had driven Molly off her rocker. Gran muttering darkly about foolish girls who were plenty old enough to know better, all the while her eyes filled with shame and distress.

She would be further from her family too, her lovely family, whom she loved so much, but who were being rather exasperating at the moment.

Could she do this? Tom would understand, she knew he would, and he would help Mum and Dad accept it. After all, it wouldn't be for ever. Pupil-lodgers stayed here for the duration of their course and then they left. Surely she would be able to afford it. She had always paid for her keep at home. Dad hadn't wanted her to. He would have been perfectly happy to support her financially, but she had insisted on paying her way.

Molly sat forward. 'Do you have room for another pupil-lodger? I'd like to apply.'

It was Cuffy Loudwater's birthday. After playtime, he was allowed to stand on the form behind the double-desk he shared with Jacob in the middle of the classroom. It was meant to be a big secret, what the classroom arrangements meant, but everybody knew. Bad boys and dimmies at the front, good girls and anyone with a hope of grammar school at the back, leaving the middle ground for those who were never going to set a pond on fire academically but who weren't going to set the school on fire either.

Jacob had spent much of his school life at the front, in the bad boys' desks. Not that he had ever kicked up a stink in class, but no one was prepared to take a chance on Thad Layton's brother. But with Thad gone, Jacob had been moved to the middle. No longer viewed as bad, and neither clever nor a dunce. Just one of the crowd. A nothing. A nobody.

This being Cuffy's birthday, Cuffy stood on the form while sixty voices sang 'Happy Birthday' and roared out three cheers. Then Miss Kirby invited Cuffy to the front of the classroom. Miss Kirby had retired, but Miss Fowler was off sick so Miss Kirby had been asked back. She was as old as the hills. She had taught Jacob's oldest sister Belinda in the olden days before the war.

The teachers had two chairs. There was the tall one behind the raised-up desk and an ordinary one. Miss Kirby sat on this and waved the birthday slipper. Leaning over, Cuffy balanced his stomach across Miss Kirby's knees, his legs wobbling on mid-air.

'Ready,' said Miss Kirby. 'And...'

The class bellowed out the numbers as Miss Kirby gently spanked Cuffy once for each year of his life, plus one extra.

'...ten...eleven...twelve, and one for luck, THIR-TEEN!'

A rosy-faced Cuffy righted himself and returned to his place, soaking up the applause. Some of the kids came from pretty awful families and the birthday slipper was the only acknowledgement their birthdays received, but Cuffy was one of the lucky ones. He had been given a bag of marbles and his mum had made ginger biscuits.

Cuffy's birthday spanking lifted Jacob's spirits, protecting him until afternoon playtime from the inevitable school-day dread of what might happen on his way home. He hadn't clapped eyes on Shirl since last week. Might Shirl have lost interest in him? Forgotten him? It was stupid to let hope flutter in his belly, but he couldn't help it. He was a nobody at school now. Why couldn't he be a nobody outside school an' all?

But on the way home, Shirl fell in step beside him and the flutter twisted into a tight knot. Of course Shirl wasn't going to let him off the hook. He had been a twit to imagine it even for a second.

'How are you, Jemima? Keeping your pecker up?'

'Yes, thanks.' He tried to sound off-hand, as if he and Shirl were mates, as if Shirl's company didn't put him in danger of pissing himself.

'Glad to hear it.' On his chin Shirl had an angry red spot with a juicy yellow centre that begged to be squeezed. 'Not had any more mad ideas about leaving our happy band, eh?'

'Course not.' He tried to laugh. It came out as a feeble croak.

'Good for you, Jemima. I'm glad you've seen sense. Only, you know what happens to them what walk away, don't you?'

'No.'

'Oh, I thought you knew. Let me tell you. You know that lad what got hit by a tram?'

'Aye. He didn't go to our school, but we had an assembly about not larking around on the roads; and Mrs Rostron at the orphanage had a go at us an' all. Why? Was he one of your gang?'

'Yep, he were one o' mine until he decided not to help out no more. And then...' Shirl drew the side of his hand across his throat.

'What? Nah...' *Nah* was one of Thad's words. When Thad said it, it was defiant and scornful. Emerging from Jacob's suddenly trembling lips, it sounded like a fart gone wrong. 'You mean, you...?'

'Me? Did I say it were me? Don't you go making accusations, Jemima, or you'll get yourself into trouble. Just take it as a friendly warning. Now listen. I'm a reasonable bloke. The people I work with are reasonable. I've told them you want to part company with us and they're sympathetic.'

'But you just said—'

'You're not paying attention. I said that lad decided to leave, without permission. That in't allowed. But you're being given the chance to leave, only you have to give us summat, as payment, like.'

'Anything.'

'It's dead easy. There are plenty of kids in that orphanage. We need another recruit. You find me a new lad and maybe you'll be allowed to leave.'

'Maybe? But you said—'

'If you don't find me a recruit, you'd best watch out for yourself in traffic. Ta-ta, Jemima.'

Shirl strode away, which was just as well because Jacob couldn't have carried on walking beside him. His knees had turned to blancmange. Had Shirl's gang really shoved that boy in front of the tram? He couldn't believe it. But what if it was true? He trailed miserably to St Anthony's. He ought to be planning what to do, but his head was packed tight with fog and terror.

As he went indoors, he saw Daniel Cropper. Cropper would sell his grandmother's soul to get to Southport. He had run away and been dragged back several times. His problem was that to reach Southport, he needed money. If he had that, he could run away properly. Would he mind how he came by the money? Not if he was desperate.

'Cropper! Daniel Cropper!' Jacob started after him. 'Hang on a mo. I've got summat to ask you.'

Chapter Eleven

WHEN THE MISS Heskeths invited Molly back to their house a few days after her interview, her heart soared when they confirmed she could have a room, only to plummet into her shoes a moment later when Miss Patience explained, 'It's rather small, I'm afraid, not even a bedroom, really. It's the box-room, but if you don't mind having limited space, you're welcome.'

From one windowless box-room to another. Was it worth it? Yes. She needed independence and Mum and Dad would never agree to her moving into a soulless bed-sitting room. Neither would she wish to. She had read about the dreaded phenomenon of bedsit-itis in *Vera's Voice*, the loneliness endured by surplus girls who had no family to live with and, on women's wages, no spare money to put towards building a social life.

Maybe something showed in her face, because Miss Patience said in her kindly way, 'You can't decide without seeing it. Let me show you.'

Molly trailed upstairs behind her. All the doors were shut, unlike at home where the Watsons automatically left doors a few inches ajar. Miss Patience opened a door and stood aside.

'We recently had the idea of turning the box-room into a bedroom for a pupil-lodger and I've made it as pleasant as I can.'

Molly peered in, expecting to see a replica of her own room.

'It has a window,' she exclaimed. She felt a rush of ridiculous excitement. A box-room with a window, and a decent-sized window at that, with two panes, one that was fixed and one – oh bliss – that opened.

Miss Patience looked crestfallen. 'I thought you might comment on the bedspread or the pictures. We even managed to squeeze in a dressing-table, so you can have a proper looking-glass. Of course that means there's no room for a hanging cupboard, but there are hooks and hangers behind this curtain.'

'It's perfect,' Molly assured her.

'Do you really think so?'

Molly took a chance. 'Was the dressing-table your idea?'

'As a matter of fact, it was. My sister thought a hanging cupboard would be more practical.'

Prudence the practical and Patience the dreamer. That seemed to sum it up. Miss Patience had gone to some trouble to fix up the new bedroom. In its days as a box-room, it certainly wouldn't have contained those floral curtains or that rug. It was all a bit of a squash, admittedly, but it was appealing – and it was hers.

'I'd love to take it. I don't want to be cheeky, but would you mind if I had shelves put up? It would be at no cost to you. My dad runs a building company. He or my brother would be happy to do the job.'

'I see no reason why not, but we'll have to ask my sister.'

Another door opened and Mrs Atwood appeared.

'Do you like the room? It's rather darling, isn't it?'

'Yes. I'm taking it.'

'Mrs Atwood, might I prevail upon you to entertain Miss Watson for a few minutes?' asked Miss Patience. 'Just while I ask my sister about the shelves,' she explained to Molly before she headed downstairs.

'Come and see my room,' Mrs Atwood offered.

It was the large bedroom at the front of the house. It had a bay window and was handsomely furnished with matching bedstead, wardrobe, chest of drawers and dressing-table. The bed was a double. Crikey. Mrs Atwood had made the room her own by throwing a fringed shawl over the back of a wicker chair, adding a set of china trinket-dishes to the dressing-table and standing a row of books along the back of the chest of drawers. A teddy bear and a formally dressed doll with real hair perched on one of the pillows. Were the art nouveau pictures hanging from the picture-rails hers too?

'It's a beautiful room,' said Molly.

'I hope you don't think I'm showing off by dragging you in here when you've just been offered the old box-room.'

'Not one bit. I'm just glad there's space for me. But this is rather splendid.'

'It belonged to the ladies' late father, I believe. He passed away not so long ago.'

'I'm sorry to hear that. What's it like living here?'

Mrs Atwood smiled. 'Pretty formal, but you'll get used to it. Miss Hesketh is a stickler for full decorum. I think she finds it hard having p.g.s. She's not the sort to unbend, so the atmosphere can be rather stuffy and topics of conversation are decidedly safe – books, the weather – in Miss Hesketh's presence, I mean. When it's Miss Patience on her own, things ease up.'

A wave of emotion passed over Molly. It was going to be a big step to leave home, to leave the place where she had always felt so comfortable, not just because Mum made the house attractive and cosy, but because the family got on so well. Living somewhere where decorum was the order of the day promised to be a considerable change.

But she knew it was the right thing to do.

*

At home, Mum helped her pack.

'Clothes and a few knick-knacks,' said Mum. 'Everything else will be waiting for you when you come back.'

'Thanks, Mum.'

'Just make sure you do well in your studies, so you fly through the course and come home soon. I'll miss you.'

'I'll miss you too. Thanks for letting me do this.'

'You're over twenty-one. I can't stop you.'

'You know what I mean. I – I need some breathing space.'

'I'm sorry if I've made you feel you need to leave,' said Mum.

'Oh, Mum.' Molly reached for her hand and squeezed it. 'Everything's topsy-turvy at the moment. This will help it settle down.'

'It'll get you away from everyone trying to make you change your mind about Norris, you mean.'

'That's part of it, yes,' Molly admitted, 'but it's exciting too. It's time I had a change.'

'Thanks very much.' Mum adopted a mock-offended voice.

'Not from you.' Molly gave her a hug. 'I never want a change from you.'

Mum returned the hug. 'Make sure you tell your dad that an' all.'

They finished the packing and went downstairs, leaving the suitcase on the bed for Tom to bring down. Dad stood up as Molly entered the parlour.

'Well, lass, I have to say this isn't how I pictured you leaving home.'

'It's only while I do this course and I'll be popping round to see you. You don't get rid of me that easily.'

Dad took her hands. 'I used to think I'd stop worrying about my children once they grew up, but I never have.'

'Don't tell me: this has made me the biggest worry of all.'

'Getting wed is what girls are meant to do, Molly, but,' Dad went on with a wry smile, 'you're not a giddy youngster with nowt between her ears. Work hard at your course and make Mum and me proud, and then come home to us, eh? Back where you belong.'

'Oh, Dad.' She tried to blink back the tears as Dad enfolded her in his strong arms.

Tom appeared, dumping the suitcase on the floor. 'Is this a private hug or can anyone join in?' Crossing the room in two strides, he threw his arms around the two of them, not spoiling the emotion of the moment but adding to it with his sturdy good humour. 'Come on, Mum, you too.' He drew her into the family embrace. 'Let's send our Molly on her way with a big hug.'

At the office, when Molly handed in her change of address, it wasn't long before Mrs Wardle, silk blossom swaying on her hat, pounced on her.

'There you are, Miss Watson.' Mrs Wardle made it sound as if Molly had just crept back in after a disgracefully long dinner-hour, when in fact she had been at her desk almost all day. 'I'm disappointed that you failed to see fit to inform me personally of your new address, but I suppose the lapse is no more than I've learned to expect from you.'

Concern flickered inside Molly. Should she have told Mrs Wardle? Or was Mrs Wardle simply taking the opportunity to have a dig at her?

Mrs Wardle sighed dramatically. The blossom shimmered. 'Evidently an apology is too much to hope for. Ah well. Since you are now residing under the same roof as Mrs Atwood, I no longer deem it appropriate for the two of you to work closely together. In future, until you can be trusted to work alone, assuming that time ever comes, you will accompany me.'

Molly smiled. It wasn't easy. The muscles around her mouth felt like stone.

'I look forward to working alongside you, Mrs Wardle.'

Mrs Wardle frowned and shook her head. Blossom fluttered. 'Really, Miss Watson, you shall have to learn to speak more clearly. For a moment, it almost sounded as if you said you were going to work alongside me, whereas, as you are fully aware, you shall be working under me.'

Oh, how true that was! Accompanying Mrs Atwood on her visits had been a pleasure. Working alongside – sorry, under Mrs Wardle was very different. When Mrs Wardle said 'under', that was precisely what she meant. Mrs Atwood had, while providing guidance, treated Molly as an equal, asking her opinion and providing her with the necessary background information before they went anywhere, enabling her to contribute effectively to the visit. Not so Mrs Wardle. She shared nothing in advance, which made Molly feel rather a twit in front of the people they went to see.

'I'll say one word to you,' Mrs Atwood whispered. 'Post-trolley!'

Molly remembered Mrs Atwood intercepting the post. 'And I'll say one word to you. Diary!'

Sneaking looks at Mrs Wardle's leather-bound diary that lay importantly on her desk meant she could ask Mrs Atwood or look up information that would enable her to be of use.

Not that Mrs Wardle gave her many opportunities.

'Observe and learn,' was Mrs Wardle's customary command, generally followed by a weary-sounding, 'in so far as you're capable.'

Molly fumed, but kept her frustration to herself. Even Mrs Wardle couldn't keep her as a trainee for ever. The more she held her tongue, the sooner she would be set free to work independently.

Keeping quiet wasn't easy, though. When she accompanied Mrs Wardle to see Mrs Fletcher, she was appalled by Mrs Wardle's attitude, which was a mixture of patronising and dismissive.

'My good woman, what a stroke of luck for you that your appearance before the Panel had to be postponed.'

'Postponed?' Molly hadn't known that.

'Indeed, yes. Two of the members were unable to attend as they were invited to lunch with the Lord Lieutenant.'

'I assume these two members are former Guardians,' said Molly.

'Naturally. Board of Health people are hardly likely to receive the honour of such an invitation.'

'Neither would they be able to abandon their work responsibilities if they did.'

Mrs Wardle gave her a hard look. So, it seemed, did her glassy-eyed fox-fur. 'What a nasty little mind you have, Miss Watson. I despair of teaching you anything. Mrs Fletcher, you know perfectly well that the Panel will take a dim view of your owning this photograph. I instruct you to sell it.' Her beady eyes skimmed the damp room with distaste. 'Do you have any other possessions that the Panel should know about? Speak up! It won't go in your favour if you keep secrets.'

Mrs Fletcher's fingers tangled together. 'Mrs Atwood said—'

'Oh – Mrs Atwood. I shouldn't pay attention to her, if I were you, Mrs Fletcher. I have had this kind of authority for many years and she's a beginner, and a flighty one at that, full of her own ideas. These modern girls! All I can say is, it's a great pity her husband died. Taking care of a husband and children would have kept her busy and out of the workplace, leaving those of us with years of charitable experience to deal with the poor and destitute.' An elaborate sigh. The buttercups on her hat trembled. 'As I was saying before you interrupted me, Mrs Fletcher, that photograph has to go.'

'But it's a picture of Mrs Fletcher's former employer's mother,' said Molly. 'It has great sentimental value.'

'If Mrs Fletcher had wanted to indulge in sentiment, she should have made a better choice of husband. Mrs Fletcher, do you have other possessions of which the Panel should be aware?'

'Well—'

'Don't beat about the bush. It will go badly for you if you withhold information.'

'I have a brooch,' Mrs Fletcher whispered.

'A brooch? Was it your intention to hide this from me? Sell it.'

'Mrs Wardle,' said Molly, 'with the greatest respect, your advice to Mrs Fletcher overturns what Mrs Atwood and I agreed to do last time.'

'Miss Watson, you forget yourself. Firstly, I do not give advice to these people; I issue instructions. Secondly, you personally agreed to nothing because you have no authority; and thirdly, Mrs Atwood is a bleeding-heart social reformer, who views these people through rose-tinted spectacles instead of seeing them for what they really are.'

'What they really are is decent folk in need of a helping hand.'

'A helping hand? A firm hand. First and foremost, a firm hand and a stiff talking-to. Only after that should they be given assistance, on the strict understanding that it will be removed if they don't prove themselves to be clean, sober, hard-working and grateful. Or perhaps you think cleanliness, sobriety, diligence and gratitude are old fashioned.'

'I think no such thing.' Molly reined in her temper. 'I simply wish to point out that Mrs Atwood said she would write to the Panel on Mrs Fletcher's behalf, asking for leniency regarding her keeping her most precious possessions. Shouldn't this be allowed to stand?'

'Be silent! Mrs Fletcher, if you desire the Panel's assistance, there must be no subterfuge. Sell the photograph; sell the brooch; and then you may be considered. Good morning. Miss Watson, come.' She might as well have said, 'Heel.'

Mrs Wardle stomped down the stairs so heavily, it was a wonder she didn't bring the decrepit staircase crashing to the floor. At the bottom, she turned on Molly.

'Contradict me again in front of one of these people and I'll dismiss you on the spot.'

Molly bit her tongue all the way back to the Town Hall. She was going to tell Mrs Atwood everything and hope she could set things to rights. Molly was at her desk for the rest of the day, but so was Mrs Wardle. Had she guessed Molly's intention?

In the end, when the other two, as well as the two colleagues who occupied the other desks, tidied up and got ready to leave, Molly stayed put.

'I'll finish writing this.' Blimey! As if she was composing a report to be presented to the Lord Mayor himself. 'I'll see you at home,' she told Mrs Atwood.

Alone, she quickly wrote an explanation of what had happened at Mrs Fletcher's and popped it in Mrs Atwood's top drawer for her to find tomorrow. Although work was regularly mentioned at home, it was only in general terms. The strictest confidentiality regarding one's place of work was one of Miss Hesketh's golden rules.

Molly left the building with a lighter heart, feeling she had done her best for poor Mrs Fletcher. Albert Square was busy with office-workers heading for home. She felt a thrill of pride. As heartily as she loathed Mrs Wardle, this knocked spots off working at Upton's.

'Evening, Molly.' Norris raised his hat in jaunty salute.

'Norris! What are you doing here?'

'Waiting for you, of course. I haven't seen you since you went to live elsewhere. We can't have you forgetting me.' He chuckled. Was there anything that didn't make him chuckle?

'I'm hardly likely to forget you.'

'That's what I like to hear. I hope you'll allow me to take you for a bite to eat. I want to hear all about your new job.'

'I'm afraid I can't, Norris. I'm expected home for tea.'

'Home?' His frown was an indulgent reprimand. 'I hope you don't call it that in front of your mum.'

Her throat tightened with guilt, preventing her from answering.

Norris had consolation at the ready. 'Don't look so stricken. I know you'd never hurt her, not knowingly anyway, and I'll tell her so the next time I see her.'

'You'll do no such thing,' Molly exclaimed. 'I can't hang about. I really do have to get back.'

'Get back? Not go home?' Norris's smile was more than a little smug. 'You've adapted your vocabulary already. I'm pleased to have helped you appreciate your error.'

She made a move in the direction of the tram-stop. Norris kept pace.

'We'll travel together. I'll pay for you as a gentleman should.'

'There's no need. I'm an independent woman now.'

'Oh, Molly, there's no such thing. There are widows and old maids. You can't call them independent when they're forced to fend for themselves. And then there are young ladies – like yourself – who have their reasons, or imagine they do. Maybe they hanker after the taste of freedom the war provided...'

Was that a veiled dig at her? Surely not. He wouldn't stoop so low. She increased her pace. So did Norris.

'...but they're acting contrary to their true natures, so it isn't real independence.'

On the tram, Norris paid both their fares by virtue of waving his coins practically in front of the conductor's nose.

'That's the way it should be,' he remarked complacently, 'a fellow treating his girl like a lady.'

Molly recalled various occasions when she had paid for herself, or for both of them, and clamped her lips together. It was in the past. It was the future that mattered.

As they approached Norris's stop, he didn't get up.

'Norris,' she said.

'Kind of you to worry about me, Molly, but I'm staying on until the terminus so I can see you home properly.'

That was too much. 'No, you aren't. I'm quite capable of seeing myself home. It's time for you to get off, Norris. I mean it. It's been good seeing you, but now you have to go.'

The sidelong look he gave her said he was weighing up his chances. 'If you insist. Never let it be said I don't listen to what you want.'

As he swung himself out of the seat, Molly gave him her sweetest smile. 'And thank you for using the word "home" a moment ago. I'm glad you realise it's my home now.'

Making her way from the terminus to Wilton Close, she didn't know which of them she was more annoyed with: Norris or Mrs Wardle. Or possibly herself. Why had she let Norris say those things to her about women's so-called independence? But then, why shouldn't he hold such views? He hadn't said anything that wasn't considered normal. She was the one who was out of step.

Chapter Twelve

PRUDENCE HAD TO bend forwards to do her hair in her dressing-table mirror. The dressing-table had a matching stool, but she never bothered with it, apart from standing on it once a year to take down the curtains to be washed. Like everything in the house, the curtains were old. How many more spring cleans would they stand before they disintegrated? Mind you, though faded, they still looked all right, because they were good quality.

A bit like herself. Faded, but good quality. Her quality was all on the inside – education, standards, duty. She had never been much to look at, even less so now. Thin and plain, bony, all angles. It was only the quality of her clothes that prevented her from looking like a scarecrow.

As always when she arrived home from the office, she unfastened her hair from its severe bun, gave it a brisk comb and put it up again. Every so often, Patience suggested she wore a looser bun for evenings at home, but that was just Patience being soppy. Anyway, they didn't have evenings at home any longer, not in the accepted sense. Weekday evenings were spent teaching and even at weekends, the house was no longer their own, now that they had their lodgers. Mrs Atwood and Miss Watson were pleasant young women, but it wouldn't do to unbend.

She fastened her bun with expert fingers. She didn't really need to look. Standing in front of the looking-glass was more habit than necessity. She jabbed in a few hairpins. She might not look like anything much, but she hadn't felt so good in years. It ought to be exhausting, travelling into town every day to do a day's work, then coming home to teach in the evenings, but it wasn't. It was exhilarating.

She had worked in the offices of Manchester Corporation for forty years, ever since she left school at the age of twelve. How clever, how indispensable, she had thought herself – office junior by day, household manager at home. She had been in charge of ordering the coal, paying the butcher's bill and organising repairs ever since Mother died. Strictly speaking, she hadn't worked for the Corporation absolutely all that time. She had left for a while. She had meant to leave for good, had intended to leave her old life behind. Oh yes, she had been full of plans and excitement and determination to build a fulfilling new life and career for herself. But the trouble with making plans was that other people and circumstances and life in general didn't know what was meant to happen and waded in and made other things happen instead. She had ended up coming back home and she had been here ever since.

Her jaw hardened. Home: the house where she had been born, the house that should by rights be hers now, hers and Patience's. It had originally belonged to Mother, who had inherited it before she met Pa. Poor Mother died young and she had left the house to Pa. When Lawrence had grown up, he left home, but Prudence and Patience had stayed put. Patience had stayed put to the extent that she had never worked outside the home, but had kept house, shopping and cooking and doing as much housework as was ladylike, the rest being undertaken by their daily, and generally pandering to Pa and his whims.

Pa and his whims! Prudence had revised her opinion of Pa considerably since the beginning of this year. You weren't supposed to think ill of the dead, but honestly! When Pa had passed away in the new year, she and Patience had taken it for granted that the house would come to them. It was only right and proper, given that it had originally belonged to their mother, but Pa, blast his eyes, had left it to Lawrence, the son of his first marriage.

A solid block of unfairness had lodged inside Prudence's chest ever since. Lawrence and Evelyn wanted her and Patience to move out, so they and the girls could take possession. Not that there was anything wrong with the house they rented, but Lawrence fancied the prestige of owning his own place. Idiot! What was wrong with renting? Far more people rented than owned their own houses. But Lawrence had an inflated opinion of himself. His success as a businessman wasn't sufficient. He wanted the title of Alderman in front of his name; and jollying along with the right people and getting a name for himself as a philanthropist by sticking his fingers in various social reforming pies was how he intended to achieve it. Owning his own home would make him look good too.

A pulse jumped in Prudence's neck as the fear that had enveloped her at the reading of Pa's will swooped through her, as it sometimes did, though she would never admit it. She was the strong one, the capable one, the one who organised repairs when the gutter got blocked or the attic skylight leaked. Patience was the sweet-natured one, the kind one. Well, she could afford to be. She had Prudence to tackle all the difficult things.

No, that wasn't fair. Being gentle didn't mean Patience was weak. In her own quiet way, she had shown her mettle in recent weeks in all she had done to involve herself in their business school and also in the way she had helped the Layton family after that dreadful fire.

Their business school: this was how they had rescued their house – yes, their house, whatever Pa's will said – from Lawrence's grasping fingers. Using Prudence's years of office experience and Patience's social skills, they had set themselves up to train girls to be office workers; and not just any girls, but surplus girls, that blighted generation whose chances of matrimony had perished in the fields of Flanders. Opening their night school had been carefully choreographed, with Lawrence, poor sap, being invited to its official opening, complete with journalists not only from the local press but also from Patience's favourite weekly paper, *Vera's Voice*. Under the circumstances, Lawrence had had no choice but to blather on about his social conscience and his dear sisters, who were going to run this business school on his behalf.

Hard cheese, Lawrence.

Since then, he had made various attempts to discredit the school, even to discredit Prudence personally – and she would never tell a living soul how deeply that had shaken her – but he hadn't managed to wrest the house back. He never would, if she had anything to do with it.

She changed into fresh collar and cuffs, the merciless starch chafing her skin as she fastened them. She used to change out of the ankle-length skirt and plain blouse she wore at the office into an equally plain dress and cardigan for the evening. Not now, though. Now, evenings were spent working and that meant being appropriately dressed.

Downstairs, the hall smelled of beeswax with a trace of the lemon Patience added to it. Patience was a good little housewife. Everything was neat and clean. Even the small cloakroom at the foot of the stairs was perfectly tidy. Not that they possessed many coats and hats and umbrellas to make a mess of it. Mrs Atwood, when she moved in, had hung up her worsted coat without smoothing it and had tossed her hat onto the shelf, but now, after the smallest of hints from Patience, who was far more diplomatic than Prudence would have been, she was as neat as they were.

Why did Mrs Atwood go out to work? Her smart coat and that oversized beret of stiffened felt suggested she wasn't exactly on her uppers. Maybe she worked because what reason had she, a youngish widow, to stay at home? It wasn't something you could ask – as Prudence had told Patience in no uncertain terms. Patience had a regrettable tendency to make pets of their pupils and having pupils living with them as lodgers increased the danger. Patience was such a softy. Prudence had no desire to be anything other than impersonal and professional towards their pupils – or anybody else, for that matter. She preferred to keep herself to herself.

In the sitting room, Patience and Mrs Atwood were talking. It was the custom of the household to gather together for a few minutes before heading into the dining room.

'Where is Miss Watson?' asked Prudence.

'She stayed on at the office to finish something,' said Mrs Atwood.

'I'm sure she won't be late for tea,' Patience added.

'I hope not,' said Prudence.

No sooner had she uttered the words than the front door was heard opening whereupon Patience excused herself to serve their meal. They all ate their main meal in the middle of the day, so this was a high tea of corned beef patties with salad. Nevertheless, they ate in the dining room, the table complete with linen, Grandmother's cut-glass six-piece condiment set on its solid silver tray, and a dainty vase of lily-of-the-valley as a centrepiece. They used the best china these days too. Why not? It had sat in the sideboard for donkey's years, kept for best and consequently never used, because they didn't lead a 'for best' kind of life; but Pa's will had changed a lot of things.

After tea, Prudence repaired to the sitting room with the pupil-lodgers while Patience cleared away. On her first day, Mrs Atwood had offered to assist, but hadn't been permitted to. You couldn't have a paying guest doing housework. She and Patience might not be rolling in money, but they had their standards. Standards were everything. Standards were what held their lives together.

After tea, the Miss Heskeths prepared to teach. Neither Molly nor Mrs Atwood had a lesson this evening, which meant they were required to absent themselves from the sitting and dining rooms, both of which were required for lessons.

'If you wouldn't mind,' murmured Miss Hesketh, as if they weren't perfectly well aware of what was expected; but that was Miss Hesketh all over, always observing the proprieties.

'Thank you, dears,' added Miss Patience. Molly had soon got used to being 'Miss Watson dear.' There was no doubt Miss Patience was fond of her p.g.s. Was it only Miss Hesketh's unyielding formality that held her gentle sister back from making complete pets of their pupil-lodgers?

The doorbell rang.

Miss Hesketh raised her eyebrows. 'I hope that isn't one of tonight's pupils. I know I impress upon everyone the importance of never being late, but really, there is such a thing as too early. It's most inconsiderate.'

Miss Patience went to answer the door. Molly and Mrs Atwood followed her into the hall to fetch their outdoor things from the cloakroom, ready to go for a walk.

Miss Patience opened the door and there was a pretty, dark-haired girl of about twenty. She wore a cherry-red loose swing-jacket that hung over a cream dress with patch-pockets in the drop-waisted skirt. A brown leather suitcase stood beside her in the porch and she clutched the handles of a tapestried handbag in slender gloved fingers.

'Oh, Auntie Patience!' Her voice wobbled on the brink of tears. 'Can I come and live with you and Aunt Prudence, please, and attend your school? Mummy says you're taking pupil-lodgers. Please may I be one? You'll fix up that old box-room for me, won't you?'

Chapter Thirteen

'LUCY, WHAT'S THIS about?' Prudence demanded the moment the pupil-lodgers departed and the front door shut behind them. 'Do your parents know where you are?'

'I left a note.'

'A note?' Prudence couldn't remember the last time she had taken Lawrence's side, if indeed she ever had, but right now she was in full sympathy with the shock and vexation he and Evelyn would experience when they read Lucy's words. 'I suppose this means we can expect them to turn up at any minute.'

'No. They're out at a function. They won't be home before midnight.'

'So you picked your moment to run away.'

'I haven't run away. Not exactly.'

'What else do you call it when you turn up on someone's doorstep and demand a room?'

'But you're my aunts,' Lucy pleaded. 'I thought you'd be pleased to have me.'

'Of course we are, dear,' said Patience, 'but it is rather unexpected.'

'It's entirely unexpected,' Prudence said drily. Trust Patience to ooze sympathy.

'I know and I'm sorry,' said Lucy. 'But Daddy is always trying to close down your business school. Fliss and I aren't meant to know, but we do.'

'Because you've been listening in?'

Lucy flushed, but lifted her chin. 'I thought if I came here, he would look more kindly on it.'

'Is that why you've come?' asked Patience. She threw Prudence a look of urgent appeal.

Prudence wasn't going to be rushed into anything. 'While we're teaching, you must make yourself scarce.' She held up her hand for silence as both Patience and Lucy opened their mouths. 'You're overwrought, child. Have a lie-down.'

Patience took Lucy upstairs. Prudence followed, just in case Patience made any rash promises.

On the landing, Lucy threw open the box-room door. 'How big is it? Oh! You've already turned it into a bedroom.' Her face glowed.

'Don't get any ideas,' said Prudence. 'It's spoken for.'

'Oh.' From glow to gloom in an instant.

'You can rest on my bed,' Patience offered.

'But not,' said Prudence, 'until after you've written a letter to your parents to say you've arrived here safely. If it goes by the evening post, they'll receive it first thing tomorrow.'

She stood by, exercising great restraint, as Patience did her mother hen act on Lucy. Then she firmly led Patience downstairs.

'Poor Lucy—' Patience began.

'Little minx, causing all this trouble.' Her tone was calculated to put a damper on the gushing Patience was barely holding in check.

'Be fair, Prudence,' said Patience. 'This isn't like her. She's a good girl.'

'I'm as fond of her as you are, but we must forget about her for now. Our pupils are entitled to our full attention.'

That was easier said than done, though. What had happened to her single-minded concentration? She might be vexed with Lucy for behaving in a dramatic way, but there was a knot of concern in the pit of her stomach nonetheless. Drat the girl.

It was a relief when, at the close of lessons, Patience showed their pupils out. Prudence hovered at the foot of the stairs, hesitating before she called Lucy down. The pupil-lodgers had come back a while ago and would be in the small breakfast room that adjoined the kitchen, playing draughts or reading. Well, they would have to remain there a bit longer.

Lucy appeared at the bend in the stairs. 'May I come down?'

'Of course, dear,' said Patience.

Prudence led the way to the sitting room. Lucy sat on the sofa. Patience sat beside her, her hand creeping towards Lucy's. Prudence dealt her sister a hard look and Patience pulled her hand back into her lap.

'So you've decided you want to learn office skills,' Prudence said briskly. 'I don't propose to discuss that, as I can't visualise your parents agreeing to it. The main question is, what are we to do with you tonight?'

Lucy paled. 'I thought I was staying here.'

'We have no choice about that, but where are we to put you? All our bedrooms are occupied.'

'Lucy can share with me,' Patience offered.

'Certainly not.' A young girl seeing a middle-aged lady in a state of undress? Absolutely not. 'Aunt Patience can come in with me and you may have her bed.'

'Thank you,' Lucy said humbly. 'Are you going to send me home in the morning?'

'I rather think I shan't need to,' said Prudence. 'I imagine your father will haul you home himself before the neighbours find out. We can all look forward to a jolly Saturday morning.'

'Oh, Lucy,' said Patience.

'Don't encourage her,' said Prudence. 'She's a naughty girl who's caused a rumpus.'

A light tap on the door heralded the arrival of the p.g.s.

'We're sorry to disturb you,' Mrs Atwood began. 'We know you're in the middle of family business.'

Family business? Family crisis, more like.

'The interruption is my fault,' said Miss Watson. 'If I'm to lose my room because your niece needs it, I'd rather be told immediately.'

Patience uttered a small cry. 'Have you been fretting about that all evening?'

'I would understand,' said Miss Watson. 'It's family.'

Mrs Atwood looked Prudence straight in the eye. 'There's nothing more important than family, is there?'

It was as if she and Mrs Atwood were the only two in the room. Prudence shook off the impression. 'I don't intend to throw over my other responsibilities to accommodate the whim of a foolish girl. Miss Watson, that bedroom is yours until you cease to be a pupil. We have determined where my niece will spend tonight.'

'Auntie Patience is giving up her bed,' said Lucy.

'I don't wish to speak out of turn,' said Mrs Atwood, which undoubtedly meant she was about to do that very thing, 'but since I'm the one person with a double bed, I'd be happy for – Miss Hesketh, is it? – to share with me.'

'We couldn't ask it of you,' Prudence said immediately.

'Why not? I slept in some pretty wretched conditions in France during the war. I think I can manage to share a comfortable bed.'

The others clearly thought it a good idea. Even so, it wasn't easy to agree. As landlady and tutor to Mrs Atwood, Prudence had no desire to accept a favour from her, but these were hardly ordinary circumstances.

'Thank you,' she said stiffly, 'though I'm not sure Lucy deserves such consideration.'

Was that unkind of her? She didn't want to be unkind, but she wanted to be in control and sometimes a sharp word helped achieve that. Nevertheless, she was dismayed to see a sheen of tears in Lucy's eyes. Humiliation at her aunt's words or gratitude for Mrs Atwood's kindness? The latter, Prudence hoped. The last thing she wanted was to make the child cry.

And that was another thing. Whatever else Lucy was, she wasn't a cry-baby. What was going on?

'The breakfast room table isn't big enough,' said Patience when Prudence came downstairs the next morning, 'so I'm setting the table in the dining room.'

'I'm helping,' added Lucy.

'I should think so too,' said Prudence.

She noted the flush of colour that rose in her niece's face. Had it been mean to put her in her place? But what else did the child expect, after turning their household upside down? It wouldn't do her any harm to feel uncomfortable. The simple fact that she had thought she could get away with it proved what Prudence had always believed, that Lawrence and Evelyn spoiled those two girls. Finishing school – honestly! Walking round with books on their heads and learning how to choose menus and arrange flowers. What about lessons in maths so they could divide up the household budget and measure for curtains? What about learning how to store winter woollies with a sheet of newspaper lining the base of the drawer to repel moths, or how to protect the house from mice, or how to mend a teapot handle and all those other bits of domestic economy at which Patience had become so adept over the years?

But Lucy and Felicity Hesketh would never need to acquire such knowledge, not if their well-heeled parents channelled them into solid middle-class marriages that set them up for life, not to mention casting a glowing light on Lawrence's quest to become an alderman. Imagine it. All those bigwigs and their glossy wives on the bride's side of the church, while the faded, old-fashioned spinster aunts sat straight-backed in the family pews at the front.

Was she jealous? Of Lawrence's comfortable life? Of everything he provided for his wife and daughters? It would be fatuous to suggest she relished being hard up, but neither did she hanker after cocktails and canapés with the social elite. Intelligent conversation and a few hands of whist with her long-standing friend Miss Kirby on a Saturday evening was more in her line.

'How did everyone sleep?' asked Patience.

'Like a top, thanks,' Mrs Atwood said promptly.

'Did you really?' Lucy asked. 'I'm afraid I tossed and turned a bit.'

Mrs Atwood lifted one shoulder in a shrug. 'I wasn't aware of it.' She turned to Prudence. 'We know you have family matters to sort out, so Miss Watson and I will make ourselves scarce.'

Prudence forced herself to nod, though her neck almost cracked with the effort. It was bad enough that the pupil-lodgers were aware of this upset – that in itself set worms wriggling beneath her skin – but to have them absenting themselves as a kindness... It was too much. The only antidote was to assert herself.

'Make the most of today,' she advised. 'It'll be your final free Saturday. By next weekend we'll have found you unpaid positions where you'll be able to spend a few hours each Saturday using some of the skills we're teaching you.'

Miss Watson and Mrs Atwood didn't hang about after breakfast – which was just as well, as the sound of a motor car entering Wilton Close was heard shortly after they departed.

Lucy chewed her lip.

Patience pressed her hand. 'Don't worry, Lucy dear. I'm sure Daddy won't be angry, just concerned.'

'Make yourself useful, Lucy,' Prudence commanded. 'Make the beds while the adults discuss this.'

'I'm an adult.'

'You haven't behaved like one. Please do as you're told.'

Lucy dragged herself to her feet, but she scampered upstairs quickly enough when Patience said, 'I'll let them in.'

A moment later Evelyn bustled into the sitting room, her loose-fitting pale-green coat with its large cape-collar swirling impressively. Her dark-green silk hat sported a colossal bow on one side but, no matter how smartly decked out she was, there was no disguising the worry in her pudgy features. It was the same with Lawrence. Tall and lean, he cut a fine figure in his double-breasted suit and silk tie, but his cheeks were more hollow than usual. If Prudence had expected to feel any satisfaction at seeing the customary complacency stripped from her brother and sister-in-law's features, she was disappointed.

Lawrence looked round. 'Where is she?'

'Upstairs,' said Prudence. 'I thought we could talk about this without her.'

'There's nothing to talk about. She's coming home.'

'Perhaps we could sit down and have a chat first.' Patience spoke in her usual gentle way. 'Please. I've lain awake most of the night worrying – as I'm sure you have, Evelyn.'

Evelyn gravitated towards the sofa, unbuttoning her lightweight linen coat and thrusting it in Patience's general direction for her to take charge of.

'I don't know what's come over her,' Evelyn declared. 'The first we knew of it was when we found the note last night, saying she had gone to be your pupil-lodger. That's absurd, of course, with her background.'

A devil stirred inside Prudence. 'The world at large believes the business school is your idea, Lawrence. What greater accolade could there be than that you send your beloved child here?'

'My daughter isn't a surplus girl,' Lawrence snapped. 'I support her in comfort and style and Evelyn ensures she meets the right sort of people.'

'Tony Palmerston and the Bambrook boy are clearly taken with her.' Evelyn gave her shoulders a proud wriggle.

'Even if she wanted to work,' said Lawrence, 'she couldn't. It would reflect poorly on me.'

'Which, naturally, is the most important thing,' Prudence murmured, then widened her eyes innocently when Lawrence glared in her direction.

'So,' said Evelyn, 'if you'll kindly call her downstairs, we'll be on our way.'

'May I make a suggestion?' said Patience. 'Why not leave her here for a visit? She's obviously in a tizzy over something. I don't imagine for one moment she really intended to join the business school. That was just an excuse. But if she's going to say silly things like that, wouldn't it be preferable if she said them here than in front of your friends? Your social connections are important, Lawrence.'

'She can't stay,' said Prudence. 'We have nowhere to put her.'

Patience's smile was as sweet as ever, but there was steel in her eyes. 'Actually, we have. Mrs Atwood has offered to share her room. Such a generous offer, I thought.'

'We can't ask a paying guest to share,' Prudence objected.

'She offered.'

'If Lucy were to stay for a visit – *if*, I say,' said Evelyn, 'she would naturally require her own room. The box-room is a reasonable size. Perhaps if you—'

'We already have,' said Prudence. 'There's a p.g. in there.'

'Ye gods,' said Lawrence. 'Have you got others camping in the attic?'

Patience turned to Evelyn. 'Won't you let her stay, just for now? You know I'll make a fuss of her. That might be all she needs to get her over this little bump.'

'What bump?' Lawrence demanded. 'There is no bump.'

'All I know is, this is where she wants to be,' said Patience. 'Can't we humour her, for the time being? It would be such a pleasure for Prudence and me to have her here.'

And somehow or other it was agreed, though Prudence wasn't entirely sure how. She suspected Lawrence and Evelyn weren't sure either.

'Thank you, Mummy and Daddy,' Lucy burbled when she was informed. 'I'll go and unpack properly.'

'Not until Mrs Atwood gets home,' said Prudence. 'She'll show you where you may put your things.'

Later, she advised Mrs Atwood, 'I suggest you set ground rules. Lucy is more accustomed to getting her own way than I should like.' It was the closest she could come to expressing her disapproval of the arrangement without uttering the words.

But Mrs Atwood failed to treat the situation with the gravity it deserved. 'I'm old enough and ugly enough to cope. She's little more than a child, after all.'

'I'm not having her sitting around doing nothing all day,' Prudence told Patience. 'You wanted her here, so it's your job to keep her busy.'

'That won't be a problem. She's promised to help me think of telephone lessons for our pupils; she's to come shopping with me every morning and walk Mrs Morgan's spaniel every afternoon; and she'll help me clean the brights.'

'I'm pleased to hear it.'

Polishing the silver and crystal was certain to send Lucy scuttling home to her life of luxury.

Chapter Fourteen

'BUT MR ABRAMS, sir, it's not fair if us girls aren't allowed.' Pigtails dangling either side of a face flushed with annoyance, young Matilda Graham gave Aaron a look that suggested that, should she become a teacher when she grew up, she would have no trouble quelling a class of sixty with a single glance. 'It's not our fault the boys have penknives as part of their uniform and we have sewing kits. We're just as capable of hacking away bits of plant.'

Aaron swallowed a smile. 'There are plenty of folk who'd say hacking isn't ladylike.'

'But, *sir...*'

'Fortunately for you, I'm not one of them. I see no reason why girls shouldn't join in, if I can lay my hands on enough gardening knives.'

It was a fine afternoon at the tail-end of June. It would be July on Saturday. School was over for the day and most of the St Anthony's children were in the playground. It was a shame the whole area was tarmacadamed. Some grass would have made it more appealing, but tarmac was sensible. The only concession to nature was the trees growing at intervals round the edge, their roots causing the tarmac to swell.

Aaron had decided that hacking back the ivy would start in the corner of the girls' playground and would progress all along the Church Road part of the wall, then turn the corner along High Lane. He had no shortage of volunteers. Picking six lads from the eager group, he promised the rest that everyone would get a turn in due course. As the boys melted reluctantly away, Aaron selected four girls.

Seeing young Matilda opening her mouth to object to there being fewer girls, he forestalled her with, 'I've got only four gardening knives – for now. Maybe I'll pick up a few more at the ironmonger's. But two girls can have the job of filling these sacks with what we cut off.' He showed the children how to cut the stems, then stationed them along the section of wall. 'Stay where I put you and make sure you cut only the stems and not your fingers.'

There was a ripple of laughter. They got started. He watched them for a couple of minutes before setting to work himself.

A bearded face appeared over the wall.

'Well, look at this. I see you've made a start at last, Abrams.'

'Bunny! Good to see you. Business gone well today?'

When he smiled, Bunny's yellowing teeth showed between his beard and his neatly trimmed moustache. 'Sold out. Shall I lend a hand for half an hour? I did say I'd help once you ran out of excuses not to get going.'

'Cheek!' Aaron grinned back. Bunny was a good sort, who would do anything for anyone. 'Come on in.'

'I'll park my wagon inside, if it's all the same to you.'

Bunny pushed his hot-potato barrow through the gates and put the brake on. Drawn by the sight of the black metal boiler, the children flooded towards him, the boys leaving their playground to rush across.

'Bunny's brought us hot potatoes for tea,' called a bright spark and a ragged cheer went up.

'No, he hasn't.' Aaron raised his voice. 'He's here to help with the ivy. Back to your games, you lot.'

With a groan, they dispersed, the girls to their French skipping and circle games, each with its own song, the boys to British bulldog and cricket.

'Let's have a butcher's.' Bunny peered over the shoulders of the children hard at work. 'You look like you're fighting your way through to Sleeping Beauty's castle. Here, you two lads, make room for a little 'un. What are your names?'

'Layton One and Layton Two, mister,' said Mikey.

'No need to call me mister. Everyone calls me Bunny, always have, always will. I'm Mr Rabbit, you see.'

'Really?' young Jacob asked.

'That's for me to know and you to find out. Now budge up and let me get cutting.'

It was surprisingly hard work, with all those strong stems intertwined and clinging tenaciously to the brickwork. Messy too, with clouds of dust that smelled of soil and age filming the air around them, to say nothing of the creepy-crawlies being flicked here, there and everywhere by the chopping, snipping and sawing.

'Ugh! Disgusting!'

Of all the times for her to turn up, here was Mrs Wardle coming through the gates, waving her hand in front of her face as if she couldn't breathe – and wasn't that Miss Watson from the sweet shop with her?

'Mr Abrams,' boomed Mrs Wardle. 'What is going on here?'

He stepped away from the wall, mopping his brow with the back of his hand. 'We're clearing the ivy. It'll undermine the brickwork if we don't get rid of it.'

'I don't mean that.' Mrs Wardle was pink and puffed up. 'I mean, just look at these children.'

Aaron gazed round with a grin of pure pride. 'It's good for them. They're in the fresh air, doing something useful – and making a good fist of it, I might add.' Mrs Wardle's puffed-up pinkness wasn't subsiding. 'If it's the blades you're worried about, it's good for them to learn to use tools properly.'

The pink deepened to puce.

'I think what Mrs Wardle means,' said Miss Watson, 'is that the children are rather dirty.'

Oh crumbs. He hadn't noticed. Faces and clothes were smeared; hair was streaked with a fine dust of soil; and as for the girls' pinafores…

'This is a disgrace,' Mrs Wardle declared. 'You might as well have told them to roll in the mud – isn't that so, Miss Watson? This will disrupt the orphanage's routine, as this washing can't wait till Monday. How many changes of clothes do you imagine each child possesses?'

'Mrs Wardle, why don't I take the children indoors so they can clean up and get changed?' said Miss Watson. 'Perhaps the maids can put the clothes in to soak.'

'And I,' declared Mrs Wardle, 'shall speak to Mrs Rostron.'

Aaron and Bunny were left standing there as the children were led away, a couple of them daring to slouch with disappointment until Mrs Wardle clipped them round the ear as she marched past on her way to blacken his name with Mrs Rostron.

The superintendent, however, took it remarkably well. Was that so as not to give Mrs Wardle the satisfaction? Impossible to tell. Mrs Rostron was discretion itself.

'I have no objection to the children helping you with the ivy,' she told Aaron. 'It will foster community spirit and pride in their surroundings; but in future they must wear old sacking aprons.'

Later on, in the Horse and Jockey, Bunny grinned at Aaron. 'You didn't get booted out, then? I be that's what that snooty lady wanted. Who is she, anyroad?'

'It's in the orphanage's charter that a member of the local Panel must be appointed as the official visitor. It started out as a means of communication, given that the Panel had often had dealings with the children's families before the children ended up in St Anthony's, but Mrs Wardle uses it as a ticket to come and go as the fancy takes her.'

'Who was the pretty lass she brought with her?' asked Bunny, taking a sup of his pint. 'Her daughter, learning how to be Lady Bountiful?'

'She works at Upton's sweet shop near the station. I can't imagine what she was doing there this afternoon.'

It was a good question. What was Miss Watson doing hanging onto Mrs Wardle's coat-tails – or should that be her fox-fur tails? Something twitched beneath Aaron's skin. Miss Watson's unusual hair colour and her intelligent greeny-hazel eyes had appealed to him, as had the generous nature that had prompted her to raise money to buy sweets for the orphans. His visit to Upton's to pay back the stolen money had left him in no doubt that the fund-raising had happened entirely at her instigation. He valued initiative and kindness in anybody and he was willing to bet Miss Watson possessed both in spades. It had been a long time since a girl had had this effect on him. He had gone back to Upton's to see her again, only to be told she had left. He had cursed himself for missing his chance, but now they had crossed paths once more. He raised his pint of bitter to his bent head to hide his smile.

Then his facial muscles rearranged themselves. Miss Watson had arrived with Mrs Wardle this afternoon and been quick to jump on the 'Aren't they dirty?' bandwagon. Was she that pompous lady's acolyte? When she had given him a piece of her mind over the penny tray, had that been less a flash of honest annoyance than a chance for her to assert herself over an inter-loper who had spoiled her plan to dispense bounty? Surely not. Surely his instincts about her integrity were right.

But she had turned up in Mrs Wardle's wake and had given that disagreeable lady her support.

There was nothing for it. Any ideas he might have had about developing a serious interest in Miss Watson needed to be stamped on and squashed flat. He had more self-respect than to allow himself to get sweet on a girl like that.

Rather to Prudence's surprise, Lucy seemed bent on settling in, making herself at home to the extent where she and the p.g.s were soon on first-name terms.

'I'm not happy about that,' Prudence groused privately to Patience. 'Lucy shouldn't treat our p.g.s so casually. It's inappropriate.'

'Why? They're all young. It's friendly. In fact, I'm considering whether to ask Mrs Atwood and Miss Watson whether I might use their first names; not during lessons, of course, and never in public; just when there's only us, en famille, as it were.'

'We aren't a family,' Prudence objected.

'We are, in a way, having meals together, spending evenings together after lessons. And it won't be for ever. The p.g.s will leave once they've finished attending our school, and Lucy will go home. Then we can return to formality with the next pupil-lodgers. But at present don't you think a less rigid atmosphere might benefit Lucy?'

'We don't run this house for Lucy's benefit.'

But apparently they did, because Patience started calling the p.g.s 'Vivienne dear' and 'Molly dear', much to Prudence's discomfort. When had she lost control of the household? That was how it felt. She liked things to be ordered and fixed. Then everyone knew where they stood. Well, they still knew where they stood with her. Patience could go round Viviening and Mollying if she must, but Prudence doggedly continued with the use of their formal names, as was right and proper.

That dreadful child! What a shocking nuisance she was.

Lawrence turned up unexpectedly one evening, though at least he had the wit to arrive before lessons started. He stood with his back to the empty fireplace, glaring down at her and Patience, as if he were the lord of the manor.

'I've come to take Lucy home.'

'But you agreed to let her stay,' cried Patience.

'I've changed my mind. I don't know what silly game she's playing at, but it's over.'

'Do I take it that your influential friends are wondering why she isn't at home?' Prudence taunted him.

Lawrence shifted on the balls of his feet. 'As a matter of fact, people have asked after her. It was that blessed Bambrook boy that started it.'

'Honestly, Lawrence,' said Prudence, 'don't you possess the gumption to tell your friends to mind their own business? You'll require gumption if you're to be an alderman or you'll never do any good. Or is it just the title you're after?'

'Prudence, please,' Patience whispered.

A white slash appeared along Lawrence's tightened jawline. 'There's nothing to discuss. She's coming home.'

'Lawrence, listen,' said Patience. 'You're concerned about appearances, aren't you? Prudence and I know all about that, believe me. We spend our lives maintaining a respectable, comfortable front when really we're living from hand to mouth and have been for years, thanks to Pa's desire to be a scholarly gentleman who didn't go out to work. Your friends must find it odd that Lucy is staying with us. Blame it on me, if you like.' Her smile wavered: evidently she wasn't as confident as she was trying to sound. 'Say I'm finding it hard coping with the business school and you've sent Lucy here to make a fuss of me and help me through. I don't mind what you say, only please let her stay. She wanted to come here and she's settled in nicely. Let her stay a little longer and we might get to the bottom of what brought her here in the first place.'

Lawrence stared at the faded carpet. 'It goes against the grain to have anyone other than Evelyn care for my daughter, but under the circumstances, I shan't give an outright refusal.' A ghost of a smile crossed his lips. 'But I won't need to, will I? Prudence doesn't want her here. You'll tell her to pack her bags, won't you, Prudence?'

Here it was, the moment she had yearned for, the moment when that dreadful child could be shipped home and domestic life in Wilton Close returned to normal – ordered, formal, predictable. About time too.

But the words that emerged from her mouth were, 'It's true I wasn't keen on her remaining here, but if Patience wants her to stay and thinks it will benefit the child, that's good enough for me.'

The afternoon sun had soaked deep into everything. In Aaron's small workshop the air was as dense as rice pudding. He had long since shed his waistcoat and rolled up his sleeves, but his skin still felt swollen with heat. If he had had a bucket of cold water, he would cheerfully have upended it over his head.

He stood back from the drawer he had just finished mending. Time for a breather. Heat slapped him as he stepped outside and made his way to the big scullery off the back of the kitchen. He dunked his arms in cold water up to his elbows before splashing his face and the back of his neck, giving himself a cursory dry using the roller-towel on the back of the door.

He returned to his workshop, rolling down his sleeves en route. Taking his waistcoat and jacket from the hook, he set his cap on his head and set off for the ironmonger's to buy the putty he needed to fix a broken window; and he would get a couple more gardening knives while he was at it. He would probably be in time to meet some of the children on their way back from school. Was it the hardest part of the day for them? When the bell rang and your classmates went off to a proper home, with a mum, how did that feel for the orphans?

Even those classmates who lived in stinking, overcrowded conditions, even the ones whose one meal a day was eaten in the poor corner at school – even they had something the orphans lacked. So Aaron made a point of sometimes meeting the kids on their way from school. Was it foolish to hope that in some small way, being met by an adult gave them the feeling that they mattered? When he was a lad, his mum had always greeted him with a smile, no matter how busy or tired she was. She had broken away from what she was doing to hug him as well, until he decided he was too old for hugs. These days, he looked at the orphanage kids and wished they could all have someone to hug them.

He was longer than intended in the ironmonger's, as Wally Poole wanted to show off a new hose director that could change from rose to jet spray with a simple wrist action. Another customer had joined in and the three of them passed the time of day for a while.

On his way back to St Anthony's, it wasn't worth putting on a spurt, as the kids would all be there by now. They attended three schools around Chorlton, as there were too many of them to dump them in one school. Did Mrs Rostron use this as a means of separating children who were likely to be trouble? He wouldn't put it past her.

Approaching the corner of High Lane, he could hear children's voices in the orphanage playground and as he rounded the corner, he saw the St Clement's School lot walking through the gates. He twitched onto his toes, ready to sprint across the road and run through them, flicking off the boys' caps and starting a mad chasing game, when Danny Cropper, at the rear of the group, hung back in a way that put Aaron's senses on alert. That lad was up to something. Not another attempt at running away, surely? He hadn't tried it since May Day and Aaron had dared to hope that the support he had provided on that occasion had helped young Danny settle down. How big-headed of him. Had Danny merely been biding his time?

Danny let the others disappear through the gates, then struck out up Church Road, head down, pace swift, the sort of walk you do when you're trying not to run.

Keeping his distance, Aaron followed, increasing his speed as Danny turned the corner onto Beech Road. He was in time to see Danny twist his face away, shielding it with his hand, as he passed Brown's the stationer's, where Mikey Layton worked in the afternoons as a half-timer. On Danny went, past what until recently had been the bookshop, all the way down, past the tea-room opposite the Trevor pub. Could he be heading for the little chippy on the corner? But the orphans didn't have any money...unless he had swiped some. Aaron's mouth tightened. Please don't let Danny have done any more thieving.

But no, the boy rounded the corner, vanishing briefly from sight. Aaron followed, Chorlton Green coming into view. It was as if Danny was leading him home to Soapsuds Cottage, but then Danny crossed onto the Green itself and sat on one of the benches.

And sat there.

Aaron stopped. Watched. Waited. The boy just sat there. To start with, he perched with a hand on either side curled round the lip of the bench. Then he sat back; or rather, he slouched. He wasn't tall enough to have his bottom at the back of the bench at the same time as keeping his feet on the grass. He opted for leaving his feet on the ground, his spine curving as he leaned backwards, his shoulder-blades resting against the back of the bench.

And still he sat.

Standing here watching wouldn't butter any parsnips, not to mention he felt as though he were spying, even if he did have the child's best interests at heart. Taking a moment to ensure he strolled rather than strode, Aaron walked over to the bench and sat down.

'Afternoon, Danny.'

'Mr Abrams!'

And that was another odd thing. Danny didn't look up until he spoke. Surely, no matter how lost in thought you were, you would instinctively glance up when somebody joined you on a bench.

'What are you doing here?' Aaron asked.

'Nothing.'

'You're meant to go straight back to St Anthony's when you finish school.'

Silence.

'It's a beautiful day.'

Silence.

'Did you feel like a walk?'

Shrug.

Aaron felt a snap of annoyance. 'If you don't intend to answer me, at least show some respect by sitting up straight.'

It was difficult to see, what with that man's cap Danny wore overshadowing his face, but Aaron caught a glimpse of red in Danny's cheek as he shuffled into an upright position; but if Aaron had hoped the lad would lift his chin and look him in the eye, he was disappointed. Danny's gaze was locked on the daisy-strewn grass.

Injecting a smile into his voice that he hoped Danny would hear, even if he couldn't see it, Aaron said lightly, 'That makes me sound like a teacher, doesn't it?'

Silence. Then, 'A bit.'

'Hallelujah! He can speak, after all.' Aaron leaned back. If he adopted a casual pose, would Danny feel more comfortable? 'Are you going to tell me what brings you here?'

The boy's pale, freckled face swung towards him. 'Are you going to report me?'

'Should I? You've disobeyed the rules.'

Danny looked away again. 'She'll give me the strap.'

'*She* has a name. It's polite to use it.'

A pause. 'Mrs Rostron will give me the strap. She says giving you the strap isn't just for punishment. It's to improve your moral fibre.'

'Aye, the people who founded the orphanage had that written into its charter.'

'What's a charter?'

'Rules, mostly; but also a way of looking at things, a set of values.'

And what a value that was. Discipline was essential, but the strap was a well-worn length of leather, one end of which sported six or eight four-inch-long cuts that fanned out when they made contact with a miscreant's defenceless palm, presumably delivering a sharper sensation than uncut leather would have done. Was this the way to instil moral fibre? His own childhood canings had been more likely to fill him with resentment or defiance; and the long-lasting effect had been to make him determined never to say, 'It didn't do me any harm' which you heard so many folk declare.

'Do sanatoriums have charters?' Danny asked.

Aaron's heart creaked inside his chest. 'The honest answer: I don't know.'

'If they do, they ought to say that sanatoriums should be everywhere, so that sick people don't have to go so far away.'

'Sanatoriums need to be in the country or by the sea, because that helps people get better.'

'Then the charter should say that there should be rooms or cottages where the sick people's families can stay, so they can all be close together.'

'Even if the sanatorium did have accommodation like that,' Aaron said gently, 'you still wouldn't be allowed to see your dad.'

'But I could be nearby.' Tears thickened Danny's voice; Aaron's throat ached in sympathy. 'Instead of ruddy miles away.'

'Language,' Aaron warned and immediately wanted to kick himself. This poor lad was breaking his heart over his sick and very possibly dying father and what did Aaron do? Reprimand him for using the strong language that afforded him a moment's release from the pain. Even so, it couldn't be permitted. 'If I hear language like that again, I'll give you a thick ear.'

Surprise blossomed inside him as Danny turned to him with a smile. 'That's what my mum used to say. Not about the bad language, because I never swore in those days, but about the thick ear. She said it, but she never did it. She was a right softy.'

'She sounds nice.'

The boy's face clouded. 'She was.' He looked away. 'Are you going to report me for swearing?'

'I'd rather not. It slipped out because you're unhappy, but you have to promise to watch your tongue in future. Does that make me a softy?'

'You're not soft, sir. You're kind. I wish...'

'What, Danny?'

Danny shrugged. 'It would have been good if someone like you had come to our house that time.'

'What time?'

Silence. Danny shifted and sat forwards. Was he about to jump up and run for it? He didn't move.

'When Mum died.'

'I see.'

'It happened while I was at school. I came home at home-time, same as usual, and a man and a lady were standing outside our house, with a suitcase packed ready. They said Mum had died and, with Dad being away in the sanatorium, they were taking me to the orphanage. They'd been inside our house and packed a case for me, and we walked straight to St Anthony's.'

'Didn't they let you go into the house?'

'They said they'd got everything I needed and the lady said they'd put in a photograph of my mum, but when I unpacked, it was a picture of Auntie Betty.'

Aaron gave Danny's shoulder a brief squeeze. What this young chap had been through. 'I'm sorry to hear that.'

Danny sat up straight and turned to him. The lad's eyes almost glowed. Aaron was startled. He had been ready for tears or despair, but Danny looked positively cheery.

'There's no need to be sorry, sir, honest. If they put Auntie Betty's picture in my case, it means they sent Mum's photograph to Dad in the sanatorium, so that's all right.'

Best not pursue that. 'Couldn't you live with Auntie Betty?'

'Stop with.' A stubborn note entered Danny's tone. 'Not live with. Stop with. I don't need to live with anyone. My dad's going to get better.'

'Couldn't you stop with Auntie Betty?'

'She's dead an' all. But there is Uncle Angus. Auntie Betty was Mum's older sister and Uncle Angus is Dad's brother.'

'Couldn't you stop with him?'

'Huh. He lives miles away. We used to hear from him sometimes and Mrs Rostron says she's in touch with him now. Anyroad, I don't need to go and live with him. Dad's going to get better and come home. I don't like St Anthony's, but it's near where we used to live, so that'll make it easy for Dad and me to find somewhere new to live. I'm not stupid. I know our old home is rented by another family now. But we can find somewhere nearby.'

Aaron hoped so with all his heart, but realistically what were the chances of Mr Cropper returning to his son? He cast about for something to say that would be acceptable to Danny, but without providing false hope. Danny didn't seem to require a reply. Perhaps he didn't want one. Perhaps he was used to ignoring what he didn't want to hear. He was watching a man in a flat cap, who was walking by with a folded newspaper under his arm. The silence lengthened between Danny and Aaron as the man went to another bench and took a seat.

Danny looked at Aaron. More confidences? But Danny said in an oddly grown-up way, 'I mustn't keep you from your work, sir.'

'And I mustn't keep you from your tea. Come along.' He slapped his palms on his knees and stood up. 'Time to make tracks.'

'Must I? Only...'

'Only what?'

'Nothing.'

'On your feet, Cropper.'

Aaron used a friendly voice, but didn't get so much as a smile in return. Was Danny going to refuse to come with him? If so, he would throw the boy over his shoulder and carry him. He had let Danny get away with a certain amount, but there were limits. Danny's mouth screwed briefly into a sulk, then he frowned. Finally he stood up. That little cleft in his chin made him look even younger.

Aaron set off, Danny by his side. The boy glanced back. Aaron looked over his shoulder. Around the edge of the Green mature trees threw welcome pools of shade. Beyond the far end, over the road, stood the handsome lych-gate with its distinctive octagonal bell-tower, that guarded the entrance to the disused graveyard on the site of what had been the original St Clement's Church. On the Green children played. Girls sat in the shade, stringing daisy chains. A young lady twirled a frilled parasol as she strolled in the company of an older gentleman with a handlebar moustache. The man in the flat cap rose from his bench and walked away.

'What's so interesting, Danny?'

'Nothing,' said Danny.

Chapter Fifteen

MOLLY SAT AT her desk, writing up notes about the visits she had been on with Mrs Wardle. It wasn't easy, when she disagreed with so much of what Mrs Wardle said, but she couldn't give any indication of that in case Mrs Wardle asked to see what she had written. Warmth rose in her cheeks at the memory of the first time Mrs Wardle had stood over her, hand outstretched, demanding, 'Give me that, Miss Watson. I wish to see it,' as if she were a schoolgirl being pounced on for passing notes in class.

The office was deathly quiet. It always was when the great lady herself was present. Behind Molly, Miss Cadman and Miss Byrne sat silently at their desks. She caught the occasional scratch of a pen. Mrs Wardle was seated behind her desk, running her eye over the minutes of a meeting she had attended, clicking her tongue every minute or two and scribbling in the margin. By the look of it, much of the next meeting would be devoted to matters arising and the committee members would be lucky to have much time over to attend to fresh business.

What a relief to escape at dinnertime. Molly ate in the canteen, then went outside to sit in Albert Square. She was wearing a new drop-waisted dress of duck-egg blue linen, its hem a whole two inches shorter than anything she had dared wear before. Vivienne had helped her to make it.

Vivienne. It felt good to be on first-name terms. Chummy. Even Miss Patience had taken to using their first names in private. It was because of Lucy. Her arrival had lightened the formal atmosphere in the house – not that you'd know it from observing Miss Hesketh. She was as starchy as ever.

'Here you are.' Vivienne dropped onto the bench beside her. 'I've been looking for you. I called at St Anthony's this morning and found them all at sixes and sevens. Have you met Miss Allan, the secretary? She's caught shingles, poor old love, and is going to be off work for some weeks. They're in need of administrative help.'

'There are agencies, aren't there, where offices can get temporary assistance?'

'There are, but Mrs Rostron doesn't want any old stop-gap. Miss Allan has been at the orphanage longer than anyone and although her work doesn't require her to have much to do with the children directly, she knows all about them – their family backgrounds and what have you. So I thought of you.'

'Me?' Molly's hand flew to her chest. 'I don't know the children.'

'You've already shown an interest by raising money for the May Day bash. Now you can step in and save the day, honing your new office skills in the process. Plus, you get to escape from Mrs Wardle's clutches. Plus plus, you could learn a lot from Mrs Rostron that would stand you in good stead. I suggested you to her and she'd be glad to have you. What d'you say?'

A dozen questions flashed through Molly's mind. 'What about my job here? I can't give it up.'

'I'm sure the Board of Health would be pleased to assist a worthy institution like St Anthony's, especially at no inconvenience to itself, since you don't have your own workload yet.'

Molly laughed. 'What a joy to be free of Mrs Wardle – and a joy to get to know the orphanage better. I'll start to build up some expertise at last.'

'Mrs Rostron is going to write to Mr Taylor with her request – in fact, her letter will already be in the post; and she's writing to Mrs Wardle as a courtesy, since she knows you're currently attached to her. They'll receive their letters this afternoon.'

Molly bounced a knuckle thoughtfully against her mouth. 'If Mrs Wardle says no, Mr Taylor will never stand up to her. If she says yes, she'll make it seem like all her own idea and expect me to be eternally grateful to her for the opportunity.'

'Exactly,' Vivienne agreed. 'So what are you going to do about it?'

Shortly after three, Vivienne sauntered into the office. Glancing up with feigned casualness, Molly caught her tiny nod. Slipping from her seat, she left the room and tapped on Mr Taylor's door. According to Miss Cadman, when he was first appointed he used to leave his door wide open so as to be available at all times to the staff, shutting it only when he was in conference, but since Mrs Wardle had moved herself into the department, he kept his door permanently shut.

'Hiding,' sniffed Miss Cadman, 'when what he should really do is put her in her place.'

'Come,' called Mr Taylor. 'Ah – Miss Watson.' Was that relief in his bright blue eyes?

'Please may I have a word?'

'Of course. Take a seat.'

Molly closed the door and sat facing him. In Mrs Wardle's absence, he was a different person. Without the scared rabbit look, you could understand what the interview panel had seen in him. He was serious, informed and well-intentioned. If only Mrs Wardle didn't put the wind up him, he might make a real difference.

She explained about Miss Allan. 'Mrs Rostron intends to ask the Board of Health if St Anthony's may have me on loan. It would give me the chance to learn something of how the orphanage runs and about the children and their backgrounds, which would broaden my knowledge and benefit me when I return here.'

'It isn't the Board of Health's duty to provide staff to other organisations. It could, however, offer you valuable training, Miss Watson, as well as assisting St Anthony's in its time of need. Perhaps we can accommodate Mrs Rostron.'

'Thank you, Mr Taylor.' She held a joyful tingle at bay: it wasn't safe to feel anticipation yet. 'There's just one thing: Mrs Wardle.'

The scared rabbit look appeared on Mr Taylor's face. He cleared his throat, a nervous sound.

'Dear me, yes. You're under her wing at present, aren't you? Maybe...'

That thought mustn't be allowed to run its course. 'Perhaps you could write her a memorandum, explaining that you've assigned me to other duties.'

She gazed at him expectantly. Dear heaven, did she have to word it for him?

There was a tap at the door and Vivienne stuck her head in, not a moment too soon.

'Pardon the interruption, Mr Taylor. I met the post-trolley in the corridor and I've got our office correspondence. There's one for you personally. I think the handwriting is Mrs Rostron's.'

'Thank you. Is, um, is Mrs Wardle at her desk, do you know?'

'At the moment she is, but she's going out presently and won't be back until tomorrow.'

'Oh, right, well... A memorandum might be in order, then. I, um, wouldn't wish to distract or delay her if she's preparing to go out.'

Back in the main office, after Mrs Wardle had departed, Mr Taylor appeared, memorandum in hand. He placed it on Mrs Wardle's blotter and backed away.

'Miss Cadman, if memory serves, you're going to the infirmary first thing tomorrow morning to meet the new lady almoner. I'll accompany you. Mrs Atwood, would you kindly make a note in the diary that I'll be unavailable all morning?'

As he left, Vivienne rose and went to the table where the diary was kept and made the required entry. Then she delved in her pocket, bringing out an envelope.

'Whoops.' Her blue-grey eyes twinkled. 'I forgot to give this to Mrs Wardle. Never mind. I'll leave it on her blotter and she'll see it tomorrow.' She pretend-sighed. 'She won't discover you've gone until after you've left for pastures new, Miss Watson. What a shame she won't have the chance to wish you luck.'

Molly arrived early at St Anthony's, determined to make a good impression. In her handbag was a new notebook, which she had purchased before going home yesterday. She had shown it to Dora last night when they went for a walk together, explaining her intention to write up all the information necessary for her Board of Health colleagues to make a better fist of assisting, not just St Anthony's, but orphanages in general. Upon her return to the Board of Health, perhaps there would be a meeting at which she would be invited to share her findings.

One of the double-gates stood open and she drew her shoulders back as she set foot in the grounds of her new place of work, but her pleasure was tempered by the sight of the building and what it represented. What a pity the orphanage wasn't a more attractive place. Its once red brick had darkened almost to black beneath coat upon coat of soot; and those ground-floor windows set so high up in the walls guaranteed that no one, not even an adult, could possibly see out without a stepladder. It was the way schools were built, only it was worse than that, because this was a home for children.

Was home the right word? Did the orphans enjoy the warm, comforting feeling of being at home or was this merely somewhere that kept them dry until they were booted out once they were old enough to fend for themselves?

'Morning.'

Startled, she spun round. Mr Abrams was by the wall, standing in a pool of clippings and twigs, a pair of lopping shears in his hands. There was an ease and confidence in his stance, as if physical work came naturally to him. Twisting stems, some of them as thick as your fist, were heaped in a pile behind him. His shirt-sleeves were rolled up. His shirt was collarless, the top button open, and not just the top button but the next one as well. Her eyes were drawn to a glimpse of chest between his neckerchief and shirt-front. She lifted her gaze to his face; his eyes were nut-brown. Having grown up among builders and labourers, Molly was accustomed to the sight of working men smeared with brick dust and paint and smelling of grime, but the orphanage caretaker sported bits of ivy and crumbs of faded soil and he smelled of earth and greenery and fresh air.

He pushed his cloth cap to the back of his head, revealing thick dark hair with the suggestion of a curl in it, and wiped the back of his hand across his forehead, causing dirt and sweat to mingle in a grubby smear of honest toil. Molly's fingers twitched, wanting to wipe the mark away. Ridiculous!

'Good morning.' How stiff she sounded. 'I'm—'

'Miss Watson. Yes, I know. And I'm—'

'Mr Abrams, the caretaker. You introduced yourself when you came to Upton's.'

'Morning. Lovely day.' A dark-haired girl of around eighteen came through the gates. Under her shawl she wore a long-sleeved dress of dark blue beneath a white bibbed apron.

'You must be the new lady – Miss Watson. I'm Carmel, one of the nursemaids. Shall I show you where to go?'

'Yes please.'

As Carmel led her away, Molly looked over her shoulder to say goodbye to the caretaker, but he was already working on the ivy, squeezing the shears together to cut out a substantial branch. Annoyance twisted inside Molly's chest. If he had waited just one moment, instead of plunging back into his work, she could have said a polite goodbye. Now she looked rude and it was too late to do anything about it.

'This is the girls' playground,' Carmel said, 'and this,' as they walked around a sticking-out wing of the building to where the maypole dancing had taken place, 'is the boys' playground. You never get girls playing here, but the boys are forever going to and fro through the girls' playground, because that's the way to the BB.'

'BB?' Was this the first piece of information for her notebook?

'The bog block.' Carmel pulled a face. 'The outside privies. Sorry, miss, but that's what the children call it. They're not meant to, of course.'

'Oh.' So much for that. 'You said you're a nursemaid. Does that mean you look after the babies?'

'Bless you, miss, you don't know much, do you? The posh folk from fifty years ago who built this place all had money and grand houses and servants to do their bidding. Their children were looked after by nannies, helped by nursemaids, so that's what we're called: nursemaids, because we look after the kids. It's got nowt to do with how old they are. We do the housework an' all, when they're at school.'

'I see.'

'We work in shifts. There have to be people here all the time, obviously. There's a dormitory we sleep in when we stop overnight. Mrs Rostron has her own bedroom for when she's on night duty and there's another bedroom that's used by the other senior members of staff. That means them as is in charge of the nursemaids.'

'Don't tell me: they're called nannies.'

'You catch on quick. I'll give you that.'

They approached the stone steps that led to the main door. Inside, a young girl hovered in the corridor. She wore a grey serge skirt and white blouse and her mousy-brown hair was fastened into a bun, several hairpins anchoring the sides in position where presumably wisps would otherwise work themselves free.

She bobbed a little curtsey. 'Miss Watson? I'm to take you to Mrs Rostron's office, if you please.'

'I'll leave you in Ginny's capable hands,' said Carmel as she left them.

Molly smiled at the girl. 'Thank you, but there's no need. I know the way.'

Ginny's eyes widened and her top teeth caught at her lips. 'Oh no, miss. Mrs Rostron told me to. This way, if you please.'

She darted ahead, as if scared Molly might ignore her and take the lead. Round the corner and up the long flight of stairs they went, then around the head of the staircase and along the dark, narrow passage. Molly wanted to pause and drink in the sight of Miss Allan's, now her, desk and cupboards, in the gas-lit alcove, but Ginny was already tapping on the door at the end.

Molly followed her into Mrs Rostron's office, nearly falling over her as Ginny dipped her knee to the woman behind the desk. Mrs Rostron raised an eyebrow as they righted themselves.

'That will be all, Virginia. Thank you.'

'Thank you, Mrs Rostron.' Ginny turned to go.

'Thank you, Ginny,' Molly said quickly. She had already been uncivil to Mr Abrams, albeit inadvertently. She wasn't about to make the same mistake again.

'You may use my coat-stand to hang up your coat and hat,' said Mrs Rostron. 'Please be seated. You seemed fazed by Virginia's curtsey. All the girls will curtsey to you, and the boys will bow their heads, the first time they see you each day. They curtsey to me, to the nannies and now to you.'

'Goodness. I'll try to get used to it.'

'You won't merely try, Miss Watson. You shall succeed. I suggest setting you to work immediately at Miss Allan's desk, so you can begin to accustom yourself to your clerical duties. After school, I'll assign a pair of the fourteens to show you round the building.'

'The fourteens?'

'Yes. When St Anthony's was founded, it took children to the age of twelve. Then the school leaving age rose to thirteen and St Anthony's was required to keep orphans for an extra year. After the war, the government in its wisdom increased the school leaving age to fourteen, so now we accommodate still older children – though you can hardly call them children at that age.'

'That must put a strain on the bedrooms and so forth.'

Mrs Rostron nodded. 'Good. You are able to think things through. And to reply to your point, no, it doesn't put a strain on the dormitories: don't refer to them as bedrooms, please. Our building is only so big and we can house only so many children.'

'So the year the school leaving age went up, you couldn't take in any new little ones.'

'We had room for a few. You asked what a fourteen is. When a child enters his or her final year at school, we refer to them here as fourteens. The boys wear a striped tie and the girls shed their grey dress and pinafore in favour of the skirt and blouse you saw Virginia wearing. On her fourteenth birthday, a girl is permitted to put up her hair. Before that, on her twelfth birthday, she starts to wear her hair in a single plait down her back. Prior to that, from starting school, the girls wear two plaits, which are fastened behind their ears. So you will always know a girl's age by her hair.'

'I'll remember.'

'I'm sure you shall.' Mrs Rostron didn't say it in the kindly, encouraging way Vivienne would have done. 'The boys are called by their surnames and the girls by their full first names. I noticed you called Virginia Ginny. That is not acceptable.'

'I won't do it again.'

Mrs Rostron tilted her head slightly to one side. Her bun looked loose, yet it remained fixed in position in spite of there being not so much as a hairpin to be seen.

'I wonder where you got the name Ginny. Virginia certainly wouldn't have introduced herself in that way.'

'It was my mistake. A slip of the tongue – trying to be friendly.'

'You are not required to be friendly with the orphans, Miss Watson. It may interest you to know that the duty rosters will inform me, to the minute, whose shifts start and finish at what time. It would be simple for me to determine whom you met on your way in, for example.'

Blimey, was she supposed to offer up Carmel on a plate?

'I don't take kindly to being fibbed to, Miss Watson, no matter how worthy the intention. I am grateful to you for stepping in at short notice – at no notice at all, in fact – but now that you're here, you're a member of my staff and will be treated as such. Perhaps you would make a start on your work. You passed Miss Allan's work station in the corridor. I'm sure you'll find everything you require. I'll answer any questions that arise, but it would be helpful if you use your common sense and get on with what needs doing. '

Do what needed doing. She could manage that…couldn't she? She would have to; she apparently wasn't going to get much, if anything, in the way of help.

It wasn't going to be altogether pleasant working in this windowless corridor, but Molly intended to make the best of it. It would be easier for her than it was for Miss Allan, with her old bones. On the blotter lay a couple of scrawled letters, with a note at the top of each, saying *Please typewrite*. Well, at least she didn't have to worry about getting started.

After turning up the wall-mounted gas-lights, she typed the letters, careful to take a carbon copy of each, before presenting them to Mrs Rostron for her signature.

'You'll find a tin of stamps in one of Miss Allan's drawers,' said Mrs Rostron. 'Please take these to the pillar-box in time to catch the midday collection. In Miss Allan's in-tray you'll find bills from the grocer and fishmonger, which you should take to the kitchen for Mrs Wilkes, the cook, to check before they are paid; though I suggest you do that this afternoon. Mrs Wilkes doesn't care to be disturbed in the morning.'

Molly located the stamps as well as a small notebook for recording their use. Investigating the desk drawers, she also came across a petty cash tin with accompanying notebook, an address book, a list of telephone numbers and a tin of lavender lozenges.

Mrs Rostron came down the corridor, dressed in a severe longline jacket and a squashy felt hat.

'Here are Miss Allan's keys. It's unfortunate on your first day that I should have to attend a meeting. I shan't be back until half past four.'

Molly sat up straight. 'I'll manage. Now I've got the keys, I'll look through the filing cabinet and cupboards and see what's what.'

'One of the nursemaids will bring you a cup of tea and a biscuit at eleven o'clock. If you make your way to the dining hall at midday, the staff dining room is just off it.'

Mrs Rostron couldn't have been gone more than half an hour before footsteps came tapping up the stairs just as Molly was exploring the stationery cupboard.

'As I warned you, Evelyn,' came Mrs Wardle's voice, causing Molly's heart to sink, 'it's rather dingy up here, so do watch your footing. Ah, there you are, Miss Watson. Settling into your temporary home, I see.'

'Yes, thank you.' Approval? Even though Mrs Wardle hadn't been consulted?

The other lady stopped at the desk. Her expensive attire and tasteful brooch and pearls showed how well-to-do she was.

'So this is your protégée, Emmeline?'

Protégée?

'How gratifying for you,' the new lady continued, 'to bring on a girl in this way. She has so much for which to be grateful to you.'

'Sweet of you to recognise it,' Mrs Wardle murmured.

Well, it was a good job the new lady recognised it, because Molly certainly didn't. Bristling, she pulled back her shoulders. Protégée? Grateful? Not on your nelly!

'Come,' Mrs Wardle said to her companion. 'I'll introduce you to Mrs Rostron. She does such a sterling job as superintendent.'

'Mrs Rostron is out.' Molly had to raise her voice, as the two ladies were already on their way along the landing. 'She won't be back before half past four.'

'That's what the girl who admitted us said.' Mrs Wardle stopped. 'I hoped she was wrong. Some of these girls aren't the brightest.' She tapped her black suede-clad toe. 'This is most inconvenient.'

Molly reached for the diary. 'If you'd care to make an appointment...'

'Nonsense. I am the official visitor. I don't require an appointment.'

'Won't you introduce us?' asked Mrs Wardle's companion. 'I should like to make the acquaintance of your protégée.'

That word again!

'Of course. This is Miss Watson, who, through the training and guidance she has received from me, has been deemed suitable to assist St Anthony's during the secretary's illness. Miss Watson, this is my friend, Mrs Hesketh, who wishes to take an interest in the orphanage.'

'How do you do?' said Mrs Hesketh.

Molly replied automatically. Hesketh? Would it be appropriate to ask? Did she want to engage in civil conversation after Mrs Wardle had claimed her as her protégée?

The moment was lost as Mrs Wardle said, 'Could you organise tea for us, please, Miss Watson? We'll take it in the office.'

'I'm not sure that's...' Molly began. She hadn't come here expecting to have to repel all boarders.

'Where else should I entertain a prospective patron?' Mrs Wardle enquired. 'In fact, Miss Watson, why don't you join us? I'm going to explain the history of St Anthony's to Mrs Hesketh. It would be of benefit to you to hear it too.'

'Maybe Miss Watson is up to her ears in work,' suggested Mrs Hesketh.

How could she claim she was when they had come across her looking through the stationery cupboard? The two ladies headed along the passage, leaving her to order the tea. Just how had she ended up in this position?

On the stairs, she met Carmel on her way up.

'I was on my way down to see about tea.'

'The tea isn't late, miss,' Carmel said immediately.

'I know.'

'We don't stop for it until eleven.'

'I know.'

'I was coming to ask you whether, if you're not too busy, you'd like to come down at eleven when the smalls have their morning milk. You could meet more nursemaids and start to learn the children's names.'

'I'd love that, but I'm expected to have tea with Mrs Wardle. That's what I was coming down for, to request tea for three in Mrs Rostron's office.'

'In the office? By, you've made yourself at home, haven't you?'

Carmel spun round and ran downstairs.

'Carmel!'

But Carmel didn't hear. No, she heard all right. She just pretended not to.

Molly retraced her steps. Carmel wasn't impressed with her and, frankly, she wasn't impressed with herself. Fancy letting Mrs Wardle steamroller her like that. Walking past the alcove, she made straight for the office, where she found the ladies had turned the two chairs for visitors to face one another.

'Here's Miss Watson coming to join us.' Mrs Hesketh sounded welcoming.

'Thank you,' said Molly, 'but I need to press on. I've sent for the tea.'

In the alcove once more, she looked through the accounts book. Dad always said that the accounts could tell you all you needed to know about a place, not just how close to the wind they sailed financially, but who were their preferred trades-men, how often they had their chimneys swept and the piano tuned, how careful or wasteful they were, and whether they paid their wages on time.

Carmel came stomping up the stairs, carrying a tray.

'Oh, you're out here, are you? I thought you were lording it in the office.' And presumably that was what she had told the world and his wife.

'I shan't be having tea with Mrs Wardle.'

'But it's all on one tray.'

'Leave it with me. I'll pour mine and take the tray through.'

If she hoped Carmel might linger for a friendly word or even repeat her earlier invitation, she was disappointed. She poured a cup and helped herself to a finger of buttery-smelling shortbread before taking the tray to the office, making herself scarce before Mrs Wardle could ask her to pour.

She drank her tea, then popped out to the pillar-box with the letters she had typed earlier. When she returned, Mrs Wardle and her guest were leaving the office.

'Miss Watson, you'll be pleased to learn that Mrs Hesketh has already thought of something to improve the orphanage and it will benefit you directly.'

'Really?'

'Indeed, yes,' said Mrs Hesketh. 'This little alcove is so dark.'

'It has gas-lights,' Molly pointed out.

'Even so.'

'Well, yes, it is rather gloomy,' Molly conceded.

'Precisely,' cut in Mrs Wardle. 'Mrs Hesketh suggests placing oil-lamps there,' indicating the top of the filing cabinet, 'and over there.' She nodded approvingly at her friend. 'I look forward to hearing your observations on the rest of the building. Miss Watson, I hope you'll accompany us on our tour.'

'Mrs Rostron has arranged for me to be shown round later on.'

'Very well, but I insist that you join us for lunch.'

'Please do,' Mrs Hesketh added. 'I would be interested to hear your impressions of St Anthony's.'

Having not joined them for tea or the tour, how could she refuse?

Later, when they came to collect her, Mrs Hesketh was full of everything she had seen. They went downstairs and into the dining room Molly had seen on the day of the maypole dancing. At one end young children sat at the tables while tots perched in high chairs, waving their fists as they anticipated each mouthful. Blue-and-white clad nursemaids looked round as Mrs Wardle led her little procession across the room to a door on the far side.

Here was the dining room for the staff. A few nursemaids shared a table and an older woman in black with a white collar and a lacy white cap tied beneath her double chin sat alone. Was she one of the nannies? Molly would dearly have liked to linger and introduce herself, but there was no chance of that, not with Mrs Wardle streaming across the room towards what looked like a stage, with a table and chairs on it.

Mrs Wardle led the way up the four wooden steps at one side and stopped behind a place that looked over the room.

'This is the top table,' she informed her companions. 'The places here are reserved for important guests and sponsors, so you are honoured to have the opportunity, Miss Watson. Do sit beside me, Evelyn. Miss Watson, would you care to sit on my other side?'

Cold fingers tapped at her ribs. Important guests? Sponsors? She was the secretary, for pity's sake, and a temporary one at that. No, she jolly well wouldn't sit beside Mrs Wardle, gazing out over the lower orders. She sat opposite the other two, but it didn't make her feel any better. Throughout the meal, her spine prickled under the darts of disapproval flung her way by the rest of the dining room.

Chapter Sixteen

T HAT SETTLED IT. There could be no doubt. Aaron had wanted there to be doubt; oh yes, he had wanted it, but after that complaint he had received from Mrs Wardle, and with seeing Miss Watson now at top table – well, he had been a fool to hope. The way she had walked off this morning without so much as a goodbye should have shown him. Miss Watson was cut from the same elite cloth as the high-and-mighty Mrs Wardle.

Having pushed the door open onto the staff dining room, he backed out again sharpish and presented himself at the long serving hatch between the kitchen and the children's dining room.

Leaning in, he caught Mrs Wilkes's eye. 'All right if I come back for mine later?'

'I'll keep a plate warm for you.'

Mrs Wilkes couldn't do enough for him ever since he had mended the mechanism in the serving hatch, so that it now slid easily up and down instead of having to be tugged with all your might.

When he returned later for his slice of meat and potato pie, made even tastier by the cook's onion gravy, Mrs Wilkes tried to stir up some gossip.

'You won't know, not having eaten here at dinner time, but that new secretary only went and put herself on top table along with the Wardle woman.'

'As long as she doesn't make a pig's ear of the clerical work, that's all I care about.'

'Aye.' Mrs Wilkes gave a mirthless laugh that showed what she thought of the new secretary. 'As long as she gets us wages right and on time, she can be as stuck-up as she pleases.'

Later on, needing his favourite chisel, which was in his toolbox in Soapsuds Cottage, Aaron set off to fetch it. It was home-time and the children were coming back from school. The St Clement's lot were already here, their school being just along the road. Now the rest were spilling in through the gates, chatting and mucking about on their way. No one wore a coat in this warm weather. They went straight indoors to hang up their caps and hats, then came back outside until teatime, except for those who had homework, which was done in the dining room and had to be completed before tea.

As he crossed the girls' playground, children ran up to him, including boys who should be in their own playground.

'Are we helping with the ivy today, sir?'

'Can I do it, Mr Abrams? You promised.'

'Later,' he said. 'I have to nip home first.'

'Oh aye? Skiving, are you, sir?' asked one bright spark and Aaron pretended to clip him round the ear, much to the delight of the rest.

He went on his way. Mrs Rostron was happy for him to come and go as he pleased, trusting him not to take advantage. He rounded the corner onto Chorlton Green to see Bunny heading his way, pushing his hot-potato barrow.

As they stopped to have a word, Aaron glanced over the road to the Green itself.

'What's he doing there?'

'Who?' Bunny followed his gaze.

'The lad on that bench. He's one of ours,' said Aaron. 'I don't know what it is about the Green at the moment, but it seems to attract our kids like a magnet. He's the second one I've found here. He should have gone straight home from school. He's under threat of the reformatory if he doesn't behave himself. I'd better go and get him.'

A man sat down at the other end of Jacob's bench and started to read his newspaper. As Aaron stepped from the pavement, there was a soft thud behind him, instantly followed by the half-metallic, half-musical sound of coins striking the flagstones. He turned back.

'Damn!' said Bunny. His leather money-pouch had fallen to the ground, spilling some of its contents.

'Never heard you swear before,' Aaron said with a grin, 'but I suppose that's what happens when you fling your worldly wealth all over the place.'

He bent to retrieve the money, wanting to spare his friend, who was older and not as spry as he had once been. Bunny tipped the silver and coppers back into his money-pouch and fastened it.

'Thanks, mate.'

Aaron turned once more to face the Green. The fellow with the newspaper got up to walk away, leaving Jacob alone on the bench, swinging his feet. As Aaron crossed over, Jacob scooted along the bench and – did he pick something up? It was such a subtle movement, it was difficult to tell. Wait – yes – he slipped it inside his trouser pocket, whatever it was.

Coming to his feet, Jacob put a foot forward to start walking, only to stop dead, mouth falling open, cheeks blazing, as he saw Aaron striding towards him. Aye, there was no doubting that look of guilt.

He didn't come on all heavy-handed. You wouldn't get the truth out of a kid that way. Aaron assumed a long-suffering attitude, with a dry edge to it that could head off in the direction of humour or might turn to steel.

'What is it about the Green these days that draws our lads like bees round a honey-pot?'

'N-nothing, sir.'

'First Daniel Cropper, now you.' He pinned Jacob to the spot with his gaze.

'I d-don't know what you mean, sir.'

Well, of course he didn't, poor kid. It was coincidence, pure and simple.

'What brings you here? You know you're meant to go straight back to St Anthony's after school.'

'Yes, sir.' Jacob hung his head, scuffing the grass with the toe of his shoe.

'Stand up straight when an adult speaks to you.' That was one of Mrs Rostron's golden rules. 'What are you doing here?'

'I just felt like it.'

'What did you pick up?'

'What?' Jacob's head jerked back in shock. 'Nowt.'

'You picked up something off the bench and put it in your pocket. Show me.'

Jacob froze. Then, chewing his lip, he drew out a sixpence. 'I never pinched it, sir, honest. It were just…lying there.'

'I'm not accusing you of anything, lad.' He let his manner soften. 'It must have fallen out of that man's pocket when he sat down to read his paper. Look – he's about to disappear down the road beside the old graveyard. If you run, you'll catch up. I'll watch to see you're all right, then you must go straight back to the orphanage. Understand?'

'But… Yes, sir, Mr Abrams.'

The boy's face twisted, showing his internal struggle, but Aaron couldn't let him keep the sixpence. It wouldn't be right.

He strolled along the Green, watching as the lad jogged away, neglecting to look before he crossed the road, increasing his speed to catch the man. There was a small pantomime, denoting explanation; Jacob pointed back at him. The man glanced Aaron's way before practically snatching the tanner from the child's hand and marching on his way. Charming!

No sign of a thank-you, no ruffling the cap on the boy's head. Still, it took all sorts.

The end of her first day was in sight and it hadn't been the unqualified success Molly had hoped for. The embarrassment of sitting at top table still made her squirm. Neither had she had the opportunity to make peace with Carmel. On top of that, Mrs Wilkes hadn't exactly welcomed her with open arms when she ventured down to the kitchen to check the tradesmen's bills.

Be positive. She had done some typing and found where Miss Allan kept everything; she had gone through the accounts and read some of the children's files, which had made her feel she had more of a grasp on matters; and she had removed some ancient, faded, handwritten labels from various drawers and shelves and replaced them with fresh typewritten ones. She didn't want to step on Miss Allan's toes, but surely she wouldn't object to that.

Hearing footsteps on the stairs, she picked up the afternoon's mail, ready to hand it to Mrs Rostron, but it wasn't the superintendent who appeared at the top of the staircase. It was Mr Abrams, carrying a pair of oil-lamps.

To her surprise, he placed one on top of the filing cabinet, making room for the other on a small table, his shoulders set rigid beneath his jacket.

'As requested. Demanded, I should say.' He turned to face her. His expression was set rigid too. 'In future, Miss Watson, if you have any complaints, I'd be grateful if you would, A, come to me directly instead of voicing them to Mrs Wardle; and, B, ask politely instead of whining.'

'Whining?' She gasped, but it wasn't breath that seared the back of her throat. It was outrage. 'I don't know what you're talking about.'

'Good afternoon,' said a new voice.

Mrs Rostron stood at the top of the stairs. Nothing about her moved, not so much as the faint lingering swish of her skirt. She hadn't just this moment arrived on the landing. Had she heard every word?

'I'll be about my business.' Mr Abram departed, his boots striking the wooden treads squarely as he ran down.

Mrs Rostron stopped in front of the alcove. 'What was that about?'

'I don't know. He just appeared with these oil-lamps.'

'Had you complained to Mrs Wardle?'

'I would never do such a thing. I don't know how – oh.'

'Explain.' Not 'Would you please explain, Miss Watson.' Just 'Explain'.

Humiliation squeezed her ribs, but she looked the superintendent in the eye. 'Mrs Wardle was here with her friend; and the friend – Mrs Hesketh – remarked on how dark the alcove is.'

'And you took it upon yourself to agree.' Mrs Rostron shifted her shabby old leather briefcase from one hand to the other, as if to make the point that she had worked hard today even if Molly's time had been frittered.

'Mrs Wardle apparently went to Mr Abrams.'

'Mrs Wardle is St Anthony's official visitor and as such enjoys a privileged position. While extending every courtesy to her, you shall refrain from expressing personal opinions in her presence.'

'Yes, Mrs Rostron.'

The superintendent headed towards her office. Molly puffed out a small breath. Thank goodness she had remembered to remove the tea-tray and put the chairs back. Was Mrs Rostron aware that Mrs Wardle helped herself to the office in her absence? Or had it never happened before? Had Mrs Wardle taken advantage of Molly's newness to take a liberty Miss Allan would have prevented?

At six o'clock, Molly fetched her things from Mrs Rostron's office, taking them to her desk to put them on. She slipped on her linen jacket, positioning her cloche hat with the aid of a small speckled looking-glass she had come across in one of the drawers. This evening she would ask the Miss Heskeths for additional lessons in the use of the telephone. Telephone lessons were taken by Miss Patience and involved holding pretend conversations about deliveries that were late or invoices with mistakes, but it wasn't more of those that she wanted. The ladies possessed a replica telephone that had been constructed for use in an amateur stage production. What Molly wanted was practice at dialling and holding the pieces correctly and not speaking into the ear-piece. She had never used a telephone until she started at the Board of Health and she had placed a call only once. She didn't want to make a clot of herself here.

As she descended the stairs, the sound of the children's chatter grew louder, a rounded, cheerful sound made richer by the dining room's warm acoustics. Was Carmel still on duty? It would feel good to give her a farewell wave over the children's heads, but it was out of the question after this morning's mis-understanding. That was something she must do tomorrow, get back on Carmel's good side. In fact, a fresh start all round would be no bad thing. She had to show the staff she was one of them and not Mrs Wardle's tame follower.

Crossing the boys' playground, she rounded the wing that formed a boundary between the boys' and girls' playgrounds – and here was her opportunity to make good on her resolve to have a new beginning. Mr Abrams was ending the day as he had started it, chopping and sawing the ivy that clung thickly to the wall.

'Mr Abrams, I'm sorry you were put to the trouble of finding extra lamps. It was nothing more than a chance remark on my part. I never imagined Mrs Wardle would act upon it.'

He regarded her. Having worn his jacket to venture upstairs, no doubt out of respect for the proximity to Mrs Rostron's office, he had shed it to crack on with this dusty outdoor task, which was probably more demanding than it looked.

'Thank you. I didn't expect an apology – especially after the way I tore you off a strip. That was rude of me and I'm sorry.'

There was a gruff note in his voice, but instead of putting her off, it made her feel drawn to him. She had taken him by surprise and she rather liked that. The strong, lean features that had been uncompromising during their confrontation now assumed a different cast, genial and kind. There was a light in his brown eyes that suggested warmth. Then his expression altered subtly, becoming serious, distant even.

'You'd best take care what you say to your friend in future.'

'My friend?' Good heavens, did he think...? She started to say, 'Mrs Wardle isn't my friend,' but a cheery voice cut across her. Norris!

'There you are, Molly. Look, here's your knight in shining armour, come to escort you home at the end of your first day.' Sweeping off his trilby, he executed an exaggerated bow, bending from the waist and all but sweeping his hat across the ground.

'How did you know I was here?' Molly asked.

'Aha.' Placing his trilby back on his head, Norris tapped the side of his nose. He wasn't going to make a secret of it, was he? And expect her to wheedle it out of him? 'I went for a pint with Harry last night. Afterwards we bumped into Dora on her way home after you left her. Good girl, Molly, for having an early night.'

Good girl? She wasn't a pet dog. 'There was no need to come and meet me.'

'Of course there was. I can't have my best girl walking home on her own on her first day, can I? What sort of fellow would I be to permit that? I'm better husband material than that, I hope.'

Husband material? And with Mr Abrams standing there listening as well. She had to get Norris away from here before he could make even more of a show of her.

Norris stepped towards her, offering his arm. Instinct prodded her, urging her to step away, but that would have looked so singular in front of Mr Abrams. She couldn't have him witnessing her and Norris tussling over her arm. If Norris was here one moment longer, she would be obliged to introduce them and she didn't want that.

Grasping Norris's arm, she spirited him through the gates and away up the road. How smart he was in his suit and trilby, with his striped tie and black lace-ups. How proud she used to feel to be on his arm. She should still be proud to be seen with such a well turned out man, even if they were no longer an official couple. Norris was dapper and personable. Not like Mr Abrams, with his rolled-up sleeves and collarless shirt. Norris wouldn't be caught dead without a collar; and if he went out this evening, he would change his trilby for a natty straw boater with a coloured band. It would come as no surprise if Mr Abrams wore that old cloth cap even for church.

'It was well worth finishing early at the office, to have the honour of seeing you home,' Norris was saying, 'and in particular to have the pleasure of your taking my arm. I found that most gratifying, Molly, and I shall tell your mother so when I see her.'

'Please don't say anything to make people think—'

'Think what? I can't help what others think, especially when they've got your best interests at heart.' When she tried to withdraw her arm, Norris clamped his elbow to his side, trapping it; her heart bumped. 'There now, don't take on. You can't blame your family and friends for wanting what's best for you. It would be a rum do if they didn't.'

This time she did wrench herself free. 'I'll be the judge of what's best for me.'

'You're tired. You've had a long day. Give me your arm and let's be friends. You owe me that, at the very least. You can't turn your back on me, not after I've been loving and faithful for so long.'

Loving and faithful. It was true. Unwillingly, but with a sense of the inevitable, Molly offered her arm. Had his always been this fleshy? She had never noticed before. Norris wasn't plump, but just now, with her hand resting in the circle of his arm, she had an impression of…flesh. And another impression: the work-hardened muscle in the caretaker's arm. What was she thinking?

'I arranged to finish work early especially to see you on your first day,' said Norris.

'That was a kind thing to do.'

'I didn't do it out of kindness. I did it to impress you with my continuing devotion.'

'Norris, don't.' This time, when she withdrew her arm, there was true resolve in it. What on earth had she been thinking, letting him have her arm? Never mind being courteous for the sake of her family. How about their showing some courtesy to her by accepting her decision? How about Norris accepting their engagement was at an end?

'Don't what? Don't love you? Don't hope to win you back? I'm not made of stone, Molly, and I tell you here and now: I'm not going to give up. If you like, I can provide a list of the people who are cheering me on.'

Chapter Seventeen

PRUDENCE HAD LOOKED forward to Saturday afternoon all week. Her long working week, both in the office and teaching in the evenings was over, and Mrs Atwood and Miss Watson now both had unpaid work to go to, just for a few hours, so they could use their new office skills for real. Not so long ago, Patience had turned squeamish at the very thought of approaching local businesses to seek placements for their pupils, but now she was used to it and turned up trumps time and again. For Mrs Atwood, she had found a place in a domestic employment agency, typing, filing and so forth, while for Miss Watson, there was the opportunity to work in the office of a hotel in Seymour Grove, with the promise that if she did well, they would let her work on the reception desk, under supervision, of course.

Not only did Saturday afternoon mean no work and no p.g.s, it also, today, meant no Patience and no Lucy. Prudence couldn't recall the last time she had had the house to herself. Normally a busy person, who frowned darkly upon others' idle hands, she sat in her armchair, allowing herself to sink back against the cushion, hands resting lightly on the embroidered arm-caps that protected the front edges of the chair's arms, and allowed the sense of stillness to sink into her bones.

She had always been content in her own company – well, there had been one time in her life when she had shed her solitary nature, like a butterfly emerging from its chrysalis, but that had turned out to be a calamitous error and she had quickly retreated into her shell. Talk about mixing your metaphors.

The doorbell rang. Her fingers tightened over the arms of the chair, pressing into Patience's exquisite crewel-work on the cotton arm-caps. She released her grip. Mustn't crease the cotton.

What if she ignored the doorbell? Who could it be, anyway, on a Saturday afternoon? They weren't the sort to have friends dropping in unexpectedly. They weren't the sort to have friends dropping in, full stop. Scraping by on very little income had always precluded the possibility of entertaining, even on a small scale, not so much as a bridge night with supper or singing round the piano followed by refreshments. Or would such ways of passing the time be considered old hat these days?

That was the sort of thing that used to take place under this roof when she was a girl, when Mother was alive and Pa went out to work. It was only after Mother died that things had changed. Pain twisted inside her chest, a remembered pain from long ago. She hadn't understood back then that Pa should have taken responsibility for keeping their household functioning. He should have ordered the coal, and had that leak in the scullery roof attended to, and found someone to mend the garden gate when one of its hinges dropped; but these tasks had fallen to her, then and ever afterwards.

Pa did employ a daily cook, but only until Patience finished school, whereupon she took on the mantle of housewife and had lived her entire life within these four walls. Worst of all, Pa had never returned to work after Mother's funeral. At first, it had seemed right that he should be at home, grieving. Goodness knows, they had all missed Mother dreadfully.

At what point had Prudence understood that Pa had inherited not only the house but also Mother's annuity? It certainly had never been explained to her when she was young. Well, one didn't explain things to children, did one? The terms of Mother's annuity were that it had to pass to her children, which meant Prudence and Patience, not Lawrence, because he was her stepson. But, being children, she and Patience weren't old enough to receive the income, which therefore had been paid to Pa to help him bring them up until they married or attained the age of twenty-five, whichever came first.

Whichever came first. As if the one that didn't come first was bound to come second. Had there really been a time when she and Patience had believed that both milestones lay ahead of them?

No matter. The point was that the annuity had gone to Pa's head. He had decided to become a scholarly gentleman of independent means. Independent means! As if the annuity was worth thousands instead of a mere hundred or so.

And it was worth less than that these days, its value having dropped like a stone during the war. Goodness only knew what their future held. Prudence dreaded retirement. Not only did she earn less than a man in the same job, but her pension would be correspondingly small too. How were they to get by? For years they had existed on a reduced level, with no indulgences permitted – barring, of course, the single colossal indulgence of Pa's idiotic way of life.

It was harder for Patience than it was for herself. She was forged from stronger metal, but Patience would have adored a bit of financial leeway, enough to provide a few creature comforts and a modest social life. As it was, their one real friend was Miss Kirby, who, after visiting them every Friday evening for years, now, because of their teaching commitments, came on Saturday evenings instead for conversation, a few hands of whist and a little light refreshment. As reduced as their own circumstances were, Miss Kirby's were even more so and they mustn't overdo their hospitality lest they embarrass her.

The doorbell sounded for a second time. Prudence fetched a sigh and pushed herself to her feet, reluctant to drag herself away from the unutterable luxury of being alone in the house. Someone tapped on the side pane of the bay window. What cheek! Her gaze flew across the room – Evelyn. Which meant Lawrence as well.

'Lucy isn't in,' she said before she had fully opened the front door.

'We haven't come to see her,' said Lawrence. 'We're here to speak to you and Patience.'

'Probably Patience more so than you,' Evelyn added.

'She's not here either.'

'Aren't you going to invite us in?' Lawrence enquired, shifting testily from one polished shoe to the other.

'Normally you march in without being invited,' Prudence retorted.

'As I am entitled to do, since this is my house.'

Waving Evelyn ahead of him, he crossed the threshold. Prudence led the way to the sitting room, feeling the invasion more keenly than usual. Her precious, solitary afternoon!

Seated on the sofa, Evelyn picked up a discarded library book.

'Lucy's?' she asked. 'She does love her romances.'

Evelyn's normally complacent features wobbled before settling into lines of sorrow. Prudence felt a tug of sympathy. It couldn't be easy for Evelyn, knowing that her daughter had chosen to live elsewhere for the time being.

'She's fine,' said Prudence. 'I don't know what upset brought her here, but there's no sign of it now, so maybe she'll be ready to return home soon.'

'I hope so.' Evelyn's voice was throaty.

'What brings you here?' ...to spoil my perfect afternoon.

'The local orphanage,' said Lawrence.

'Ah yes, you've taken an interest in it, haven't you, Evelyn?' Prudence let their surprise stretch out for a moment before putting them out of their misery. 'I believe you met Miss Watson, the temporary secretary. She's one of our pupil-lodgers. She asked if you were any relation.'

'An agreeable girl. I'm sure the tuition she receives from you will stand her in good stead.'

'Praise? You must want something.' She looked at Lawrence.

Unabashed, he crossed one leg over the other, making himself at home in Pa's old armchair. 'I do, as it happens. It would be inconvenient for Evelyn to have much to do with St Anthony's, because of our living a few miles distant.'

'Then why go there in the first place? Oh, don't tell me. She was doing a spot of toadying on your behalf.'

'You employ such a disagreeable turn of phrase at times.' The way Evelyn lifted her chin and sniffed might have suggested something in the oven was burning. 'I was most certainly not toadying. I was invited to go there in the company of Mrs Wardle, who is well known for her good works.'

'Mrs Wardle and Evelyn are friends,' said Lawrence, 'and I don't mind saying that Mr Wardle is a useful fellow to know.'

Wardle, Wardle... 'Oh yes,' Prudence said, 'you found him most useful when Pa secretly wrote his new will, leaving everything to you.'

'That's beside the point. Diggory Wardle—'

'Diggory? What sort of name is Diggory?'

Lawrence's jaw set. 'He knows many of the councillors. He sits on various committees and is chairman of more than one of them. He is au fait with many charitable initiatives.'

'Does he know he's going to help you become an alderman?' Her honeyed tone was calculated to get on Lawrence's wick.

'As I say, he's a useful fellow to know. I'm pleased that Evelyn has been invited to take an interest in his wife's charitable concerns.'

'I bet you are,' Prudence murmured.

Lawrence threw a dark look her way. 'The fact that this may be of benefit to me in the long run is an unexpected bonus.'

Unexpected? Just whom did he think he was fooling?

'It is gratifying when one's womenfolk support one's ambitions.'

'But Evelyn won't be supporting them, will she, as you live too far away.' Dear lord, she knew what was coming next.

'We'll make a donation in the form of offering to pay for new pinafores or something,' said Lawrence, 'but I still require to be represented in the orphanage on a regular basis.'

'Don't look at me,' Prudence said obstinately.

Lawrence looked her straight in the eye.

Just before the hour of eleven struck on the grandfather clock in the gloomy passage downstairs, Molly set her paperwork aside, anchoring it beneath a glass paperweight, and hurried down to help at morning milk time. Since taking Carmel to one side to apologise for getting swept up in Mrs Wardle's wake, she had been accepted by the nursemaids, much to her relief.

At home, when she had remarked on getting along well with the staff, Miss Hesketh had frowned.

'I wasn't aware that there were other clerical workers at St Anthony's.'

'There aren't. I meant the nursemaids.'

Miss Hesketh had raised a single thin eyebrow. 'Be careful, Miss Watson. You have a position to maintain. You aren't there to fraternise with lowly members of staff.'

How old fashioned. Molly had looked away lest her face should betray her. Obviously, a secretary in a company dominated by men would have to watch her Ps and Qs to ensure there was no familiarity, but surely it was different in a setting like St Anthony's.

At any rate, she didn't intend to be stand-offish. She had checked with Mrs Rostron that joining the nursemaids and children at specified times was acceptable.

'I don't imagine Miss Allan felt a need to do so,' she explained, 'but I believe it would help me understand St Anthony's better.'

Mrs Rostron had given her a considering look and tapped the end of her pen on her blotter. 'Very well. You may join the smalls for morning milk and you may occasionally assist in supervising the children at their homework, your other duties permitting.'

Arriving in the dining room now for morning milk, she greeted the smalls. Now that they were used to her, they brightened at her arrival. A couple of tots came in a waddling rush to fling their chubby arms round her legs.

She bent down to unpeel their fingers. Her arms ached with the need to scoop them up and cuddle them, but it was against the rules.

'They have to be treated all the same,' Carmel had told her. 'If you hug one, the whole lot might come swarming at you, wanting to be held, and then what would you do?'

Hug them all, of course – but she couldn't say so.

'Stand up, stand up,' the nursemaids encouraged the little ones. 'What do we do when we see Miss Watson?'

The wobbly attempts at bows and curtseys turned Molly's heart to wax.

'And what do we say? Good morning...'

'Good mor-ning, Miss Wat-son.'

It was like being a teacher. Now that the formalities were out of the way, she could sit down. At her first appearance at morning milk, she had attempted to help pour, only to have Nurse Eva remove the jug from her hands.

'You mustn't, miss. You're above such things.'

Now Eva handed her a cup of tea while Carmel and the others handed round beakers of milk to the smalls, who sat cross-legged in a circle on the floor.

'I'm gasping for this.' Carmel plonked herself onto a chair. Reaching for her tea, she drank deeply. 'Eh, I needed that.'

'Busy morning?' Molly asked.

'Always.' Leaning forward, she eyed the children in mock-exasperation. 'This lot run us ragged.'

The children giggled, milky moustaches on show.

'What about you, miss?' Eva asked. 'You've been with us a week now. Have you settled in?'

'I think so. It wasn't so easy to start with, not least because folk thought I was Mrs Wardle's handmaid, but that's behind me now. I'm learning more every day.'

'Starting to feel part of the furniture, eh?' said Eva.

'I started another job as well on Saturday afternoon – not paid work,' Molly added quickly. 'Part of the course I'm doing is that I have to gain experience of relevant work, so Miss Patience Hesketh finds suitable jobs for us, just for three or four hours a week.'

'Even though you've got this job here?' asked Carmel. 'What work is it?'

'Clerical work in a hotel.'

'Johnson Four,' said Eva, 'don't slurp your milk. It's not polite.'

As much as Molly felt she was settling in, there were things that still gave her a jolt. Hearing the boys addressed by their surnames was one of them. It was one thing to call the school-age lads by their surnames – but the smalls? It didn't feel right.

The doorbell clanged. A minute later, Nurse Louise, who was on housework duty, came down the couple of steps into the dining room. Crossing to the group, she lowered her voice so the smalls couldn't hear.

'Her majesty's arrived.'

Soft groans greeted this.

Molly stood up. 'I'd better get back upstairs.'

'Aye, quick smart.' Carmel gave her a sympathetic smile.

As Molly rounded the newel post at the top of the stairs, Mrs Wardle was in front of the alcove, her hand hovering over the paperweight. Was she about to read the documents?

'Good morning, Mrs Wardle.' She went to stand behind her desk, feeling like the last line of defence before the castle was stormed. 'May I help you?'

'Where have you been? You shouldn't be away from your post.'

'I've been at morning milk.' Not that it's any of your business, she added in her head.

'At morning milk?' The berries on Mrs Wardle's hat trembled indignantly. 'You forget yourself, Miss Watson. The Board of Health has released you for the purpose of attending to clerical duties, not to racket about with the orphans.'

'I have Mrs Rostron's permission,' Molly said stiffly. It was all she could do not to fold her arms. 'She wishes me to acquaint myself with the daily life of St Anthony's.'

'Really?' Mrs Wardle sniffed so deeply Molly could have sworn the pelt rippled on her fox-fur.

The office door opened and Mrs Rostron came along the passage.

'Mrs Wardle, this is an unexpected pleasure. Miss Watson, please would you type this report as a matter of priority?'

'Yes, Mrs Rostron.' Molly took the densely written sheets of paper.

'Miss Watson tells me she joins the children for morning milk,' said Mrs Wardle.

'Indeed. It was her own idea. I approve.'

'Her own idea? Well, that doesn't surprise me.' Oh no. Was she about to lambaste Molly for acting beyond her remit? 'That'll be my training, you know. I showed her the necessity of thinking things through carefully. It is gratifying to see her using her initiative.'

Molly's nails bit into her palms. How dare Mrs Wardle take the credit? Was Mrs Rostron fooled?

The superintendent merely said, 'Miss Watson is giving satisfaction. What brings you here this morning, Mrs Wardle?'

'I'd like to make an appointment. I wish to discuss the Cropper boy.'

'Again? Very well. I have a free half hour now, as it happens. Daniel Cropper's file, please, Miss Watson.'

Molly retrieved it, her skin prickling at the memory of wrongly accusing the boy of theft. Did the others remember that too?

They disappeared into the office, closing the door. Molly got on with typing the report. Her typewriting had improved with practice, thanks to the extra time she put in at home each evening, clacking away on one of the business school's two machines after lessons had finished.

Presently, the office door opened. Mrs Rostron accompanied Mrs Wardle as far as the alcove.

'I've signed these.' Mrs Rostron handed Molly a couple of letters. 'Would you post them at once, please? Perhaps you would like to show Mrs Wardle out.'

'Of course.' Was it obvious her teeth were gritted?

With the two of them waiting for her, there was no chance to titivate in front of the looking-glass. She pulled the cloche into position, smoothed her hair and hoped for the best. Mrs Wardle preceded her down the stairs, turning to her at the bottom.

'What is your opinion of the Cropper boy, Miss Watson?'

Molly remembered the last time she had expressed an opinion in Mrs Wardle's presence. 'I can't say I know him.'

'You were quick enough to blacken his name over that business with the missing money. Well, you're wise to keep that one at arm's length. He's a runaway, as you know.'

'As far as I'm aware, there haven't been any incidents recently.'

'He does appear to have settled, that's true.' Mrs Wardle sounded grudging. 'Not that that means anything. It would be a mistake to let our guard down.'

Distrustful creature. Why couldn't she think well of the boy, be glad he seemed to have accepted his lot? Molly opened the heavy front door. Mrs Wardle swanned out. Molly followed her down the steps onto the playground. There was something sad about a playground that was empty of children.

'I firmly believe,' said Mrs Wardle, 'that it would be in Cropper's best interests to be sent to live with his uncle in Cumberland. It's where he'll end up anyway, when his father dies, so why wait? The end of the summer term is fast approaching. It's a good time to move him on.'

'Is his father going to die?'

'Almost certainly. Poor people do. One could call it a waste of money to send them to the sanatorium when they have so little hope of recovery, but there are charities that fund these things, no matter how ill-advisedly.'

'Are you suggesting the poor aren't worth helping?'

'Charities and the authorities have limited resources. It behoves those of us in positions of influence to ensure that funds are spent in the most appropriate manner.'

'That's—'

'That's what? Unfair? It's the way of the world. Would you rather funds were squandered? As an employee of the Board of Health, you have a duty to understand these things. Take the Cropper boy, for example. Mother dead, father as good as. Despatch him to the uncle, say I, and be done with it. While Cropper remains here, there is the constant threat that he might run away again. He may not have made any attempts recently, but don't let that blind you. He's a naughty boy and naughty boys don't change. Furthermore, while he's here, he's taking up a space in the orphanage – a space that could be offered to an orphan in need.'

'I consider Daniel Cropper to be in need.' That poor lad, separated from his surviving parent. He must be beside himself.

'In need of what, Miss Watson?' Mrs Wardle stopped in the gateway and turned to her. 'A parent and a home? Both await him in Cumberland. He could start his new life and another child could be brought to St Anthony's. What possible objection can you raise to that?'

Put like that – none.

Chapter Eighteen

FRIDAY LOOKED SET to become Molly's favourite day. It saw her at her busiest, concentrating her hardest. Friday was pay day and she had to check everyone's hours against the rosters and calculate their wages and deductions, filling in the relevant paperwork and inserting the money into small square brown envelopes, each one carefully labelled with the recipient's name.

It took all morning and part of the afternoon. Then came the task, as pleasant as it was responsible, of distributing the wage packets. For this, she had a leather bag on a long strap to carry everything around the building. Nannies and nursemaids, cook and kitchen maids, each had to sign for her wages and place her envelope, in Molly's presence, into her locker; and Molly had to have her own wages checked by Mrs Rostron. Later, the staff not on duty today would pop in between five and six to collect theirs.

When she finished handing out the wages to the women on duty, there was one person left on her list. The children were back from school now, those of them that came home at half past three. Some of the older ones were at their half-time jobs, which they wouldn't leave until five or six. At this time of day, homework was under way in the dining room while the remainder of the children were kept outside out of the way, apart from a handful who had been chosen to take part in a new activity.

As Molly opened the front door, Miss Patience and Miss Kirby came towards her across the playground, weaving their way around the edge of a game of cricket.

Molly smiled in greeting. 'Are you here to read to the children? It's good of you to volunteer.'

'I'm here to read to them,' said Miss Patience, 'but Miss Kirby is going to get them to read to her. She used to be a teacher, you know.'

'Come in,' said Molly. 'Nurse Carmel and Nurse Philomena have taken the children to one of the common rooms.' She hailed one of the boys, who was waiting his turn to bat. 'Sullivan! Please take our visitors to the junior common room.'

As they disappeared indoors, it was her turn to make her way around the edge of the cricket match. It was another hot afternoon. She pushed her hair behind her ears. In the girls' playground, children were helping Mr Abrams clear the ivy.

'You're doing a grand job,' she told them. She had been shy of addressing the children at first, but now it came naturally. 'You've cleared the whole of the wall beyond the gates.'

'They're not bad little workers,' said Mr Abrams, 'apart from this one.' He flicked off a lad's cap and tousled his hair. 'This one's bone idle.'

'*Sir!*' the boy protested, but he was obviously delighted.

Seeing the wages-bag, Mr Abrams nodded. To the kids, he said, 'That's it for today. Thanks, everyone. Boys, clean your penknives like I showed you. Cropper, will you gather the blades and secateurs into the box and bring it to my workshop?'

Molly walked with him to the workshop, which was tucked away in a corner at the back of the grounds. Grounds! That sounded like the orphanage stood in rolling parkland instead of a tarmacked corner plot.

'You have a way with you, talking to the children,' Molly observed.

'A bit of individual attention goes a long way.'

'What about treating them all the same?' A twist of annoyance clenched unexpectedly inside her. Why should Mr Abrams get away with being different?

He shrugged. 'It's different for me.' Had he read her mind? 'I don't work with them the way everyone else does. The way I see it, the more interaction they have with adults the better.'

'And your interaction is matey and jokey while the rest of us obey the rules.'

They had reached his workshop. A long, low building, it stood in front of the high walls at the rear of St Anthony's, not far from where the dustbins and pig-bins were located at the back of the kitchen.

Mr Abrams turned the key in the lock, but instead of opening the door, he looked at her. She hadn't been this close to him before. His nut-brown eyes were flecked with gold and there were two vertical lines between his eyebrows. His frown now showed how deeply they were gouged – a legacy of the war?

'You make it sound as if I dress up as a clown and throw custard pies. A spot of larking about does no harm.' He pushed open the door, but didn't stand back for her to enter. 'If Mrs Rostron raises no objection to my conduct, I don't see that it's your place to do so.'

Her ears burned. Automatically she lifted her hand to pull her hair forwards and hide them – or would that merely draw attention to her discomfort? What had made her take exception to Mr Abrams's way with the children? To tell the truth, she admired it. She should be glad – she *was* glad that the orphans, surrounded by female staff, had a decent man on the edge of their lives. Masculine influence could make such a difference; not the strict, nose-to-the-grindstone influence of their schoolmasters, but a kinder attitude that bolstered their home lives.

'I'm sorry. I spoke out of turn. I find it hard sometimes, keeping my distance from the children, and seeing you being so familiar with them... It was wrong of me to object. I can see how much it means to them.'

His gaze softened. The frown lines cut into him by the war melted away to be replaced by a web of fine lines beside his eyes.

'Like I say, it's different for me. I think it's good for the kids to have a man around.'

'A man who pays them a bit of attention.'

'It's not just me. You know Bunny, the hot-potato man?'

'Everyone knows Bunny.'

'He's helped with the ivy once or twice. There's so much discipline in the children's lives – rightly so – but they need to know you can josh around a bit and still get the work done.'

Rays of golden light brightened the grim area. The sound of the children's voices back in the playground seemed to recede. Molly's pulse raced and a trembling inside her legs made them feel weak.

Mr Abrams stepped back. 'After you.'

Cold washed through her – surprise, disappointment; annoyance at herself. Had he seen, had he sensed, the way she had been drawn to him in that moment?

The inside of the workshop was thick with heat. The rich scents of wood and oils swarmed up her nose, together with the comforting smell of beeswax. After the brilliance of the afternoon sunshine, the workshop was gloomy. She blinked, adjusting her eyes, as she twisted at the waist to open the flap of the leather wages-bag.

Mr Abrams cleared a space on a work surface. 'It's clean. This is where I draw plans.'

She laid down the wage packet. So what if she had put all the other packets into the recipients' hands? Unfolding the list of staff on duty this afternoon, she smoothed it, pushing it in his direction.

'Do you need a pen?'

'I've got one, thanks. That makes a change,' he added as he signed.

'What does?'

He ran a finger down the line of signatures, which included a couple of Xs. Neither of the scrubbing women had learned to write.

'Being the last to sign. All my life, I've been the first to do everything.' He gave a mock-bow. 'Aaron Abrams, at your service.'

'I've always been one of the last, being a Watson. One of my teachers used to sit us in alphabetical order and make us line up in alphabetical order, so I was always at the back. I used to long to be at the front.'

'I was the other way round. I wanted to be at the back.'

'Did you have an alphabet-mad teacher as well?'

'I was at the front because I was one of the naughty lads.' His grin made the years fall away from him, allowing her to glimpse the boy he had once been. 'I wasn't interested in writing copperplate or learning the kings and queens of England by heart. I wanted to be outdoors, running about.'

'Were you good at physical drill?'

'I don't know that I was any good, but I enjoyed it. What I remember most about drill is the swimming lessons.'

'Your school went swimming?'

He laughed. 'No such luck. We learned to swim by lying across chairs and moving our arms and legs. To this day, I wonder whether my technique would keep me afloat.'

Molly joined in his laughter. He was good company, interesting and amusing and...and she would like to know him better.

A clatter of footsteps shattered the moment. Daniel Cropper

burst in, making even more of a disturbance by whirling to a standstill.

'Sorry, sir. Sorry, miss. I forgot to knock. Here's the box.'

'Thanks. Off you go.' Mr Abrams – Aaron – put the box on a shelf. 'Now there's a lad who could do with a spot of attention.'

She didn't want to talk about Daniel Cropper. She wanted to rekindle the friendly laughter they had shared. Oh, this was ridiculous. She was ridiculous. She knew better than this. Only flighty girls gave male colleagues the glad eye. Moreover, the simple fact that Aaron clearly had no wish to recapture the moment showed it had meant nothing to him. She would do well to remember that.

'Daniel Cropper? He could have all the attention he needs, if he went to live with his uncle in Cumberland.'

A brief laugh escaped him, a sound of surprise, of being taken aback. 'And you'd know what's best for him, would you? You, who've known him all of five minutes.'

'You don't have to have known him for long to be aware of his situation. Mrs Wardle told me about his uncle—'

'You really are in her pocket, aren't you?'

'I can think for myself, thank you. When I'm given information, I form my own judgement. I never thought I'd hear myself say it but, in this case, I agree with Mrs Wardle.'

'She knows nothing about it; and if you agree with her, neither do you.'

'A very mature argument, Mr Abrams.' Molly thrust her list into the wages-bag and slapped the flap shut. 'I think you've let the children's affection go to your head.'

There! An excellent parting shot. She threw open the door.

'Miss Watson.'

Drat! If she had been a fraction quicker, she could have pretended not to hear. As it was, she was forced to look over her shoulder. The low-ceilinged room emphasised Aaron's lean height.

'He isn't called Daniel.'

A frown tugged her brow. 'Of course he is.'

'You claim to know about him. Then you should know he isn't Daniel. He's Danny.'

A young lad ran in Molly's direction as she retraced her steps to the front door. It was Layton Two. He wasn't a good-looking lad, like Layton One. You wouldn't think they were brothers, to look at them; and evidently the differences ran deeper, since the older boy was trusted to have a half-time job while the younger one was under threat of being packed off to the reformatory if he failed to behave himself. Theirs was one of the files she had read, so she knew all about the Laytons, including Thaddeus, whom Mrs Rostron hadn't had even one day at the orphanage before deciding to send him to the reformatory.

'Miss, miss.' The boy skidded to a halt in front of her. All the other children were rosy and glowing with health in this fine weather, but Layton Two – Jacob – was grey and tired-looking. Molly felt a stab of concern.

'Did you want something?' she asked.

'Please, miss, will you help me with summat?'

'Of course, if I can.' How pleasing to be asked. It meant she had been accepted.

'Will you – will you ask Mrs Rostron if I can change schools? I still go to my old school in Stretford and...' Jacob chewed his lip. 'If I could go to school here in Chorlton, it'd be easier for me to see my mum.'

Poor lad. 'Come indoors and tell me properly.'

Inside, she was at a loss as to where to take him. Homework was going on in the dining room, reading in the junior common room. Her alcove upstairs was out of bounds to children. She settled for sitting on the stairs.

'I miss my mum something rotten.' Jacob stared straight

ahead, not looking at her. 'My dad left us, you know, so there's only her. I hardly ever see her, but if I could move to one of the Chorlton schools, I could mebbe see her after school. She lives near the rec, in a road called Wilton Close.'

'Wilton Close?'

'Aye. D'you know it?'

'I should. I live there.'

He twisted to face her. 'That's lucky, isn't it, miss? It sort of puts you on my side. Will you ask Mrs Rostron?'

No wonder his skin had that grey look. So many changes had assaulted him all at once. The father had absconded; the family had nearly been wiped out in a fire; and now their mother couldn't keep them, which was why Michael and Jacob were here at St Anthony's. Jacob must be in turmoil.

'I'll speak to her for you.' She pulled in a breath, proud that Jacob had chosen her to help him.

'Thanks, miss.' He bounced to his feet, eyes shining, the extent of his delight taking Molly by surprise.

'I can't promise anything,' she said but doubted whether it sank in before the lad rushed away. She let out a sigh and her shoulders dropped. Jacob Layton, Daniel Cropper... How fortunate she was to have grown up in a stable, healthy family.

She ran upstairs. The staff who weren't on duty today would soon appear to collect their wages. Was there time to have a word with Mrs Rostron first?

She knocked at the office door.

'Come.'

The superintendent was bent over her desk, writing something that no doubt Molly would be required to type up in due course. Pinching the bridge of her nose between thumb and forefinger, Mrs Rostron squeezed her eyes shut for a moment.

'Is there a problem?'

'It's Jacob Layton.'

'I expected you to ask about an administrative matter, not a child. Have a seat. What's this about?'

Molly sat, folding her hands in her lap. 'He wants to leave the school in Stretford.'

'And he will – at the end of the school year. I've made arrangements for him to attend St Clement's in September.'

'Couldn't he change schools now instead?'

'Why the rush? School finishes the week after next.'

'He could end the year with the children he'll be with at the start of next year. That would help him, surely; save him from the anxiety of being new in September.'

'My, he has got round you, hasn't he?' Mrs Rostron laid down her pen. 'Have you seen the Layton boys' file? Then you'll know what they have suffered. Keeping them at their old school has provided a modicum of continuity at a time when everything else in their lives has undergone disruption. That's important to their well-being.'

'Surely being nearer to Mrs Layton would also benefit their well-being.'

'Ah, is that the reason he gave you? Tell me how attending a Chorlton school would make things better regarding his mother.'

'He could see her on his way home.'

'You are aware of the rule about coming straight back here from school, are you not, Miss Watson?'

'It need be only for a few minutes...'

'And what of the other children we accommodate who aren't orphans? Should they also be allowed to see more of their families? Or do you propose one rule for Jacob Layton and another for the rest?'

'Of course not.' Infuriating woman! Was she trying to make Molly look daft?

'What if the families aren't available at that time of day? Or if they live too far away? Would it interest you to know that the Layton boys are the only ones with a parent on the doorstep?

And what of Michael Layton? Is he also to be found a school place in Chorlton? Then there is Mrs Layton to consider. She is employed. Do you think her mistress wishes her to be distracted from her duties every day after school? And then there are the orphans. Are they to have their noses rubbed in their orphaned state every school day?' Mrs Rostron paused, tilting her head enquiringly on one side. 'Have I made my point, Miss Watson?'

'Yes, Mrs Rostron.' The last time she had felt like this was when she had been summoned to the head's office for passing notes in class.

'Moreover, there are other reasons to keep the Laytons at the school in Stretford.'

'Such as?'

'Are you questioning my judgement?'

'I'm sorry if it sounded like that, but I should like to understand.'

Mrs Rostron nodded. 'There was another brother.'

'Thaddeus.'

'Thad the thug. Jacob was entirely under his influence and indeed is now here on probation while he shows me what he's made of. The two oldest children in the family, who are adults, have told me how Thaddeus hated Michael, which meant Jacob used to hate him too. Now that Thaddeus's undesirable influence has been removed, I want Jacob to see Michael with new eyes. By sending the pair of them to Stretford together every morning, I hope to create a bond between them. Michael is an admirable young man. Jacob could do a lot worse than give him the allegiance he used to squander on Thaddeus.'

'I hadn't realised there was so much to it,' Molly admitted.

Mrs Rostron's smile was wry. 'People seldom do. Anyone can see what's on the surface. It takes experience to see what's underneath.'

Mrs Rostron moved, preparing to continue with her work. Molly sat forward, placing her fingers on the edge of the desk.

'May I ask about Daniel Cropper? I know about the uncle in Cumberland.'

'Do you indeed? And what do you think I should do?'

She spoke evenly, wanting her opinion to sound measured and worth listening to. 'Daniel will be sent to live with his uncle if his father dies, won't he, so why not send him now? That way, if his father dies, at least Daniel will have had the chance to settle into his new life first, which might make his bereavement less painful; and if his father lives, Daniel can come back and they can be together, Daniel having been cared for by family in the meantime.'

'You seem eager to see the back of him.'

'I believe children are better off with their families.'

'I agree – as a general rule; but Daniel Cropper doesn't fit in with the general rule.' Mrs Rostron sighed quietly. 'So few children do. How do you think Daniel would feel, were he to be packed off to his uncle now?'

'Surely he'd prefer to be with family than here? No one wants to be in an orphanage.'

'Oh yes, such frightful places,' Mrs Rostron murmured.

'I mean...'

'I know what you mean, Miss Watson. What if I told you Daniel Cropper has no wish to be sent to his uncle?'

'Has his uncle been unkind to him – or to his father?'

'Mr Angus Cropper is a respectable, law-abiding individual, who has made something of himself, unlike Daniel's father.'

'All the more reason to hand Daniel into his care.'

'You're seeing things on the surface again, Miss Watson. There's more to the children who live here than what's written in their files.'

Molly bridled. 'I hope I don't see any child that way.'

'Don't you? That remains to be seen. Let me tell you about the Cropper boy. The reason he doesn't want to live with Uncle Angus is because he wants to be on hand for his ailing father.'

'But he isn't. He's here in Manchester and Mr Cropper is in Southport.'

'Daniel feels more on hand here than he would if he were spirited away to Cumberland. If he were to go there, it would, in his mind, be like admitting his father is going to die; therefore he is desperate to stay put. Staying here also allows him to hope for his father's recovery.'

Molly spoke carefully. God forbid she should sound heartless. 'Am I right in thinking Mr Cropper's chances are slight?'

'Is that a reason to dash the boy's hopes? There are plenty of people in authority who would pack him off to the uncle's without a second thought, and give themselves a pat on the back for doing it. I should be disappointed to discover you were one of those people, Miss Watson.'

The odd mixture of criticism and compliment held Molly silent.

'Knowing his uncle is there in the background,' continued Mrs Rostron, 'gives Daniel a kind of security. He knows he is wanted. He knows that if the worst happens, he has somewhere to go. Even though he doesn't articulate this to himself, nevertheless it is there deep down in his self-knowledge.'

Molly leaned closer. 'Do you think so?'

'It isn't something that appears in any report, because it isn't a fact that can be proved. But, as I said before, I have to see beneath the facts.' Sitting up straight, she rearranged her papers. 'Are there other children about whom you wish to interrogate me or may I get on with my work?'

Molly rose. 'Thank you for your time.'

'Perhaps it will stop you jumping to conclusions in future.'

The superintendent held her pen poised as she re-read what she had written. It was dismissal. Molly went to the door, but before she could leave, Mrs Rostron spoke.

'I wonder. Were they your own opinions – or Mrs Wardle's?'

Chapter Nineteen

MOLLY SPENT SATURDAY morning with Mum. She had popped home regularly and was pleased and reassured to find her parents were genuinely interested in her studies and her job. This morning, she was able to settle in for a good natter because Mum had no cooking to do since Dad always brought fish and chips home on Saturdays for a hearty nosh-up before setting off to watch Tom play football or cricket, depending on the time of year.

'Gran's over at Auntie Faith's this morning,' said Mum, as they made a pot of tea, slipping automatically into their old routine of Mum seeing to the teapot while Molly got out the crockery. 'She'll be sorry to have missed you.'

'And I'm sorry not to see her,' Molly answered, 'but I'm not sorry to have avoided a morning of hints being dropped like bricks about what I've let slip through my fingers. That's why I didn't tell you I was coming.'

'Oh, Molly.' Mum paused in the larder doorway to throw her a look in which sadness, exasperation and concern tussled for top billing.

'If Gran had known, you can bet Norris would have found out. You know how often Gran bumps into his mother at the tripe shop and the grocer's.'

'Mrs Hartley has always been good to your gran.'

'And to me an' all.' Her conscience gave her a nudge. 'I ought to call on her.'

'See that you do.' Mum slid the quilted tea-cosy over the pot. 'Eh, it's a messy business when an engagement ends. I never thought it would happen to one of my lasses.'

'Steady on. You'll be dipping your toes in the shocking and shameful waters next, like Gran.'

Mum stopped in the middle of stirring her tea. 'How can you make light of it, Molly? It is a shock and a shame when a girl isn't engaged any more. You don't know what it's been like round here.'

'You make it sound like I've moved to the ends of the earth.'

'And I'm still here, still using the local shops, being asked how you are and have you seen sense yet and what are the chances of you meeting another man at your age?'

'There isn't another man!'

Mum's gaze homed in on her. 'That sounded a bit like protesting too much.'

'No it didn't.' Molly picked up her tea, practically sticking her nose into it. 'Why is everybody so keen to marry me off?'

'It's what everyone wants that cares about you.' Mum opened the cake-tin, releasing the delicious spicy-sweet aroma of cinnamon. 'I want all my children to get married. I love to see Tilda and Chrissie with their families and I want the same for you and Tom. Even if you do meet someone else *eventually*,' she added in response to Molly's glare, 'you'll likely be too old to have children. You're twenty-seven.'

'Thanks for reminding me.'

'I'm serious, love. Carry on the way you are and the only way you'll become a mother is by marrying a widower who needs a new mum for his kids.'

Was that true? She wanted children, she really did. Was Norris and his parsimony a price worth paying to become a mother?

No.

Or would she one day look back and wish?

'I didn't come to talk about my failure in the marriage stakes.'

'When we've finished our tea, I'll show you the dress I'm making for Lottie. Such a pretty print, and it'll wear nicely for a good few years.'

It would need to, as it would be passed from one girl to the next, not just in Chrissie's family but in Tilda's too, until it ended up in the patchwork box. Oh, the joys of hand-me-downs. Molly remembered only too clearly Chrissie insisting on a pink fabric that Molly knew would look hideous with her own strawberry-blonde hair when her time came. Lucky Lottie, being the oldest in her generation.

At half-twelve, Molly set off to intercept Dad on his way to the chippy, so he would get a portion for her as well. They returned home to find the table set with salt and vinegar and a plate heaped with bread and butter, and Tom coming downstairs, having washed off the grime of a morning spent on the building site.

'This is like old times,' said Dad, taking his place while Mum and Molly unwrapped the layers of newspaper and the mouth-watering aroma filled the air. 'It's good to have you home, Molly. Are you stopping for the afternoon?'

'No, I have to get over to Seymour Grove.'

'Oh aye, the hotel. I was forgetting.'

'I don't like this business of you doing a second job,' said Mum. 'Isn't it enough that you work Monday to Friday?'

'Most of the business school pupils work on Saturday mornings as well, then have to set off for their Saturday afternoon placements. When I'm back at the Board of Health, it's what I'll be doing. It's a luxury working just weekdays at St Anthony's. No other member of staff has it so cushy.'

Tom walked her to the bus stop.

'Doing well, Molly? No regrets?'

'Don't you start.'

'I'm not trying to steer you back to Norris. I only want to make sure you're all right.'

'I'm sorry. I should know you better than that.'

'No regrets, then?'

'None. Well – I do wonder what the future holds and I'd be very sorry if I ended up not having a family of my own, but—'

'But not with Norris? Fair enough. You ought to make it clear to him, though.'

Molly looked at him in surprise. 'I already have. Believe me, when I told him, I left no room for doubt.'

'He's telling folk he's going to win you back.'

Her groan came all the way up from her toes. 'Who has he told?'

'Dora, for one. Gran, for another.'

'And I bet they encouraged him.' Her throat tightened in frustration.

'Do you want me to have a word with him?'

'Thanks, but there's no need.'

Drat Norris. How could he put her in this position? But then, she had put him in a crummy position by ending their engagement.

At the hotel, her first duty was to help the housekeeper check a consignment of linen that had come back from the laundry. Molly wasn't convinced that counting pillow-cases could be called office work, but she didn't object. Then she returned to the office, which, for once, was empty.

The door flew open and Mr Dallimore, the chief reception-ist, appeared. 'Can you prepare Mr Hodge's bill, please? Room twenty. He's leaving early.'

'Yes, of course,' but she was talking to thin air.

Fortunately, she knew what to do. Sliding two blank bills with carbon paper in between into the typewriter, she found the records of when the Hodges had arrived and which meals they had taken in the hotel, double-checking her maths before twisting the knob on the side of the machine to wind the bill around the drum and into her hand. Folding the top copy, she took it through to the reception area, where Mr Dallimore was in conversation with a smartly dressed couple the same sort of age as Mum and Dad. Well, he wasn't talking to the couple, exactly, just with the lady while the gentleman stood there, nostrils flaring impatiently.

'I'm sorry we have to depart sooner than expected,' Mrs Hodge was saying. 'My husband's business, you know.'

'Flora,' murmured Mr Hodge warningly, as if she were about to divulge deadly secrets.

'I hope you found everything to your satisfaction,' said Mr Dallimore. 'Ah, here is your bill, sir.'

Mr Hodge examined it so closely that Molly felt impelled to remain in case he had a query.

Mrs Hodge prattled on. 'If our son-in-law were as successful in business as my husband, he would be able to afford to rent a larger house and we could stay with them. Not that we aren't comfortable here, but it would be so convenient.' She heaved a misty-eyed sigh. 'I should so love to stay with Alicia. That would make our visits to Manchester perfect.'

Yes! There it was in Molly's head, a wonderful new idea. Thank you, Mrs Hodge. It would indeed be perfect, if she could bring it into being.

Molly mulled it over all through the Sunday sermon. The more thought she gave it, the better it seemed. She couldn't wait for Monday, so she could propose her idea to Mrs Rostron.

On Monday, she excused herself from morning milk and took Eva, who was on housework duty, to one side to explain what she needed. Eva led her upstairs to where the children slept. The boys' and girls' dormitories were in different parts of the building, each reached by its own stairs. The wooden hill, as it was called, led to the girls' dormitories and the soldiers' trail to the boys'. On a separate landing in between were the bedrooms used by the night staff; and tucked away, down half a dozen shallow steps and round a sharp corner, was a small, empty room that might have been intended as a box-room, except that its position was so inconvenient that it wasn't used for anything other than gathering dust.

'I don't know if this is what you're after,' said Eva, 'but I can't think of anywhere else.'

'It's perfect,' Molly exclaimed.

'If you say so, miss.'

Now all she had to do was wait for Mrs Rostron to return from a meeting with the superintendents of other orphanages and officials from the Board of Health. Molly had briefly felt miffed when Mrs Rostron didn't invite her along. After all, she worked for the Board of Health – except that she didn't, did she, not at the moment.

When Mrs Rostron returned, she stopped typing to look up with a smile.

'Would you like a cup of tea?'

'That would be most welcome. A pot would be more welcome still.'

Molly slipped downstairs to organise it. She would gladly have carried the tray upstairs, but Mrs Wilkes wouldn't hear of it. No one would have dreamed of asking Miss Allan to do such a thing and that meant Molly mustn't do it either.

Mrs Wilkes rang a bell. Eva appeared and was given the tray. Feeling vaguely guilty, Molly made sure she got upstairs first so she could open the office door.

When Eva left, Molly lingered.

'May I speak to you when it's convenient? I have an idea.'

'This afternoon, after the smalls have been checked by the nit nurse.'

Molly smothered a sigh. Evidently an expression of interest in hearing her idea was too much to hope for, though that probably said more about her own excitement than it did about Mrs Rostron's personality. Since the superintendent had set her straight about the Layton and Cropper boys, Molly had started to see her in a new light, admiring her for knowing the children inside out; and if she was inclined to be short with people, maybe that was plain tiredness, since she often worked long into the evening even when it wasn't her turn to do night duty.

When the time came to present her idea, Molly felt more than ready as she took a seat in front of Mrs Rostron's desk.

'There's a small room upstairs that's standing empty. I wondered – that is, I suggest turning it into a bedroom so that a parent or other adult relative of one of the children could stay overnight.'

Mrs Rostron's expression didn't give away anything. 'Go on.'

'For instance: Mrs Layton. I asked Michael about her work hours. He says that after tea on Saturday, her next duty is to prepare Sunday lunch; so once in a while she could come here on a Saturday evening and be with her boys, stay overnight and see them again at breakfast. Daniel Cropper's uncle could come, perhaps for more than one night; and there are other children with family, including some of the orphans.'

'What of the orphans with no living relatives? What of the children who do have relatives, but the relatives don't want to know?'

'Is that a reason to deprive the other children? Surely it would be good for all the children, whatever their circumstances, to see family affection. Yes, it might sadden some of them, but it will also set them a good example of the kind of loving support they can give to their own children when they grow up.'

Mrs Rostron's eyes narrowed thoughtfully. 'I'll consider it – if you can tell me how it is to be paid for.'

'I wondered if Mr Abrams would construct a bed-frame, a wash-stand and so forth. That would save money.'

'Save money? What money? I hope you don't imagine the materials could be paid for from the orphanage budget.' Mrs Rostron smiled, then glanced at the papers on her desk: the interview was clearly coming to an end. 'Come and see me again when you have found the money – if you find it.'

The words didn't seem like a ringing vote of confidence, but Molly refused to be put off, especially when she remembered Mrs Rostron's smile. Had that been intended to encourage her? Or possibly challenge her? If so, it was a challenge Molly had every intention of rising to.

She discussed her idea that evening with Vivienne.

'It pains me to say it,' said Vivienne, 'but you might try Mrs Wardle. She has her fingers in any number of charitable pies.'

Molly pretended to flinch. 'It's funny how something can be a good idea and a bad idea at the same time.'

The next morning, she went in search of Aaron to share her plan. Having failed to think through the money side of her project before speaking to Mrs Rostron, she wasn't going to make the same mistake with Mrs Wardle. Dad would have her guts for garters if he knew she hadn't costed the work in advance.

Aaron was up a ladder, sanding down a window-frame. The pane glistened in the morning sun. There was a refreshing edge to the air today and the playground, instead of being heavy with the smell of hot tarmac, rang instead with the aroma of trees in full leaf.

Not wanting to disturb him, Molly was about to walk away when Aaron took off his cap and rolled it up, but when he pushed it into his pocket, he missed and the cap tumbled to the ground. Rescuing it, Molly looked up and met his eyes. Would he stay put up the ladder? They hadn't parted on the best of terms last time.

He came down. Molly pressed her lips together to keep herself from smiling.

'Yours, I believe.' She offered him the cap.

'Thanks.' He smiled. 'You could have made more of an effort to catch it before it hit the ground.'

That broke through her restraint and she laughed. What was it about them that made them get along with one another? Was he aware of it too? It felt so easy. Natural. Comfortable, but with a blade-sharp edge of excitement.

Aaron said, 'I'm pleased to see you.' He was? Her heart leaped. 'I ought to apologise.' Oh. Was that all? 'Last time we spoke, I overstepped the mark. I stand by what I said about Danny Cropper, but I apologise for the way I said it.'

'I'm sorry about the disagreement as well,' said Molly, 'the difference being that I don't stand by what I said. I've found out more about his circumstances since then and I was wrong before.'

'Good of you to say so.' Was that admiration in his eyes? 'Does something need mending?'

'Beg pardon?'

'Were you looking for me?'

'Or was I just passing by when I rugby-tackled your cap? I was looking for you, actually. When you've got a few minutes, I'd like to ask for your help with something.'

'Let me finish this and I'll come and find you. Shall you be at your desk?'

In the event she was at morning milk. Aaron came and sat on the floor with the smalls, who giggled and squirmed in delight.

'You mustn't sit there, Mr Abrams,' Carmel cried.

'I can and I am.' Over the children's heads, he said quietly, 'I don't want them growing up feeling scared of me, me being the only man about the place. But if I sit here,' he added in a louder voice, gathering the children's attention, 'shows I'm one of them, because only smalls are allowed to sit on the floor at milk time.'

'You're not a small,' said Johnson Four. 'You're a big.'

'Only on the outside,' said Aaron. 'Inside, I'm very small.'

'Inside, are you teeny-tiny?' asked Jessica.

'Inside, I'm so teeny, you can hardly see me. That's why I have to be big on the outside.'

'You'll have to sit on a chair, if you want a cup of tea,' said Philomena. 'Nanny Duffy is on the war-path this morning and she won't be amused if I serve you tea on the floor.'

Aaron pulled a face for the children's benefit. 'Looks like I have to pretend to be big.'

'Don't worry,' Jessica consoled him. 'We know you're teeny-tiny.'

'That makes me feel a lot better.'

After milk, Aaron accompanied Molly from the dining room. 'What did you want help with?'

'First, I need to show you something. This way.'

She led him up the wooden hill to the unused room, where she explained her idea.

The warmth of his smile took her by surprise. She felt fluttery inside and had to remind herself that his approval was for her idea, not for her personally.

'If I can raise the funds,' she said, 'would you build the furniture?'

He looked round. 'It'll be cramped. The bed has to go along here and I can squeeze in a little wash-stand at the foot.'

'And shelves and pegs on the walls,' Molly added.

'I'll work out the cost, including for whitewashing.'

'And I'll find out what the bedding will cost, and fabric for curtains.'

Going downstairs one flight, she peeled off to wend her way through the twisty-turny passages to her alcove, leaving Aaron to head straight down. How good it felt to have him on her side. Would there be the opportunity for them to work together properly on this – or, having heard her plan, would he simply get on with it with no further reference to her, if and when she secured the sponsorship?

Mrs Wardle came to St Anthony's the next day. 'Good morning, Miss Watson. Mrs Atwood tells me you have a plan that may be of interest to me.'

'If you give me a minute to ask Mrs Rostron if I may leave my desk, we can go downstairs and talk about it.'

'Aren't we going to discuss it with Mrs Rostron?'

'I've already done that and received her consent.'

'You should have approached me first and asked me to speak to Mrs Rostron on your behalf, assuming I approve of your scheme, that is.'

Did this impossible woman think Molly couldn't manage without her?

Soon they were seated in a corner of the empty staff dining room. Mrs Wardle looked round with pursed lips. Clearly, only Mrs Rostron's office was good enough for her.

Molly explained her idea.

'And you wish me to find the funds to pay for this?'

'Yes, please. Here are the costings.'

Mrs Wardle didn't even look. 'You may put your figures away, Miss Watson. This is an orphanage, not a hotel. The very idea!'

And that was that. Molly duly reported back to Mrs Rostron.

'If Mrs Wardle says no,' said the superintendent, 'you have little chance of success. A venture such as this will be of interest only on a local level.'

Molly didn't feel ready to give up, though just then she didn't see what her next step could be, especially if Mrs Rostron didn't see fit to supply any ideas. Or was Mrs Rostron testing her?

At home that evening, after lessons finished, she shared her disappointment.

'I'm sorry to sound like a wet blanket, but it's such a let-down. Do any of you have any idea whom I might approach?'

'Perhaps the local churches,' Miss Patience suggested, 'although they already have such commitments.'

'I'll ask at the office tomorrow,' Vivienne offered, 'in Mrs Wardle's absence, of course.'

'No need for any of that,' said Miss Hesketh, causing them all to look at her. 'Leave it to me.'

Chapter Twenty

JACOB'S BODY STILL felt all screwed up inside with disappointment. He had pinned his hopes on the new lady, Miss Watson. He had judged her to be a soft touch and he had been right. With his sad tale of missing his mum, he had got round her straight away. It had troubled him to use his need for his mum in that way, but what choice had he had? But his ploy hadn't worked. He wanted to hate Miss Watson for letting him down, but some deeper instinct told him she would have done her best. Then again, what use was her best if it hadn't got him what he wanted?

Oh, if only she could have talked Mrs Rostron round, how much better his life would be. He wouldn't have to walk home from school in Stretford any more, wouldn't have to worry whether Shirl would be there as he turned each corner. The worst thing was when Shirl came upon him from behind, throwing his arm round Jacob's shoulders and falling in step – no, Shirl didn't fall in step; he carried Jacob along with him, his longer stride forcing a faster pace and causing Jacob to stumble as he made the adjustment. In his head, he didn't adjust. In his head, he wrenched free and spun away; in his head, he faced Shirl, stood up to him, told him to sod off; but that was only in his head. His body went along with it and he felt feeble. Cowardly. Terrified. Jemima.

Recruiting Daniel Cropper hadn't got him off the hook.

'But you said, if I found someone for you, I'd be able to pack it in.' It had taken all Jacob's resolve to force the words out. His insides were shaking. Any moment now, his outside would be shaking an' all.

'Nah, I never said nowt of the kind.'

'You did...' It had been a whisper; barely even that, more of a dying breath.

Shirl had laughed in that matey way he had. 'I said we might let you bugger off and leave us, but only might, nothing definite. And I only said it to make you find me another lad.'

It had been all Jacob could do to hold in the tears that wanted to burst forth. If he let even one tear slip through, next news he would be howling like a babby, he knew it. He couldn't let that happen. No matter how scared he was, no matter that his thin body ached with dread, like having toothache all over, he had to put on a front, had to look like he didn't care. That was important. Thad used to kick the shit out of weedy lads who showed their fear.

'Fair enough,' he had managed to say. Pretending to see Shirl's side. Pretending to agree. Coward. Jelly-belly.

'Good for you, pipsqueak. I like a fellow who can take it on the chin. And to show you that you're still one of us, here's a little job you can do for me.'

And Shirl had slipped a packet into his sweaty hand. Automatically he had transferred it to his pocket and had gone on his way, dimly aware of the rest of the world, but separated from it by the roar of fear in his ears.

There had been a couple of jobs since then. More or less than there would have been, had Cropper not also been making deliveries? There was no knowing.

Bloody Miss Watson. She should have tried harder.

Bloody Thad. If he hadn't been such an out-and-out rogue, Jacob wouldn't be in this mess now.

Oh aye, and wouldn't you rotten well know it? Here was Shirl, unpeeling himself from the brick wall he had been leaning against. Any moment now, he would grab Jacob round the shoulders in that one-armed hug that might look jolly and brotherly from a distance, but was downright brutal when you were on the receiving end. He made an effort to dodge away, but since he also had to try to look like he wasn't dodging away, he couldn't move far and, lo and behold, Shirl's arm slung itself round his shoulders and clamped itself into position.

'Afternoon, Jemima. Good day at school? Why do you even bother going? Me, I haven't set foot in school since I were ten.'

Was that true? Or just a way of sounding tough? Even Thad had attended school. Well, on and off.

'Still, if you're at school, you must be having lessons, right? It's time to show how clever you are, time to use some of that eddycation.'

Jacob tried and failed to throw off Shirl's arm. 'What d'you mean?'

'I gotta job for you, pipsqueak. And it's the same as your old job, taking a little packet for me, but it's different to your old job, cos you have to take it to a different place.'

'Oh aye?'

'Aye. Weren't you going to tell me?'

Was it his imagination or did Shirl's arm tighten? 'Tell you what?'

Hell's bells, it wasn't imagination. Like lightning, Shirl's arm moved from his shoulders to his neck. Squeeze, squeeze, can't breathe.

'About the orphanage bloke what saw you on Chorlton Green when you was working for me, of course.'

'Oh, that.' Squeeze, squeeze. Jacob blinked at top speed to stop his eyeballs popping out. 'I...I...' He tugged at Shirl's arm. 'Let me... I can't talk if you...' Squeeze, squeeze, can't breathe.

Shirl let go so suddenly, it was all Jacob could do not to drop to the flagstones. He doubled over, gasping, chest heaving, legs wobbling. Snot poured from his nostrils. Grabbing his handkerchief from his pocket, he wiped his face clean, taking a few secret swipes at his eyes to dash away the tears he mustn't let Shirl see.

Bloody Thad. This was his fault.

Shoulders square, Shirl dug his hands in his pockets, elbows sticking out. He might be built like a brute, but he was light on his feet. Perfect for swaggering.

'Well, that tops it all. "Oh, that," he says. "Oh, that." Yes, that, you idiot brain. You was seen by a bloke who knows you, a bloke what works at the sodding orphanage. And it didn't occur to you to tell me? Didn't occur to you that this might be dangerous, eh? Eh?'

'He...he didn't see what was going on, honest.'

'Didn't see? Oh well, that's all right then. Pardon me for making a mountain out of a molehill.' Shirl swept closer, right up to him. One moment he was three or four feet away, next he was dead in front, toe to toe, practically standing on Jacob's feet, his face pushed so close his spots could have jumped ship and embedded themselves in Jacob's flesh. 'You dummy, you idiot, you *Jemima*. How d'you know what he saw, eh? Did he tell you? Did he say, "Well then, young Layton, what a fine day it is and I don't know what you're doing here where you're not meant to be, but I'm sure there's no harm done"? Well? Did he say that? Did he?'

'I know he never saw owt, because—'

'Because what?'

'Because all he saw were me picking up the tanner the man left.'

'He saw *what*?'

Jacob pressed damp palms down his trouser legs. 'That's all he saw, honest to God. And he made me run after the man and give the money back. If he'd...if he'd seen owt else...'

'Are you sure that's all he saw?'

Shirl's face swam in front of Jacob's. No matter where Jacob looked, there it was. He nodded. Gulped. Please let this be over. Please let him not get beaten up. It hadn't been his fault, that time on the Green. He hadn't done anything wrong. He hadn't betrayed Shirl or the gang. Freezing cold water poured into Jacob's puny chest. His heart stopped. That boy who had been killed by the tram...

'Honest injun. He saw nowt else, I swear. How d'you know about him, anyroad?'

'Oh, let me think.' Shirl swaggered away and back again. 'Could it be because you had the wit to tell me? No, wait, it weren't that, cos you're too stupid, aren't you? I said, aren't you?'

'Yes,' Jacob breathed.

'Louder. I can't hear you.'

'Yes.'

'Aye, you're a dimwit, but fortunately for you, me and the price of coal, Danny Cropper has his head screwed on. He told me. He said he'd been seen by yon caretaker and he hadn't been able to deliver his packet as a result. Bloody lucky for him he did tell me an' all, or I'd have broke both his legs. I'd have thought he'd made off with my packet, you see? You do see, don't you? Only you're so thick, I never know what you understand and what you don't. Anyroad, I saw Danny-boy yesterday, just to slip him a little summat to pass on, and he told me something very interesting. Can you guess what it was, Jemima?'

Hell's bells and burnt toast. Why hadn't it occurred to him to tell Shirl himself? He had blurted it out to Cropper when there were just the two of them in the washroom, but he should have thought to tell Shirl. Now he looked stupid for saying nowt and...and what if he looked disloyal? Untrustworthy? What if Shirl decided he wasn't worth the trouble? That boy who had been hit by the tram...

'He told you Mr Abrams had seen me on the Green.' How sulky he sounded, but it wasn't the sulks. It was fear.

'He did – and d'you know why he did? Because he's got summat between his ears, that's why. Unlike you.' Shirl flicked the side of Jacob's head, once, twice, a third time. 'Is there anything in there?' He blew into Jacob's ear. 'Did that come out the other side?'

'Stop it!'

'Whoa there! Did you tell me to stop? Did Jemima just dare tell me what to do?'

'I'm sorry, Shirl. I'm sorry.'

'Well, I'm not sure about that. If you're really sorry, you'll beg pardon on your knees.'

'Shirl…' Shame writhed in his gut.

'Of course, if you're not sorry, well, who knows what might happen?'

Jacob slumped to one knee. At least it might look from a distance like he was tying his shoe-lace. His knee felt warm where a playtime graze had opened up and started bleeding again. Perhaps dirt would get in the wound and go all the way to his heart and kill him.

'Both knees, pipsqueak. If it's worth doing, it's worth doing properly. Didn't they teach you that at school?'

He shuffled onto both knees. Now he was down here, he wanted to get it over with as fast as he could. 'Beg pardon, Shirl.' He made sure to say it out loud. He didn't want any of that 'Louder. I can't hear you' tripe that Shirl was so fond of.

'That's better.' Shirl hoisted him to his feet so abruptly that he almost fell down again. 'This caretaker johnny has seen Danny-boy on Chorlton Green and he's seen you, so that's the end of Chorlton Green. So – and this is where you have to pay attention and show that you aren't as thick as horse-shit after all – the new place for delivering – and this place isn't for Danny-boy; he's being given somewhere else;

this is just for you – is the bench near the cabbies' hut outside the Lloyds.'

'The Lloyds?' squeaked Jacob. 'I can't go up that way. It's too far from the orphanage.'

Shirl shrugged. 'It's no further than Chorlton Green, just in a different direction.' He grinned. Bad breath spewed over Jacob. 'Here's your packet. Off you go to the Lloyds, like a good girl. See you next time, Jemima.'

'How do I look? Will I do?' In the centre of the sitting room carpet, Lucy twirled on the spot, showing off her evening dress. Goodness, the money Lawrence lavished on those girls! The price of those cream kid shoes alone would have fed the Wilton Close household for a week.

'You look like an angel,' said Patience. Typical.

'If angels go in for sparkly gold thread and gold fringing,' Prudence remarked.

Patience tutted at her before gazing once more at Lucy. Prudence didn't miss her soft sigh. Ever the besotted aunt. And it wasn't just their niece she was besotted with: she was head over heels with the dress too. Prudence didn't give two hoots about swanky clothes, but Patience was dazzled by the sight. Not that the sight came their way very often.

And Lucy did look delightful, though why girls these days wanted to wear these drop-waisted dresses was beyond Prudence. Loose-fitting clothes might be less restrictive, but give her smartness any day; and if starch and stays were uncomfortable, so be it. It was a question of standards. Standards were everything.

The sound of a motor approaching made her glance up.

Lucy danced to the bay window. 'Here's Daddy now.'

'Come away from there, please,' said Prudence. 'We don't gawp from the window in this house.'

'She's excited,' Mrs Atwood murmured as Lucy hurried to open the front door. 'She's spending the evening with her family.'

'She could spend a great deal more than that with them if she went home,' Prudence said drily. She didn't wish to be unkind, but it needed saying. It especially needed saying because Mrs Atwood should keep her nose out of other people's family business. It was odd, because she didn't strike Prudence as a nosy parker in other respects, but this wasn't the first time she had barged in with her two penn'orth to make a remark about families. Prudence didn't care for it. It felt like an infringement of her privacy.

Squeals came from the hallway as Lucy and Felicity greeted one another. Honestly, what a fuss. Prudence loved Patience dearly, but she had never greeted her with squeals. She turned her face aside. What an old misery she was.

The door was thrown open and Evelyn swanned in, resplendent in her satin-lined velvet cloak which streamed behind her, revealing heavy silk in a rich green underneath. The girls followed her in, arms linked, as if they would never be parted again, with Lawrence bringing up the rear, ushering them all before him.

The room felt stuffed full. The girls perched on the arms of the sofa and Lawrence stood with his back to the fireplace. Mind you, the seats didn't have to be all occupied for him to do that. It was his favourite position.

'Where are you going?' Patience asked.

'To dinner with the Palmerstons,' Lawrence said without so much as a flicker – as if he hadn't persuaded the Palmerstons to send their daughter Thomasina here earlier this year in an effort to infiltrate their pupil-lodger scheme. 'It's an important evening, which is why I require the whole family to attend.'

'What makes it so important?' Prudence asked, rather thinking she knew the answer.

'Among others, Alderman and Mrs Edwards will be present. He is retiring from his position at the end of this year.'

'And you wish others to see you as his replacement.'

Lawrence wouldn't be drawn. 'If they should see me in that light, it would be an honour to bow to their judgement.'

'I'm sure it would.'

'You all look splendid, I must say,' said Patience.

'Have we got a few minutes?' asked Lucy. 'Fliss, come and see my room.'

'Hold your horses,' said Prudence as the girls jumped up. 'It isn't your room to invite others into, Lucy. It is Mrs Atwood's room, which she is generously allowing you to share for the time being.'

Lucy had the grace to look abashed. Prudence was almost sorry for the reprimand. Almost.

Mrs Atwood laughed. 'Feel free. I shan't mind.' As the girls left the room, she came to her feet. 'I'll join Molly in the dining room. She's squeezing in some typewriting practice before lessons start. I'll see how she's coming along. Excuse me.'

It was a graceful exit, Prudence had to give her that, leaving the family members together.

'Who else will be there this evening?' Patience asked.

'Judge Armitage, Mr and Mrs Wardle – speaking of whom,' said Lawrence, 'I hope you have obliged me by arranging to support that orphanage in some way.'

'I now read to the children once a week,' said Patience.

Lawrence huffed an exaggerated sigh. 'Is that all?'

'Our dear friend Miss Kirby accompanies me.'

Lawrence snorted. 'I don't mind telling you I'm most disappointed. You're respectable spinsters of this parish. In your own small way, you can claim to have a certain standing. Couldn't you do more than read a book and take a friend?'

Normally Prudence would have been hopping mad before he had said even half of this, but not today. Lawrence had played straight into her hands.

'I have the ideal opportunity for you to…' she mustn't say *ingratiate*, 'do something for St Anthony's that will be of far greater use to them than sending a sister with a story-book; something that will be a lasting testament to your legendary social conscience and your desire to undertake good works.'

'The last time you speechified in this way, Prudence, it was to inform me in front of a room full of newspaper reporters that I had set up a business school I knew nothing about.'

She smiled. 'Yes, that was a gratifying moment.'

'What's this about?' Lawrence asked sharply. 'Spit it out.'

'Really, Lawrence, anyone would think you don't trust me. You want to impress the Wardles and your other cronies by making a grand gesture to benefit the orphanage. It so happens I have the perfect opportunity for you and you'll find it's a great deal more impressive than weekly story-telling.'

Chapter Twenty-One

M OLLY COULD HARDLY believe her ears as Mrs Rostron read the letter to her. Mr Lawrence Hesketh, the husband of the lady Mrs Wardle had brought to St Anthony's on Molly's first day, had offered to sponsor the bedroom for a visiting parent or relative.

> *...Blessed as I am to live in my own home with my wife and two beautiful daughters, I regard it as both a duty and a privilege to extend to the less fortunate the possibility of spending more time with the children of their family. I should be grateful if all bills could be sent to me at the above address and I hope you will permit me to visit St Anthony's in due course when the room has been made ready for occupancy, so that I may see for myself the accommodation that is going to make such a difference to the lives and hopes of some of the children in your care...*

Mrs Rostron laid the letter on her blotter; Molly glimpsed strong, sloping handwriting in black ink.

Mrs Rostron looked at her. 'Did you approach Mr Hesketh yourself?'

'No, but he is the brother of the Miss Heskeths who run the business school I attend, and who are also my landladies, so they must have mentioned it to him.'

'A word of warning, Miss Watson. I am not pleased that you discussed orphanage business outside these four walls. That was inappropriate; indeed, it was downright unprofessional. I appreciate that in this particular instance, no harm was incurred and in fact St Anthony's and its children will benefit, but that does not make it right. Kindly remember in future that orphanage matters are confidential.'

But no amount of telling off was going to take the wind out of Molly's sails. Her plan was going to come into being, it really was. Her pulse quickened. She wanted to rush in search of Aaron and share her splendid news. He would be delighted too. Maintaining her composure, she nodded gravely.

'I understand, Mrs Rostron. It shan't happen again.'

Mrs Rostron put the letter to one side. 'I'll compose a reply to this and give it to you later for typing.'

Molly returned to her alcove. Gloomy it might be, and stuffy, and cramped, but who cared? Not Molly Watson. She had just made a difference. When she left St Anthony's and returned to her post at the Board of Health, she would take with her the private satisfaction of having left behind her something that would have a lasting effect on life in the orphanage. Maybe she would have the opportunity to suggest similar arrangements at other orphanages. Maybe she could specialise in working with children. The thought was appealing, reaching deep inside her to a need she hadn't known she possessed.

Later, on the way back from taking letters to the pillar-box, she couldn't resist heading for the workshop. The door stood open. She knocked and leaned inside, her toes just touching the threshold.

'May I come in?'

'I'll come out. I could do with a breather. Is there something I can do for you, Miss Watson?'

'There most certainly is.' She couldn't restrain a broad smile. Her whole face seemed to be crinkling with happiness. 'You can build a bed-frame and a wash-stand...'

She didn't get any further. He made a move and, for one breathless moment, she thought he was about to scoop her up in his arms and swing her round, but then he stepped away.

'Congratulations! That's excellent news. Let me fetch my diary and I'll see when I can get started.' He grinned. 'Don't worry. I shan't keep you waiting. This is far too important.'

He went back into his workshop. Molly stood just inside, watching. He picked up a rag to clean his hands, then plucked a tatty book from a shelf, patting the side of his head as he did so.

'I sometimes keep a pencil behind my ear. Ah, here's one.' Picking up a pencil from among the things on a work surface, he clicked it against his teeth as he frowned over the diary. 'I'll get the materials tomorrow and come in early the next morning to make a start.'

'I can't ask you to do that.'

'You're not. I'm offering. I believe in this project of yours. I want to have it up and running as soon as possible.'

This project of yours. The words warmed her through and through. She wanted to clasp her hands together like an excited child.

Her high spirits stayed with her all day, making her feel more a part of the orphanage. Goodness, but she would be sorry to leave when her time was up.

Six o'clock came and she gathered her things to go home. Aaron, as was often the case, was hacking away at the ivy on the wall. By now, he and the children had cleared as far as the wall beside the bit of no-man's-land between the girls' and boys' playgrounds.

Seeing her, he paused, letting the lopping shears hang by his side and mopping his brow with the back of his other hand.

'Off home?' he asked.

'She is indeed.' And here was Norris coming through the gates. His voice was jolly, but his eyes were sharp, missing nothing. Not that there was anything for him to spot. Molly's breath hitched as if she had been caught out.

She spoke quickly – too quickly. 'Norris, what a surprise.'

'A good one, I hope.'

Unaccountably self-conscious, she felt forced to perform introductions. 'Norris, this is Mr Abrams, the caretaker of St Anthony's.' She turned to Aaron. 'This is Mr Hartley, my...friend.'

Norris chuckled. 'More than a friend, I think you'll find. Much more than a friend.' He nodded at Aaron. 'Don't let us keep you from your work.'

Aaron glanced from Norris to Molly and back again. 'I won't.' With a deft movement, he lifted the shears back into both hands and positioned them ready for the next chop.

Molly tried to catch his eye. 'I'll see you tomorrow.'

'Will do.' A brief glance her way and then his attention was back on his work.

She walked through the gates, not wanting to leave so abruptly, but it was the only way to be sure Norris couldn't take her arm. She didn't want him to take her arm in front of Aaron. Oh, how ridiculous. Her heart clouted the wall of her chest.

'Have you taken the afternoon off work again, Norris?'

'Guilty as charged.' More chuckles. 'You don't blame me, do you? You should be flattered. It isn't every girl who can treat her fiancé the way you've treated me and still have him treating her with such devotion.'

'You're not my fiancé any more.'

'Maybe, maybe not. I haven't given up yet.' He chuckled. 'Never let it be said you aren't being given ample opportunity to change your mind. And there'll be no hard feelings when you do.'

When. Not if. When.

'I'm not going to change my mind. I wish you'd accept that, Norris.'

'Someone got out of the wrong side of the bed this morning. Have you been in a nowty mood all day? That's not like you, Molly. It's a good job I know you so well. It's a good job I know this isn't the real you.'

She stopped and faced him. 'Listen carefully, Norris. This is the real me speaking. Our engagement is over and will never be reinstated. Is that clear? I'm sorry to have hurt you, but it's over.'

His mouth slackened; he shook his head. Swallowed hard. His Adam's apple jerked above his starched collar.

'Is there…is there someone else?'

'What?' The question caught her by surprise. 'No, of course not.'

Norris pulled in a deep breath. He nodded slowly. Had he taken her seriously at last?

Molly had to smile at herself as she stood in the room that was now being referred to as the relatives' room. For all her romantic ideas of supporting those children who had an adult to visit them, the first step couldn't have been more mundane: the room needed a thorough clean.

Mrs Rostron declared, 'It's an opportunity for some of the older girls to use their skills.'

All the girls were taught cleaning as a matter of course, along with basic cooking, so that they would grow up to be competent housewives. They also learned mothercraft, using the babies, tots and smalls for practice. But the cleaning had additional importance, because many of the girls would be put into service when they left the orphanage.

'This was always the case,' said Mrs Rostron, 'but even more so now. There's a servant shortage these days, thanks to all those girls who went into the munitions. During the war, their ideas changed. Many of them refused to go back into service afterwards – as though it isn't a respectable job, with prospects too, if you work hard. Anyway, their newly enlightened views,' and these words were uttered in a wry tone, 'are a boon to us, because it's easier for us to place our girls.'

St Anthony's even had a room, called the parlour, which was set aside specially for this purpose. Never mind cleaning: it could just as easily have been used for history lessons, because entering it was like stepping back in time. The parlour was as crowded as the fussiest, most over-stuffed Victorian sitting room, complete with wax fruit and flowers beneath glass domes, embroidered and tasselled cushions on the buttoned upholstery, and numerous books and knick-knacks displayed on shelves and in cabinets and niches. Dark-leaved plants, a china tea-service, crocheted antimacassars and more brass than you could shake a stick at, all had to be cared for, as well as the polished floorboards, rugs and soft furnishings. Dominating the room was a vast fireplace with three over-mantel shelves covered in ornaments; and the girls cleaned the grate every morning and tended the fire regularly during the day.

'I'll ask some of the girls who are most likely to benefit from the relatives' room,' said Molly. In quiet moments, she had taken to flicking through the children's files, identifying those who had relatives who might have the desire and the cost of their fares to come and visit.

'Firstly,' said Mrs Rostron, 'you shan't ask. You'll choose. Secondly, it's immaterial whether a girl might have a relation to visit her. This is a job that needs doing. When our girls leave here and are in employment, or are lucky enough to find husbands, they won't be able to pick and choose their favourite tasks and ignore what they find hard, inconvenient or unpleasant.'

The girls brushed the floor, walls and corners with a variety of hard- and soft-bristled brushes, then set to with hot water and scrubbing-brushes, the tang of soda crystals lingering in the air to mingle with the diluted vinegar that was used to bring the windows from dull to sparkling.

'When it's dried out, I'll do the whitewashing with a couple of the boy-fourteens,' said Aaron, as they crossed paths in the playground when Molly was returning from the pillar-box.

'I'm coming in on Saturday to help the girls make the curtains,' she said.

'When you've got a few minutes, come to my workshop and I'll show you the plans for the furniture. You can choose the design you want for the headboard.'

How intriguing. She hadn't expected any sort of choice to be involved. She would have suggested coming to look now, except that Mrs Rostron had made it clear that preparing the relatives' room was not to compromise her duties as secretary.

As she went upstairs to return to her alcove, a figure appeared at the top.

'There you are at last, Miss Watson,' boomed Mrs Wardle. 'I've been waiting for you.'

'I wasn't aware you were coming this morning.'

'I don't require an appointment. In my capacity as official visitor, I'm permitted to come and go as I please, which is essential if I am to oversee the day-to-day running of this orphanage.'

'I wasn't aware that was within the remit of the official visitor,' said Molly. 'I thought of the official visitor as more of a general friend, looking for ways to assist the orphanage and reporting any matters of concern to the Committee. Am I mistaken?'

'What you are, young lady, is impertinent. You've kept me waiting with no word of apology. I hope you won't make me regret allowing you to have this position in Miss Allan's absence.'

Heat flushed through Molly's body, swooping into her muscles. 'It was Mr Taylor's decision to send me here.' It was an effort to keep her voice quiet. Be professional. Don't let her rile you.

Mrs Wardle remained in position at the head of the stairs, looking down on her. Molly took a few more steps upwards, but halted when Mrs Wardle didn't budge. That dratted fox-fur slipped on her shoulder, its glassy eyes staring down at Molly.

'Is there something I can help you with?' Molly asked, fastening a glacial smile in position.

'Help? You? After the way you have let me down?'

'Then if there's nothing I can do for you, please would you step aside, so I can return to my desk.'

'Telling me to step aside – the very idea! I haven't finished with you yet.'

This was ridiculous. Molly tried a different tack. 'Mrs Wardle, if you'll just tell me what I've done that has upset you, we can discuss it; but I really can't imagine—'

'Oh, can't you? Did I not say that having a room for visiting relations was inappropriate? Did I not make it clear that such a project was emphatically not to go ahead? And yet what do I find? You have gone behind my back and the room is to be established. Such impertinence. Such – such arrogance. Yes, arrogance. For you, an inexperienced miss, to set yourself up as knowing better than I do, with my years of charitable work, is insupportable.'

'Mrs Rostron doesn't think so. She agrees with me that it will be of benefit to the orphans.'

Molly made herself take a breath. She mustn't get into a slanging match with the orphanage's official visitor. Mrs Wardle was in a position of influence here, not to say power. Mrs Rostron had to work alongside her and would have to do so for a long time after Molly had returned to the Board of Health. She mustn't put that in jeopardy.

'Mrs Wardle, perhaps we could find somewhere more comfortable and discuss this—'

'Don't imagine you can butter me up.'

'I didn't think that for one moment. Allow me to show you the room, so that you can—'

'I don't need to see it, thank you. My mind is made up – as yours should have been after I made my position clear to you. How dare you go behind my back? Who gave you the funding, anyway?'

'A kind benefactor.'

'A deeply misguided benefactor, you mean. You pulled the wool over his eyes, didn't you? You should have referred him to me. It was your duty to do so, both as the secretary here and as an employee of the Board of Health under my guidance and jurisdiction.'

Jurisdiction? She had always known Mrs Wardle had an inflated idea of her own importance, but this really took the biscuit. Nevertheless, she remained calm – on the outside, at least. Inside, her heart was pounding. It was galling to try it, but maybe a touch of flattery would do the trick.

'Mrs Wardle, you of all people have the orphans' best interests at heart. Won't you consider the matter from the children's point of view, and that of their families? Think of poor Mrs Layton, who has lost so much this year – her husband, her home – and now her family has been split apart, and all through no fault of her own. Wouldn't it be a good thing for her to spend more time with her sons? Just an occasional evening and breakfast?'

Mrs Wardle issued a gruff laugh. On her hat, tiny flowers – it was too gloomy here on the staircase to see precisely what kind they were – shivered.

'For your information, Miss Watson, Mrs Layton is a feeble creature who is content to sit back and let others do everything for her. I know this because my friend Mrs Hesketh informed me. It was one of her sisters-in-law who arranged for the Layton boys to be taken in by St Anthony's and her other sister-in-law who found Mrs Layton a position in a neighbour's house. If Mrs Layton wishes to be worthy of assistance, she should apply herself to improving her moral fibre.'

'Then what about the Sullivan children? They have a grown-up half-brother who comes to visit them once a year. Think what it would mean to them if he could stay overnight.'

'What, and build up their hopes that he might take them to live with him? You have a strange idea of kindness.'

'The Cropper family, then.' Surely there was something she could say that would win round this intractable woman. 'Mr Angus Cropper is going to have his nephew to live with him when…when the time comes. Living so far afield, he could only visit if he stayed overnight. It would provide the chance for—'

'Don't tell me: for Daniel Cropper and his uncle to begin to forge an unbreakable bond.'

'I hope so,' Molly said stoutly.

'Daniel Cropper is an undeserving nuisance and if the uncle had anything about him, he would have taken steps to over-ride Mrs Rostron's decision to keep the boy here.'

That was it. Molly had had enough. She was tired of being looked down on by this disagreeable woman. How dare she call herself charitable? How dare she claim to have at heart the best interests of those poor and disadvantaged folk who relied on her and her kind to give them a leg up?

She stood tall, thrusting back her shoulders so that, even though she was obliged to look up at Mrs Wardle, her stance was one of resolve and independence.

'Excuse me, Mrs Wardle. I have matters to attend to.'

'You are not excused. I haven't finished yet.' Mrs Wardle seemed to swell, as if barricading the top of the stairs.

Molly smiled at her, then turned and ran lightly down a few steps, before pausing to look back.

'One last thing, Mrs Wardle. The Cropper lad's name isn't Daniel.'

'What?'

'He's called Danny. I thought you'd like to know.'

This time next week, school would be over. This time next week, he would be out of Shirl's grasp. All summer he would be free and, come September, he would start at St Clement's and never see ruddy Shirl again. And if Shirl made him do a delivery or two before the end of term, so what? He could manage that. He would keep his trap shut an' all; he wouldn't tell Shirl he was going to school in Chorlton in the new school year. Let Shirl hang about waiting for him as much as he liked. He would never find him, would never think of walking down to Chorlton. Even if he did think of it, why would he? Surely Jemima wasn't worth that much bother.

The gloom that had weighed him down in recent weeks had lifted a little and Jacob dared to look ahead, not just to the summer holidays, not just to being freed from his tie to Shirl, but to being able to settle properly into his new life. He wanted normality. He wanted what Mikey had. Mikey worked hard without being a swot and he had a half-time job. Jacob fancied one of those. He had never even considered such a thing when he was with Thad, but now he liked the idea.

He and Mikey both had July birthdays, but both right at the end of the month after the holiday started, so they had never had the birthday slipper at school. Mikey was going to be thirteen and Jacob was going to be twelve. Twelve was the age when you could go half-time at school if you could find an employer to take you on in the afternoons. Imagine! In September, he might not only go to a new school but also to a job, if he could find one and if Mrs Rostron gave her permission. Their sister Belinda had helped Mikey get his job. Would she help him too?

Looking forward to something instead of existing in a fog of dread made him almost giddy at times and he had been ticked off once or twice at the orphanage for larking around, but he couldn't help it. The relief was almost more than he could comprehend.

But the relief turned tail and dashed back into its den pretty sharpish when Shirl appeared on the way home from school. All it took was one glimpse of Shirl's swagger, one eyeful of those blackheads and yellow-headed spots, and all Jacob's fears storming came back to churn his stomach and turn his brain to mush.

Shirl clapped him on the shoulder so hard he staggered. 'Good to see you, pipsqueak. Ready to do a job for me, are you?'

'Yes.'

'That's what I like. Loyalty. Willingness. Cooperation.' Shirl fell in step beside him as though they were the best of mates. 'Looking forward to the end of term, are we?'

'Yes.' And to never seeing you again, you bully.

'Hark at me. "Looking forward, are we?" As if I bother with school! Nah, my school days are long since over. My work never stops, you know. You do know that, don't you, pipsqueak?'

No, he didn't know and he didn't want to. Jacob chewed the inside of his cheek.

'That weren't one of them remarks that doesn't need an answer,' said Shirl. 'It was a question. You do know, don't you, that I don't stop my job just because it's the school holidays? Wait.' He slapped his forehead with the palm of his hand. 'Yes, it was one of those remarks not needing an answer, cos we all know the answer, don't we? I said, don't we?'

The inside of his cheek was swollen. He would have to be careful how he ate or he would chew a socking great hole in himself.

Shirl let out a roar of laughter. 'Go on. Say yes. You've said yes to my other questions. Looks like yes is the only word you can remember.'

'Yes.'

Shirl cupped a hand behind his ear. 'Didn't quite catch that.'

'Yes.'

'Good lad. Good little Jemima. So tell me this: what are you saying yes to?'

'Um...'

'Are you telling me Jemima doesn't know? And yet, Jemima said yes. See, I like that. I appreciate that. Trust: that's what it shows. Obedience.'

Jacob hauled out a crumb of self-respect from somewhere. 'What d'you mean?'

'You mean, what have you said yes to? Think about it. If my work doesn't stop, then yours doesn't either. How could it?'

'But I won't see you, will I? I don't live round here. I'm only here because of school.'

'You're not telling me they keep you locked up inside that orphanage place all summer long, are you? Course they don't. I bet they'd let you out to visit a friend from school.'

'I don't have that kind of friends.'

'Didn't your Thad let you have friends? Well, you know something, Jemima, I'm not like that. I don't mind you having friends, especially friends that help you do your job properly. It's like this, see.'

Shirl looped his arm round Jacob's shoulders. Jacob tensed. One wrong word from him and that arm wouldn't be round his shoulders any more, it would be round his neck.

'You're going to make an arrangement with someone from your class to go round to his house once a week in the summer holidays. If I have a job for you, I'll meet you on your way home.' Shirl whipped away his arm so swiftly that Jacob almost spun round. 'And you know what I'm going to do for you, Jemima? I'm gonna let you choose what day of the week. How's that?'

Aaron picked up one wooden saw-horse in each hand and took them outside into the sunshine. One of the first jobs he had done when he became caretaker here was to clear the area outside the workshop, an area his predecessor had used as a dumping ground for leftover bits and pieces. Aaron had salvaged what he could and treated the children to a bonfire with the rest. Now the area was an extension of his workshop. Nothing was left lying about and he swept up after every job.

He set up the saw-horses the right distance apart, making the calculation by eye. Not like when he was a nipper, working for coppers after school in the wood yard, and needed to use a yardstick for every measurement. The door he was working on was standing propped up against the workshop wall. Grasping its edges firmly, he lifted it and swung it round, placing it across the saw-horses, adjusting it to find the right position.

Then he went indoors to fetch his tool-caddy with all its wood-handled instruments. When he stepped outside again, Miss Watson – Molly – was coming towards him. He shouldn't permit himself to think of her as Molly; suppose it slipped out. Neither should he permit himself a swift glance to admire her slender, upright figure and that unusual colour of hair that he still couldn't put a name to. Not fair, not gold, definitely not red but with perhaps a trace of red in it, giving it that rich hue. The colour seemed to crackle in the sunshine – it really was time to stop looking, if he was going to have daft thoughts like that.

She smiled as she approached and he couldn't help smiling back. He ought to keep his distance, but – well, it was only a smile. Only. As if.

'Morning.' He touched his cap to her.

'Morning.' She glanced at the contents of the tool-caddy. 'They look old.'

'They were my father's tools.'

'What's the matter with the door?'

'Nothing – oh, I see what you mean. No, I'm not mending it. I'm making it. The door on the BB is warped and damaged, so I'm building a new one.'

'I hadn't realised you were...'

'More than a handyman?' The way she pulled herself up before she could put her foot any further in it was endearing. 'I'm a carpenter and joiner and I have the papers to prove it.'

'I didn't mean to suggest—'

He waved his free hand, dismissing it. Putting down the tool-caddy, he turned to her, determined to focus on the task at hand and not those hazel-green eyes. 'You've come to see my plans for the furniture for your room.'

She laughed. 'It isn't my room.'

'It's your idea and you found the money for it. That makes it your room.'

'Actually, someone else saw to the money side of it for me. But yes, I've come to see the plans.'

'I'll bring them out here.' Better than looking at them in the workshop; better than being forced to stand closer to her. 'It'd be a shame to waste the sunshine.'

He fetched the plans, laying the top one on the door. As Molly leaned over, he heard her breath catch. Surprise? Did she like his work? Or was that breath a little hitch of disappointment? Surely she wasn't going to do a Mrs Wardle on him and declare that the visiting relatives wouldn't require – in other words, deserve – anything more than a plain little wash-stand.

The one he had designed stood on squat round feet and had a square base, with four barley-sugar twisted legs stretching up to the top, where there was a hole for the wash-bowl to sit in the middle, a small towel-rail along each side and a hinged looking-glass at the back.

'Don't you like it?' he asked.

'How can you ask? Of course I do.'

'Only you looked at it for such a long time, I thought you must be trying to dream up something polite to say.'

'It's a beauty. It's far more than I expected.'

'All rooms deserve the best furniture and since this is costing only the price of the materials and I'm giving my time for nothing, there's no reason why this wash-stand shouldn't be stylish.' He pulled out another sheet of paper from underneath. 'Here. You need to choose the design for the headboard. I can carve either of these into the board.'

Molly shook her head. 'My dad and my brother are builders. If they could see these... You're a true craftsman. You can't imagine how this has cheered me up. I've gone from a run-in with Mrs Wardle, who thinks the relatives' room is a disgraceful project that should be stopped immediately, to... this. These.' She indicated his drawings. 'You're going to turn the room into something special and remarkable. I'm grateful to you.'

Her eyes were shining, her face radiant. Aaron almost gulped.

'It's a pleasure to work on this project.' How formal he sounded, how stilted. What he meant was, *It's a pleasure to work with you*. But he couldn't say that, mustn't give any indication of what was going on inside him. 'That time you came before you started as secretary, when you arrived with Mrs Wardle and found the children helping me with the ivy and they were all covered in clippings and dust, I thought you were her flunkey.'

'You never!'

'I did. It was the way you whisked the kids off to get them cleaned up.'

'As I recall, I was trying to get them out of an uncomfortable situation. The way Mrs Wardle had a go at you in front of them was inappropriate and I wanted to defuse the situation. You didn't really think I was her flunkey, did you?'

He nodded.

'Well, I hope you realise now that I'm not.'

'I don't think there's any doubt about that,' he said. 'There is one other thing I'd like to tell you.'

'Oh, lord. What now?'

'It's not about you. It's about me, something that I did.' He let out a breath. 'The day I came to Upton's to return the stolen money, I said Danny Cropper wasn't the thief.'

'I remember.'

'And you were so taken aback and guilt-stricken that you didn't think to ask who the real thief was.' He stopped.

'It hardly matters now.' But that little wrinkle of the nose told him her curiosity was piqued.

'It was Danny. He stole it just the way you said he did, by coming into the shop along with a load of other children.'

'Why didn't you say so? Do you have any idea how bad I felt? Not to mention what Mrs Rostron must have thought of me for flinging accusations around.'

'I'm sorry, but I had to protect him.' Would she understand? 'He tried to run away that day, wanting to reach his dad in Southport. I found him and brought him back and told his school and Mrs Rostron that I'd found him playing truant locally.'

'Why not tell the truth? It's not as though it was his first attempt at running away. No one would have been surprised.'

'Exactly. He'd already been in enough trouble. I felt sorry for him, poor kid. He's lost his mum and been sent here, and all he wanted was to get to his father.'

Her eyebrows gathered in, but not in censure. A softening in her eyes said that she understood. 'So you covered up what he'd done.'

'Which involved lying to you and I'm sorry for that.'

'Thank you for telling me.'

His pulse raced as his gaze caught hers. Entranced but fluttering with nerves, he strove to break the moment, reaching out a hand to indicate one of the carvings he had sketched on the top piece of paper.

'I prefer...' he began at the same moment as she reached out to point, saying, 'What about...?'

Their hands brushed, awakening his skin, filling him with new consciousness and longing. Would she move closer? Might her hand...? His own hand moved, ready to meet hers halfway.

Molly took a step backwards, away from him, away from the moment. Had she felt something in that moment? If she had, she clearly wanted nothing from it.

Aaron cleared his throat and bent to fiddle with something, anything, in the tool-caddy. When he straightened up, he flicked a casual hand over the paper. 'This one, then?' Picking up the sheets, he rolled them up loosely.

'I'd better get back to my desk.'

'I'd best get on as well.'

But he didn't, not immediately. He watched her walk away, his heart yearning after her. She still wasn't wearing an engagement ring. That Hartley bloke needed his bumps feeling. He had claimed to be 'much more than a friend', so wasn't it about time he did something about it? If Aaron had been engaged to a beautiful, capable, resourceful girl like Molly Watson, he wouldn't wait five minutes. He would buy her the best ring he could afford so that the world could see how proud he was.

Chapter Twenty-Two

SWINGING A BROWN-PAPER parcel from her fingers by its string, Molly headed for the orphanage, enjoying the early sunshine and the snap of freshness in the air after a dash of rain overnight. As she walked along Beech Road past the rec, the green scent of the rain-washed grass and privet hedges was rich and pure, comforting and invigorating at the same time. It was a day for being outdoors. That was what Dad would have said, but he would also have said that if there was work to be done, it mustn't be put off. Honour your commitments. It was one of the reasons Perkins and Watson was in such demand for its services. Customers appreciated reliability.

Walking through the orphanage gates, she looked automatically for Aaron, who so often started his days with a spot of ivy-clearing. There was no sign of him – well, of course not. Not on a Saturday. He worked the same days she did, Monday to Friday.

She went to find the fourteens who had been assigned to make the curtains, under her supervision, for the relatives' room. Originally, she had also intended that they should make a curtain to go around the lower half of the wash-stand, but having seen Aaron's design, she had ditched this idea. Aaron's wash-stand would be a good-looking piece of furniture and ought to be seen in its entirety.

Rounding a corner, she almost bumped into him. She danced backwards instinctively. What if they had bumped into one another? What if his hands had reached to hold her steady? Mad thoughts!

'I was just thinking about you.' What had made her say that?

'Something good, I hope.'

'Well, not so much about you as about your wash-stand.' What an idiot she sounded. 'What brings you here on a Saturday?'

'I was about to ask you the same question. I told the kids I'd take them to the rec for a game of rounders to celebrate the start of the summer holidays. Want to come?'

'I'm here to supervise the making of the curtains for the new room.'

'I won't keep you, then.'

'Enjoy the rounders. It sounds fun.'

A lot more fun than being stuck indoors making curtains. It didn't seem fair on the girls she had chosen. Should she offer them the chance to play rounders instead? No, Mrs Rostron wouldn't approve of that. Bunking off from a job wouldn't be good for their moral fibre, no matter what the circumstances. Honour your commitments. Molly sighed. That was all very well for an adult, but these were children and their lives were so regimented.

Now that the school holidays had begun, the fourteens were scarily close to the end of their time at St Anthony's. How did they feel? A child with a family could leave school one day and start work the next and come home to the same place. Not so the orphanage children. An essential aspect of placing them in employment was securing their accommodation. All too soon, the girls would be live-in maids in houses and hotels. A few had been found positions as apprentice shop assistants in one of the big department stores in town, which had a dormitory on the top floor where their unmarried girls could live. It was a matter of going from one institution to another for these girls. Every year a number of boys joined the army; this year's contingent was leaving on Monday. Others had been found jobs as apprentices to various trades, as long as they were allowed to sleep under the counter at night. That was the question that coloured every possible job: where was the child to sleep? With no family to care for them, they had to be placed in jobs that included somewhere to lay their heads.

A rising clamour of young voices rang through the corridors, showing the popularity of the outing to play rounders. Molly went in the opposite direction and entered the girls' teaching room, where they learned sewing, knitting and patchwork as well as darning and other repairs. They also copied verses from the Bible in their best script and worked out how to keep a family on a low wage, tackling stacks of budgeting questions that looked far more challenging than any maths problems that had ever confronted Molly at school.

The three girls rose as she came in and dipped their knees to her. She still hadn't got used to be curtseyed to.

'Good morning, girls,' she said, taking off her jacket and hat. 'Thank you for giving up your Saturday morning, especially on such a beautiful day. If we get a move on, we can get this finished by midday and you can have the afternoon to yourselves. Have you got the scissors there, Beatrice? Would you like to open the parcel?'

At least they liked her choice of fabric. That felt like a good start, though Molly's conscience tweaked her. She should have taken the girls with her to the shop to choose. Too late now.

'Let's go upstairs and I'll show you how I measured the windows.'

As cramped as the relatives' room was, for some reason it had two windows. Goodness, but it was going to be chilly in there come the winter. Would it be an imposition on Mr Hesketh's generosity to add an extra blanket to the list?

Back in the teaching room, it soon became obvious that, once the girls had been given instructions, they knew what they were doing.

'It's a nice change to make curtains,' Ruth remarked.

'Better than darning,' agreed Beatrice. 'I'm sick to death of darning the boys' socks. I think they should be taught to darn their own.'

Presently, the door opened and one of the kitchen maids put her head in.

'Please, miss, Mrs Wilkes says she needs a telephone call to the grocer to ask them to send round a tin of baking powder. Dolly's only gone and dropped ours all over the floor and walked in it.'

'Please tell Mrs Wilkes she's welcome to use the telephone.'

'What, Mrs Wilkes? She wouldn't know one end from t'other. She means for you to do it, miss, if you please. Lipton's for preference, but otherwise Aero Baking Powder.'

'I'll see to it.' She got up, glancing round at the girls. At this stage, they didn't need her.

Upstairs, she placed the call. As she walked away, the telephone rang. For a moment, she considered not answering. After all, Mrs Rostron wasn't here today, which meant that, but for the chance that had brought her upstairs at this moment, there would be no one here.

Returning to the desk, she lifted the ear-piece and brought the mouth-piece close to her lips.

'Good morning. St Anthony's Orphanage.'

'I must speak to Mrs Rostron. Is she available?'

'She isn't on duty today. May I take a message?'

A pause, filled by a few faint crackles.

'There hardly seems any point.'

'Who am I speaking to, please?' Molly asked.

'This is the sanatorium in Southport.'

Molly went tingly all over. She straightened. 'Is there news about Mr Cropper?'

'Well, if Mrs Rostron isn't there...'

'You're speaking to her secretary. Has Mr Cropper...has he passed away?'

'No, but things don't look good, if you understand me. Mrs Rostron might wish to prepare the son for bad news. Or she might want to wait until it's over to tell him.'

'Thank you. I'll do what's needed.'

She would indeed. Ending the call, she replaced the earpiece in the holder on the side of the stick and sat perfectly still. Her heart beat steadily, reverberating through her body, filling her with the warmth of resolve. It was time to act. She pulled the telephone towards her and asked the operator to connect her to the Grove Hotel, tapping a fingernail against the desktop as she waited.

'This is highly unsatisfactory,' declared Mr Dallimore when she told him she wouldn't be able to attend that afternoon.

Hanging up, she knew there would be consequences. Her absence from her Saturday afternoon placement would cast the business school in an unfavourable light, but she couldn't think about that now, any more than she could think about the far more important and severe consequences likely to rebound on her here in the orphanage.

What she intended to do was right, she had no doubt about that. It needed to be done and it needed doing right now, this very minute. But she couldn't do it without money. She had only a handful of change in purse, but when she had done the wages yesterday, Mrs Rostron hadn't been here, which meant that, with her own wages unchecked by the superintendent, Molly had put her brown wages-envelope in her drawer. Unlocking the drawer now, she removed the envelope, slit it open and took out her money.

She couldn't tell anybody what she was going to do, yet neither could she go without leaving word. She bit her lip as she weighed her choices. Choices – as if she had loads. Actually, there was one and only one. Hope surged inside her. It didn't matter that there was only one if it was the right one; and it was, oh, it was. No question. She would leave a note for Aaron. He of all people would understand.

She scribbled a few lines, slipped the sheet into an envelope and wrote *A Abrams Esq* on the front. Running downstairs, she went in search of the smalls, finding them with a couple of nursemaids under the supervision of Nanny Mitchell. That was a relief. Nanny Mitchell was kinder than Nanny Duffy.

'Nanny, please would you make sure that this letter is given to Mr Abrams when he comes back from the rec? It's important that he receives it.'

'I can send one of the fourteens to the rec to deliver it.'

'No, it can wait until he comes back.'

One last thing and she would be ready. She returned to the teaching room, hearing giggles as she opened the door though the girls fell silent, heads down over their sewing, when she walked in.

'I'm sorry, girls. I've been called away. If you finish the pattern-matching, so that the curtains look the same when we hang them, and prepare the lining, we can finish off another time.'

'Yes, miss.'

Grabbing her hat and jacket and slinging her handbag over her arm, she hurried from the building and across the playground, heading for the rec. When she arrived, she took a moment to compose herself outside the gates. She must give an impression of calm and normality. Planting a smile on her face, she walked in, her smile automatically expanding into one of genuine pleasure at the sight of the children's game, which was in full swing, with Aaron as umpire and some of the nursemaids sitting in the shade under the trees with the children who had been run out.

Molly made her way around the edge towards those under the trees. Carmel was sitting slightly apart from the rest. Molly went to her, bending quickly to speak to her before Carmel could politely spring to her feet. A few murmured words was all it took. No explanation was necessary, not when the secretary spoke to a nursemaid.

'I need to take Daniel Cropper.'

'Yes, miss.'

It couldn't have been better. Danny was a fielder in the deeps, easy for her to approach without having to say anything to Aaron.

'I want you to come with me,' she said softly.

'But I'm playing, miss, and our team hasn't batted yet.' His face turned up to hers, with an obstinate look that almost smoothed the dent in his chin.

Molly took a side-step, placing herself between the boy and the game, ensuring her back was to the other fielders, so no one would catch so much as a breath of what she said. Not that anyone was near enough, but even so.

'I'm …' A wodge of emotion the size of a tennis ball clogged her throat. She had to squeeze her words around it. 'Danny, I'm taking you to see your dad.'

Danny's eagerness was hard to bear. Molly sat opposite him in the swaying train compartment, her heart torn in two by the transformation she had witnessed. She remembered the first time she had seen him; she had thought then that, if only he didn't look wary, his face would fall naturally into a cheerful expression. It turned out she had been right. Look at him now. Even overshadowed by the man's cap he wore, his pale skin was flushed with anticipation, his eyes aglow. He was positively good-looking.

From the moment his eyes had widened when she promised to bring him to his father, he had burbled non-stop about his beloved dad.

'He used to be a night-watchman. Well, not to start with. Before the war, he worked in a factory, but I don't really remember that. After he came home from fighting, the only job he could get was night-watchman.'

'Where, Danny?'

'Not just for one place, one factory or what have you. You know how sometimes they have to dig a hole in the road? Someone has to watch over it at night to make sure nobody falls in. That's what Dad did.'

'It's a responsible job.'

Danny gave her a knowing look. 'Tell that to the bosses who pay it so poorly. My mum had to take in washing because Dad couldn't earn enough. Not that I'm complaining, mind, and Mum never did neither.'

'You sound proud of him.'

'Aye, I am. There was this one time he organised a dads versus lads football game up our road. To make it fair, the grown-ups weren't allowed to run. I don't know how he did it, but he borrowed a real football from somewhere instead of using a rag-ball. That was the best game of football ever – well, until the ball went through Ma Lambert's window and she chased the whole blinking lot of us down the street, waving her rolling-pin and shrieking blue murder.'

At last Danny subsided into his thoughts, his gaze turned towards the window. Did he see the landscape flying past or was he lost in memories of happier times?

His silence provided a not entirely welcome opportunity for reflection. Her fingers tightened around the handles of the handbag in her lap. What awaited her on their return? Rather than dwell on that, she focused on the child opposite her. Was it her imagination or had his narrow oval face filled out?

Could happiness have plumped up his skin? She smiled at the sight, but her pleasure quickly turned to worry. Oughtn't she to prepare him? Was it fair, was it right, to let his spirits leap so high? But how did you tell a child he was being taken to his father's death-bed? In her head, Mrs Rostron said, 'It takes experience to see what's underneath.' She would know what to say, or not say, in this situation.

Oh lord. She had made off with Danny without so much as a by-your-leave, based on nothing more than an instinct that had flooded her bloodstream, giving her no choice but to act. What if instinct had played her false?

A loose, tingly feeling uncurled in her stomach, but the fear she felt wasn't for herself. It was for this poor lad now in her care. A measure of confidence returned. She must concentrate all her thoughts, all her efforts, on giving him the support he needed to get through whatever today held.

'Danny.' She waited for his eyes to swivel her way.

'You're not allowed to call me Danny. You're meant to call me Daniel. Actually, you're meant to call me Cropper. That's the rules.'

'I know. And when we get back to St Anthony's, I'll obey the rules again, but just for today, wouldn't you rather be called Danny?'

He shrugged – fearing a trick question?

'My name is Molly. It's short for Margaret, but no one has ever called me that. If anyone did, I wouldn't know who they were talking to. So I know what it's like to have your name shortened and to feel that that's the name that belongs to you.'

Danny nodded. 'I was always called Danny until I landed up at the orphanage. Mum and Dad called me Danny and so did the neighbours and my mates at school, but I'm at a different school now.' He gave her a speculative look. 'Can you keep a secret, miss?'

'As long as it isn't something Mrs Rostron ought to be told.'

The brightness of his smile, the way his eyes glowed with mirth, almost took her breath away. Such a good-looking boy! This was how he was meant to be, not ground down with worry and loss.

'You wouldn't be able to spill this secret, miss, not after calling me Danny.'

'Oh aye?' She ought to be stern, but her lips twitched.

'Aye. You see, Mr Abrams calls me Danny an' all. Not when there's anyone else about, like, but when it's just the two of us…which means almost never. But there were two times when he could have got me into deep trouble and he didn't and he called me Danny. He's a good sport.'

'Yes,' she agreed. 'He is.'

Trust Aaron to do his best to help the lad. One occasion would have been after the theft of the money from Upton's. Apparently Danny had needed further support since then. Many a person wouldn't have helped Danny a second time, would have felt he wasn't worth the bother if he couldn't learn his lesson from the first occasion; but Aaron had a bigger heart than that, a greater understanding.

'And then there's this lad that sometimes calls me Danny-boy,' Danny added.

'A friend of yours?'

He squirmed on the fuzzy upholstery. 'Just someone I see sometimes.'

They must be nearing Southport by now. If she intended to give him an inkling of what to expect, she must get on with it.

'Danny, listen. You understand that your dad is very poorly, don't you?'

'Course, miss. That's why he were sent to the sanatorium. He'd have died if he'd stayed put in our house, what with the damp and the stench of the gas-works. That's what Mum said.

That's why she made him say yes when the doctor found a charity to pay for him. She said it was his only chance.'

Molly's heart dipped. Danny's quick response, half cheerful, half obstinate, the set of his chin, the trust in his eyes, all said that the sanatorium was going to make his dad get better, however long it took.

Oh, Danny.

Cords of anguish tightened in her throat. She wanted to reach for his hand. She wanted to sit beside him and gather him to her.

Sitting up straight, leaning forwards a little, she held his gaze as she spoke gently.

'Danny, this is important. I know how much you want to see your dad, but you need to know before we get there that he is very ill.'

'I know that, miss.' The cleft in his chin deepened stubbornly.

She pressed on. 'There was a telephone call from the sanatorium this morning. They...they're worried about him. He's worse than he was and I'm afraid he might be...slipping away. Do you understand?' Her heart thudded. Please don't let her have to be more explicit.

'Look, miss.' Danny sat up, pressing his forehead against the window, squashing the peak of his dad's cap. 'Are we there? Is this Southport?'

Chapter Twenty-Three

THE FIRST TAXI driver refused point-blank to drive them to the sanatorium. Molly's flesh prickled: suppose no one would take them? But she hadn't brought Danny all this way just to fail so close to the end of their journey. Marching purposefully towards the next taxi in the rank outside the station, she made the same request.

'No need to sound so fierce, miss,' said the driver. 'I don't mind going there, but only as far as the gates. You'll have to walk up the drive.'

'Is she taking that child to the san?' said a woman's voice and Molly looked round to see a pair of well-dressed ladies walking past, arm in arm. 'Disgraceful.' The speaker wobbled her shoulders in a dramatic shudder. 'If he catches his death – and I mean that in the most literal sense – on your head be it, young woman.'

Tossing her head, she pulled her friend on their way, leaving Molly staring after her. How could she say something so hurtful, so damaging, in front of a child?

Turning quickly to Danny, she urged, 'Don't listen to her. We'll be perfectly safe.'

Danny ignored her, not out of rudeness, but because he was so fixed on what he had wanted for such a long time. 'You'll take us, mister?' he asked the driver.

'Aye, son. Get in.'

'I've never been in a motor car before,' said Danny, but there was no display of excitement, just concentration that grew more intense by the minute.

As the taxi headed out of town, Danny looked round in agitation.

'Where are we going?'

'It won't be in the town itself,' Molly told him. 'It'll be in the countryside close by.'

'So that the townsfolk don't catch anything?'

'So that the patients have peaceful, healthy surroundings with plenty of fresh air. That's why it's near the sea.'

True to his word, the driver dropped them next to a high brick wall at the foot of a hill. Tall wrought-iron gates stood closed but not locked, each metal pole topped with an arrowhead. Molly paid their fare, adding a tip. She wanted to take Danny's hand to give him reassurance, but he was already pushing the gates open. They clanked, the sound mingling with that of Danny's boots crunching on the gravel drive.

Molly hurried after him.

Above them, partway up the hill, the sanatorium was a long, low building, just a downstairs and an upstairs, presumably with accommodation for the staff under the roof. The windows were large. All along the front of the building stretched a wide verandah on which people lay in beds or reclined in basketwork chairs. Beside Molly, Danny tensed, his head turning swiftly. Lord, if he was hoping to see his father, then he really hadn't absorbed her words on the train, had he? So much for trying to prepare him.

Going up the steps to the verandah, Molly was unpleasantly warm after walking so quickly uphill. It had been breezy in town, but there was no breeze out here: the hill must provide shelter. She approached the double doors, the top two-thirds of which were glassed, which meant the door-knob was unusually low and she had to bend her knees to reach it.

There was no reception desk. A woman in a white uniform dress with a nurse's winged headdress appeared through a doorway.

'Can I help you? Have you made arrangements to visit a patient?' She frowned at Danny. 'We don't permit children to visit.'

Molly gave Danny a nudge and he removed his cap respectfully, screwing it up in fingers that couldn't be still. His feet couldn't keep still either.

'Does the boy need to visit the lavatory?' asked the nurse and it wasn't a kindly enquiry.

'No, thank you,' said Molly. She glanced down at Danny. She didn't want to say this in front of him, but there was no choice. 'Someone from here rang St Anthony's Orphanage in Manchester first thing this morning, with news of one of your patients, a Mr Cropper.'

'Yes?' The nurse's eyes sharpened.

'This is his son, Danny. I've brought him to see his father.'

'This is most irregular.'

'I realise that, but we've come a long way and Danny hasn't seen his dad for some months. Couldn't you please make an exception?'

'We don't allow—'

'You don't allow child visitors – yes, you said. But...' Oh hell, there was nothing for it. Placing her arm lightly around the boy's shoulders, she said, 'The person on the telephone said that Mr Cropper is...might be fading. I've brought Danny to see him.'

'What d'you mean, fading?' The swiftness with which Danny turned to face her almost dislodged Molly's arm. She held on tighter.

'I'm sorry, sweetheart. I tried to tell you before, but I didn't use the right words and, anyway, I don't think you wanted to hear them. Fading means...it means the doctors and nurses have done everything they possibly can to help your dad get better, but he's too ill and they think...he might not live much longer.'

'You mean he's going to die?' Danny demanded. 'Like Mum.'

'I'm afraid so,' Molly whispered, peering anxiously into his face, expecting him to crumple; but Danny's face was a mask. She looked at the nurse. 'Please. You heard him. He lost his mum a few weeks back. That's why he's living in the orphan-age even though he isn't an orphan.'

The nurse's manner softened. 'Sad to say, it looks like that's the most appropriate place for him.'

'You don't mean...?'

'No, Mr Cropper's still with us...for now.' The nurse stepped across the corridor and opened a door. 'Sit down while I see what I can do.'

Like the corridor, the floor of the room was covered in linoleum. On the wall was a poster with a picture of the head and shoulders of a man clutching a handkerchief to his mouth. At the top it said in thick black capitals PREVENT DISEASE. Beneath the picture were the words *INFLUENZA and TUBERCULOSIS are Spread by Thoughtless Coughing, Sneezing and Spitting.* Thoughtless spitting? Ugh!

Too anxious to sit, they awaited the return of the nurse. Molly watched Danny from the corner of her eye. Should she speak? Try to offer comfort? But his closed expression told her not to attempt it.

Two sets of footsteps sounded in the corridor. Molly placed a hand on Danny's shoulder to remind him not to go flying towards them. The nurse reappeared, preceded by another nurse, this one in a dark blue uniform, her starched headdress more elaborate.

The first nurse barely had time to say, 'These are the people I...' before the newcomer, having briefly taken in their appear-ance from head to toe, said, 'I understand you've come a fair distance to see Mr Cropper. I can honestly say it's the first time one of our charity patients has had visitors.'

'May we see him?' Molly asked. 'Just for a minute.' Her hand tightened on Danny's shoulder as the boy made a movement of protest. 'Danny lost his mother a few weeks ago, so this is even more important.'

'How old are you, boy?'

'Nearly eleven, miss.'

The nurse glanced at her colleague. 'Undersized. Well, since you've come all this way, I'll permit it just this once.'

Molly forbore to say that this once was all they required. 'Thank you.'

'Nurse Peters will show you where to go.'

They followed Nurse Peters along the corridor towards the back of the building. Presumably the verandah was saved for paying patients, or possibly for those for whom there was still hope. They turned a couple of corners; the corners were rounded, not angled. The joins between floor and wall, and wall and ceiling, were curved as well – nowhere for dust and germs to hide.

As they rounded another corner, Nurse Peters came to a halt.

'Mr Cropper is along here. You need to be quiet.'

Further along was a door, but instead of opening it, Nurse Peters took them to a window alongside it.

'You can see him from here.'

Molly looked through at a plain white room, again without an angle to be seen. On the far side, French doors were open to the fresh air. There was no furniture except for a bed containing a still figure, arms neatly lying by his sides on top of the bedclothes. Good God, had he already passed away?

'I can't see, miss,' said Danny. 'Can I go in?'

'That's not allowed,' said Nurse Peters. 'You might catch it.'

'If you open the door, could he stand in the doorway?' Molly begged. 'I promise not to let him set foot inside.'

'I'll fetch a stool for him to stand on. You're on your honour not to budge from this spot.'

'We won't,' Molly promised.

A minute later, Nurse Peters returned with a wooden stool, which she placed beneath the window.

'There. I'll let you have a few minutes.'

As she walked away, Danny jumped onto the stool. It wobbled and Molly instinctively put out her hands to steady him, but he was already leaning towards the window that separated him from his dad, his fingers resting on the sill as if he were about to play the piano, his nose glued to the glass.

'He doesn't know we're here.' Danny tapped on the pane, then tapped louder. 'Dad! Dad!'

'Keep your voice down or we'll be asked to leave.'

'There's no one else here.'

No one else here. The words cut into Molly's heart. Poor Mr Cropper was known to be dying and there was no one else here. If she hadn't brought Danny, there truly would be no one here at all. A sense of resolve speared through her. Bringing Danny had been the right thing. She had known it all along, but now the knowledge filled her bones.

'He went to live in the lean-to when he knew what was wrong with him,' said Danny, his eyes never leaving the figure under the bedclothes.

'He what?'

'You can't stay with other folk when you've got what he's got. You have to keep yourself separate, so he went to live in the lean-to.'

In the lean-to. Molly shut her eyes against the picture in her head. How ignorant she was about the lives of the poor. For all that she was employed by the Board of Health, she still had so much to learn. And she would learn it. She was going to be a useful and effective member of staff, someone the poor were glad to see, because they knew she could be trusted.

The hairs stood up one at a time along her arms. Had Mr Cropper's chest stopped moving? Had he…? Was he…? The tiniest rise and fall sent relief cascading through her. A sideways glance at Danny showed he hadn't shared her fear. The boy's forehead was fastened to the window, his breath steaming the pane. He took a moment to lean away and rub the glass clean before leaning against it once more.

'D'you think he knows we're here?'

Molly wanted to say yes, not because she believed it but because she wanted Danny to believe it; but Danny wasn't the sort you could lie to and get away with it. If he detected an untruth, his reaction would be scorn and disgust.

'I don't know. I hope so.'

Clenching his fist, Danny rapped his knuckles sharply on the glass. 'Dad!'

Molly snatched at his hand, trying to still it, but he wrenched it free and carried on banging. What if he broke the glass?

'Look, miss – look!'

Danny went utterly still as, inside the room, Mr Cropper slowly, agonisingly slowly, turned his head. Molly held her breath, her heart beating strongly as if it could beat for Mr Cropper too. His head was turned towards the window – well, not quite, but if he moved his eyes, he would see his son.

'He's looking. He's looking!' cried Danny, raising himself on tiptoe and plastering himself against the pane.

Could Mr Cropper see? Could his eyes focus? Could he… could he give some indication that he knew Danny was here with him as his life drew to its close? Anything, a nod, the smallest movement of his hand. Molly willed him to make a sign. There was nothing, but that didn't mean he couldn't see.

'Wave to him,' she urged Danny. 'Give him a big smile. We haven't come all this way to show your dad a long face. A smile will cheer him up.'

She stared again at Mr Cropper, willing him to make a sign, just a small acknowledgement that Danny would remember with love and gratitude for the rest of his life, but still there was no signal. She focused on the sick man's chest. Nothing. No movement. Wait – yes, a breath. Shallow, barely there, but a breath nonetheless.

'Hey, Dad, I'm here,' Danny called, mouth close to the glass. He swung round to face Molly. 'D'you think he'll get better now? He's got a reason to, hasn't he, now that he's seen me?'

'Oh, Danny...'

She didn't know what to say and even if she had known, she couldn't have said it without bawling. Tears were clamouring for release and it was all she could do to keep them locked in. Fortunately, Danny didn't require an answer. He had looked her way for no more than a couple of seconds before turning his attention back to the beloved dad he had waited so long to see.

'Look!' It came out not as an exclamation but on a pro-longed breath as Danny plastered himself against the window. 'Dad's hand – he's moving.'

Molly stared. The child was mistaken – no, wait. Mr Cropper's arms lay flat on top of the bedding and the fingers of the hand nearer to the window had lifted ever so slightly, the palm still on the bed. The fingers didn't wave or even wiggle, just lifted a fraction, then dropped back. But it was enough. It was a message from father to son.

'He knows you've come to see him,' Molly whispered. 'That proves it.'

Blowing out a long, slow breath to compose herself, she resumed her task of watching Mr Cropper's chest. Nothing, nothing...a shallow breath. Nothing, nothing...a shallow breath. Nothing, nothing...nothing...a shallow breath. Nothing, nothing...nothing. Nothing. The tiniest movement of the chest. Nothing. Nothing...Nothing.

She counted to a hundred.

Nothing.

'Danny, stay here, will you? I won't be gone long. Promise me you won't move.'

She went in search of Nurse Peters, finding another white-uniformed nurse on the way.

'Excuse me. It's Mr Cropper. I think...I think he might have died. Could you please come?'

'Of course. I have to fetch the doctor to pronounce life extinct. Wait here for me.'

Molly did no such thing. She went straight back to Danny, touching his arm. When that didn't rouse his attention, she gently shook it.

'It's almost time to go. Wave to Dad and tell him goodbye.' The backs of her eyes were red-hot as her locked-in tears surged. She fought them down. This wasn't her situation; it wasn't her grief. She had to be strong for Danny.

'I'm not ready yet.' The face he turned to her was twisted with fury.

'I know, but you have to come now. Look, here's the doctor to check up on your dad. That has to be private. It's the rules. Say goodbye and come with me.'

Danny looked through the window again. 'Bye, Dad.' He waved vigorously. 'I'll be back after the doctor's been.'

Molly grasped his arm and at last he climbed down, the nurse and doctor arriving outside the room at the same moment. The doctor walked straight in, but Molly stopped the nurse.

'This is Mr Cropper's son. If we wait in the room by the front door, could you please come and tell us...'

It looked as if the nurse might say no, but she nodded and followed the doctor. She closed the door behind her, which was just as well because Danny pulled in that direction, but Molly held onto his arm.

'I know how much you want to stay, but don't let me down now. They let you in even though they don't allow children to visit. Don't spoil it or – or it'll prove to them they were right in the first place and the next time a child is brought here to visit their mum or dad, they won't be allowed.'

That got through to him and he permitted her to lead him away. Back in the room where they had started, Molly left the door open. Danny slumped onto a chair, hunched over. His shaking shoulders suggested that tears were falling, but everything about him demanded to be left alone. Molly stayed on her feet, taking a few paces every now and then, unable to be still. When would the nurse come? Had she forgotten them?

Footsteps. Molly went quickly to the open doorway, but Danny was quicker.

'Can I go back?'

The nurse brushed past him. Addressing Molly, she said, 'You were right. Mr Cropper has passed away peacefully.'

Like a whirlwind, Danny threw himself in front of her. 'Passed away? You mean Dad's dead? He can't be. I was just there, with him… He can't be.'

Molly caught hold of his shoulders. 'I'm so sorry, Danny. He's gone.'

'Gone? You mean he's died? He's dead?'

She nodded. 'You were there with him right till the end. Your face was the last thing he saw. He knew you were with him.'

'But I wasn't.' With an almighty push, he freed himself from her hands. 'I wasn't there. The doctor came and you took me away. You made me leave him and I wasn't there. He needed me and I wasn't there. You made me leave him – you – you made me – and I wasn't there.'

There they were at last, trailing through the summer twilight. Aaron ran up the road to meet them. They looked exhausted, the pair of them. Well, it was hardly surprising after such a long day, though the amount of time must have been nothing compared to the emotional impact on Danny of losing his father. Had they got to the sanatorium in time? Ever since he had opened Molly's note shortly before midday, Aaron had been able to think of little else.

Slowing as he reached them, Aaron felt pulled in a dozen different directions. It had been one hell of an afternoon. He had tried to conceal Danny's absence and might have succeeded if Jacob Layton hadn't looked round for Danny in the dining room at dinner-time. At that point, Aaron knew he had to confide in Nanny Mitchell. What the end result would be when Mrs Rostron was informed, he didn't like to think.

Right now, that didn't matter. All the mattered was that Molly had brought Danny back safely. The poor lad looked done in, shrunken, his clothes hanging off him. Molly held herself upright but the strain in her face was clear to see and the hazel-green of her eyes had turned to sludge.

'You're back. That's good.' Aaron put on a cheerful voice for Danny's benefit. 'Let's get you indoors and you can tell me what's happened.'

He looked at Molly over the boy's head. She gave him a slight nod. Yes, Danny's dad was dead? Yes, they had got there in time? He wished Danny was younger so he could pick him up and carry him. As it was, all he could do was sling a friendly arm around the boy's shoulders.

'I'm under orders to take you straight to the nannies' sitting room.'

'Oh, no,' said Danny and the look on Molly's face said the same.

'You aren't in trouble, son, but you've had a long, hard day and Nanny Mitchell wants to see that you're all right.'

He glanced at Molly. The fiancé would have the job of seeing that she was all right, blast him. There was nothing Aaron wanted more than to sit quietly with Molly beside him on a sofa, so he could put his arm round her and listen while she poured out what had happened, let her lean against him, hold her if she wept. He wouldn't take advantage. He wanted only to be the one she turned to, the one she needed, the one she relied on now and always.

Blast the fiancé.

Carmel was waiting for them outside the nannies' sitting room.

'Nanny Mitchell says to go straight inside. She's doing her nursery visit at the moment. I'm to arrange for a tray for Danny. Sweet tea with egg on toast.'

'Thanks, Nurse Carmel.' Aaron opened the door for the others and followed them in. 'Sit down, Danny.'

Danny looked round uncertainly. The nannies' sitting room was small and cosy, a place for the nannies to retreat to for a private word or a cup of tea. No child ever came in here and Danny's rigid posture and the way he repeatedly fisted and loosened his hands was the picture of unease.

Aaron pressed the boy into a chair. 'Sit. You too,' he added to Molly.

Clutching his cap between his fingers, Danny suddenly sprang upright in the chair, his back pencil-straight. 'Mum's photograph. What about Mum's photograph?'

'What photograph?' asked Molly.

'There was a photograph of his mum that Danny is sure was sent to the sanatorium for his dad.'

'After she died, the man and the lady that brought me here said they'd put her photograph in with my things, but they hadn't. They'd put Auntie Betty's picture in instead. So that means they must have sent Mum's picture to the sanatorium for Dad.'

Aaron met Molly's frown and shook his head. Don't let her disabuse the lad of his fantasy. No, of course she wouldn't.

'What will happen to Mr Cropper's effects?' he asked.

There was a pause before Molly answered. 'Because of the nature of his illness, the clothes he arrived in will now be burned.'

'But not the photograph,' said Danny. 'The picture were inside a frame with glass in front, so it wouldn't have got any germs on it. No one will have coughed on it or spat on it. That was what it said on that poster. No thoughtless spitting. Can you get the picture back for me? I don't mind having Auntie Betty's picture, because she were my mum's older sister that fetched her up after my grandma died, but I want Mum's picture too. I don't mean no disrespect to Auntie Betty, but Mum's is more important.'

'Of course it is,' said Molly. 'Are you sure it was sent to the sanatorium?'

'Course it was. Stands to reason.'

Aaron and Molly exchanged a hopeless glance.

Molly came to her feet. 'Tell you what. You stay here and I'll place a telephone call to the sanatorium. How about that?'

'Thanks, miss.'

Aaron opened the door for her, stepping outside and holding the door shut behind him as he whispered, 'Goodness knows what happened to that picture. The people who brought Danny here told him they had given him his mum's photograph, but when he unpacked, it was Auntie Betty's instead.'

'We'll have to play along,' she whispered back. 'I'll make it as easy on him as I can.'

She disappeared and Aaron returned to Danny. The determined glint in the lad's eyes said he had pinned his hopes on having his mum's picture restored to him.

A few minutes later, Molly slipped into the room. Without looking at Aaron, she went straight to Danny. She sat beside him and, before he could object, took his hand in hers, capturing his gaze with hers in a way that held him still and quiet.

'I've spoken to Nurse Peters at the sanatorium. You remember her? She told me what a great comfort it was to your father to have your mum's photograph close by. She said that when he was stronger, he used to look at it for hours on end while he remembered all about his life and the family he loved so much.'

'Me and Mum.'

'You and your mum. The thing is, Danny – and you can blame me for this, if you like – they didn't know at the sanatorium that you'd want the photograph afterwards, so they put it in your dad's coffin with him. When someone dies at the sanatorium, they're put in a coffin straight away. It has to be like that, because of all those sick people. I didn't know about the photograph, you see, or I'd have asked for it; and now it's too late, because it's in with your dad. So...' She swallowed, blinked.

Aaron stepped forward, kneeling in front of the pair of them. 'So they're together. I know how much you wanted the picture, Danny, but it's in the next best place. Is that all right?'

Eyes brimming, Danny nodded. His body lurched and Molly caught him in her arms as, with an almighty sob, he gave in to his grief.

Chapter Twenty-Four

HELL'S BELLS AND burnt toast. Cropper's old man couldn't have chosen a worse moment to pop his clogs. What if Daniel was too upset to do the job? Would Shirl make Jacob do it all on his own? Or – and this seemed highly likely – would Shirl not give a monkey's about Daniel's bereavement and insist he did it anyway? Jacob wouldn't put anything past Shirl, up to and including shoving an unreliable kid in front of a tram. An animal scream started to build up in his depths. He tensed every muscle he possessed to hold it in. The thought of that boy who had been splatted by the tram haunted him day and night. Had Shirl pushed him? Had he?

The one good thing about old man Cropper's death was that the funeral was happening miles away in Southport, so it was nothing to do with Daniel. Even so, Jacob felt itchy inside. It wasn't right to be buried so far from your folks, with no one to come and see you on a Sunday afternoon. Having spent his entire life yawning over how blinking boring it was to visit graves, especially on Christmas morning, he was surprised by how unsettling he found it to think of Daniel Cropper not being able to go and see his dad's headstone. If he had one. Maybe Mr Cropper would be given a pauper's burial; or maybe the sanatorium had its own cemetery, like the work-houses used to.

'Bet you anything he's been cremated,' announced Philip Eckersley. 'That's what they do when you die of a terrible disease. If they bury you, the disease will make the ground go all rotten, so they have to burn you instead. And if you're poor, they just stick you on the bonfire.'

'Really?' gasped Jacob. Surely not.

'Really. And them that die close to Bonfire Night are saved up and put on top of the bonfire like so many guys.' Eckers-like nodded and Jacob didn't dare challenge him in case it turned out to be true. Eckers-like sounded deadly serious.

They said prayers in church on Sunday morning for the repose of Mr Cropper's soul and everyone looked at Daniel, causing Nanny Mitchell to utter a soft but compelling murmur of reprimand that had all eyes front and centre in an instant.

Back at St Anthony's, Jacob got Daniel on his own.

'You're still going to do it, aren't you?'

'Do what?'

Was he being thick on purpose? 'The job. Shirl's job. You know.'

'Oh, that.'

Oh, that? *Oh, that?* How could he be so off-hand? 'You have to do it,' Jacob insisted, his voice low and urgent. 'You know what Shirl's like. You might be safe with your uncle a million miles away, but Shirl will take it out on me if you don't do this job. I'm the one who got you involved.'

Jacob had another reason for wanting Daniel by his side. This job was the worst ever. Not that he knew the details yet. But he sensed it.

'There'll be no more delivering for you, Jemima,' Shirl had said.

'But I thought...' He had just got used to trailing along to the bench by the cabbies' hut in front of the Lloyds, and now he wasn't going to do it any more? He ought to be pleased. He ought to be ruddy well running round in circles and jumping for joy, but he knew Shirl better than that by now.

'Nah, best not, not with you and Danny-boy Cropper both being seen on Chorlton Green.'

'Then why did you send me to the Lloyds? I mean, if I'd already been seen—'

'Are you questioning my decisions, Jemima?' Shirl delivered a swift slap round the back of Jacob's head that made his teeth snap together with a sharp click. 'Are you suggesting I don't know what I'm doing?' His hand hovered threateningly.

'Course not.' Jacob had done his best not to flinch but couldn't stop his face screwing up in anticipation of a second blow. At that point he couldn't tell what the ruddy heck was going on. First he had been given a new delivery place, now he wasn't going to be sent there again. What had Shirl got in store?

What Shirl had in store had turned out to be far worse than anything that Jacob had gone through so far.

'You and Danny-boy are going to do a job together,' Shirl had told him. 'An important job. How does that sound? He's not a lily-livered scaredy-cat like you, so you should be pleased. He's the one who should be kicking up, having to work with a Jemima instead of a real lad.'

What this job was, Jacob didn't know and neither did Daniel. Not that Daniel seemed bothered.

He shrugged. 'I don't need the money no more, now my dad's dead.'

Panic streamed through Jacob. 'But—'

'I only did it for the money. I was saving up to run away to Southport.'

'You can't leave me to do it on my own. 'Sides, Shirl'd never let you. You don't know what he does to boys what try to leave.'

'I won't be here for him to do anything to me, though, will I?'

Daniel Cropper wouldn't be at the orphanage much longer, because his uncle was going to come and fetch him. Daniel was going to be adopted. He was going to live miles and miles away, nearly in Scotland, the lucky bugger, where he could forget all about Shirl and his jobs. He would be safe.

And Jacob, pathetic Jemima, would be left here all on his own.

Molly slept poorly on Sunday night, full of worry about facing the music on Monday. She hadn't said anything in Wilton Close about her escapade with Danny Cropper. Miss Patience would be deeply sympathetic to the child's plight and would understand Molly's reasons for spiriting him away, even if she didn't condone them; but Miss Hesketh wouldn't be so generous. She was a stickler for the rules. Molly hadn't breathed a word to Vivienne either, not wanting to delve into the rights and wrongs of the situation, especially when there were likely to be so many more wrongs than rights; though no amount of wrongs could outweigh the simple, inarguable right that Danny Cropper and his father had needed to be reunited in those final moments of Mr Cropper's life. Or did that make her sound holier than thou?

Monday was another fine morning. Molly set off earlier than usual. If she could be at her desk before Mrs Rostron arrived, then she would have the chance to tell the superintendent what had happened before Mrs Rostron could hear it from anybody else. Owning up would surely go in her favour.

No such luck. As she rounded the top of the stairs and walked along the dingy landing to her alcove, the superintendent's door opened and Mrs Rostron appeared. She didn't leave the doorway, but merely said, 'I'd like to speak to you, please, Miss Watson.'

Molly experienced a dropping sensation in her torso, but she held her shoulders back and her chin up as she walked towards the office door. Mrs Rostron had closed it, which meant she had to knock and wait, even though there could have been no doubt that she would obey the summons immediately. A taste of Mrs Rostron's displeasure? No doubt.

'Sit down.' Barely allowing time for her to do this, Mrs Rostron began. 'I'm aware of what took place on Saturday. Nanny Mitchell was responsible for St Anthony's all weekend and she sent for me yesterday to inform me.'

'Oh. I had hoped to be the one to tell you.'

'Indeed? And you considered it to be something that could wait until Monday?'

That stung. 'Given that I brought Danny back safely, yes.'

'Danny? So, on top of removing the child from the premises, you have also developed a personal relationship with him to the extent of bestowing a pet-name on him.'

'With respect, Mrs Rostron, it isn't a pet-name. It's the name he was known by before he came here.'

Mrs Rostron lifted her eyebrows. 'You took it upon yourself to take Daniel Cropper to Southport. You had no authority to do so and the fact that you did it without reference to Nanny Mitchell shows that you were aware you were acting irresponsibly.'

'I did leave a note.'

'I believe so. Tell me, to whom was it addressed?' As if she didn't know.

'Mr Abrams.'

'An interesting choice. You left word, not for the person in charge, but for the caretaker. You attend the local business school for surplus girls, don't you, Miss Watson?'

That took her by surprise. 'Yes.' What now?

'So that is where you learn your work practices. I've a good mind to write and complain.'

'Oh please don't. This is nothing to do with the Miss Heskeths.'

'Have they taught you nothing about your responsibility to your place of work?'

Heat prickled the inside of her cheeks. 'Of course they have. The first duty of an employee is to act with integrity at all times.'

'And yet you saw fit to remove a child from these premises and make off with him.'

'That makes it sound like a kidnapping.'

'You took a child with neither the knowledge nor the consent of the person responsible for his welfare, who on that particular day was Nanny Mitchell, acting in my stead.'

She tried a different tack. 'I realise I—'

'Let's forget the present tense, shall we? You said "I realise". Wouldn't it be honest to say "I realised" – unless you're going to pretend you didn't realise at the time the nature of what you were doing?'

'No, I'm not going to suggest that.' The muscles in her shoulders had tightened to the point where they might snap if she made a wrong move. 'All I'm saying is that perhaps integrity isn't necessarily all that straightforward. Taking Daniel Cropper to the bedside of his dying father was the right thing to do; and to that extent, I did act with integrity.'

'With compassion, perhaps; with impetuosity, certainly. As for integrity: people who act with integrity aren't reduced to leaving notes for the caretaker when they ought to explain the situation in person to the member of staff in charge.'

'But—'

'But what? But Nanny Mitchell wouldn't have given her permission? Of course she wouldn't. It isn't her place to make decisions of that nature. Such a decision would be mine alone… had I been permitted to make it. This is what should have happened on Saturday morning. When you answered the telephone, you should have fetched Nanny Mitchell immediately; then she, not you, would have held the conversation with the sanatorium, at the end of which she would have sent for me, so that I could place my own call to the sanatorium and decide how to act.'

'May I ask,' Molly ventured, 'what you would have done?'

'Are you seeking reassurance that your little adventure was the right course of action? I can assure you of one thing: had I spoken to the sanatorium, my side of the conversation would have been a great deal more informed than yours could possibly have been. Would I have taken Daniel Cropper to Southport? The point is, Miss Watson, that it was my decision to make, not yours.'

'I realise I acted impulsively. I apologise.'

'You apologise for the impulse but not, I note, for the action. Not that it makes any difference. You cannot possibly remain here in the capacity of secretary if I cannot trust you implicitly, and clearly I cannot.'

Molly's skin tingled from head to toe. 'Mrs Rostron...'

'And now you should take yourself off to the Town Hall. By the time you arrive, I will have spoken to Mr Taylor on the telephone.'

Dismissed. Sacked. Not given notice. Just told to go and not come back. Molly didn't know whether she was more shocked or ashamed. She had known she was – what? Taking a risk? Acting beyond her responsibility? – when she took Danny to Southport, but she had never pictured this as the outcome. A dressing-down, yes, but not dismissal.

As if her interview with Mr Taylor wasn't painful enough, who should barge into his office but Mrs Wardle. Typical. As outraged as she had been by Molly's transgression, she was equally vexed, it seemed, with poor Mr Taylor.

'This is what comes of not listening to me at the interview stage,' she berated him. 'I told you Miss Watson wasn't suit-able, but did you listen? No, you did not, and now look where we are. The reputation of the Board of Health hangs in the balance, thanks to your preferred candidate.'

Mr Taylor made an effort. 'I think that's an exaggeration, don't you?'

'No,' Mrs Wardle snapped. 'If this Board of Health gets shut down and the old Board of Guardians reinstated, we'll all know whom to blame, won't we?'

'I really must protest,' bleated the hapless Mr Taylor. 'There is no question—'

'Defending her, are you? Defending the creature who has let us all down so badly, not to mention publicly.'

Two pairs of eyes swivelled in her direction; three, if you included the glassy eyes of the fox-fur. Molly stood up, clinging to what remained of her self-respect.

'If you'll excuse me, I'll leave now.'

'I haven't said half of what I intend to say,' boomed Mrs Wardle.

'And yet I understood it as if you'd said every word,' Molly murmured, making her way from the room and shutting the door on Mrs Wardle's wrath.

She tried to slip away unnoticed, but Vivienne pounced on her, demanding to know what had happened. Feeling by this time like a wrung-out dishcloth, she pulled Vivienne out of the department's territory before she spilled out the sorry tale to her friend.

'What were you thinking, taking the boy like that?' Vivienne exclaimed. Her blue-grey eyes were full of concern, but there was censure in her voice too, which Molly knew she richly deserved.

'We can't discuss it now. You have to get back into the office or I won't be the only one in trouble. Just one thing. Don't say anything at home. Leave it to me to tell the ladies.'

'Wouldn't dream of saying a word. It's your news to tell. Oh, Molly.'

To her surprise, Vivienne gave her a hug before hurrying back the way they had come. Molly watched her go, almost unbearably moved by the show of affection. She headed downstairs – for the final time. She had lost her job. She had to stop on the stairs, too wobbly to trust herself not to stumble. Oh well, this wouldn't get the baby bathed. She had to break the news to her family as well as the Miss Heskeths. But first, she had to collect her few bits and bobs from St Anthony's. What were her chances of getting in and out without seeing anyone?

But her conscience wouldn't permit that.

Stopping Carmel in the corridor, she asked where Nanny Mitchell was.

Carmel's eyes widened. 'With the smalls. Is it true you've been...you're leaving?'

'I'm afraid so. I need to see Nanny Mitchell first. Would you mind asking her?'

Carmel scurried away, returning to say, 'You're to wait for her outside the nannies' room.'

Standing outside the nannies' sitting room was like waiting outside the headmaster's office. Nanny Mitchell swept down the corridor without acknowledging her. She opened the door, throwing a brusque 'Come in' over her shoulder.

Molly followed her into the room where, less than forty-eight hours earlier, she had held Danny in her arms while he sobbed his heart out. How was he coping with his loss? Nanny Mitchell sat down, perching her ample behind on the edge of a chair, as if prepared to leap up and dash back to her duties at the first opportunity.

'I want to apologise for what happened on Saturday,' Molly began.

'I should think so too,' snapped the usually genial nanny. 'Do you have any idea of the position you put me in? You ignored my authority.'

'I know.'

'No, you don't. Mrs Rostron has questioned my ability to take responsibility for St Anthony's in her absence.'

Molly caught her breath. 'But it wasn't anything to do with you.'

'It was – or should have been. You should have come to me as soon as you took that telephone call. The wrongdoing was completely on your side, but it occurred while I was in charge and that makes it my responsibility. I had to go to Mrs Rostron's office and explain myself.'

'Explain yourself?'

'You rode roughshod over my authority, so I had to face a discussion about whether I'm fit to carry that authority. You can't leave someone in charge if the staff don't respect them.'

'But I do respect you.'

'So much so that you sneaked off to Southport with one of the children, leaving your confession for the attention of the caretaker, if you please.'

Molly was stumped for something even halfway adequate to say.

'You may well stand there gawping,' sniffed Nanny Mitchell. She stood up. 'And now I'll return to my work.'

Before she could reach the door, Molly put her hand on her arm. Nanny Mitchell slowly turned her head and looked down at Molly's hand until Molly let it drop away.

'I'm truly sorry for the trouble I caused,' she said quietly. 'All I could think of was what Danny – Daniel Cropper needed most.'

'Well, I hope it was worth it, Miss Watson, because you've paid a high price.'

'Will you tell Dad for me?' A knot of guilt ached in Molly's throat, but she had to ask. She had to lump the horrible responsibility onto Mum's shoulders. To make it worse, Auntie Faith was here to witness the Watsons' shame. No – her presence made it better, because Mum would have someone to lean on when Molly left. But it also meant that Gran would soon know, and Dora, and everyone. Mum and Dad would have no time to huddle together and get used to it in private.

Mum roused herself from the crumpled position she had slumped into in the armchair, hauling herself upright. 'Oh aye? Too ashamed to tell him yourself? I'm not surprised.'

'It's not that. I have to get back to Wilton Close. In fairness to Vivienne, I have to get there before she does.' Should she wait for Miss Hesketh to get home from the office or ought she to tell Miss Patience as soon as she arrived? Or would that be a slight to Miss Hesketh? 'I can't wait for Dad and Tom. I'm sorry.'

'Sorry, she says.' A bitter laugh escaped Mum's lips.

'Eh, come on now.' With one hip perched on the arm of Mum's chair, Auntie Faith leaned over and rubbed her sister's back.

'Can you at least see how it happened?' Molly appealed to them both. 'Can you understand how much I wanted to help that little boy?'

'Of course we can,' said Mum. 'We're not stupid. But – it got you sacked, Molly. There's never been anyone sacked in our family before.'

Molly closed her eyes. 'I know.' She opened her eyes again; she mustn't appear sorry for herself.

Auntie Faith shook her head. 'You gave up your engagement to go your own way and get a job – and now you've been sacked. What's happened to you, Molly? You were always such a sensible girl.'

'I did what I thought was right. Danny Cropper hadn't seen his father in months and, in between times, his mother died. I took him to be with his dad at the end, which was the right thing to do; but I acted way beyond my authority and that made it wrong.' She looked at Mum. 'I'm so sorry to have let you down.' She stood up. She hated to leave Mum in this state. 'I really do have to go.'

To her surprise and profound relief, Mum stood up and put her arms round her. Her body melted against her mother's familiar shape. Her smell was familiar too: soda crystals and cucumber hand cream, the smell of childhood, the smell of home, of love, of approval.

'Molly, you're my daughter and I'll always love you, whatever you do; but just at the moment, when I think what this is going to do to your father, I can hardly bear to look at you.' She disentangled herself and gave Molly a gentle but determined push. 'Off you go, love.'

Distress robbed her of the ability to breathe. In a dream she allowed Auntie Faith to take her to the front door. The step down onto the path felt deeper than usual, causing an odd swooping sensation. Auntie Faith's hand on her arm made her glance round. Auntie Faith stood on the step, pulling the door to behind her.

'On my way home, I'll call on Tilda and Chrissie to save your mum having to do it.'

'Thanks.'

She looked past Molly, as if hordes of nosy neighbours might be lurking behind the hydrangeas. 'You do realise you've got a way out, don't you? Norris would have you back in a flash.'

Chapter Twenty-Five

MOLLY HAD BEEN pretty certain Miss Patience would express compassion for Danny's plight. What she hadn't taken into account was the depth of her own gratitude and relief when this happened. After the emotional hammering she had endured that day, Miss Patience's gentle but steadfast sympathy for Danny filled Molly's heart to overflowing. Tears welled behind her eyes.

'It doesn't matter how sorry we all feel for the boy,' Miss Hesketh declared. 'Nothing alters the fact that Miss Watson behaved with a complete lack of regard for her professional responsibilities.'

She couldn't put it off any longer. 'I have to warn you that you might receive a letter from Mrs Rostron.' All eyes swung her way and she gulped. 'She suggested that my lapse was owing to a lack of correct teaching on your part.'

Miss Hesketh's pale eyes narrowed. 'Did she, indeed?'

'That doesn't mean she'll definitely write,' said Miss Patience.

'That's beside the point,' snapped Miss Hesketh. 'She has linked our business school with Miss Watson's conduct and it behoves us to defend ourselves. If people start saying we give our pupils the wrong ideas, it'll ruin us.' She eyed her sister. 'And you know what that would mean.'

Molly looked from one to the other. What would it mean? It was all she could do not to drop her head into her hands. An apology, yet another one, hovered on her lips, but Miss Patience spoke first.

'You do see, Molly dear, don't you, that we have to protect our reputation? What do you suggest, Prudence?'

'I'll have to make an appointment to speak to Mrs Rostron.' Miss Hesketh turned to Molly. 'Is she on duty at the weekend? Not that I want to wait that long, but I have no choice.'

'Yes, you do,' piped up Miss Patience. 'You can entrust the task to me. I'll take a copy of our prospectus and some of our lesson plans and – I'm sorry, Molly dear, but it has to be done – I'll assure Mrs Rostron that we are as shocked and disappointed as she is.'

Molly nodded. It had to be done, she could see that, but she felt as if her skin were being peeled away, leaving nothing but raw shame.

'Don't apologise to Miss Watson, Patience,' Miss Hesketh said crisply. 'It is she who should be apologising to us.'

Which made Molly start to apologise all over again, but Vivienne, having sat silent throughout the conversation, spoke across her.

'I'm not defending what Molly did. She acted unprofessionally and that's that; but she did it with the best of intentions. She'll be paying for her mistake for a long time to come, but who can blame her for wanting to reunite father and son in the father's final moments? Family matters more than anything – doesn't it?'

'I'm sure the little boy will always be grateful to you, Molly,' said Lucy.

'Unfortunately, that won't pay the bills,' Miss Hesketh remarked drily.

'I realise I'll have to leave here,' said Molly. Was there no end to the repercussions her transgression had unleashed? 'I won't be able to pay you my rent or my business school fees, so I'll have to go.'

'But not quite yet,' said Miss Patience. 'Your rent is paid until the end of the week. You must stay until then. Allow yourself a breathing space.'

Everyone looked at Miss Hesketh. She was the one who would make the final decision.

'I wouldn't blame you if you showed me the door immediately,' said Molly.

'You made a serious mistake,' said Miss Hesketh, 'and I feel personally let down, but I prefer to lead my life according to the principles of common sense and Christian charity rather than Victorian melodrama.'

'Thank you,' Molly whispered.

'No office will employ you after this,' said Miss Hesketh, 'but if you can find another employer who is prepared to give you a chance, I'll write a conditional reference and after that it will be up to you to explain your misdemeanour as best you can.'

For the first time that day, a little of Molly's burden eased.

She had never been more exhausted in her life. Losing her job and having to tell people had left her drained. That night she went to bed expecting not to sleep a wink, only to plunge into a deep slumber. She woke with the dawn chorus and, for the tiniest fraction of a second, her heart lifted before reality crashed around her. No job and, shortly, no home. Well, she would have a home, obviously. She would go back to her parents, dragging her shame behind her like Marley's chains.

It was a long day. Miss Patience kept her busy, giving her mending to do and asking her to polish the brights.

'I ought to be out looking for another job,' said Molly.

'Give yourself a day to recover,' advised Miss Patience.

'Did Miss Hesketh say that?'

'No, Molly dear. I did.'

It was a strange day. For the first time in her life since she left school, she didn't have a job to go to. Her life had been left hanging.

When Miss Patience and Lucy went out to do the daily shopping, Miss Patience wouldn't hear of Molly's accompanying them.

'No, dear, stay at home and have a rest. Plenty of time to face the world later.'

Shortly after they returned, Miss Patience went out once more.

'To get *Vera's Voice*,' Lucy told Molly. 'Auntie Patience buys it every week.'

'The first time I heard of the business school, it was in *Vera's Voice*.'

At first Molly was glad to hide away, but by the afternoon she felt ready to face the world again, though, with Miss Patience fussing over her and being such a sweetie, it would have felt rude and ungrateful to sally forth in search of a new job; but she would definitely do so tomorrow. Would she end up back in a shop? A picture formed in her head of the new girl at Upton's not working out and herself ending up back where she started. *You do realise you've got a way out, don't you? Norris would have you back in a flash.* Oh, how had things gone so wrong?

She must go and see her parents this evening. Talking to Dad face to face was the least he deserved.

She helped clear away after the meal and then went upstairs to get ready. The doorbell rang. That couldn't be one of the pupils already, could it? It must be later than she had thought. She brushed her hair, curling it under as much as it would go. She ran down the first half of the stairs, turned the corner and – stopped dead. There, in the hall, Aaron stood, cap in hand, looking up at her.

'Look who it is,' said Vivienne. 'Mr Abrams has come to see you.'

'I hope you don't mind,' he said, 'but Mrs Rostron gave me your address so I could bring you something from Danny. A letter.'

Molly came the rest of the way down. 'You've not chosen the best moment, I'm afraid. The house is busy turning from a home into a school.'

'You could sit in the breakfast room,' suggested Vivienne.

'No.' Molly reached into the cloakroom for her jacket and cloche hat. 'I need some fresh air. Let's pop into the rec.'

As they left Wilton Close, Aaron said, 'I was shocked to hear you lost your job.'

'Thank you.'

'I was going to explain to Danny, but Mrs Rostron had already told him. I gather she was kind to him. She said it wasn't his fault that you wouldn't be coming back.'

Once again Molly heard those words in her head. *Anyone can see what's on the surface. It takes experience to see what's underneath.* Trust Mrs Rostron to make sure that Danny didn't feel he was to blame for her losing her position.

They entered the rec by the gate on Cross Road. Here was where Aaron had organised the rounders match. Those trees beside the hedge had provided shade for the nursemaids to sit and watch.

'Shall we sit down?' Aaron guided her to a bench. 'Here.' From his pocket he took a folded piece of paper.

Molly's hand trembled as she unfolded it.

Dear Miss Watson

Thank you for taking me all the way to Southport to see Dad.

I am glad I saw him before he died and I think he was glad to see me too. Mum would have been pleased we were together.

I will never forget what you did for us.
Love from

Danny x

Molly's eyes filled. Losing her job was a matter of bitter regret, but she could never be sorry for taking Danny to see his father.

'Thank you for bringing this,' she whispered to Aaron. She couldn't look up in case he saw her tears. 'If you get the chance, please tell Danny I'll treasure his letter.'

She bent her head over it again, as if re-reading, but actually she couldn't see a thing.

'St Anthony's won't be the same without you,' Aaron said softly.

'Please don't be kind or I'll howl.' She tried to laugh and had to sniff instead.

'Well, I'm certainly not going to be anything other than kind. Come here.'

He opened his arms and she slid into them, nestling against his chest, fumbling awkwardly in her pocket until Aaron, keeping one arm securely around her, produced his handkerchief with his other hand and pushed it between her fingers.

'I promise I haven't used it to clean oil off my bicycle chain.'

Her shuddery breath turned into a half-laugh.

'That's better. You have a good cry if you want to.'

'No, really, I'm fine.'

'Liar.' He spoke softly into her hair. With her ear pressed to his chest, she could feel the rumble of his voice. 'I'm your friend, Molly Watson. Whatever happens, I'll stand by you and be proud to do so.'

'Really?' she breathed.

'Always.'

The moment drew out. Molly's fingers, resting lightly on his chest, ached to slide around his ribcage to his back and cling to him. She moved her face, lifting it ever so slightly, then stopped, waited, her heartbeat loud and slow, the blood in her veins taking her longings on a journey around her body. Aaron neither moved nor relaxed his hold, but she sensed withdrawal. Had she made a terrible mistake?

'I apologise,' he said. 'I know you have a fellow. I don't wish to... I would never...'

'It's not what you think,' Molly whispered. 'I'm not spoken for.' But, oh, how she wanted to be.

And at last, at long last, Aaron moved, just the tiniest movement, as his face angled down towards her – no, not quite, but almost, just enough of a movement for her to respond to if she wished.

And she did wish. Oh, she did.

Raising her face to his, she felt his breath on her cheeks, her lips, as his mouth slowly moved towards hers.

'Oy! What the ruddy hell's going on here? Get your hands off her, you brute!'

Startled, Molly moved, or did she? Did she break away from Aaron or did he put her from him as he came to his feet? Norris – Norris! – was approaching at a brisk trot, brows knotted beneath the brim of his hat; he was waving a fist – actually waving a fist in outrage.

'Norris, stop it. Calm down.'

'Calm down?' he blustered. 'You sit there canoodling with this man and— Oh my goodness! I've just realised who you are.' He squared up to Aaron. 'You're the fellow from the orphanage – the gardener chappy, aren't you? I remember you doing something with the ivy.'

'Mr Abrams is the caretaker,' said Molly.

'And he was certainly taking care of you!'

'Norris!'

'I know what I saw.' He reached for her arm, but she stepped away. 'I've just heard about your job and I came here out of the goodness of my heart and I find – I find...' He wagged a furious finger at her. 'You promised me faithfully. You swore there was no one else – and what do I find? How could you, Molly? And in public, too! Well, I hope you know what you're taking on,' he spat at Aaron. 'Has she told you her secret, eh? Has she told you what she did in the war?'

After landing a hefty shove on Norris's shirt-front to bowl him aside, there was nothing in Molly's way, yet she felt like she was having to push past enormous obstacles to get out of the rec and back to Wilton Close. She fumbled with her key, trying to insert it in the lock. Next news, the door was opened from within and there was Vivienne. Molly ducked her head, trying to get inside without showing her distress, but Vivienne caught her shoulder and turned her round.

'What's happened?'

Molly waved her hand, an awkward movement, trying to warn Vivienne off. Somehow the hand ended up covering her own mouth. She darted upstairs to her room and closed the door. Her emotional turmoil was such that she expected to hurl herself full-length onto the bed, but somehow she merely sank onto the edge and sat there. Her limbs were impossibly heavy, yet there was a lightness, an emptiness inside her. All around the space was a jagged boundary. If she were to move even a fraction, blade-sharp pain would tear her to pieces from the inside outwards.

Norris had told her secret.

He had sworn never to reveal it to a living soul, never never never.

But that was when they were engaged, when it was in his interests to keep silent.

Norris had told. Norris had blabbed.

There was a soft knock on the door. Molly flinched inwardly. Her head was lowered, but her eyes shifted. It was the only movement she could make without shattering into a thousand pieces. In the doorway stood Vivienne, her expression warm with concern. She didn't ask; she just came inside and sat on the bed. Molly tilted towards her as the mattress dipped.

'What's wrong?' Vivienne asked. 'It's obvious something has happened.'

Molly remained utterly still, floundering through mounting distress.

'It's hard to believe a letter from Daniel Cropper could have this effect,' Vivienne prodded gently.

The pain of speaking almost made her throat creak. 'It was a sweet letter, but I was upset and Aaron... Mr Abrams put his arms round me and – and Norris, my old fiancé, saw us and—'

'He didn't cause a scene, did he? It's none of his beeswax, if you're not engaged any more.'

Molly shut her eyes, but that only made Norris's words roar more loudly in her ears. *Has she told you her secret, eh? Has she told you what she did in the war?* She opened her eyes again and her gaze landed on the floor.

'He's been hanging on as if I'm going to go back to him.' How flat her voice sounded. Shouldn't she be having hysterics? 'In the end, I made it clear that I wouldn't and he asked if there was someone else, so of course I said no. There wasn't. There isn't.' She glanced at Vivienne; but if Vivienne had formed an opinion based on Molly's admission of being found in Aaron's arms, nothing showed in her face. 'When he saw us in the rec, Norris had a go at me.'

'As I said: none of his business.'

'It's worse than that. He...he announced to Mr Abrams that I have a secret, that – that something happened to me in the war.'

Vivienne nodded, but didn't answer at once. She wasn't the sort to rush into hasty responses – or judgements. It was one reason she was so good at her job.

'Did you stop him blurting it out?'

'No, I – I ran for it.' She scrubbed a palm over her face. 'God, what a fool. If I'd stayed put, I might have stopped him. As it is...' Nausea swirled in her stomach. 'He's telling Aaron all the gory details right this minute.'

What would Aaron think of her now? His good opinion, which she seemed to have retained even after Saturday's escapade, would be trodden in the mud by the time Norris had finished.

'You don't know that for certain,' Vivienne said quietly. 'Maybe Mr Abrams' – and her use of his title made Molly realise she had blundered into using his first name – 'didn't let him. I can't claim to know Mr Abrams well, but he's always struck me as a decent sort. I'm not making light of your situation. Please don't think that. I'm only saying that, even though you think you know what happened after you left, you may not be right.'

'Norris swore to me that he would never speak of it again. He swore.'

'And you believed him.'

'Of course. It would have reflected poorly on him if it had got out. But it was something I had to tell him when he wanted us to get engaged. He had a right to know.'

'Then he's an out-and-out louse if he breaks your confidence now,' Vivienne declared.

'Bless you for that.'

Vivienne's robust support caused a stirring of warmth deep inside the cold that had invaded Molly, but Vivienne didn't know what she had done. Would she stand by her if she knew? Would anyone?

'Let me help you off with your jacket and hat,' said Vivienne, 'and I'll take them downstairs for you, then you can have some thinking time.'

Rising, Molly peeled off her things, but instead of handing them over, she discarded them on the bed.

'Don't go. You're being so kind and un-nosy, and I do appreciate it, especially the un-nosy bit, but I don't want to be on my own.' She sat down again. 'Part of me has been all alone since it happened. Even when I told Norris, I knew I was still alone. Before I told him, I thought – I hoped he might share it with me, but that was just me being daft. What man would? He forgave me and that was the end of it.'

Oh hell.

'I'll have to tell my parents,' she realised. 'Whether or not Norris actually blabbed this evening, I can no longer trust him to keep quiet, so I must tell Mum and Dad.'

Dread was sour in her mouth. What would they say? What would they think of her? Need the rest of the family know? Gran would die of shame.

Oh cripes. If she turned up at Mum and Dad's, they would assume she was there to face the music about losing her job, whereas...

She sucked in a breath. 'I want to tell you what I did.'

'You don't have to. I'm just trying to say the right things to help you through, although,' Vivienne added with a gentle smile, 'that might be easier if I knew what I was dealing with.'

'I want to try it out on you,' said Molly. 'I've never told anyone apart from Norris and I need to talk about it before telling my parents.' A fresh wave of fear shivered through her shoulders. 'The Miss Heskeths will throw me out.'

'Not necessarily. What did Miss Hesketh say? Common sense trumps melodrama.'

'But morals trump everything.'

'What's this about, Molly? Pictures are forming in my head. You should tell me before I latch onto the wrong idea.'

Molly looked at Vivienne, but had to look away before the words would come. 'It's very simple. During the war, I was a driver in London. There was a soldier. He was handsome and amusing; he was good at drawing and he was interested in bats.'

'Bats?'

'Not cricket bats. Flying bats. He lived in an old house in the countryside, with bats in the attic. Once a year, he and his friends had a night-time picnic on the lawn and counted the bats as they flew out from under the eaves. He told me that the first time we met. I thought him quite mad.'

'He sounds interesting. Fun.'

'He was – both. I soon stopped thinking he was mad and started thinking,' and her voice dropped of its own accord to a whisper, 'he was the most wonderful man I'd ever met. I'd been walking out with Norris before the war and we'd been writing to one another. After I met Toby, I had to write to Norris and say...' She shook her head.

'A hard letter to write,' said Vivienne.

'It's horrible to write to a serving soldier to say you've met someone else, but I had to do it. I wanted everything between Toby and me to be perfect. I didn't want Norris on my conscience.'

'You'd fallen in love.'

'I adored him. If he had lived, I'd be his wife now and it wouldn't have mattered if he'd come back with limbs missing, or blinded, or gassed. But he was killed going over the top and I was left behind to have his child.'

'You had a baby.'

'A little boy. He was perfect and I had to give him away.'

'You poor love. Your poor baby.'

Molly roused herself. 'But he wasn't poor, was he? He was lucky. That's how I've always thought of it.' How she had trained herself to think of it. Forced herself to think of it. 'He went to a decent family to be cherished and appreciated and in all probability spoilt rotten by a mother who couldn't have children of her own. A mother with the one thing I didn't have – a husband.' She looked squarely at Vivienne. 'You should understand. You said you were adopted. You know how important adoption is, how successful it can be.'

'My parents loved me and were proud of me and the feeling was entirely mutual.' Vivienne pressed her hand. 'I hope your son is as content and secure with his adoptive parents as I always was with mine. I can have no greater wish for him than that – and no greater wish for you.'

A tiny squeak of a hinge made them both look up. The door, which had been ajar, opened and Lucy appeared. Her face was drained of colour and looked rather ghastly. Oh lord. Had she heard everything? Molly tried to swallow but it wouldn't go down. Was Lucy shocked? Disgusted? Was this a foretaste of censure to come from all sides?

'Lucy!' Vivienne exclaimed. 'Have you been earwigging? That's a low-down trick. I'm ashamed of you.'

Lucy couldn't take her eyes off Molly. 'You had a baby? Out of wedlock?'

'You're not to breathe a word,' Vivienne commanded.

Lucy's face started to crumple. Molly was startled. Vexed, too. What did Lucy have to cry about? Molly was the one facing social ruin if her story was spread around.

Lucy said, 'Please help me. I don't know what to do.'

'Whatever it is—' Vivienne began brusquely.

'I'm having a baby.'

Chapter Twenty-Six

ALTHOUGH SHE DERIVED a great deal of satisfaction from imparting her knowledge to her pupils, Prudence always experienced relief when Patience saw them out at the end of the evening's teaching. The business school provided a useful, not to say essential, service to this new breed of surplus girls, who would benefit from being able to apply for jobs of a superior nature to those they were already in. Not to mention the essential service the school performed in enabling her and Patience to remain here in the home they had lived in all their lives, the home indeed that she viewed as being morally theirs, even if the law thought otherwise; but all that didn't mean it wasn't tiring. To work all day in the office and come home and teach all evening was a lot to ask of anyone. Not that she ever complained. She wasn't the complaining sort. Besides, what choice was there?

Patience sighed as she closed the front door. 'Another evening over with. Come and sit down and I'll make you a drink.'

Patience was a fusspot, a looker-after, but at the end of a long day, it wasn't disagreeable to receive a bit of cosseting – again, not that Prudence would ever admit it. A quiet thank-you sufficed. And it made Patience feel better to be permitted to indulge her. After all, what did Patience do all day but look after the home? And her contribution to the business school, important as it was that the pupils practised their telephone skills, could hardly be compared to the intricate knowledge of typewriting and book-keeping, invoices and minutes, filing and letter-writing, that formed Prudence's contribution to their endeavour.

No sooner had she sat down in her armchair than the door opened and all three girls not so much came in as crept in, looking subdued, and Lucy looked positively wretched. She tried to hang back, but Mrs Atwood urged her in. They all sat down, squeezing together onto the sofa, glances flickering between them like a bunch of inexperienced office juniors who had made a terrible blunder that she would have to sort out. It was all she could do not to tap her foot. It was vexing enough to feel like this at work; she didn't expect to face it at home.

'Lucy has something to tell you,' Mrs Atwood said, not seeming at all like an office junior. She had a composure, a quiet authority, that inspired confidence. 'But before she does, we ought to wait for Miss Patience.'

Prudence eyed Lucy sharply. The girl hung her head.

'Are we about to get to the bottom of what really brought you here?'

'Please,' Mrs Atwood murmured, 'if we could just wait for Miss Patience.'

Of course. Wait for Patience, the kind one, the soft-hearted one; the one who would pour oil on troubled waters and leave it to her older sister to make the difficult decisions and say the things that needed to be said.

As Patience manoeuvred the door open, a tray in her hands, Miss Watson got up to help her.

'Thank you, Molly dear – oh. You all look very serious. Has something happened?'

'I rather think it must have,' said Prudence. 'Lucy apparently has something to tell us.'

'Should I pour first?' asked Patience.

'No.' Prudence wished she didn't sound quite so snappish. 'Sit down and let's hear what Lucy has to say.'

But it was Miss Watson who sat up straighter. 'Would you hear me out first?'

'Really, Miss Watson, it's our niece we wish to hear from.' A thought occurred to Prudence. 'I hope you don't have something to add to what you told us on the subject of why you were dismissed from your job.'

The girl flushed. Not the prettiest sight, given the colour of her hair. The blush made it look brassy.

'No, it's not that. It's...something else.'

'Tell us, Molly dear,' said Patience. 'You're among friends.'

'I hope I still will be when I've told you.' Miss Watson rubbed her palms on her thighs. 'It's difficult for me to tell you this, but, as my landladies, you're entitled to know, because – because you may want me to leave immediately.'

'Heavens,' breathed Patience. 'You're scaring me.'

'If nothing else, you've given yourself a dramatic build-up,' Prudence said. 'Now kindly tell us without beating around the bush.'

'Very well.' The girl lifted her chin. She had rather fine cheekbones. 'During the war, I was away in London.'

'Doing your bit,' Patience said approvingly.

'Doing my bit. I met a soldier, a very nice chap, and we became...involved. When he returned to France, he was killed.'

Patience breathed a soft 'Oh' of sympathy.

'And I was left on my own and...in trouble.'

'In...? Oh!' Patience coloured deeply.

Prudence's heart beat hard and slow. Memories piled up in her head. 'What happened?'

Miss Watson blinked several times and sniffed; Mrs Atwood thrust a hanky into her hand. Miss Watson pressed it to her nose and discreetly wiped.

'I, um, I had the baby adopted. It was a boy. I gave him away.'

Oh, the shame. Deep down inside Prudence was cold as ice, but at the same time heat raced around her body. An unmarried mother. An unwanted child – or perhaps not unwanted, though that was immaterial. The shame, oh, the appalling shame.

Patience looked at her, waiting for her to speak. When she didn't, Patience said, 'This has come as a great shock to us. I don't know what to say.'

'I'm sorry if you feel I came here under false pretences,' said Miss Watson. 'I've kept it a secret all this time and tried to put it behind me, but…I think the secret may now be out and I wanted to be the one to tell you. I'm sorry. The last thing I want is to bring shame on you.'

'What should we do?' Patience looked at Prudence.

They all looked at her, awaiting her judgement. She was known for being the first to wade in with her opinions and her criticism.

'Before you consider that,' put in Mrs Atwood, 'perhaps you should listen to Lucy.'

Lucy promptly burst into tears.

Dear heaven, had there ever been an evening like it? And had there ever been a more impossible girl than Lucy? Why wouldn't she tell them who the father was?

'You have to tell us,' Prudence insisted as the discussion dragged on long into the night while rain beat against the windows and the temperature dropped. 'How else are you to marry him?' Horror washed through her. 'He's not a married man, is he?'

'Of course not,' Lucy cried indignantly. 'What sort of girl do you think I am?'

Prudence lifted her eyebrows. 'That's a dangerous question to ask, considering that you've got yourself into trouble.'

'Prudence, please,' Patience murmured. 'You're not helping.'

'Aren't I? I beg everyone's pardon, but it seems to me that the person who isn't helping is Lucy. Here she is, *enceinte*, and refusing to name the father. Good lord, it isn't the window cleaner or some such, is it?'

'Aunt Prudence!' It was almost a shriek.

'Well, what are we supposed to think?' she demanded.

'Lucy.' Mrs Atwood stuck her oar in. 'Will you explain to us why you won't name the father?'

Lucy looked away, sighed, fiddled with her bracelet. Patience stirred, about to speak, but at a signal from Mrs Atwood, she subsided.

'I...I don't love him. I mean, I like him. I'm awfully fond of him, but I'm not in love.'

'I think the time has passed for that to be a consideration,' said Prudence.

'Has it?' Having spent most of the evening not meeting anyone's gaze, Lucy swung round to face her. 'Have I got to get married because of one mistake?'

'When the mistake has these consequences,' Prudence said, 'yes, absolutely.'

'Does he know?' asked Miss Watson.

'No.'

'You haven't told him?'

'No. If I did, he'd want to do the decent thing, obviously.'

'Then why not let him?' asked Miss Watson. 'If you're so fond of him, and he's a good sort, what's the problem?'

'The problem,' Lucy insisted, 'is that I'm not in love with him.'

'Then how come...?' asked Miss Watson. An indelicate question, but Prudence wanted to hear the answer.

Lucy shifted uncomfortably – not easy, given how crushed together the three of them were on the sofa. 'It's as I said. I'm very fond of him, always have been, and it's entirely mutual. In fact, I think it might be more than that on his side.'

'You mean he loves you?'

'That's what made me realise. If he loves me and we get married, he'll get everything he wants; but I...I won't, will I? I'll be married, but I won't be in love with my husband.' As Prudence leaned forward, Lucy hurried on. 'Please don't say it's a bit late to think of that now.' Good heavens, did Lucy just dare to forestall her? 'I don't know what to do.'

'Lucy, dear, what choice is there?' asked Patience. 'As a respectable girl, you have to do the right thing.'

'Marry a man I don't love?'

'Darling, yes, and consider yourself lucky that he's happy to do right by you. You make him sound a pretty good sort.'

'Such a good sort that he has taken advantage of a young girl,' said Prudence.

There was a spiky silence in which the others looked away from her frank stare.

'He didn't take advantage.' There was an underlying note of sulkiness in Lucy's voice. 'It was both of us. We got carried away.'

'This is getting us nowhere,' said Prudence. It was a novel experience not to be able to get to the bottom of something. Her incisive mind and famous determination usually got her the answers she required. 'What are we going to do? You can't stay here, Lucy. I have to protect the good name of this house.'

'I won't go home,' Lucy retorted. 'Daddy will make me tell.'

'Someone has to.'

'If we fail to tell your parents about this, if we simply keep you here as if nothing has changed,' Patience said more gently, 'they'll never trust us again. You know how difficult things are between Daddy and us. Keeping you here wouldn't help us in the long term, I'm sorry to say.'

'So your precious business school matters more than I do?'

'That's unfair, Lucy.' It was unusual to hear Patience speaking so firmly. 'You know how much you mean to us. You must do or you wouldn't have come here when you needed... I'm not sure now what you needed.' Her voice slid into a sad monotone.

'I think you came here to hide, didn't you, Lucy?' said Mrs Atwood. 'You're hiding from your parents so they don't find out; hiding from the whole situation, trying not to think about it, wishing it had never happened.'

'But it has happened,' stated Prudence, 'and we have to face it.'

'I'm not going to name the father,' Lucy said softly.

'Perhaps Evelyn will have an idea who it is,' suggested Patience.

'No!' cried Lucy. 'You mustn't ask her.'

Mrs Atwood looked at Prudence. 'What are you going to do?'

Cheek! As if it was any of her business. Prudence made a point of addressing Patience.

'The child looks done in. I'm sure you can be relied on for Ovaltine and tucking-in duties. Tomorrow I'll start making arrangements for Lucy to go away – not back to Lawrence and Evelyn,' she added more loudly as Lucy started to protest, 'though, goodness knows, that could come back to haunt us. When you came here, Lucy, Aunt Patience and I promised to take care of you and this is how I propose to do it.' She turned to Mrs Atwood. 'Tomorrow, at work, please could you find the whereabouts of a respectable home for unmarried mothers?'

'A bad girls' home?' Lucy burst out. 'You can't send me to one of those. They're horrible places and the girls are treated abominably. Everyone knows that.'

'As I was saying,' Prudence resumed, 'I should be grateful, Mrs Atwood, if you'd locate a private home, one where families of the better sort send their daughters in this situation. If Lucy intends not to name the father, she needs to face up to the alternative. I think you were right when you said she came here to hide. Well, the time for hiding is over. When I go to the office tomorrow, I'll explain that I have a family emergency to deal with and arrange to take a day off, so that I can take Lucy to the home. If I find it to be clean and comfortable, and if the girls seem reasonably content and well cared for, then I'll leave her there.'

Aaron had long since given up trying to sleep. Lying on his settee, with his knees hooked over the arm and his feet dangling, was hellishly uncomfortable. Maybe he would suggest swapping round tomorrow night, so he could have the bed while Danny had the settee. The lad wouldn't mind, he was sure.

In fact, the idea of camping downstairs might cheer him up a bit. He needed it, poor chap. Aaron had overheard one of the nursemaids whispering that she didn't see why Cropper should have taken his dad's death so hard.

'The father was in that sanatorium for almost a year. That's a heck of a long time in a young child's life.'

Never mind that it wasn't the caretaker's job to take issue with the nursemaids, Aaron had stopped and said, 'Just because young Cropper hadn't seen his dad in months doesn't mean he should be unaffected by his loss. Just because all of us adults weren't surprised when Mr Cropper died doesn't mean Daniel expected it to happen. Anyway, he had seen his dad, hadn't he? Miss Watson took him.'

'Took it upon herself to take him, you mean,' Nurse Eva had retorted, 'against all the rules. Maybe she did more harm than good. Maybe that visit is the reason Cropper's taken it so badly. Maybe it stirred up all his old memories and feelings about his dad.'

'Memories and feelings that would otherwise have stayed buried, you mean? I think it's obvious they weren't buried. He muddled through with his mum for all that time; then he suffered the huge shock of losing her, which meant his dad was all he had left. Why else do you think he made all those attempts at running away when he first came here? He loved and missed his father and his mum's death made those feelings all the stronger. For what it's worth, I think Miss Watson did the right thing.'

'Do you indeed?' Nurse Eva raised her eyebrows at him. Had he spoken too warmly in defence of Molly? It was too late to take it back – and he wouldn't if he could.

What was her secret from the war? He swung his legs round and sat up, easing his shoulders as he placed his feet on the floor. His muscles quivered – and not just from being in a easier position. Anger stirred within him at the memory of the ex-fiancé being ready to blurt it out. No wonder Molly had skedaddled. He had wanted to run after her but it had been more important to make sure the ex-fiancé – Norris – hadn't done so. Had Norris expected him to lap up the juicy details? What an oaf. What a – it was an old-fashioned word, but what a cad. Fancy threatening a lady in that way, after she had entrusted her secret to you. Throwing that punch had been deeply satisfying. Norris would have a shiner as a souvenir for several days to come.

Aaron stood up and stretched, releasing the last few twinges from lying in such an awkward position. If only he could have gone to see Molly today after work. He had wanted to, had spent most of the day anxiously looking forward to reassuring her that he hadn't listened to her secret and had no intention of pressing her on the subject, but that had proved impossible in the end, because of bringing young Danny home with him.

It turned out that, since being brought back on Saturday, the poor lad had been roaming St Anthony's at night, unable to settle or sleep and, while there had been a certain sympathy for him, that hadn't stopped him getting into hot water. That was the trouble with having started his St Anthony's career as a persistent runaway. He had got himself a reputation. However compassionate the nannies and nursemaids in general might feel about his bereavement – and Nurse Eva's crisp opinion wasn't typical – there was an underlying feeling of *Oh no, not Cropper again* when he took to trailing round the building in the middle of the night, having to be followed and returned to bed time after time and then not staying where he was put.

Aaron had gone to see Mrs Rostron.

'Why not let him come home with me to Soapsuds Cottage at the end of each day? No offence to the ladies working here, but it might help him to have the company of a man. He and I rub along quite well.'

'I have observed you with the children when they help with the ivy,' Mrs Rostron had replied in a dry voice. 'It seems to me that you rub along with most of them, as you call it. That in itself isn't a reason to single out Cropper.'

'Aye, well, there's more to it than that.' And he had been obliged to explain about bringing Danny back from Victoria Station on May Day.

'So he wasn't playing truant from school? It was another of his attempts to run away. I am most displeased to think that you misled me – downright lied to me, in fact.'

'I apologise for that, but I reckoned the boy had landed in the soup enough times already and I wanted to prevent it from happening again.'

'By lying to me, his guardian. You are a member of my staff, Mr Abrams. If I cannot trust you and rely on you, I will dismiss you. Is that clear? Are there any other deceptions you wish to tell me about?'

'It was just that one time.'

'Hm. One time is too many. That, however, is beside the point just now. Your idea of taking Daniel Cropper home with you at night, as a way of helping him through this difficult time, is worth considering, not merely for his sake, but for that of the other children and the staff, who are on edge in case of more nocturnal activities. Besides, if he has a few nights in an ordinary dwelling, it will make his transition into his uncle's home less of an event.'

'Have you sent for the uncle?'

She gave him a look that warned him not to push his luck by asking questions.

So here Danny was now. Maybe getting him out of the orphanage had been the right thing to do, or maybe he was just plain worn out, but – for now at least – he was dead to the world. Either that or he was lying awake fretting. Aaron clicked his tongue. Should he check?

He had left a lamp burning low in case Danny should take it into his head to go for a wander. Not that there was anywhere much to wander to in a two-up two-down. Aaron had opted to sleep downstairs just in case Danny had tried to leave the cottage. Better safe than sorry. Otherwise he would have slept on the floor in the other upstairs room, which he used for storing books, tools and the small pieces he was working on. He had a dream about Soapsuds Cottage – that one day it would become Soapsuds House. His elderly neighbour, Mrs Mulvey, was possibly going to move in with her daughter Hetty's family. If she did, would it be possible for Aaron to take over her house and have the pair of two-up two-downs converted into a four-up four-down, just right for a family?

He stood at the foot of the tight little spiral staircase. Danny had been enchanted when he saw it. When Aaron told him, 'I'm pleased you like it. I built it,' the lad's face had shone with surprise before a new respect had settled on him.

Aaron put his foot quietly on the bottom tread and made his way up to stand in the bedroom doorway, keeping to one side, so that if Danny woke, there wouldn't be a huge shadow looming over him; but there was no danger of that. The boy was out for the count, limbs flung in all directions, like a starfish. Aaron couldn't help smiling.

It was raining hard and the room had cooled considerably. Aaron stepped across and pulled the window shut, fastening it softly. The curtain was damp against his arm. He had left the curtains open on purpose so Danny wouldn't be in pitch darkness.

Danny stirred, muttered something. Aaron stilled and waited. Danny flipped over onto his side, knees bending, legs curling up. When he was certain Danny wasn't going to wake, Aaron returned to the doorway, unable to resist looking back. There was something special and deeply moving about watching a child sleeping; something that normally only a father would be privileged to do.

He went back downstairs.

Chapter Twenty-Seven

PRUDENCE THREW OPEN her bedroom curtains. Her room was on the side of the house, her view, across two side-passages, that of the side of next door's house, its light-grey pebble-dash now darkened to charcoal after a night of heavy rain, which hadn't let up with the morning. The sky was dark, swollen with heavy purple clouds. It was going to be one of those days when it didn't get properly light, the sort of day one associated more with winter than summer.

She went downstairs. Until a few weeks ago, she and Patience used to carry their bedside electric lamps downstairs every morning and stow them away tidily in the cupboard under the stairs, an echo of the way they had carried their night-time oil-lamps downstairs every morning. It had been when their first pupil-lodgers had questioned this practice that Prudence, feeling prickly with foolishness, had called a halt to it. It was so easy to carry on doing things just because one had always done them. She was in her fifties now – her early fifties, her very early fifties, Patience would have said. Poor Patience was dreading entering her own fifth decade. Why waste time dreading what couldn't be avoided?

Why indeed? Not that that stopped the feeling of heaviness inside her as she contemplated what she had to do today.

Being challenged by Mrs Atwood didn't help.

'Could I have a private word?' asked Mrs Atwood.

'Come into the sitting room.'

Prudence led the way in. It occurred to her to remain standing to show she had no intention of allowing this conversation to last long – well, it couldn't anyway, since they both had to go to work – but she dismissed the impulse as unworthy. It was the kind of thing Lawrence might do.

She sat in her usual place, knees and ankles together, back straight. Mrs Atwood was wearing her olive-green dress. She always dressed smartly, though not in a way Prudence quite approved of for work. A white blouse and dark skirt had always been good enough for her – indeed, for generations of office women. But these new younger women…

'What did you want to say?' she asked. Having the first word could be as important as having the last.

'Do you still wish me to find a place for girls who are in trouble?'

'A respectable place, yes; a place where the girls are of a certain class. I believe such places exist.'

'I'm sure they do, though I've never been asked to find one before. The people I normally deal with…' She let the words trail away.

'Do you doubt your ability to find one?' Prudence employed a sharp tone.

'Of course not. I simply wished to find out if you are sure about this course of action.'

She bristled. 'You clearly have something to say on the subject, Mrs Atwood.' She directed a hard stare at the young woman, expecting her to look away – people normally did.

But Mrs Atwood didn't. 'I should like to know more of what you intend.'

'It's none of your business.'

'Pardon me, but you have made it my business, at least up to a point, by seeking my assistance in finding an appropriate home for fallen girls.' Mrs Atwood spoke with her habitual quiet confidence, the manner which Prudence usually thought well of, but which in the present circumstances was annoying.

'Is your assistance dependent upon my explaining myself to your satisfaction?'

Mrs Atwood's eyes flickered and a hint of colour tinted her cheeks. 'Certainly not, Miss Hesketh. I've agreed to help you and I will.'

Prudence considered her. There was a lot more to Mrs Vivienne Atwood than quiet confidence. She was a caring person as well. She had a warm heart; not a soft, soppy heart like Patience's, unable to resist any lame dog that crossed her path, but a heart both sensitive and sensible – a cross between Prudence's own and Patience's.

'Were I to keep Lucy here, it would undoubtedly cause damage between myself and my brother. Our relationship is governed by various considerations and those, Mrs Atwood, really are none of your business.' Or had Lucy blabbed to the p.g.s? The little minx. Surely she had greater family loyalty than that. 'Were Lucy to remain under this roof, I should be obliged to send for her parents and there would be uproar, which would benefit no one; whereas by removing her, I can provide her with breathing space.'

'Thinking time.'

'Just for a day or two.'

'Shall you remain with her in the home?'

'Good lord, no. I have obligations here.'

'So you'll leave her all alone. You'd do that to her?'

'I hope this isn't the way in which you speak to those people to whom it is your job to give guidance and assistance. I rather expected the new Board of Health to be above making people feel guilty or inadequate.'

The barb hit home. Mrs Atwood pressed her lips together for a moment. 'Believe me, Miss Hesketh, no one could describe you as inadequate.'

'Are you suggesting that I should feel guilty?'

Instead of glancing away, Mrs Atwood looked directly at her. 'Do you?'

'What a bizarre suggestion; almost offensive, if I may say so. Why might I feel guilty? I'm doing my utmost to contain the situation. As to Lucy's being left alone, she'll be in the company of other girls in a similar predicament and staff who presumably have heard it all before.'

'And that will give her something to think about, will it?' Mrs Atwood made no effort to dampen the challenge in her voice.

'At present, all she seems to think about is concealing the father's identity, so yes, I hope it will.'

'How can you be so...'

'Be careful how you finish that question, Mrs Atwood.'

'So clinical.'

'Would you prefer hysteria?'

'Of course not.' Her brow clouded and she shifted uncomfortably.

Prudence had had enough. It was time to put an end to this and go to work.

'Allow me to sum up, Mrs Atwood, after which this discussion will be at an end. I will send Lucy away for what you are pleased to call thinking time. This weekend I'll have the difficult task of informing her parents of her condition. I'll also explain that I've taken the liberty of booking her into a suitable home, where I hope she'll appreciate the wisdom of naming the father. Moreover, Lucy's absence from here will protect her from her parents' initial rage and distress. It's the most I can do for her.'

Mrs Atwood almost spoke – almost, but not quite. But she didn't need to speak. It was obvious what she meant.

Is it?

'What my brother and sister-in-law decide to do after that will be up to them. I should be obliged if you could make your enquiries this morning and meet me as soon after midday as possible beside the statue of Prince Albert to hand over the information. That will enable me to place the necessary telephone calls before returning to my desk by one o'clock.' She came to her feet. 'And now, Mrs Atwood, I see there should just be time for me to have breakfast before leaving for the office. Shall you partake also or would you prefer to stay in here, dwelling on my shortcomings? I beg your pardon. That was uncalled for.'

Mrs Atwood rose. 'You are a formidable woman, Miss Hesketh.'

'I've had to be,' said Prudence.

Molly trudged round to see Mum and Dad, collar up, rain streaming all around her off the umbrella, splashing onto her galoshes. Vivienne had suggested leaving her visit until the rain let up, maybe tomorrow or the next day, but her conscience couldn't have borne that. Imagine if it came out – and it would – that Norris had ceased to keep her secret on Tuesday evening and she had left it until Thursday or Friday or even the weekend before pulling herself together sufficiently to face her parents.

'You've finally come to see me, have you?' said Dad. 'Two days is a long time to wait when my daughter has been dismissed from her post.'

'I know. I'm sorry. I couldn't come yesterday – and actually, it isn't that which brings me here today. It's something else.'

'Something else?' He wasn't impressed. 'Are you telling me that something worse has happened? Worse than getting the sack?' His voice deepened the way it used to when they were children being told off.

'Please, Dad, come and sit down. Mum needs to hear this as well.'

How she managed to get the words out, she didn't know. She had thought that, having already told Vivienne, it would be easier second time around, but it was far worse. Mum and Dad stared at her, dazed and incredulous. When Dad lumbered to his feet and went to stand at the window, staring out, his back to the room, darkness swirled inside her. What a disappointment she must be, and an incomprehensible one at that. Look at Tilda and Christabel, who had both followed the rules without a murmur, marrying young and starting their families, enjoying married life – the way girls were supposed to, the way you grew up expecting your life to turn out.

And what had she done? Gone off to London in the war; then come back and entered into a long engagement, which she had backed out of halfway through, in spite of everything that was said to convince her otherwise, in favour of embracing a life of spinsterhood and office work, only to be dismissed from her post. And to top it all, now she had admitted the full truth of what had happened to her in London.

What was Dad seeing as he gazed from the window? A little lad running about on their small lawn? The grandson he had never had. The grandson he had been deprived of even before the child was born; in that moment when Toby was shot and killed and fell over backwards into a crater full of water. At least, she hoped he was killed outright. That was what his friend had told her, had sworn was the truth. All she could do was hang onto the hope. The thought that he might have fallen into that crater and drowned...

At last Mum said, 'Well, now we know. I always knew there was something. You and Tom both came back...different. It's easy to understand why a man would be changed, but not a girl, especially one who never left these shores.' Then she uttered the words that left Molly flabbergasted. 'You know what you should do, Molly. Tell your brother. Help him understand he isn't the only one carrying something inside him. He's only nipped out to fetch your dad some baccy. He won't hang about in this weather.'

And that was what she did. Upstairs, sitting together on Tom's bed in the big bedroom that, as a child, she had shared with her two sisters, Molly, exhausted by now, shared her tale with her brother. If Mum had expected Tom to reciprocate with a heart-rending tale of his own, it didn't happen. Tom, wonderful Tom, devoted all his attention to her story and hugged her at the end.

'I love you, little sister, and I don't blame you one bit. These things happen in wartime. All kinds of things happen and afterwards we pick up our lives and carry on.'

'Oh, Tom.'

'Tell you what. I'll have a quiet word with Norris.'

'No, don't.'

'He needs to be reminded that this has to remain a secret. Dad will probably want to come too.'

'Tom, *no*.'

'He's your father. He'll want to protect you, same as I do. Leave it to us. We won't hang, draw and quarter him...unless we have to.'

She tried not to smile. 'I'm sure he won't cause any trouble. He just reacted on the spur of the moment.'

'Well, he needs to be told that on any future spurs of the moment, he must bite his tongue, even if it means biting it off.' Sitting beside her, with one arm snugly around her, Tom spoke close to her ear. 'Would you like to tell me what caused this particular spur of the moment?'

She was on her feet in an instant. 'No. And you're not to ask Norris.'

'Wouldn't dream of it. In fact, if he tries to tell me, I'll wallop him for ungentlemanly conduct.'

'Oh, Tom, where would I be without you?'

'Tell you what. Let's never find out.'

*

The train chugged through the countryside. The rain was pouring down here too, just as it had been when they had started their journey from Wilton Close first thing that morning. The view from the window should have been pretty, but the rain had darkened everything beneath brooding black skies, turning grassy slopes to bottle-green, dry-stone walls to the colour of cold ashes and villages into unwelcoming blotches humped in sodden valleys beside swollen rivers that nudged the undersides of old stone bridges arching over them.

'It looks as though there may be floods,' Molly observed.

'Yes, indeed,' said Miss Hesketh. 'It isn't just in our area that it is a possibility. I hope the Mersey won't overflow its banks.'

'If it does, it's more likely to happen in the West Didsbury area than in Chorlton,' said Molly. 'When Ees House was built for the Kimber family, a lot of drainage work was done in the Chorlton part of the meadows. That was when they put in the overflow system for Chorlton Brook as well.' She smiled. 'Trust a builder's daughter to know things like that.'

If she had hoped her remark might raise a response from Lucy, she was disappointed. The last thing she had expected was to be asked to accompany Miss Hesketh when she took Lucy to the home that Vivienne had found. In fact, Vivienne had found two. Miss Hesketh had made telephone calls to both and had chosen this one: the lady who ran it had sounded more sensible, apparently. Was a dose of good sense what Lucy needed most? Probably. Anything to get her to name the father. Or would some fuss and kindness be more likely to produce that result? But if you ran a place of that nature, maybe fuss and kindness wasn't what the parents wanted for the daughters who had let them down so badly.

What did Mum and Dad think of her now? No, she wouldn't dwell on that. She must give Lucy all her attention today, just as Tom had given his to her yesterday evening. Not that it had been possible to give Lucy any meaningful attention so far, as the three of them were sharing their six-person compartment with two others, an elderly woman whose face was as lined as a walnut and a middle-aged woman, who was presumably her daughter.

When the train slowed and pulled into a little country halt, the two women rose, the younger one gathering their belongings, and, with a polite nod of farewell, slid open the compartment door, not without difficulty.

'Allow me.' Molly stood to close the door behind them. They smiled their thanks and disappeared along the narrow corridor.

A couple of minutes later, doors slammed, a whistle blew and, with a lurch, the journey recommenced. Now it was just the three of them together. Molly caught Lucy's glance of apprehension. Did she expect her aunt to deliver a wigging?

Miss Hesketh rose. 'I am going to stand in the corridor for a while,' she announced, as if this was a perfectly normal thing for a lady-traveller to do. 'This may be an opportunity, Miss Watson, for you to impart to Lucy information she may need, regarding her condition.'

Crikey! Was this why she had been brought along? To give Lucy a quick lesson in what to expect from pregnancy and the dreaded childbirth? And...giving up the baby afterwards? Good manners brought Molly to her feet to heave the door open for Miss Hesketh to step outside. She tugged it closed and sank back down onto the seat.

'Well!' She looked at Lucy. 'I wasn't expecting this.'

'Weren't you?' Lucy asked sharply.

'No, but if there's anything you want to ask, now is the time.'

Lucy shrugged. Molly couldn't blame her. She must be feeling overwhelmed. Lucy made no effort to pose questions and Molly was content to leave it like that, except that...

'There's one thing I want you to know. Giving away my son for adoption was the hardest thing I've ever had to do.'

Lucy cast her eyes heavenwards. 'If this is your way of trying to make me name the father—'

A fierce ball of heat burst into life inside Molly's chest. 'I realise that your situation makes it hard for you to think of anything or anyone but yourself, Lucy, but it might surprise you to know that I would never – never – use my child to trick you or blackmail you.' The heat was white-hot. 'Do you have the first idea how honoured you are to hear me speak of my baby?'

Lucy looked alarmed, almost fearful, at her outburst. 'Honoured?'

'Yes,' Molly declared. 'You're meant to be ashamed to give birth to an illegitimate baby, but what I felt when my son was born was an explosion of love and pride and amazement, coupled with the desperate sorrow that his father would never see him. As for having him adopted, I don't know what you're meant to feel about that. Relieved? Grateful? I was grateful that my son was going to be part of a respectable family, a proper family with two parents, but mostly what I felt was regret and shock and a grief so intense I thought I would die. But I didn't. I packed my bag and went back to my old life. It was the oddest thing. I stepped back into my old life and carried on as normal, but everything was different, because I was different and have been ever since.' She gave Lucy a hard look. 'As for you, madam, you're quite possibly the most self-centred person I've ever met.'

'Oh...' Lucy's eyes filled.

'Don't bother with the waterworks. I'm not interested. Refusing to name the father, feeling sorry for yourself because you're not in love with him – you shouldn't be thinking of yourself. You should put your baby first. That's what I did, what I had to do, why I gave him up. You've got a husband waiting in the wings. Can you even begin to imagine how much I longed for my chap not to have died, how much I wanted it to be a case of mistaken identity and for him to walk through the door?'

Anguish coursed through her, almost cramping her muscles. She rubbed her arms, trying to keep from trembling. A sheen of perspiration glowed all over her skin, leaving it cool and goosebumpy.

'I probably shouldn't have said all that. I didn't even realise I was thinking it. I'm sorry if I upset you, but I'm sorry only because you're pregnant and supposed not to get upset. I don't take back a single word.'

Rising, she made to slide open the compartment door. It stuck. With a final flare of anger – she wasn't going to be defeated by a damn door, for Pete's sake – she lugged it open and peered out. Miss Hesketh was further along the corridor, looking out of the window.

'Would you like to come back in, Miss Hesketh?'

She resumed her seat. Miss Hesketh returned, making no effort to conceal the speculative look she aimed at her niece. Did she put Lucy's pale face down to a scary description of childbirth?

Molly sat back. She was drained; her limbs felt sluggish. It was an effort to rouse herself when the train pulled into another station and Miss Hesketh, peering through the window, announced, 'Here we are. Look sharp.'

The sky was low and heavy, but at least they didn't emerge into pouring rain. Instead the air was a damp mist of the finest drizzle. Molly picked up Lucy's suitcase and followed the others out of the station into a cobbled square, in the centre of which was a majestic conker tree surrounded by a circular bench. The station frontage took up one side of the square; the other three sides were occupied by a hotel with an arched porch and mullioned windows, a mock-Tudor hostelry with a slightly overhanging first floor, and pretty shops with scalloped-edged awnings over their windows – or at least they would have been pretty if summer hadn't given up and let the world turn dark and wet.

'There's a tea-shop over there,' Lucy said hopefully.

Miss Hesketh gave her a sideways look. 'We aren't on a day trip. I daresay we'll be offered refreshments when we arrive at our destination.'

'Are you looking for a taxi, madam?' The porter had come outside.

'Yes, please,' said Miss Hesketh.

'Jimbo drives the local taxi. He'll be propping up the bar. Should I fetch him for you?'

'Propping up the bar?' questioned Molly.

'Not to worry, miss. He doesn't get blind drunk any more, not since he drove into the magistrate's garden wall. Where should I say you want to go?'

'Thank you.' Miss Hesketh's voice was crisp enough to cut a hole in the drizzle. 'If you'll kindly alert him to our presence.'

'Aye, will do.' With a glance at the single suitcase, the porter trotted away.

Molly and Miss Hesketh exchanged looks over the case. Was it a dead giveaway? When people arrived, one of them a young girl, with only one suitcase between them, did the locals all jump to the same conclusion?

Outside the mock-Tudor building, a thin man cranked up his motor car and it trundled round the square to stop beside them. When he leaped out to pick up the suitcase, Molly sniffed deeply. Well, he didn't reek of beer, so presumably their lives were safe in his hands.

'Where to, ladies?'

Miss Hesketh murmured, 'Maskell House, please,' then entered the vehicle with all the dignity of a duchess and none of the desperate shame of someone with a fallen girl to dispose of. You had to admire her, all the more so when you considered she was a maiden lady.

The journey was conducted in silence. Molly felt sick. She remembered this silence. It had been her silence once, the silence of dread and desperation and having no choice. The car went over a bump in the road, jolting her thoughts. For a moment, just for a split second, she was back in that other taxi with Danny, heading for that other destination, her stomach in knots with the anxiety of getting him to his father's bedside in time. She had had no idea of the extent of the trouble that would get her into. Would it have stopped her if she had known? All that had mattered at the time was doing the right thing for Danny; but what if she couldn't get another job? And any job she did get wouldn't be a patch on the one she had lost.

Beside her, Lucy lifted a hand to her cheek – to brush away a tear? Guilt was growing inside Molly for the way she had harangued the poor girl on the train. Whatever had possessed her to let rip like that? She should have kept her mouth shut. Ought she to apologise properly? Lucy looked stricken, her eyes dark with fear. Encased in the cherry-red swing-jacket she had been wearing the evening when she had landed on the doorstep in Wilton Close and turned the household upside down, her chest rose and fell perceptibly in short little breaths, interspersed occasionally by a longer, deeper sigh.

'Here we are,' said Jimbo. How many families had he brought to this place? Was it all in a day's work to him?

He steered the motor through a gateway with a sturdy wooden gate that might have belonged to a farm, and up a short driveway with deep lavender beds on one side and a rather rough-looking lawn with several sets of garden tables and chairs on the other. The car pulled up in front of a large house, the sight of which instantly brought Aaron to mind, because much of it was covered in ivy.

Never mind waiting for the door to be opened, Miss Hesketh was out of the motor almost before Jimbo had applied the brake.

'Come, Lucy.'

Lucy scrambled out after her. Molly emerged through the other door, which Jimbo was just in time to grab hold of, even if he didn't manage to open it for her. He lifted out the suitcase from the luggage box on the rear of the vehicle.

'I'll carry this in for you.'

He was up the steps and ringing the bell before Miss Hesketh could say yea or nay. They followed him up the steps. Miss Hesketh paid him and, speaking quietly, but not so quietly that Lucy didn't catch her breath and clutch Molly's arm, asked him to return in one hour.

The door opened and a maid admitted them through a small lobby with built-in bench-seats to either side that probably lifted up for the storage of outdoor shoes, and into a hall with a tiled floor and a table in the centre, bearing a vast and highly fragrant flower arrangement of roses and lilies and goodness knows what else besides, that wouldn't have been out of place at a society wedding.

'Miss Hesketh? This way, please. Mrs Ayrton is expecting you.'

Molly hovered beside the suitcase.

'That will be taken upstairs for you,' said the maid before heading for a door leading to one of the front rooms. She knocked and stood aside for them to enter an attractive room with generously proportioned armchairs and a green-tiled fireplace with a glassed over-mantel display case. From one of the chairs rose a middle-aged woman with improbably black hair, dressed in a mid-calf-length checked dress with a wide collar.

Trust Miss Hesketh to get in the first word. 'Mrs Ayrton? Prudence Hesketh. How do you do? This is my niece, Miss Lucy Hesketh, and this is Miss Watson.'

'It's a pleasure to meet you.' Mrs Ayrton gave a Lucy an appraising glance. 'I expect you would you like some refreshment after your journey. It will be here directly. And we can talk about Lucy's stay here.'

It was bizarre. They sat in the comfortable armchairs, with an array of triangular-cut sandwiches on a couple of low tables between them, exactly as if this were a social occasion. Molly eyed the food hungrily. She was starving, but felt she couldn't dive in when the others were nibbling so daintily. Or were they all secretly dying to stuff themselves?

Mrs Ayrton talked about the home she ran and the daily lives of the girls. Hearty country walks seemed to be the order of the day – 'until it becomes uncomfortable. Fresh air is so important. I've never subscribed to the view that mothers-to-be should sit around with their feet up.'

Well, that certainly put this place in context. In her sphere of life, Molly had never known any mother-to-be who was able to indulge herself by sitting around with her feet up, apart from Tilda's sister-in-law, but she had had medical reasons for doing so. She glanced at Lucy, whose rigid posture and pallid skin made her look plain terrified.

Mrs Ayrton showed them the sitting room, where three or four girls in their late teens or early twenties were reading or chatting while another played the piano, her arms extended because her considerable girth meant she had to have the piano-stool pushed further away than normal from the instrument. Then Mrs Ayrton opened the door on what she called the busy room, which boasted a billiard table in the centre and green-baize card-tables in the bay windows. On shelves were boxes with snakes and ladders, ludo, backgammon, draughts and something called the Landlord's Game, which Molly hadn't heard of. Other shelves had stacks of old magazines, while a row of sewing boxes and knitting bags was lined up in front of one of the window-seats. Half-finished jigsaws lay on a couple of low tables by the fireplace and another table offered a Ouija board.

Lucy's bedroom was on the second floor, its knick-knacks and trinket-boxes, pretty floral cushions in the balloon-backed rattan chair and watercolours on the walls, all suggesting that this room belonged to someone in particular rather than being somewhere for a guest. Perhaps an impersonal guest room might have seemed daunting and unwelcoming to a vulnerable girl facing weeks here, but Molly wasn't sure she would have relished moving into a room filled with clutter that wasn't her own.

She gave Lucy a bright smile. 'Isn't it pretty?' She went to the window. 'Look – apple trees.'

Lucy had said barely a word since their arrival at the station. By now, she had completely clammed up. Molly's heart yearned towards her, but she mustn't say or do anything to tip Lucy over the edge into the floods of tears that were no doubt building up.

Downstairs once more in the sitting room, Miss Hesketh explained that she would pay the bill for Lucy's first few days. 'After that, Lucy's father must decide what to do for the best.'

Molly politely avoided looking at her. She wasn't stupid. The Miss Heskeths might live in a genteel way, but there wasn't much money keeping them afloat. If they footed the bill for the first few days, it would represent a significant outlay for them. With luck, their brother would reimburse them.

The hour was almost up. Miss Hesketh kissed Lucy's cheek and told her to be a good girl. Molly gave her the swiftest of hugs, but her throat was too constricted for her to be able to utter any words. Not that she would have known what to say.

The maid tapped on the door and announced the arrival of the taxi.

'Thank you,' said Mrs Ayrton, 'and would you kindly take Miss Lucy up to her room and she can show you where she would like you to put her things. Miss Hesketh, Miss Watson, permit me to show you out.'

And Lucy was whisked away in one direction while Mrs Ayrton escorted Molly and Miss Hesketh to the front steps.

'So pleased to have met you. Don't worry about Lucy. My staff and I will take good care of her.'

Jimbo opened the car door and they climbed in. Molly felt weighed down and breathless. The motor pulled away down the drive. She was on the side of the car where the lavender bed was and the herby-sweet scent filled her senses. The bed was alive with bees hard at work.

The motor passed through the open gate and turned onto the rutted country lane. Molly resisted the temptation to look over her shoulder. Along the lane, they passed through a hamlet clustered around a crossroads with an ancient stone cross and then between high grassy banks boasting vast clumps of pale-lilac bachelor's buttons and drifts of soft-yellow lady's bedstraw that must have swayed in every breath of breeze before recent rains had flattened them.

'I think Mrs Ayrton's establishment is all we could have hoped for,' said Miss Hesketh. 'My sister will be pleased when I describe it to her.'

'I'm sure she will.' Molly made the effort to join in. 'Lucy's room is very comfortable.'

'I daresay. Too fussy for my taste.'

'But Miss Patience will enjoy hearing about the ornaments and the pictures and so forth. It'll make her feel Lucy is in an agreeable place.'

'Lucy's parents will have nothing to complain of when they see the house,' said Miss Hesketh.

'No, indeed.'

'Mrs Ayrton provides a pleasant environment for the girls in her care; and it is a discreet distance from any other habitation, so the girls can be taken out for walks without being stared at.'

'And there is plenty in the house to keep them occupied,' Molly added.

'Yes. I have to say I'm very pleased with the house and its location. It seems ideal.' Miss Hesketh leaned forward and raised her voice. 'Mr Jimbo, would you please turn this vehicle round at the first convenient place and take us back to Maskell House. Thank you.'

Chapter Twenty-Eight

SUMMER HOLIDAYS WERE meant to be the best time of the year and this would have been a wonderful summer if all Jacob had to think about was mucking about with his friends and spending time with Mikey. Mikey was popular in the orphanage and the other children were well-disposed towards Jacob because he was Mikey's brother. How different it was to when he had clutched onto Thad's coat-tails. Everyone had been scared of Thad and Jacob had been the most scared of the lot. He didn't want to seem like a sissy, but it felt good to have a big brother who was kind and funny. Already there were whispers among the children about what a good head boy he would make. Thad would have laughed his socks off. Thad would have viewed a possible head boy as a toady and a swot. But Jacob knew better. He admired Mikey as well as liking him.

The trouble was he was under Shirl's thumb. He had moved from one thug to another and Shirl was scarier because of what he made Jacob do. With Thad, he had stolen off other kids and off the market, had pinched flowers from graves and sold them at the cemetery gates for coppers to the poorer sort of folk, for whom the appearance of the family plot was a constant juggling act between pride and economy. All that felt like child's play now. Delivering the strange little packets on his own was frightening. Well, he wasn't going to be alone for today's job, was he? Daniel Cropper would be with him.

Yes, but after that Cropper was going to go away to live with his uncle. Lucky beggar! A proper home, and no more working for Shirl. What more could anyone wish for? Jealousy created flashes before his eyes that dazzled his vision.

He was on his way to Cuffy's for the afternoon, as dictated by Shirl. 'I bet they'd let you out of the orphanage to visit a friend from school,' Shirl had said – commanded. Accordingly, Jacob had asked Cuffy if he could come round and play now and again in the summer.

Cuffy had shrugged. 'Yes, why not? Any time you feel like it.'

But that wouldn't do, either for Shirl, who wanted a regular arrangement, or for Mrs Rostron, because she wasn't happy unless she had full control of every aspect of the orphans' lives.

'It has to be a definite day and time,' Jacob explained to Cuffy. 'We're not allowed out unless there's a reason.'

'A reason?'

'Aye. Like going to the library.'

'The library?' Cuffy spluttered with laughter, covering Jacob's face in a faint mist.

'I don't mean I go.' Strewth, what an idea. Reading was for school, not for pleasure. 'That's just an example. Some kids go every Saturday, but in the holidays they can go in the week as well.'

'What other reasons are there?'

'You can ask to go to the park to play on the see-saw and the roundabout, or to the rec to play cricket; but you can't just ask to go out. If I said, "May I go to Stretford and see if Cuffy's home?", the answer would be no; but if I said, "Cuffy's asked me round to play" that would be all right.'

They had agreed that Jacob would go round on the Thursday of the first full week of the holidays and Jacob had duly reported this to Shirl, scared silly that Shirl would sense the waves of relief leaking from him because of knowing how much Shirl-free time lay ahead between now and then.

Getting permission to go to Cuffy's hadn't been as easy as he had imagined. It was one thing, apparently, to let the children go out and about nearby, but quite another to let him trail over to Stretford. Jacob had kicked himself. Why hadn't he thought of saying that to Shirl?

No one had ever asked for permission to go to Stretford before and Nanny Mitchell had handed the matter over to Mrs Rostron.

'We do allow the orphans who attend Chorlton schools to accept invitations from their school-friends,' was Mrs Rostron's verdict, 'so it's only fair to extend the same privilege to Layton Two.'

So today after dinner, he walked to Stretford and spent the afternoon playing out in Cuffy's road. Playing out was grand, and who cared about a bit of drizzle? He hadn't played out since before Thad went to the bad. Mrs Rostron's idea of playing out involved either the orphanage playground or the rec or Chorlton Park, certainly not larking around up and down the street. It was daft, really, when you thought about it, because if an orphan was invited round to play with a school-chum, they would always play out. It was what you did; what your mum told you to do to get you out from under her feet.

Sometimes the Church Road children would loiter near to the orphanage gates on purpose, while the orphans within begged them for invitations to come out and play in the street, invitations that might or might not be forthcoming. Sometimes the Church Road inhabitants would hang about just for the sense of power it gave them. Even though there was loads more space in the playground, everyone wanted to play outside in the road. It was the 'proper' place to play. Everyone knew that.

Jacob had a top-hole afternoon. He knew most of the other kids from school, apart from those who were too young to have started yet. They ran relay races and played ticky off the ground and hide and seek. The kickstone was the wall under Cuffy's front window and Jacob, running for its safety, yelling 'Kickstone, one, two, three,' at the top of his voice, took a mighty leap at it, imagining it was Shirl's rotten head on the receiving end of the flying drop-kick, only for a brick to drop out of the crumbling wall; but even this, after the first wash of panic, turned out to be fun, causing much sniggering as they forced it back into its hole, not quite all the way in, but far enough to keep it there for the time being. Next time it fell out, no one would know the help it had had from Jacob Layton.

Mrs Loudwater was really nice too. She gave Jacob a slice of bread and dripping. Jacob had wanted to ask if he could come again the same time next week, but he didn't like to with the bread and dripping in his hand, in case it sounded like that was the real reason he was asking.

It was a wrench to leave. The kids in Cuffy's road lived in houses, however shabby, and had families of their own. Maybe their family lives weren't anything special. Jacob knew all about that. His own family had specialised in bickering, but now that he had lost both home and family, he understood how much they had meant to him. As he made his way back to St Anthony's, he felt weighed-down and tired, and not because he had been running round all afternoon.

'Heading for home, Jemima?' Shirl stepped out in front of him, making him stumble to a halt, almost tripping over his own feet in his effort not to bump into the bigger boy. 'Had a good time with your mates?'

'Aye,' he said, adding, 'Thanks,' as an afterthought, in case Shirl picked on him for his lack of manners. It didn't do to show lack of respect for Shirl.

'And now you can have a good time doing me a favour,' said Shirl. 'Here.'

Jacob automatically took the packet. It was bigger than usual. Heavier an' all. He shoved it in his pocket and felt the seam give way. He took it out to move it to his other pocket, the one without the string, the penknife, the handkerchief the orphanage made him carry and the marble Cuffy had lent him.

Shirl grabbed it back. 'Whadder yer think you're doing, idiot-brain, waving it around for all to see?'

Jacob's gaze flew in all directions, but there was no one about. Course not, or Shirl wouldn't have handed it over. Gingerly he transferred the parcel to his other pocket. It was a snug fit but was hidden from view.

'Danny-boy all set to go with you?' asked Shirl.

'Yes.'

'Two lads out together in the school holidays is less obvious, less suspicious-looking, to those of us with suspicious minds. You're to take it to the meadows.'

'I can get there down Limits Lane.' It wasn't far. It was on his way back to the orphanage. And he didn't need Daniel Cropper.

'No, not down Limits Lane. You've got to take it right into Chorlton. Do you know that garden village place, Chorltonville? Just before that, there's a path what goes down a slope onto the meadows.'

'I know. That's the way they take us from the orphanage onto the meadows for walks.'

'For walks? Lucky you, I don't think. The path has trees and bushes on both sides and it'll be a quagmire after all this rain, but you don't have to go down it. Wait at the top. The packet will be collected.'

'We can do that,' said Jacob.

'Yes, *we* can, by which I mean Danny-boy can cos he's got guts, and you can cos you'll trail along behind him.'

Jacob stiffened in resentment, but it was true. 'Cropper's going to be waiting for me when I get back. We can slip out right away.'

'And back in time for bread and jam at teatime,' sneered Shirl. 'Nope. You've to take it later on. Be at the head of that path at seven o'clock sharp.'

'We can't—'

'You can. You have to.'

From somewhere came the sound of a policeman's whistle. Shirl looked round. 'Got to go.' And he legged it.

The hairs lifted on Jacob's arms. Was that bobby's whistle for Shirl? But now he, Jacob, was the one carrying the packet. Hell's bells. Better scarper.

It had been one of the longest days of her life. Prudence, normally so aware of living economically, splurged out on a taxi to take them home from Victoria Station. The thought of catching a bus and then walking, after the exhausting day they had all endured, was too much. Besides, Lucy needed to get home and be put to bed.

As they climbed out of the taxi in Wilton Close, the front door was thrown open and Patience came pattering down the path in her carpet-slippers to open the gate.

'Lucy! You've brought Lucy home. Oh, Prudence.' She gave a great gasp, which sounded dangerously as though it might be followed by a spurt of tears.

'Announce our business to the neighbours, why don't you?' Prudence remonstrated in a fierce undertone, grasping her sister's arm and leaving Miss Watson to scoop up Lucy and bring her indoors. 'Please will someone put the kettle on.'

'I will.' Mrs Atwood appeared from the sitting room. 'Oh! You've brought Lucy back. Oh my goodness! I never expected—'

'A cup of tea would be most welcome, thank you, Mrs Atwood.' Was she the only person present capable of keeping things moving? 'Yes, I've brought her back, as you can see.'

'But... No, Miss Patience, allow me. You sit down; I'll put the kettle on.'

But Mrs Atwood still hovered, cluttering up the hall while Patience shepherded Lucy into the sitting room and Miss Watson saw to the coats.

'What's the time?' Prudence glanced through the doorway at the clock on the mantelpiece. 'It's not quite six. What brings you home so early, Mrs Atwood?'

'I'm playing truant, I'm afraid. I had to call on a widowed mother in Fallowfield this afternoon and I couldn't bear to go back to the office. I wanted to be here to comfort Miss Patience. I knew how hard today would be for her.'

'It's not been easy for any of us,' said Prudence.

'And you've brought Lucy back. May I ask?'

'What you may do, Mrs Atwood, if you would be so kind, is put the kettle on. Thank you.'

Only self-respect and an unshakeable belief in the importance of standards prevented Prudence from collapsing into her armchair. On the sofa, Lucy sat wrapped in Patience's arms, leaning into her like a child. Well, she was still a child in many ways. Certainly immature: all that nonsense about not naming the father and wanting to be in love. A child having a child of her own. Poor Lawrence and Evelyn. This would devastate their comfortable, self-satisfied lives. Would they pin some of the blame on her for not leaving Lucy at Maskell House? Well, if they did, they did. And if they wanted to ship Lucy back there, that would be up to them, but leaving her there had been more than Prudence could bear to do.

Mrs Atwood brought in a tray of tea and started pouring, which was really Patience's job, but she was busy hugging Lucy and didn't look like stopping any time soon.

'Was the place just frightful?' Mrs Atwood asked, serving herself last and sitting down with her cup and saucer.

'Not at all. Why would you think so? It was perfectly decent, wasn't it, Miss Watson?'

'It was comfortable and clean and obviously the girls were well looked after,' Miss Watson agreed.

'I thought maybe I'd chosen somewhere horribly unsuitable,' said Mrs Atwood.

'On the contrary.' Prudence spoke matter-of-factly. It was annoying that Mrs Atwood should be inserting herself into the upset in this manner. 'Maskell House is everything it should be and if my brother deems it the appropriate place for Lucy to see out her time, I won't have any doubts or reservations on the subject.'

Lucy raised her face from Patience's chest for long enough to whisper in a quavering voice, 'I don't want to go back.'

'You may not have an option,' said Prudence, again matter-of-factly. Sometimes it was tiring being the one in charge.

'Let's not worry about that now,' said Patience. 'You're back home and that's what matters. A warm bath and bed, I think, don't you, Prudence? And I'll bring up something on a tray. Then you need a good night's sleep. Come along.'

Unwinding herself from Lucy's clutches, Patience eased herself off the sofa and helped Lucy to her feet. Miss Watson got up too.

'You see to Lucy, Miss Patience. I'll bring the suitcase upstairs, and then shall I make a start on our meal? I don't know about you, Miss Hesketh, but I'm famished.'

'I ought to offer to do the cooking,' said Mrs Atwood, as Patience, Lucy and Miss Watson left the room. 'I will when Molly comes down.'

'Thank you.' It went against the grain to permit one of the p.g.s into the kitchen, but needs must. 'If you'll excuse me, I must go and tidy myself.' She rose from her seat. Goodness, her bones were tired. She would be glad to get to bed tonight.

Mrs Atwood put out her hand and almost – almost – touched her, pulling her hand back at the last moment. 'May I ask why? Why did you bring Lucy back?'

Prudence stiffened. 'That is a question my sister and brother are entitled to ask, but no one else.'

'Please, I'm not being nosy. I – I need to know.'

'I beg your pardon? "Need" is an interesting choice of word.'

Mrs Atwood's hands shook; she clumped them together in her lap, then used them to cover her mouth and nose. This was ridiculous. What was going on?

'I think it's time to end this conversation,' Prudence said in the voice that had quelled many a colleague over the years.

She made to leave the room, but Mrs Atwood broke down in tears.

'Mrs Atwood!' Really, this was too much.

'I'm adopted, you see. That's why I want to know.'

'I fail to see…'

'I always knew I was adopted. My parents made sure I knew it made me extra special. Bless them, they gave me such confidence.'

'If Lucy's predicament has brought your adoption to the fore, I suppose that's only to be expected, but I'm disappointed in you if you intend to wallow in your adoption, as if you are the person in the centre of this crisis, while the rest of us are thinking about Lucy. I thought better of you than this, Mrs Atwood.'

The younger woman gazed up at her from swimming blue-grey eyes. When she spoke, her voice was surprisingly steady.

'It wasn't until after my mother passed away last year that I found my birth certificate and decided to trace my real mother. That's what brought me here.'

'It doesn't say much for your dedication to your new job, if it was merely the means to bring you here to Manchester.'

'Not here to Manchester. Here, to Wilton Close, to this house.'

Unease stirred. 'What are you talking about?'

'My birth certificate.' Mrs Atwood swallowed. 'It says *Mother: Prudence Winifred Hesketh. Father unknown.*'

Chapter Twenty-Nine

AARON WAITED FOR the final stragglers in the dining room to finish their tea and leave. Instead of going home, he had had his tea here today in order to organise games for the children to while away the evening at the end of another wet day.

When Danny came up to him, Aaron gave him a smile, wanting to tousle his hair, but restraining himself. He mustn't do anything that suggested favouritism.

'Would it be all right if I stop here at St Anthony's tonight instead of coming to Soapsuds Cottage?'

That was a good thing, wasn't it? Danny must feel more settled, but Aaron experienced a stab of disappointment. He was growing attached to Danny. Well, he could jolly well unattach himself. It wasn't appropriate. It wasn't fair to the other children. Moreover he was laying himself open to an emotional wrench when Danny went to live in Cumberland.

Speaking of which, where was Uncle Angus? Shouldn't he have come by this time to take Danny to his new home? Mr Cropper had passed away last Saturday. Now it was Thursday, more than enough time for Uncle Angus to show his face.

Tea was over. This week's table monitors wiped down the long tables and swept the floor, working under the eye of Nurse Philomena, then Aaron took charge.

'Move this table against the wall and put that one at right-angles to it. Layton One and Appleby, bring that table over here. Lift it up, lads! Don't drag it along the floor. And I want the chairs spread about all over the place. We're going to play pirates,' he announced, causing a frisson of excitement. 'Will everybody please check that everybody else is wearing slippers.'

He grinned at the ensuing skirmish. A game of pirates would be fun, but he would much rather have the evening free to go round to Wilton Close. He had called there during his dinner-hour. The door had been answered by a middle-aged lady with grey hair, whose face would probably have been kind if she hadn't looked so worried. He had made it sound like he had an official reason for coming from St Anthony's, not wanting to land Molly in hot water for having a follower calling.

'Miss Watson isn't here today,' the lady told him.

'Do you know when she'll be back?'

'I'm afraid not. She's out all day.'

Looking for a new job? Having an interview, maybe? She deserved it if anyone did.

It was time to start the game.

'Everyone sit on the floor and listen.' A soft thudding sound echoed round the dining room.

'When the game starts, the floor will be the sea. The tables and chairs are rocks and shipwrecks. You have to keep out of the sea. If so much as your little toe touches the water, you're out. If one of the pirates catches you, you're out. When there are two sailors left, they'll be the next pair of pirates.'

'Who are the pirates to start with, sir?'

He chose the head boy and the head girl.

'Catherine can't be a pirate,' called out Johnson Two. 'She's a girl.'

'It's a well-known fact,' Aaron replied, 'that girl-pirates are more ferocious than boy-pirates. Right, if your birthday

344

is in January, February or March, find a rock and stand on it…'

Soon the game was in full swing, with the children moving nimbly from one piece of furniture to another while trying to evade the pirates. Presently only a handful of sailors remained. Aaron was pleased to see Danny was among them. He deserved a spot of fun after everything he had been through. Wait a minute. It looked like he was putting himself in the way of being caught. No, that couldn't be right. But it was. He was letting Catherine catch up with him. Yet Aaron could have sworn he was enjoying the game. Hang on a sec – was he putting himself in danger to save Johnson Three from capture? That was kind of him, giving the smaller lad a chance to carry on playing.

Shortly afterwards the second game was under way, Aaron keeping an eye out for cheating or accidents. Where was Danny? He had probably nipped out to the BB, but he ought to have asked permission. Aaron's gaze sharpened. Was Jacob Layton…? Yes, he was missing too.

'You two.' He crouched beside a couple of boys who were already out, sitting with their backs against the wall. 'Nip up to the junior common room and see if Cropper and Layton Two are there, will you? And if not, try the dormitories.'

'We're not allowed in the dormitories until bedtime.'

Aaron said in a jokey way, 'There's a lot of things you're not allowed to do, but I wouldn't put anything past those two. They're not in trouble. I just need to know where they are. Get a move on or you'll miss the start of the next game.'

Those were the magic words. The boys raced away, returning a few minutes later to report that there was no sign of Cropper and Layton Two.

'We even went to the BB.'

'Thanks, lads.'

He smiled at them, but couldn't prevent a prickly feeling scuttling across his skin.

As if from a huge distance, Prudence was aware of Mrs Atwood speaking. Well, no, not so much speaking as weeping, hiccupping and stammering. She made an effort to focus, but how could she when her heart, frozen at first, was now pounding fit to burst? In any case, did she want to focus? Did she want to listen? How could this possibly be real?

Mother: Prudence Winifred Hesketh. Father unknown.

All those years of being unsympathetic and critical towards others, positively judgemental at times. But the person she had always, albeit in darkest secrecy, judged most harshly was herself.

When Mrs Atwood had uttered the fatal words, Prudence had sat back down. No, not sat. That suggested she had been in charge of her knees, and she hadn't. They had turned to mush and she had dropped, simply dropped. If she had been further from the armchair, she would landed in an undignified heap on the floor.

Mother: Prudence Winifred Hesketh. Father unknown.

Father unknown: that was a lie. The father had been very much known, thanks to her and her utter stupidity.

With a wrench, she homed in on Mrs Atwood's babbling.

'...that's why I took such an interest in poor Lucy, d'you see? I know you thought me the most frightful busybody, but I had to know. I had to understand – I still do. I thought – I thought the way you treated Lucy...would help me understand what happened to you when – when you were having me.' Mrs Atwood's blue-grey eyes now longer swam with distress. Her voice was pitched low, words spilling out. Her hands moved, making gestures, expressing themselves in their own instinctive way. All at once, she stilled. The uncertainty left her. Her voice was sober. 'I thought the manner in which you dealt with Lucy would show me what you thought of your own past and your own child...' She spread her hands. 'Me.'

Me.

Vivienne Atwood – her daughter.

Her *daughter*.

The years fell away. Prudence's insides swooped and her thoughts jumbled together like pieces in a jigsaw puzzle box. Like a jigsaw, they would come together; they would build a picture, a story. Her story. Her secret.

Vivienne Atwood. Blue-grey eyes. Cool, confident manner. Smart clothes.

My daughter.

What a name to choose. Vivienne! Prudence wouldn't have thought of that in a hundred years. She would have chosen – no, she wouldn't. She hadn't chosen anything, not even as a secret solace.

Vivienne Atwood.

My daughter.

The gabardine was way too roomy. It was like old times, the youngest lad having to grow into too-large cast-offs. That was one good thing about the orphanage. They put you in clothes of the correct size. The gabardines were Daniel's idea.

'They'll keep us dry and – how's this for a clever wheeze – they're a crafty disguise. If there's any bother, the cops will be on the look-out for a pair of grammar school bods.'

'The cops?' Did the flip of panic in Jacob's stomach make itself heard in his voice? It was all right for Daniel Cropper, making off-hand remarks about the police. He hadn't been there to hear that police-whistle earlier. Shit shit shit.

'Well, anyone who sees us, anyone who's asked if they saw owt.' Daniel shrugged as if it didn't matter and Jacob was ashamed of his cowardice. 'Not that anyone's out in this weather that doesn't have to be.'

Attempting a swagger, Jacob said, 'It's the closest I'll ever get to grammar school.'

The orphanage set aside the money to send two boys to grammar school – two at any one time, not two per school year. So you could be the brightest lad in the universe, but it wouldn't do you a blind bit of good if there were already two boys at the grammar. No one else from the orphanage could go until one of them left.

'Who the heck wants to stay on at school until they're fifteen?' he added. 'Not flaming likely.'

It was a good job the gabardines were too long because the rain chose that moment to come down in stair-rods. He hunched inside his coat, turning up the collar, for all the good it did. His cap moulded itself onto his skull. They must look less like grammar school boffins and more like drowned rats as they squelched their way across the Green. They went past the old churchyard, where the road sloped downwards. Jacob dug his hands in his pockets. One wet hand bumped into Shirl's packet and he quickly drew his fingers out again. He couldn't risk getting into a jam for handing over a damp packet.

The road widened as they passed the Bowling Green. It said Bowling Green Hotel on the sign, but it was a pub an' all. Daniel gave him a shove that nearly sent him stumbling into its wall.

'Hey!'

'Keep your voice down,' hissed Daniel. 'Don't look round – I said, don't look – but Bunny is over the far side of the road, sheltering under the trees.'

'You're kidding. Has he seen us?'

'Dunno, but keep your face turned the other way until we get right past.'

Jacob put on a spurt – or did that look too obvious? He sloshed through a puddle and cold water seeped through his shoes and soaked his socks. A little further on, walls sprang up on either side of the road, with two sets of handsome gates opposite one another. The gates on the other side were shut, but those on this side stood open. Up ahead, through a grey veil of rain, beyond the stretch of farmland, was the corner they must turn to get to the top of the path where they would be met. A few minutes and it would be over. Oh, thank heaven. He would pay proper attention in church for ever more if they could just get this delivery safely over and done with.

'Blimey!' exclaimed Daniel.

A bobby had come round that corner, the very corner Jacob had been focusing on. A police-whistle sounded – or was that just in his head?

'In here.' Daniel grasped his arm and dragged him through the open gates.

'We can't,' Jacob hissed. 'This is rich folk's property. What if there are guard dogs?'

But Daniel didn't let go. 'This is a hospital now, since the war. Come on.'

The drive was topped with gravel and their footsteps made a crunching noise that sounded like thunder in Jacob's ears, but as soon as they were past the gates, Daniel pulled him over to the right, where gravel gave way to soft ground – ground that wasn't meant to be soft. Jacob's shoes sank into it. Just ahead the ground fell away and there was a river.

'Is that part of the Mersey?'

'Don't be stupid. It's the brook.'

'Chorlton Brook? But the brook's shallow.'

'Not after all this rain, dimwit,' said Daniel. He headed down the bank. 'Over here: we can hide behind the bushes until the policeman's gone past.'

'Do you think he's after us?'

'How can he be? We haven't done anything yet.'

'We haven't, but the man we're meeting might have,' said Jacob. 'What if he's been caught?'

'It might just be a bobby on the beat.'

'Or it might not.' He wished he hadn't said that. Now he sounded like a coward.

'Careful.' Daniel pulled him backwards. 'Don't go too far that way. Look.'

Jacob had been too busy looking back he way they had come. Now he looked ahead.

'Ruddy heck, what's that?'

It was a giant hole beside the brook. About four or five feet across and – well, who could say how deep? There was water in it. As he watched, more sloshed over from the swollen brook, spattering the rounded sides of the hole.

'That's an overflow hole,' said Daniel. 'There are several of them along the length of the brook.'

'How do you know?'

'My dad used to be a night-watchman and if there was rain like we've had the past few days, he'd hope for the job of watching the overflow holes to see how high the water rose in them. He had to walk from one hole to another all night. He'd come home soaked to the bone in the morning and it'd take him two whole days to warm up properly. He took me on a walk once to show me where all the holes are and we sneaked in here to see this one.'

The ground shifted slightly beneath Jacob's feet and he stepped further away from the hole. He tried to peer round the bushes, only to get slapped in the face by a twiggy mass of wet leaves. He spat out some drips, wriggling as others made their chilly way down his neck.

'D'you think it's safe to go yet?'

'I'll take a look.'

Jacob pulled Daniel's sleeve. 'No – don't.'

Daniel jerked away and it was impossible to know exactly

what happened next because it happened so fast, but there was a slither, a whoosh of panic, a wild whirling of arms – and an almighty splash as Daniel fell into the hole and vanished under the water.

Chapter Thirty

AFTER THE LONG day she and the others had had, and the sandwiches she had felt unable to tuck into at Maskell House, Molly was as hungry as a hunter. The rain streamed down the windows of the Miss Heskeths' small kitchen. In the centre of the window-sill was a blue bud-vase and over in the corner, behind the curtain – out of sight of Miss Hesketh's eyes, perhaps? – stood a bottle of hand lotion. Molly plucked the onions and potatoes from the vegetable rack and started peeling. Potatoes first, and while they were parboiling, she tackled the onions, sniffing lustily and blinking. She melted a pat of butter in the frying pan; the chopped onion sizzled as she added it. Then she dashed outside to cut some herbs, any herbs, she didn't care which, not in this rain, from the flower pots on top of the coal-bunker.

Back inside, she filled the kettle and put it on to boil, then went to fetch cornflour from the pantry. The house didn't have just a pantry-cupboard, but a proper walk-in pantry, which was bigger than the small kitchen seemed to merit. Her hand hovered in mid-air as she located Oxo cubes and cornflour; then she spotted a tin of Bird's custard powder and took that as well. There were some Granny Smiths in the vegetable rack. Potato and onion soup with as much bread as could be spared without denuding tomorrow morning's bread-board, followed by stewed apple and custard. That would be satisfying.

As she stirred the onions, their tang making her mouth water, there was a frantic knocking at the kitchen door, which burst open so suddenly she thought the wind must have blown it, but a woman in a black dress and white apron stood there, shifting from foot to foot as though about to dash inside. It took Molly a moment to place her: the Layton boys' mother. Molly had seen her when she had been allowed into St Anthony's to see her boys for half an hour. She worked over the road in the Morgans' house.

'Mrs Layton, is something wrong? Did you want the Miss Heskeths?'

'You're the lady that works at the orphanage, aren't you? Have you seen our Jacob? My youngest?'

'No. Why? I don't work there any more.'

'Yon caretaker said...'

'Mrs Layton.' Aaron's voice: Molly's heart gave a little skip in spite of the bizarre situation. 'Evening, Miss Watson.'

Molly nodded at him. Dressed in a shapeless jacket that apparently did duty as a raincoat, and with his cap jammed on, he walked purposefully up the side-passage.

'Come in, both of you,' she said. 'What's happened?'

'Danny Cropper and Jacob Layton have taken it into their heads to go out.'

Molly caught her breath. 'You mean they've run away?' As Mrs Layton gave a strangled gasp and pressed a hand to her throat, Molly wished she had been more tactful, but how could you ask such a question tactfully? And it was the obvious one to ask, given Danny's history.

'There's no reason to think that,' Aaron said stoutly, with a glance at the frightened mother. 'I was playing games with the children and next time I looked, they'd gone. I've organised search parties and Mrs Rostron has gone to the police station.

I came to see if they'd called on Mrs Layton. When I mentioned coming here next, Mrs Layton beat me to it.'

'They haven't been here.'

'Do you mind if I look in the garden shed?' He strode away without waiting for a reply, returning to say, 'It was worth a try. Miss Watson, may I leave Mrs Layton in your capable hands while I carry on looking?'

'Of course,' said Molly, immediately followed by, 'No – wait. I'll come with you. Mrs Layton, let's take you back over the road so that if Jacob comes to find you, you'll be in the right place.'

'I'll take her,' said Aaron, 'then I'll come back for you.'

'I'll meet you outside.'

Quickly, Molly removed the onions and potatoes from the heat and went to the sitting room, where she found Vivienne looking like she had been crying and Miss Hesketh, silent and colourless. Not a row, surely? With a hasty 'Excuse me,' she darted up the stairs. Lucy was in bed. Miss Patience sat beside her, patting her hand. She looked up as Molly came in.

'I've started some soup, but I have to go out. Two boys from the orphanage are missing and I said I'll help look.'

'Oh, my goodness,' fluttered Miss Patience. 'Yes, go, Molly dear. I'll see to things here.'

'Thank you. And – Miss Hesketh and Vivienne are in the sitting room. I'd leave them alone for now, if I were you.'

Running downstairs, she grabbed her shoes from the shelf in the cloakroom, slipping her galoshes on top, then unhooked her mackintosh and flung it on, tying the belt tightly before reaching for her hat. She opened the front door and ran down the path to the gate just as Aaron appeared from the house over the road. She ran towards him, then stopped dead. What was she thinking? Had it looked as if she expected, wanted, to be caught in his arms?

They fell in step, Molly hurrying to keep up with his long stride.

'I've already tried my cottage,' he told her, 'but we'll go back there now, just in case. Danny has spent a few nights there with me since he lost his dad, so he knows where it is. That's why I tried your house. Jacob knows where his mum works, obviously, so he may know you live over the road. I thought – I hoped Danny might have taken it into his head to go to you, as being the person who helped him get to the sanatorium.'

'Where are others looking?'

'Nanny Mitchell and the nursemaids are staying at St Anthony's to look after the kids. I've sent the fourteens out in twos to various places around Chorlton, to have a look and come straight back. My cottage is near the Green, so after we've tried there, we'll head down Hawthorn Road. You can get onto the meadows at the end and we can walk across to Limits Lane, where the cottage was burned down that had the Layton family in it.'

'It'll be like walking on a sponge, going over the meadows.'

At the other end of the Green, Aaron guided her round the corner towards the last one in a row of cottages. He opened the front door and walked straight through to look out of the back door. Molly glanced round, trying not to be nosy, especially in the current situation, but the chance to see Aaron's home was too great. Though small, it was neat – well, that was no surprise. He kept his workshop meticulously tidy. The parlour had a settee and there was a drop-leaf dining table under the sash-window, with upright wooden chairs pushed underneath. Designed and made by Aaron? But what caught her gaze, and held it, was a spiral staircase in the corner.

'The boys aren't out the back,' Aaron said as he returned, 'and there's no sign of them having been there. Let's try the meadows.' He closed the front door behind them. 'Wait a minute. I'll ask old Mrs Mulvey next door if she'll keep an eye out.' Stepping across, he knocked on the neighbour's door and quickly explained about the missing lads.

His elderly neighbour expressed concern and promised to keep an eye out. 'Let's hope they're just having a lark. Boys will be boys.'

'Let's hope so,' said Aaron, but the tightness about his mouth told Molly he was as worried as she was.

When Daniel resurfaced, spluttering and coughing, relief poured through Jacob from his scalp right down to the soles of his feet and he almost burst into tears. Instinctively he sprang to the edge of the hole, but the ground was slick, sending his feet scudding, and he had to throw himself backwards so as not to follow Daniel into the water. More water from the brook slopped over the top of the hole, drenching Daniel and making him cough and gasp.

Jacob crawled to the edge. The face that stared up at him was wide-eyed with terror, but Jacob had his own fears to contend with. What if the ground gave way and tipped him in as well? Inching forward on his tummy, the ground slobbery-wet and squelchy beneath the front of his soaked gabardine, he got as near to the edge as he dared and thrust a hand downwards.

'That's nowhere near,' cried Daniel.

Jacob shuffled forwards another inch, but it wasn't enough. Daniel seemed miles away. The water was up to his chest. There was a surge in the brook and more water poured over the edge, dousing him.

'Come nearer.' Jacob flexed his fingers, trying to elongate them. 'Then you'll be able to reach.'

'I can't. I'm stuck. My foot's stuck. I can't move.'

'Wiggle it.'

'It's stuck, I tell you.'

'Well...' Well what? Damn damn damn. 'Wait a minute and then try again, but gently.' That would do it. It had to. It was bound to. 'And I'll...' What could he do? His brain was frozen. He couldn't think. 'I'll use my gaberdine as a rope and pull you out.'

'It's no good. I can't move.'

'Just try.'

Hauling himself to his knees, Jacob undid the belt and fiddled with the buttons, making sure to lean away from the hole as he did so. Did that make him look cowardly? Self-preservation wasn't cowardly, not really. They would be in an even worse mess if he fell in an' all. As he started to roll up the gabardine lengthways, his hands found a lump in one of the pockets. Shirl's packet! As more water cascaded over the edge into the hole and Daniel yelled at him for help, Jacob fumbled his way into the pocket and pulled out Shirl's packet. Somewhere deep inside him, guilt wriggled. What sort of monster was he to worry about a rotten packet when Daniel was trapped in the overflow hole with water pouring in?

He managed to roll up the coat, but as he dangled it over the edge, trying to cast it in Daniel's direction, it unravelled. He could almost hear Thad's voice sneering at him for having had such a damn fool idea in the first place and for being too much of a cack-handed idiot to carry it out properly. He heaved the gabardine out onto the side. It flapped against him, heavy and wet. He pushed it away.

Wiping rain from his face, he called down to Daniel again. 'Have you got your foot loose?'

Daniel's only reply was a glare that would have made Jacob recoil, except that he was lying flat out. But he recoiled inside. Daniel needed him. He was Daniel's only hope and he was useless.

'Do something!' yelled Daniel.

What the hell was he supposed to do? He couldn't run for help in case that copper really was looking for them. But if he stayed here, the water in the hole would rise and...

'Hang on. I'm going for help.'

He scrambled to his feet, slipping and sprawling in the mud. Scrabbling his way backwards from the hole, he got to his feet and, bending almost double so that his hands could help him, he clambered up the bank, almost swooning with relief when he regained the gravel drive. He dived out between the gates, scudding to a standstill in time to throw himself against one of the stone gateposts. With his back plastered to it, he peered round to see if the policeman was still there. No sign. There were houses down that way, opposite the farm, but the copper might be down there too, so Jacob went the other way, back towards the Bowling Green. He would pound the door down if he had to.

As he careered through sheets of rain towards the pub, he thought he heard a voice, but of course he couldn't have. It must have been Thad in his head. Then a hand clamped onto his shoulder and he almost shrieked in fear as he was swung round – Shirl? Thad? The copper? No, it was –

'*Bunny!*' His knees buckled with relief and Bunny yanked him upright.

'What's up?'

He had never heard Bunny sound so sharp. Sharp meant capable and Jacob felt bolstered by it.

'It's Daniel Cropper. He's fallen into the overflow hole and the water's coming in. He's stuck. He can't get out. Please help us.' He made a grab for Bunny's hand, but Bunny was already on the move.

'Show me.'

And off Bunny went, with Jacob racing behind, trying to keep up and stop Bunny from overshooting the gates.

'Here! He's in here!' Jacob was forced to shout when it looked like Bunny would go straight past.

Bunny gave him a look he couldn't fathom. 'What were you doing in here?' He strode through the gates. Who would have thought that shambling, good-natured Bunny could stride out like that? Jacob bumbled along beside him.

'Down here. Be careful. It's slippy.'

But the slipperiness seemed only to affect Jacob. Bunny didn't break his stride. Jacob burst through the sopping bushes in time to hear Bunny exclaim, 'Well, bugger me!' as he dropped to his knees and shuffled forwards, then slumped onto his stomach, reaching out an arm.

'I can't.' Danny's voice was thick with panic. 'I'm stuck. My foot's stuck. I can't move.'

Jacob jammed his hands into his armpits, trying to hold himself in one piece. Time seemed skewed. Had it sped up or slowed right down?

Bunny hissed something under his breath and scrambled up, almost losing his balance as his feet got tangled in Jacob's discarded gabardine. His hand plunged to the ground to steady himself, then he came upright.

'You stay here,' he ordered Jacob. 'I'll fetch help.'

Jacob watched him vanish, wanting to call him back. He didn't want to be left alone. He was useless, a complete dud. More water spilled over into the hole, deluging Daniel, who emerged spluttering and crying. Jacob felt like crying too. His chest was hot and tight.

Please let Bunny be in time.

Chapter Thirty-One

'WON'T YOU PLEASE talk to me about it?' Mrs Atwood spoke softly. Her initial distress had subsided and, though she looked drawn, her posture was upright, her manner composed; but how composed was she on the inside? 'If you refuse, I want you to know I shan't trouble you with it again.'

'You mean you aren't threatening me with exposure,' Prudence challenged her. Why react so sharply? Why couldn't she take a leaf from Mrs Atwood's book and speak in a moderate voice? Mrs Atwood's voice was almost gentle.

The snub brought a flicker to the steadiness in Mrs Atwood's eyes, but in no other regard did her manner falter. 'I'm not threatening you with anything. I wouldn't dream of it. Might it help if I talked a little to start with, while you overcome the shock? At the very least, you're entitled to an explanation for my presence here, even if you elect not to confide in me afterwards.'

'You said you found your birth certificate after your mother's death.' The sound of Prudence's heartbeat ought to have been running amok in her ears, but instead it was rock-steady in her chest, sending solemnity around her body. 'After Elspeth's death.'

'Elspeth,' breathed Mrs Atwood.

And there it was. Acknowledgement. Admission.

Elspeth. Dear Elspeth from long ago.

Mrs Atwood's hand fluttered to her chest and pressed against it, fingers splayed. She gave a little shake of the head, her breaths quick and shallow. She pursed her lips as if about to whistle and blew out a stream of air.

'Yes,' she said. 'Elspeth. My mother – my adoptive mother. I want you to know I couldn't have had a better mother; she was my true mother in every way that mattered – in every sense but one.'

Prudence nodded. She had never doubted that Elspeth and Graham would make good parents. In the midst of her turmoil and fear all those years ago, it was the one certainty she had clung to.

'As you know,' Mrs Atwood continued, 'I was widowed in the war. I was working in one of the family hotels at the time.' She glanced at Prudence. Waiting for an acknowledgement that Prudence remembered the hotel business Elspeth had married into? 'I loved my husband dearly and I was dreadfully upset to lose him, but part of my bereavement was the sense of futility. What was the point of working in a hotel when things were happening that were so much more important? I lived with that feeling for some time without telling anyone until finally I decided to do something about it. I flirted with the idea of war work, but I wanted something permanent, so I went to work for a charity called Projects for the Ignorant Poor. Have you heard of it? They do good work, but the name says it all: Ignorant Poor. The charity had an attitude that I found frustrating. I did my best, though.'

Of course she did. Elspeth and Graham would have instilled that into her at an early age. Possibly – oh, it was madness to entertain the thought – she had no business thinking it – but might some of Vivienne's determination to do her best be a tiny Hesketh legacy running through her veins?

Good lord. Vivienne. Not Mrs Atwood. Vivienne. She had thought of her as Vivienne. It was part of the process of admission. No, it was more than that. It was part of the process of acceptance. No – not the process of acceptance, but acceptance itself.

My daughter.

Vivienne.

'After the war, I got out of PIP as fast as I could and went to work for a local corporation in their housing department. I thought it would be a useful and interesting job, and it was, but there was a limit to what I was allowed to do, being a woman. I soon found out that I'd never be allowed to be involved in the new Housing Committee, organising the street improvement schemes and slum clearances. I stayed in that job for a year, so that no one could say I hadn't given it a jolly good go; then I moved into what, during the war, had been the rationing department, which now looked after matters such as providing extra milk to expectant mothers and making sure that, in families where the children were entitled to free school meals, the children actually ate them on the school premises instead of bundling them up and taking them home. I found as well that if I used my initiative, there was scope for me to extend my day-to-day duties, as long as what I did centred around working with families.'

Prudence nodded. 'So that no one, by which, of course, I mean no man, could claim you were working on something that was unsuitable for a woman.'

Mrs Atwood – Vivienne – leaned forward with a smile. 'Exactly.' There was a suggestion of relaxation about her, as if she felt the worst was over and now the two of them could make a fresh start. Could they? 'Last year, as I said, my mother passed away.'

'I'm very sorry.' And she was. She hadn't seen Elspeth in years. They had parted knowing there would never be contact of any description between them. Yet knowing she was dead made the world a smaller place. A tiny piece chipped off Prudence and vanished for ever, leaving her diminished.

'I found my birth certificate, with your name on it. I didn't know what to do. I didn't know if there was anything I could do, other than ask my father, and how could I do that, so soon after Mother's death? So I let it be and returned to work. I was already interested in trying for a position in one of the new Boards of Health. I thought it would give me the chance to do the kind of thing I was already doing, and more besides. Then, a few months ago, in the spring, I saw that article in *Vera's Voice* about this business school – and there was your name. Goodness, my heart has given a little jump, just thinking of it. Naturally I told myself that it might not be you; it might simply be someone with the same name.' Vivienne sucked in a breath. 'That was when I approached my father.'

'Graham.' Yes, Graham. The man who had taken on his wife's friend's child to bring up as his own. It took a special sort of man to do that. Had she realised it at the time? Truly understood it? Or had she been too embroiled in her own desperate situation?

'I told him about the birth certificate and the article and asked if you had lived in Manchester and had a sister called Patience. He said yes. He said you had worked in one of the family hotels for a time, up in Scotland; he remembered Miss Patience as well; he said she once came to visit you.'

'Yes.' That had spelled the end of everything. If Patience hadn't come...

'I carried on as normal. I didn't make any plans to contact you, if that's what you're thinking. I didn't make any decisions, either way. Part of me thought I should leave well alone; but then the position came up in the Board of Health in Manchester and it all seemed to fit in perfectly. I wrote to you, care of *Vera's Voice*, asking if you took resident pupils and – here I am. I'm truly sorry for any deception on my part, but I couldn't risk being told to go to blazes. Then, when Lucy admitted to her condition, it all got rather overwhelming. I had this idea that the way you treated her would show me how you regarded what had happened to you and how you felt about your own child...about me.'

'I see.'

'That's my side of the story. Are you going to tell me to go to blazes?'

Molly and Aaron passed the handsome lych-gate at the entrance to the old churchyard and turned the corner to walk down the road, where the rain raced down the slope faster than they did, Molly's galoshes and Aaron's boots raising a splash with every footfall. Aaron took her arm in a light but firm grip.

'Careful. Don't slip.'

At the bottom of the slope, Aaron started to guide her across the road so they could head down Hawthorn Road and reach the meadows. They were now walking into the rain and Molly ducked her face, freeing herself from Aaron so she could wipe away a lock of hair that had become smeared across her cheek. Before they could reach the far pavement, a yell made them look round. Bunny!

'You didn't say Bunny was out searching,' she said as they swung round to hurry in his direction.

'He isn't. I hope he doesn't need anything. We can't stop and help him. The boys are our priority.'

When they met in the road, Bunny bent right over, gasping to catch his breath and waving a hand to show the urgency of what he needed to say. He brought himself upright, still struggling for breath, his face red with exertion.

He pointed back the way he had come. 'Emergency – one of your lads.'

'What's happened?' Aaron was already on the move.

'Wait. We need...tools. I was on my way to...the Bowler.' A couple of puffs and he brought his breathing under control.

'Young Layton and another lad…He's fallen in the overflow hole. His foot's stuck and the water's rising.'

'You two go on ahead,' Aaron ordered. 'I'll bring whatever tools they've got.' He strode in the direction of the pub, throwing the words over his shoulder.

Molly started to run, but Bunny couldn't keep up with her. She slowed and looked round. 'Where?' she demanded.

'Through the open gates on the left. Turn right immediately. Through the bushes. Yell and the boys'll hear you.'

As she began to run, she heard him call a warning to be careful. The tall gates giving access to Brookburn House were indeed standing open. She darted inside and swerved to the right, pushing her way through soaked bushes and undergrowth, spluttering and shielding her eyes as stems and branches covered in saturated leaves sprang at her. She burst out the other side, her stomach swooping as she slipped to a standstill, waving her arms to regain her balance.

The scene before her turned her skin clammy all over in a way that was nothing to do with the rain. Jacob was on his knees at the edge of a deep hole, inside which, up to his armpits in water, was Danny. Her entrance made Jacob look round. He got up, but maybe being crouched like that had given him pins and needles, because he wobbled and picked his feet up a few times. She went straight to the edge of the hole, just as another surge from the overfull brook washed over the side. For one horrifying moment, Danny vanished. Then his head bobbed into view again.

'Hang on,' Molly called. 'Help is on the way.'

She looked back the way she had come. The bushes shifted and swayed. Thank goodness! But it was only Bunny.

Another gush of water tipped into the hole, landing squarely on Danny's head. Pushing out breaths at triple the normal speed, he stared up at her, his eyes huge with fear. More water poured in – and more – and Danny's shoulders vanished from view. Where was Aaron?

She couldn't stand it any more. She sat down on the side of the hole, legs dangling.

'Wait! You can't,' called Bunny, but she paid no attention.

'I'm coming in,' she told Danny, whose gaze was riveted to her. 'I'll try not to splash you.'

He nodded. She tried to turn round and hold on to lower herself in gradually, but with a whoosh she plunged downwards. Shock – freezing – panic – then she found her feet and stood up, gasping, trying not to look as terrified as she felt. The surge of water she had caused had made Danny swallow some and he was coughing and gasping. She stepped across and placed herself behind him, rubbing his back in big circles to ease his breathing.

'Listen to me.' She put her mouth close to his ear when his breathing had steadied as much as it was likely to under the circumstances. 'I'm going to stay here, behind you, and I'll lean forwards to protect you, so any water that comes over the side will land on me instead of you.'

Danny gulped and nodded. His body shook in a series of shivers that rocked him from head to toe. Molly put her arms around him.

'Help is on its way. Mr Abrams is coming. He has to fetch some tools first, so we can—'

Her words vanished in a huge gasp as cold water doused her from above. She hunched over Danny, holding him tightly. More water dropped on top of her – and more. The weight of it was astonishing. She braced herself, pulling Danny closer to her as his thin body crumpled.

'Hang on, Danny. Not long now.'

He gulped and gagged. The water sloshed around his chin.

'Tilt your head back. That's right. Just a bit longer. You can do it.'

Oh, where was Aaron?

'Just a bit longer.'

Well, she hadn't sent Vivienne to blazes, so that meant, it could only mean, that Prudence was about to speak the words that had never been spoken in all these years. She had come home from Scotland, telling herself she had left it all behind; telling herself to look ahead, to build a new life for herself. Except that the life she had built hadn't been new. She had simply stepped back into the old life she had left behind. And here she had been ever since. Lord, how many years?

'There isn't much to tell. It's the same old story that must have happened to so many girls. No young men were queuing up for me at the front door and I knew they never would. Most girls in that position, I suppose, learned to accept such a fate and resigned themselves to living at home with their parents; but I had other ideas.' She adopted a light, crisp tone that invited neither comment not sympathy. 'I was clever; I excelled at my job. I decided to forge a career for myself, which was no small thing in those days, I can tell you. It's hard enough now, but it was significantly harder then. In those days, a female employee wasn't even allowed to be on her own with a male employee; and if two people found themselves together, you can guess which one of them had to leave the room.'

'Things have moved on,' murmured Vivienne, 'though not nearly as much as they need to.'

'Agreed. At the start of the year in which I was due to turn twenty-one, I promised myself that I was not going to spend my birthday in the same job or even under the same roof. I was going to strike out on my own. If I was bound to be a spinster, I was jolly well going to be one with an interesting life.'

'Was that when you went to Scotland?' asked Vivienne.

'Not quite as immediately as that. There was a girl I had been friendly with at school. She married young and – I don't know why I'm speaking of her in this distant way.'

'You mean my mother – Elspeth.'

'She and your father started married life in the West Country, where Graham worked in one of his family's hotels. They had moved to Loch Lomond the previous year so he could have a promotion. I had told Elspeth in a letter that I realised I would be working for the rest of my life and she wrote to say that the Loch Lomond hotel had a vacancy for a receptionist. I applied.' She almost laughed, except there was nothing in this story that was worth laughing about. 'It must have been the longest, most detailed letter of application in history. It all had to go in my letter, you see, because I couldn't possibly go all that way just for an interview. But it worked. I was offered the post.'

'And you went to Loch Lomond.'

'That summer, yes.'

Loch Lomond. Endless skies of azure blue dotted with puffs of white cloud above the waters of the loch and its green islands. Closing her eyes as she inhaled that wonderful, pure air; wishing she could bottle it and keep it for ever; knowing she didn't need to, because she was never going to leave.

'And that October, on my twenty-first birthday, I...met someone. A man.'

Vivienne made the tiniest movement, leaning forward slightly. Pure instinct.

Prudence went cold. She had the feeling of being rooted in position, unable to move. And she did want to move. She wanted to run away. Good lord, what was she doing, talking like this? Speaking of things that had gone unspoken for thirty years. She had to hold her breath, because otherwise every last gasp of air in her lungs would rush out in one go, leaving her to suffocate. Buried memories that hadn't been taken out and looked at in years flashed through her mind, startling in their vividness. Other memories too. Not real memories of actual events, but pseudo-memories, all the might-have-beens, the dreams, a thousand pieces of madness.

Her jaw clamped shut. She had to work it in tiny circles to force it to move apart.

'You were born the following September. Elspeth and Graham had offered to adopt you. The plan was that Elspeth would announce she was expecting a happy event. I was to keep working as long as was feasible without arousing suspicion as to my condition and then I would leave Loch Lomond, ostensibly to be sent to another hotel to cover a period of staff sickness. In due course Elspeth would discreetly disappear on holiday and return with a baby that would be registered as hers and no one would be any the wiser. And I would move on from the "other hotel" to work in another one in the family business, well away from Elspeth and Graham and their new family.'

'It sounds as if that isn't what happened.'

'Unfortunately, no one thought to inform you of the plan. I was staying in a cottage in the middle of nowhere, being cared for by a woman who was to deliver the baby, but in the final month I became extremely ill and needed more attention than she could provide. I ended up in a cottage hospital and that's where you came into the world. The following day, the regis-trar of births, marriages and deaths appeared at my bedside. He was responsible for a large area and spent three days a week travelling around the hospitals and workhouses, gath-ering information for his records. The hospital had already supplied him with some details, which I wasn't in a position to deny. All I could do was supply my middle name and decline to name the father.'

'What about my name?'

'That didn't have to be chosen immediately. I left that to your parents to decide upon. The point is, I was never sup-posed to be on your birth certificate. If our plan had worked, I would have handed over my newborn child to Elspeth, and Graham would have gone to the registry office to register you as the daughter of Elspeth and Graham Thornton.'

'And I would never have found you and we wouldn't be here now.'

Rain streamed down the windows. The evening was drawing in early, filling the room with gloom.

'Thank you for telling me,' Vivienne said formally. 'The question is: what do we do next?'

Chapter Thirty-Two

S TARVED AND CLEMMED. That was what Gran sometimes said, meaning cold and hungry. Starved didn't mean starving hungry. It meant cold. Clemmed was hungry. Well, right now, Molly was proper starved, reet starved. Bloody hell, more starved than she had ever been in her whole life. More starved than she had known it was possible to be and still be alive.

Another slosh of water from above hit her head and shoulders. It couldn't make her any colder. That wasn't possible. But each extra quantity of water put Danny in greater danger. He had tilted his head back, trying desperately to keep his mouth above water. She cradled the back of his head, brushing away small waves that threatened to slop over his face into his gasping mouth.

'Keep still,' she urged, but he couldn't help it. His body was shaking with cold, with fear and exhaustion. His eyes were glazed. How long could he hold on?

'Molly!' Aaron's voice.

She threw her head back. 'Aaron! Quick!'

He wasn't alone. Others were with him, but she couldn't look at them, had to switch her gaze back to Danny's face and keep it fastened there, as she tried to stop water getting to his mouth.

'Don't move. I'm coming down.'

Lowered by willing arms from above, he arrived beside her without a splash. Nevertheless the water swirled and Danny gagged.

'I'm going to see what's what down there,' said Aaron. 'We'll soon have you out, Danny.'

Taking a massive breath, he sank beneath the water. Molly felt him bump against her. She braced herself to stand still as his body crammed into the space at her feet and his hands moved purposefully, feeling, assessing. The water broke as he stood up. Again, Danny spluttered. Tears and snot and water.

'It's a socking great root.' Aaron swept his wet hair off his face. He looked up at the anxious faces surrounding the hole. 'Pass me the crowbar, will you? Be brave, son. A couple more minutes and you'll be out of here. Promise.'

Taking the crowbar, he disappeared once more below the water. Molly whispered in Danny's ear. She had no idea what she was saying. Down by her feet, Aaron moved, bumped, steadied. Then there were other movements, some jolts against her legs that she had to withstand to keep Danny's position secure.

More water overflowed from the brook. Danny cried out, his voice cut off by a gurgle as water went down his throat. Then, from beneath, there was a sensation of movement and the lad started to struggle, arms flailing as he was freed. Aaron burst through the surface of the water, thrust the crowbar into one of the waiting hands reaching down from above and lifted Danny out of the water to be grasped and pulled to safety.

He turned to Molly. 'Are you all right?'

She nodded. She felt sick and chilled to her soul, but she had never felt more all right in her life.

'Reach up and they'll pull you out,' said Aaron, but she couldn't. She could barely move, certainly couldn't lift her arms that high. Next thing she knew, Aaron's hands were at her waist and she was lifted upwards to be grabbed by willing hands and dragged onto the wet ground. She wanted to lie there for ever, but Danny mattered more. She sat up. One of the men had wrapped him in a coat and picked him up.

'He needs a doctor,' she said.

'I think Bunny's gone to fetch one,' said Jacob.

The men reached down and, with a huge heave, raised Aaron up onto the ground. He went straight to Danny, looking into his face.

'You're safe now.'

'Not quite,' said the man holding Danny. 'He needs to see a doctor.'

'Jacob says Bunny has gone to get one,' said Molly.

'Well, I think he has,' said Jacob.

'Let's get everyone back to the Bowler,' said one of the men. 'Hot drinks all round.'

'And this young man needs to be put to bed with a hot-water bottle,' said Aaron, still standing close beside Danny.

Molly hauled herself to her feet. Jacob picked up a grubby, wet gabardine from the ground and draped it over his arm. He flung her a guilty glance and she smiled to show it didn't matter.

'Come along, Jacob.'

But Jacob was busy patting the coat.

'What is it?' asked Molly. 'It doesn't matter if it's damaged.'

'I had something in one of the pockets and it's gone.'

'Honestly, as if that matters after what has just happened.'

'No, I remember. I took it out and – it should be over here, where the gabardine was.'

'There's nothing there now.'

'You don't understand. I have to find it.'

'What I understand is that it doesn't matter in the slightest. Come along.'

Aaron appeared at her side. 'Take my arm. You're frozen. You should be seen by the doctor as well.'

She tried to walk, but her legs wouldn't obey her and she would have fallen over had Aaron not caught her. He scooped her up in his arms and carried her. When they reached the Bowling Green, the landlady popped Molly into one of her own nightgowns and wrapped her in not one but two blankets before settling her in a cosy armchair beside a crackling fire, with her feet on a stool on the hearth. Jacob, wrapped in blankets, curled up in a chair opposite. Meanwhile, Danny had been put to bed with hot-water bottles.

And still the doctor hadn't arrived.

'I don't know what Bunny's playing at,' Aaron said testily, 'but I'm not waiting any longer. I'll go and knock for Dr Keen myself. I'll bring him back with me if I have to drag him by his hair.'

Molly nodded. There was a mug of cocoa on the table beside her, but she hadn't touched it yet. Her fingers hadn't thawed out.

'I've sent one of the men to St Anthony's and another to the police station, so Mrs Rostron will probably arrive any minute now. A bloke has gone to Wilton Close as well.' Aaron glanced at Jacob, who was gazing fixedly into the flames, then dropped his fingers to her shoulder and pressed gently. 'Well done. Danny couldn't have managed without you.'

He lifted his fingers away. Her own fingers wanted to race after them and cling on. She bunched them into a tangle in her lap, hiding them in a fold of the blankets. She concentrated on her shoulder, trying to re-live the moment of his touch.

'Will you sit with Danny while I'm out?'

'Of course.'

She came to her feet, but her body wasn't quite her own again yet, and she stumbled. Aaron caught her, holding her to him to steady her. She stayed there, wanting to relax into his embrace. He put her gently from him, ducking his head to look into her face to check she was all right. She nodded. God, what a twit she was. Fancy leaning on him like that, as if she was no better than she should be. If Jacob had seen, it would be all over St Anthony's before you could say knife. And if he told his mother... But Jacob was still looking into the fire, apparently lost in thought, his mouth twisted, half of his lower lip turned inwards beneath his teeth. Poor lad. His family had been in a fire a few weeks ago and now he had been involved in an incident where another boy might easily have lost his life.

'Can you manage the stairs on your own,' Aaron asked her, 'or do you need an arm to lean on?'

'I'm fine, thank you.' She would be too, certainly until he was on the other side of the front door. After that, she would crawl upstairs if needs be.

'Don't let Danny fall asleep,' said Aaron. 'He's trying to drift off, but I think he ought to stay awake.'

'Surely sleep heals.'

'I don't know if this is sleep or unconsciousness. He's shivering in spite of the hot-water bottles and he's confused. You know yourself how cold that water was, and he was in it for a lot longer. I don't think this is as simple as putting him into bed and warming him up. Maybe the doctor will want to send him to hospital. Wherever he spends the night, I'll be at his bedside.'

'So will I,' said Molly.

Patience looked round the sitting room door. 'Molly started some soup, then she had to go out. I've finished it and Lucy has had some. Would you like some?'

'You can come in, you know.' Prudence was shocked to hear the way she instantly reverted to her crisp, impatient manner. After the way she had opened her heart to Vivienne, shouldn't she be a different person?

Patience inserted herself into the sitting room, but left the door open. 'If you must know, Molly said there was a bit of an atmosphere in here. I don't want to intrude.' She looked at them, not nosily but with concern. That was Patience all over. She was a good person, a much better person than Prudence.

'We've been discussing something important,' said Prudence.

'Why don't you leave some soup to keep warm for us,' suggested Vivienne, 'and we'll serve ourselves in a little while.'

'Of course,' said Patience. 'I'll be upstairs with Lucy.'

The door closed softly. Prudence looked at Vivienne.

'Thank you for understanding the need for privacy.'

'Did you think I would blurt it out?'

'There hasn't been time to think about anything. Nevertheless, we do need to decide what we're going to do next.'

'I'd understand if you want me to find somewhere else to live. After all, I came here under false pretences.'

'Do you wish to leave?' Prudence asked. Now that Vivienne had heard the shabby story of her birth, was that the end of it for her? Was that all she had come for? A slice of truth? For a moment, Prudence's heart forgot to beat, simply forgot. She didn't want it to be over. To her surprise, she didn't want it to be over, but she couldn't say so. She couldn't put that kind of pressure on Vivienne, mustn't make the girl feel guilty for stirring up more than she had intended.

'I'd prefer not to, if you're happy for me to stay.'

'Good. Then please stay.'

'Thank you. I will.'

How formal they were. But formality was what Prudence did best. It had been by maintaining formality that she had coped. Be strong. Be distant. Be efficient. Don't let anyone get too close. It was how she had got by in the early days and then it had become normal, the way she was, the way everyone expected her to be. After all, she had always been rational and critical. Her heart had never been soft and yielding like Patience's, and growing up with Lawrence had sharpened her tongue.

'I'd like to get to know you better,' said Vivienne, 'if that would suit you.'

'You have no idea how much that would suit me.' Prudence threw the words out before she could change her mind. 'This has come as an enormous shock and I hardly know what to think, but I do know this. I want to have this chance. I've spent thirty years trying my hardest not to think about you. Now you're here and I don't know what to do. All I know is, I want to do something and that means having you here. I don't want you to go away. I don't want this to be over.'

Vivienne's eyes brimmed. 'I know. I'm the same. I may have had far longer to think about it, but now that it's actually happening, it seems that having spent ages thinking about it is no preparation for the real thing. We need to sleep on it.'

'Sleep? I don't think I'll sleep a wink.'

'Let's give ourselves time to see what happens, to get to know one another, to ask questions.' Vivienne pressed her lips together. 'I noticed you said nothing about my father – my real father.'

'No, I didn't. And I won't. Please don't press me on the subject.' Most of what was going to keep her awake tonight was going to be to do with him. What a mess it had been.

'Very well. I'll make myself be satisfied with knowing about my real mother.'

'I'd like to hear more of your parents. I assume they moved away from Loch Lomond. You have an English accent. Are you going to tell your father you've met me?'

'I'll visit him. He's in the Brighton hotel now.'

'He may well not want you to live under my roof.'

'We'll see. Anyway, that's for the future.'

'Are you happy to leave it that we shall simply get to know one another and see what happens?' asked Prudence. 'It seems rather woolly.'

Vivienne laughed. 'Woolly or not, there is one thing we have to decide immediately. What are we going to tell other people – if anything?'

Pretend that the most momentous event of her life hadn't happened? She had spent almost her entire adult life doing that. Something inside her wanted to give up pretending, but that was impossible.

'The truth must be kept a close secret. I can't possibly... My reputation...'

'Of course. I've a suggestion that I hope you won't mind. What if we were to tell people we've discovered, through conversation, that I'm the daughter of an old school-friend of yours? That would be perfectly true.'

Warmth spread through Prudence's frame. After the revelations, she felt exhausted but in a satisfied way.

'Yes, that would work, wouldn't it? Thank you for thinking of it.'

'Should we go and have some of that soup? Miss Patience will worry if we leave it.'

'Yes, let's, and you can tell me about where you grew up.' As Prudence was about to open the door, she stopped and looked at her daughter. Her daughter. 'There's one last thing. May I call you Vivienne?'

Chapter Thirty-Three

WHEN DOCTOR KEEN left, having promised to return first thing in the morning, Mrs Rostron insisted Molly should go to bed and Aaron was quick to back her up.

'Mrs Rostron is right,' he said. 'You've been very brave, but now you need looking after.'

'Danny is in my charge,' said Mrs Rostron. 'I'll sit with him.'

'Fetch me if there's any change,' said Molly.

Shutting the door behind Molly as she reluctantly left the room, Aaron said, 'I'll stay up with you, Mrs Rostron, though, heaven knows, it ought to be his uncle. Where is that fellow, for pity's sake? If he had done his duty and fetched Danny immediately, the lad wouldn't be in this situation now.'

Mrs Rostron lifted a disapproving eyebrow. 'Danny?'

'Yes, Danny. That's what his parents called him, what everyone called him until he came to St Anthony's.'

'We have our rules, Mr Abrams, as you are well aware.'

'I know.' He spoke in a conciliatory voice. 'Rules are essential, but maybe this one should be reconsidered. It was dreamed up by toffee-nosed do-gooders years ago.'

'It's been a stressful evening.' Mrs Rostron was as unflappable as ever. 'Therefore I'll make allowances for your outspokenness, but,' and she eyed him levelly, 'I will not tolerate criticism of or opposition to orphanage rules under ordinary circumstances. I suggest you remember that. Now then,' she added briskly, 'I suggest we share out the hours of the night. I'll sit with Danny until three o'clock, if you'll take over then.'

A long night followed. Aaron lay on the bed in the room that had been provided for him, but he didn't sleep. His mind was teeming with questions. He had to make time to speak to Molly. Circumstances had already obliged him to wait too long. But what would her reaction be to what he had to tell her?

What had Danny and Jacob been up to? Larking around, obviously, but what a place to choose – and in the pouring rain, too. Was this why Danny had said he didn't want to come to Soapsuds Cottage tonight? So that he and Jacob could sneak out and indulge in a spot of mischief?

Where was Bunny? Had some accident befallen him as well?

And where was Uncle Angus? His orphaned nephew needed him.

He couldn't wait for three o'clock. He crept back into Danny's room before two.

Mrs Rostron looked round as the door opened. 'He seems comfortable.'

'Go and lie down. I'll wake you if there's any change.'

He sat watching Danny, leaning forward each time the boy stirred and muttered, his face screwing up as he slept; leaning forward also when he didn't stir for some time. At last daylight came, bringing with it an edge of dazzle after the recent days of gloom when it had rained cats and dogs most of the time. Aaron drew back the curtain upon rain-washed skies of pale blue and early sunshine filled with promise.

'Mr Abrams,' said a quiet voice from the bed.

Aaron's heart expanded as he turned round. 'Danny!' He went to the boy.

The child slipped a hand into his. 'Have you been here all night?'

Aaron squeezed his hand and put it down on the covers. Mustn't show favouritism.

'Some of it. Mrs Rostron was here too.'

'Mrs Rostron? Coo.' Danny's face clouded. 'Was she waiting for me to wake up so she could give me a wigging? I s'pose me and Jacob will get the strap for getting into a fix.'

'Mrs Rostron sat beside you for hours because she was so concerned. So was Miss Watson.'

'Miss Watson kept my face out of the water.'

Aaron smiled. 'She's a heroine.'

'And you cut me free,' said Danny. 'You're a hero.' He looked shy. 'Thank you.'

'The correct thing to do is shake hands and tell one another how brave we were.'

That raised a chuckle and Danny shook hands.

'I think we're both jolly fine splendid chaps, don't you?' said Aaron.

'Hear hear,' came a voice from the doorway.

Molly stood there, the high collar of her borrowed night-gown showing beneath the dressing gown tied tightly round her slender figure. Her hair was rumpled in a way that suggested she had used her fingers as a comb. Was this how she looked every morning? Fresh-faced and glowing, with messy hair? He would very much like to wake up beside her and find out every morning until death did them part. But it all depended upon her reaction to what he had to tell her. Would it scupper his chances for ever?

'Mr Abrams says you're a heroine,' said Danny and Aaron had the pleasure of seeing her blush.

'You seem better,' she said.

'I am, thank you.'

Mrs Rostron walked in, looking as neat as ever. Had she actually lain down? The brief glance she afforded Molly sent the girl scurrying from the room.

True to his word, Dr Keen arrived early and pronounced Danny none the worse for his ordeal.

'But if you're going back to St Anthony's today, young man, it mustn't be by Shanks's pony.'

'It can be by the laundry pony,' said Aaron. 'They have a pony and cart for deliveries and they owe me a favour for repairing some table-legs. I'll pop round there now and ask.'

On his way back from making the arrangements, he was met in the pub doorway by a policeman.

'Mr Abrams? Mr Aaron Abrams? Would you accompany me to the police station, sir? We have some questions for you.'

'There's a lady here for you,' the landlady said to Molly with a smile. 'Considering we have only a couple of commercial travellers staying here at present, our hotel rooms have never been so busy!'

The landlady was followed into the room by Vivienne, carrying a valise. She hurried to Molly's side.

'How are you? We heard what a brave thing you did. Look, I brought you some fresh clothes. Yesterday's will need to be laundered a dozen times, I imagine.'

Clean clothes! Bliss. 'Can you hang on and walk back with me or do you have to get to work?'

'I'll drop into the newsagent's at nine o'clock and telephone the office.'

'I'd hate to think of you getting into trouble on my account.'

'In trouble? For helping a heroine? Not only that, but a heroine who helped save an orphanage boy. It'll be fine. Anyway, I'm not going to work until I've told you my news and I'm not going to do that until we get home, so chop-chop. Don't look so worried. It's good news.'

'If your face is anything to go by, it's wonderful news.'

'Yes, it is.'

When Molly was ready, she went to say goodbye to Mrs

Rostron. She and the boys were waiting for the laundry's pony and cart. Oddly, considering what he had been through, Danny looked brighter than Jacob, who looked washed-out and pathetic.

Molly spoke quietly to the superintendent. 'Would you like me to take Jacob to Wilton Close to see his mum? I'll bring him to St Anthony's afterwards.'

Mrs Rostron glanced at Jacob. 'That would be a kindness. I wonder where Mr Abrams is. I thought he would be back by now.'

The maid who was clearing the breakfast table spoke up. 'He went off to the police station. A bobby called for him.'

'A bobby?' Jacob exclaimed.

'They probably want a statement from him about last night,' said Mrs Rostron. 'It's nothing to worry about.'

'They'll probably want a statement from you as well,' Vivienne told Molly. 'We could pop in there on the way past and ask.'

'Could you take me to Wilton Close first?' asked Jacob.

'Certainly not,' said Mrs Rostron. 'The police station is on the way there.'

Jacob turned away, but not before Molly has seen the tears that had sprung to his eyes.

'Make yourself useful,' she said brightly. 'You can carry this.' She handed him the valise.

They thanked the landlord and landlady and set off.

'I can go on my own to Wilton Close,' said Jacob, 'while you go to the police station.'

'No.' Molly and Vivienne spoke together.

'We'll be two minutes in the police station,' said Vivienne.

'I'll wait outside for you.'

'No, you won't. We're responsible for you and you'll stay where we can see you.'

'What's this about?' asked Molly.

'Nowt, nowt.' He blinked rapidly, his chin sinking almost to his chest.

'There's a guilty conscience, if ever I saw one,' Vivienne murmured. 'What can he be so worried about?'

They kept him waiting. On purpose? To make him anxious? Aaron wasn't anxious – well, not in a guilty way, though he was definitely unsettled and confused. What was going on? The bobby hadn't answered any of his questions on the way here. The police station's heavy door had swung shut behind the two of them and the bobby had presented him to the desk sergeant, who had checked his name and address.

'What's this about?' Aaron had asked.

'This way, please, sir.'

Unlocking and lifting the flap in the wooden counter, the sergeant had showed him to this small room where he was now, and left him here. The room boasted a table in the centre with an upright chair on either side. Frustrated at not knowing what was happening, Aaron had thought, rather bloody-mindedly, that he wouldn't sit down; but after waiting for goodness knows how long, it seemed ridiculous to stay on his feet, so he took a seat.

At last the door opened and a man in plain clothes walked in and sat down. He was followed into the room by a different bobby. They were both older men. The bobby positioned himself by the door. Did they expect him to make a dash for it?

Displaying a Bolton accent, the plain-clothed chap introduced himself as Inspector Woods and asked Aaron to confirm his name and address.

'I've already told the desk sergeant.'

'And now you can tell me...please.'

'Aaron Abrams, Soapsuds Cottage. Will you kindly tell me what this is about?'

'I was rather hoping you could tell me, Abrams.' Abrams, not Mr Abrams.

'I don't know what you're talking about.'

'Where's Hobart Carstairs?' The inspector fired the question at him.

A frown tugged his brow. 'Who?'

'You do a very good job of looking confused.'

'Probably because I am confused, Inspector. I repeat, what's this about?'

'The whereabouts of Hobart Carstairs. I repeat, where is he?'

'Haven't the foggiest. Never heard of him.'

'Is that so?' The inspector bared his teeth in a pretend smile. 'Let's make it easier for you, then, shall we? Tell me what happened yesterday evening.'

That, he could do. He described how the two lads had gone missing and how he and Molly had been intercepted by Bunny.

'Bunny and Miss Watson went straight to the brook while I went to the Bowler to ask for whatever tools they possessed.'

'And then you and a group of men from the Bowling Green, including the landlord, went to the brook. Miss Watson was in the overflow hole with the trapped boy. Was Bunny there?'

'Yes. He was next to the hole.'

'You're sure?'

'Positive. When we all came bumbling through the bushes, he looked round and said something, though I couldn't tell you what. "Thank goodness" or "At last," that kind of thing. I was more concerned with getting into the water and rescuing the lad.'

'And while you did that, no doubt all eyes were upon you.'

'I wouldn't know. I was busy freeing Danny Cropper's foot.'

'When you were pulled out from the overflow, was Bunny there?'

'I didn't see him, but then I wasn't looking for him. Then someone said he'd gone for a doctor.'

'But you didn't wait for the doctor to arrive.'

'We couldn't, not with Danny and Miss Watson soaked to the bone. We carried them back to the Bowler and, after a while, I went for the doctor myself.'

'Because you knew Bunny hadn't.'

A tingling sensation ran up and down Aaron's arms beneath his skin. It was all he could do not to scratch. 'What?'

'Because you knew Bunny hadn't.'

He almost spluttered. 'I knew no such thing. I don't know what he did or where he went. I thought he'd gone for the doctor – we all did. Then no doctor arrived and I went for one myself.'

'Where did you think Bunny was?'

'I don't know, I tell you. I thought he'd gone for the doctor.'

'But you knew he hadn't, because otherwise why would you have gone yourself?'

'I did that later, after Bunny didn't come back.'

'Took a chance, didn't you? On that young lad's life? Withholding a doctor from him when he needed one most.'

Now he really did splutter. 'How dare you! I fetched Dr Keen as soon as I realised—'

'Realised what, Abrams?'

'That we'd waited a long time.'

'Oh aye, a long time. Plenty long enough to assist Bunny.'

'I don't understand.'

Inspector Woods banged his fist on the table so hard that it moved a couple of inches, its feet scraping on the bare floorboards. He thrust his face forwards.

'It's time to stop playing games, Abrams. Bunny legged it and you helped him by pretending to fall in with the general assumption that he'd gone for the doctor. It was a pity for you that the boy was in a ropey condition, or you could have let the pretence continue even longer.'

Aaron's mouth dropped open. Confusion rolled around inside his head. 'Bunny legged it? What in the name of all that's holy are you talking about?'

'Where is he now?'

'How many times? I don't know.'

'I'll ask you again, Abrams. Where is Hobart Carstairs?'

'And I'll tell you again. I've never heard of him – unless...' Chill washed through him. 'Are you telling me that Hobart Carstairs is Bunny's real name?'

'Full marks for your prowess as an actor, but it won't wash with me. Where is he?'

'I – don't – know!'

The inspector sat back, drumming his fingers on the table, his eyes filled with thoughts. Aaron would have given a great deal to be able to read his mind. What the hell was going on? And what part was he meant to have played?

When the inspector spoke, it was in a measured voice, as if he were considering the matter even as he uttered the words, but Aaron wasn't fooled. Inspector Woods knew exactly what he was about.

'I could lock you in one of our cells and leave you to think things over, but I'm not going to do that...for now. I'm going to let you go, but don't get any funny ideas, because I'll be keeping a close eyes on you at all times.'

'You're going to have me watched?' It was unbelievable. Everything about this was unbelievable.

'Good day, Abrams.'

The inspector rose to his feet. By the door, the policeman, who, come to think of it, hadn't moved a muscle all through the interview, opened the door and the inspector walked out.

The copper looked at Aaron. 'This way.'

Stunned, Aaron hauled himself to his feet and followed Inspector Woods along the passage. As they approached the front desk, the copper behind Aaron caught his arm, bringing him to a standstill.

'One moment, if you please.'

Christ, what now?

'If you'd make way.'

The corridor suddenly felt crowded. There were men behind them, two bobbies and a civilian – Aaron's head swung back for a second look. That man: he had seen him before, but where? His gaze followed the trio up the corridor.

'Know him, do you?' asked the inspector. 'Don't bother denying it. It's written all over your face.'

'I don't know him,' Aaron said stiffly, 'but he looked familiar. I've seen him somewhere, but I can't think where.'

'Very convenient.'

Aaron started to say, 'It's true,' but what was the point? 'You wanted me to see him,' he realised. 'You wanted to see if I recognised him.'

'And you did. Thank you for confirming our suspicions.'

'What suspicions? If you'd only tell me what's going on—'

'You aren't doing yourself any favours, Abrams. This innocent act is wearing thin. What's going on there?'

They both turned to look in the direction of the front of the police station as a loud voice – a child's voice, but still jolly loud – was raised in a howl of fear and rage.

The moment they set foot inside the cop shop, Jacob clapped eyes on the man from Chorlton Green and all his worst fears swooped over him. Miss Watson and Mrs Atwood had just pretended to be kind, pretended to be taking him to see Mum, but really it was a plot to get him into the police station to be arrested. Hell's bells and burnt toast, and every other swear word you could think of.

'You tricked me!' he howled. 'You tricked me!' He hardly knew what he was doing as he swung round and confronted Miss Watson. Her eyes were wide with shock. Well, bully for her. Had she really thought he would meekly let himself be handed over to the police. 'You brought me here to be arrested. You – you...bitch!'

In the shocked silence that followed, a ripple ran through Jacob's face, widening his eyes as he realised what he had said. 'Bitch' was a bad word, a Thad word. He had never said it before in his whole life, not even about a lady-dog, not even when he had had Thad there to protect him. Some words you just didn't say and 'bitch' was one of them, and now he had said it, and in a police station an' all.

Panic streaked through him and he tried to run. It was a stupid thing to do – he knew he didn't stand a chance – but what else could he do? A hefty hand landed on his shoulder, sending fear streaming through his veins. Pure fear, dead cold. Tears burst out of him. Tears and snot and panic flew in all directions.

Then – different hands, a kind voice, Miss Watson's voice filled with concern, even after what he had called her. Concern he didn't deserve. He didn't deserve anything. He was an bad 'un, like Thad. Aye, and he would end up in the reformatory, like Thad. Old Rostron would be glad to see the back of him.

And he had wanted to turn over a new leaf, he really had. He had wanted to leave all that stuff, all the Thad stuff, well and truly behind him. He had ached to be like Mikey. Mikey was good fun and everyone liked him and he had his head screwed on right. He would never have got himself into hot water like this.

Not like Jacob. Not like stupid, pathetic Jemima.

'What's all this?' A copper loomed over him, cramming his gaze with tunic and gleaming buttons. 'What d'you mean by coming in here and using foul language about a lady?'

'I'm sorry, officer,' said Miss Watson. 'He's with us. I don't know what's got into him.'

'I'll take him outside,' said Mrs Atwood.

As Jacob turned towards the door and freedom, a gasp was wrenched out of him, dragging his lungs halfway up his gullet.

He made a lunge for the door, but a hand swiftly pulled him round and he found himself looking, not at a tunic, but at a tweed jacket and waistcoat. He caught a whiff of tobacco. He didn't dare raise his eyes.

'Now this is interesting,' the man said. 'Who is this lad? He recognised the prisoner. It's no surprise that Abrams recognised him, but this boy?'

Astonishment jerked Jacob's head up. Behind the man he recognised from Chorlton Green was Mr Abrams, with a copper standing beside him in a way that suggested – nah, not possible. Mr Abrams couldn't have done owt wrong.

The suited man gave him a little shake, not a hard one, but a meaningful one. A don't-mess-with-me shake.

'How do you know this man?'

For a split second, Jacob thought he meant Mr Abrams, but he didn't. He meant the chap from the bench on the Green.

'I – I don't know him.'

'Yes you do and don't tell me otherwise. I saw you recognise him. I saw your eyes and mouth pop open. So tell me the truth. How do you know him?'

Jacob's mouth twisted as he chewed his lip. How could he get out of this?

'Come on, son,' said the man. 'I'm a police inspector and you're obliged to tell me the truth. We know about the thefts. We know about Hobart Carstairs – or Bunny, as you probably call him.'

'*Bunny?*' It came out as a squeak. Really? *Bunny?* Behind the thefts?

'And we know the part played by Bill Thompson here.'

Bill Thompson: the man from the Green? Jacob squirmed. He had to escape, but he was trapped. If he had never followed Thad's lead in the first place, Shirl would never have picked on him, and he wouldn't be here now. A great wave of fear and guilt washed over him. He didn't understand what was happening; he didn't care what was happening. All he knew was that he would end up in the reformatory.

If Shirl didn't kill him first.

Molly rushed to Jacob as he threw himself into a corner and slid down the wall into a sobbing heap on the floor. She tried to put her arms round him, but he shook her off.

'I'm Inspector Woods,' said the plain-clothed officer, 'and I want to question this boy.'

With a howl, Jacob scrambled to his feet and huddled close to Molly.

Vivienne stepped forward. 'Not without an adult who is known to him.'

'I'll do it,' said Aaron.

'You're under suspicion yourself,' said one of the policemen.

Aaron? Under suspicion? That was another shock to contend with. Aaron was the most steadfast, trustworthy man she knew. How could anyone suspect him of anything? Suspect him of what?

Putting her arms around Jacob, Molly offered, 'I will.'

'You helped save Cropper,' Jacob wailed, 'but you can't help me, Miss Watson. No one can.'

Molly intercepted looks flying in all directions between the various adults; not as Jacob's supporters on one side and the police on the other, but as baffled, concerned adults in the presence of a distressed – no, a distraught child.

But Vivienne murmured to her, 'It's better if I do it.' To Inspector Woods, she said in her clear, confident manner, 'I'm Mrs Atwood from the Board of Health. This child is Jacob Layton, whose family is known to me. I'll remain with him for now, but you may not question him until Mrs Rostron arrives. She is—'

'I'm aware of who she is, thank you. A sensible woman. Fetch her, would you, Constable Timms?'

'You'll find her at the Bowling Green,' said Vivienne, 'but she might not be immediately available, as she's with Daniel Cropper, who came close to losing his life last night. Miss Watson, would you kindly fetch Jacob's mother? She ought to be here too. She has yet to be reunited with her son, Inspector. Moreover, as his mother, she should be present while you question him.'

Molly remembered Mrs Layton from yesterday evening. 'Mrs Layton might be a little emotional.'

'A hysterical mother is the last thing we need,' commented Inspector Woods.

'On the contrary, sir,' said Vivienne, 'a hysterical mother is precisely what this situation calls for. Her presence will provide a constant reminder to you that you are dealing with a child.'

The door opened and another policeman walked in. 'The van's here to take the prisoner.'

With a shriek, Jacob hurled himself across the confined space towards the door, and straight into a burly copper just the other side of the threshold, who propelled him back in.

'What have you done, son?' the burly copper asked with a grin. 'Pinched an apple off the market?'

Inspector Woods had clearly had enough. He barked out orders in all directions. 'Get Thompson out of here. The sooner he's locked away on remand the better. Mrs Atwood and young Layton, sit on those chairs over there. Constable Burton, guard the door. If that young whippersnapper gets to his feet, sit on him.' This was said with a kindly glance in Jacob's direction, but Jacob was hunched over as if he had stomach-ache. 'Sergeant, get Mrs Layton's address from these ladies and bring her here, then bring Mrs Rostron as soon as she's free. Miss Watson, please remain here. I need a statement from you about last night.'

'If you can wait for your statement,' Molly suggested, 'why don't I go and sit with Danny Cropper, so Mrs Rostron can come here at once?'

'Very well.'

Molly glanced at Aaron, seeing frustration and concern in the taut lines of his body and the darkness in his eyes. He hadn't been offered the chance to help. What was he suspected of doing?

Chapter Thirty-Four

I T WAS ROTTEN of her to think it, but this upheaval over the Layton child, and the way Vivienne and Miss Watson were all gingered up over it, made it easier for Prudence to introduce the idea of Vivienne's being the daughter of her long-lost friend. It removed some of its impact.

Patience, of course, was thrilled, all the more so because she had met Elspeth all those years ago when she had travelled up to Loch Lomond for that holiday to see Prudence in her new surroundings. Patience's delight, as touching as it was, was also painful to witness, but Prudence firmly set her guilt aside. This was a time for celebration, even if the true nature of the celebration had to remain a secret.

'How did you work it out?' Miss Watson wanted to know. 'Vivienne said it just emerged through conversation.'

'There'll be plenty of time to discuss that later,' Prudence replied. 'I want to hear more of this rescue in which you were involved. What were the boys doing at the brook in the first place?' Should she be ashamed of exploiting their misadventure? 'I want you to know, Miss Watson,' she added, 'that I'm proud of you.' And that wasn't diversionary tactics. It was the plain truth.

As for Lucy – well, actually it was difficult not to feel a flicker of amusement. The child had been so self-absorbed that she was almost miffed at Vivienne's supposed new identity and the incident by the brook. Honestly, did she expect all attention to be locked on her? Maybe it would make her view her position in a more realistic way. Maybe.

After tea, Prudence walked to the newsagent's and sat in the little booth to place a telephone call to Lawrence to ask him and Evelyn to come round in the morning.

'What's wrong?' he barked down the line. 'Is it Lucy?'

'It isn't something to discuss over the telephone.' Operators weren't permitted to listen in, but one never knew.

'We'll be there in half an hour.'

'Lawrence, wait—'

But he had hung up, leaving her to hurry home at an unladylike trot to prepare the household for the inevitable explosion.

'If you wait upstairs, Lucy dear,' said Patience, 'Aunt Prudence and I will tell Mummy and Daddy for you.'

But Lucy said, 'Thank you, Auntie Patience, but no. This is for me to do.'

'Well!' Prudence exclaimed. 'What a turn-up for the books. I'm gratified to see you have some backbone.'

Lucy pursed her lips in something approaching a pout. 'I've had backbone all along. How else could I have held out against naming the father?'

'That's not backbone,' said Prudence. 'That's pure idiocy.'

Mother: Prudence Winifred Hesketh. Father unknown.

Who was she to talk? But it had been different for her. Her decision hadn't stemmed from idiocy. It had been her only possible course of action.

When Lawrence and Evelyn arrived, Lucy faced them alone in the sitting room. Prudence set up the typewriters on the dining table and laid out her teaching notes, but her ears were flapping. Not that it would have taken much effort to hear Evelyn's howl of distress.

Patience flinched. 'Ought we to go in?'

'Not yet. We should give them as much time as we can before lessons.'

'How are we supposed to concentrate on teaching?'

'We must. Our pupils rely on us.'

But Vivienne solved that problem.

'Will you allow Molly and me to do the lessons tonight? We'll do everything here in the dining room, so you can be as long as you need to in the sitting room.'

'We appreciate the offer,' Prudence began, 'but—'

'Good. That's settled.' Vivienne smiled brightly. 'We've written notes about some made-up problem families and we'll discuss them as if we're in a meeting, while the girls have a go at writing minutes. Please let us do this for you.'

The breath caught in Prudence's throat – goodness, when was the last time that had happened to her, if ever?

Shortly before their pupils arrived, Prudence and Patience joined Lawrence's family.

Lawrence swung round, confronting them as if this was their fault.

'She won't tell us who the father is.'

Evelyn touched her temple as if warding off a bad head. 'Lawrence, don't, please. We've been over and over this. We have to decide what to do.' Her normally complacent features mashed together.

'If she won't name the father, we can't have a wedding,' said Lawrence. He loomed over Lucy, who shrank into the depths of the armchair, fingers clutching the arm-rests. 'It was Eric Fordyce, wasn't it – wasn't it?'

'Lawrence, stop!' Evelyn insisted. 'How many more of our friends' sons are you going to accuse? She isn't going to tell us and our haranguing her doesn't help.'

'She'll have to go back to that home Prudence found,' Lawrence declared.

'Daddy...' Lucy whispered.

'You can't come home with us,' said Lawrence. 'What would the neighbours say? Not to mention that I won't have Felicity contaminated by this. That leaves...' He glared at Prudence.

'Maskell House,' she supplied.

'But, Daddy, Aunt Prudence didn't want to leave me there.'

'What's wrong with it?' Lawrence demanded.

'Nothing that I could see.' Prudence spoke mildly. Normally Lawrence's raised voice was guaranteed to bring out her sarcasm, but not today. 'I'm sure it's eminently suitable.'

'Then that's where Lucy will go.'

'You're her parents and it's your decision, of course,' said Prudence, 'but there is another possibility. Leave her here – for now, at least.'

'Oh, Prudence.' Patience's hand crept across and touched hers.

Prudence grasped her sister's hand warmly. 'Let her stay for as long as is feasible. Provide her with some clothes that are on the large side, to conceal her condition. When is she due?'

'She says December,' said Evelyn. 'Apparently...it happened only once.'

'Only!' muttered Lawrence.

'Mummy!' squeaked Lucy.

'What do you say?' asked Prudence. 'May she stay here?'

'Why would you have her?' Lawrence demanded. 'You, of all people, Prudence. You're so judgemental. I should have expected you to sling us all out with instructions never to darken your doors again. You've always been so quick to point out what's right and wrong, especially as it applies to other people's behaviour.'

'Sometimes it isn't a question of right and wrong,' said Prudence. 'Sometimes it's simply a matter of doing the best you can.'

After church, Molly was due at Mum's for Sunday dinner, but first she went to Norris's house, where Mrs Hartley, a frilled

apron protecting her Sunday best, answered the door, flinch-
ing a little as she saw who it was.

'Molly, this is a surprise.'

'Good morning, Mrs Hartley.'

'I don't know about that, about it being good, not after the
way you've treated our Norris.'

'I've come to see him. Is he in?'

'Want to get back together, do you?'

'Please, I need to speak to him.'

'Who is it, Mother?' Norris appeared in the narrow hallway.
'Oh – Molly.' His chin jutted forward. 'What brings you here?'

Molly frowned. It looked like... 'What happened to your eye?'

'Nothing. Silly accident. I walked into a door.'

'Can I have a word, please? In private.'

Mrs Hartley tossed her greying head. 'Don't mind me.' She
retreated along the hallway to the kitchen.

'May I come in?' asked Molly.

'I suppose so. It's better than standing on the step. The
fewer people who see you, the better.'

'Norris!'

'Well, what did you expect after the way you were carrying
on last time I saw you?'

Molly started to object, but changed it to, 'Are you going to
let me in, then?'

He stood back to permit her to walk in. There was a pause
before the door shut behind her. Had he just stuck his head
outside to see if they were being watched? She didn't want to
know. Without waiting to be invited, she went into the front
parlour, stopping in the centre to turn round.

'This won't take long, but it is important. I want your assurance that you won't tell anybody else about what happened to
me during the war.'

'I've already given that assurance to Tom and your dad.
There was no need for you to send them round, you know.'

'I didn't. Tom wanted to come – and I imagine Dad did too.'

'And what d'you mean by asking if I've told anybody else? You think I've been going round telling all and sundry, do you? Well, I haven't. I haven't told anyone at all.'

Relief trembled through her. 'Apart from Aaron – Mr Abrams?'

'Aaron, is it? Very cosy. You swore there was no one else.'

'And it was the truth. Not that it's any of your business, Norris. We aren't engaged any more.'

'Oh aye, you made that very clear. Canoodling in public, I ask you.'

'We weren't canoodling. I was upset and he was comforting me. There's no need to look like that. It's true. Come on, Norris. You know me better than that.'

'I thought I did.'

She threw up her hands. 'This is ridiculous.' With an effort, she returned to the point of the conversation. 'You say you told nobody except Mr Abrams about what happened during the war.'

'I said,' Norris replied, 'that I told nobody, full stop.'

'You didn't tell Mr Abrams?'

'No. I'm a gentleman even if it turns out you aren't quite a lady.'

Molly ignored the slur. 'Thank you for that. And...' It was humiliating, but she had to ask. 'Have you mentioned my so-called canoodling to anyone?'

'I'm not a gossip. You should know that.'

Guilt made her start to soften, but she hardened swiftly when he spoke his next words.

'Besides, it would have made me look foolish. I don't want to be known as the man who spent years engaged to a girl who turned out to be a flirt.'

Was that what he thought of her now? Truly? Or was it his way of saving face? Molly gave Norris a polite smile, refusing to appear embarrassed even though she was squirming inside.

'Thank you, Norris. You've put my mind at rest. I'll leave you to enjoy your dinner.'

He saw her to the door.

'So you don't need to confess all to your new chap now.'

Yes, she did.

Chapter Thirty-Five

A FTER THE EXTRAORDINARY goings-on in the police station on Friday, Aaron had been permitted to go home. Even now, on Monday morning, he still felt rattled. It had taken all his willpower to steer clear of St Anthony's over the weekend. Much as he wanted answers, he mustn't hound Jacob for information, not least in case Inspector Woods accused him of putting the lad under pressure. But it was hard staying away when he wanted to see Danny. He knew the boy was all right, but somehow knowing wasn't enough. He wanted to see him and spend time with him, just to make sure.

Now, under the bright morning sunshine, he was helping the grocery chap unload his delivery, ferrying sacks and boxes from the cart to the kitchen's back door, when Inspector Woods came stalking down Church Road and turned in at the gates, sparing Aaron no more than a glance, his closed expression forbidding any acknowledgement.

Aaron immediately put on a spurt with the groceries, then hurried upstairs. Since Molly had left – left! Been chucked out, more like – Mrs Rostron had had the more able nursemaids taking turns to do a spot of clerical work, much to the annoyance of the nannies, who were deeply displeased at having their girls commandeered. The nursemaids weren't best pleased either, as far as Aaron could tell, and the wish for Miss Allan to make a full recovery and return to her duties was so strong you could almost taste it.

Nurse Carmel was seated behind Miss Allan's desk, fiddling resentfully with a stack of papers. 'I'm meant to put this lot in alphabetical order,' she groused. 'I've never been so bored in my life.'

'Is Inspector Woods in with Mrs Rostron?'

'Yes.'

The office door at the end of the landing opened and Mrs Rostron appeared. 'Nurse Carmel, would you— Oh, there you are, Mr Abrams. I was about to send for you. Would you come in, please?'

In the office, she and Inspector Woods sat on either side of the desk. Aaron wasn't offered a seat.

'Why do you need me?' he asked, wanting to take the initiative.

'Personally, I don't,' said the inspector, 'but Mrs Rostron insists.'

'I do indeed,' she replied. 'Mr Abrams, it seems the police have got to the bottom of certain events. Since you, a member of my staff, were inconvenienced by their suspicions, I think it proper that you should hear what Inspector Woods has to say.'

'I'm here as a courtesy to you, Mrs Rostron,' said the inspector. 'I believe you're entitled to hear this, as it concerns two of your boys.'

'Two? I was prepared to hear about Jacob Layton, but...'

'The other is Daniel Cropper.'

'Is this connected to the boys' escapade?'

'I fear so, madam. There have been thefts over the past couple of years from folk in Stretford and Urmston. All small things – jewellery, watches, pens. Nice pieces, but small. The police over that way never found the culprit and never recovered the missing things. It now transpires that the stolen items were immediately brought into Chorlton, which is a different police area, and from here they were taken across the Mersey into Sale, which is in a different county. It's no wonder the Stretford police couldn't trace them.'

'Very regrettable,' said Mrs Rostron, 'but what has that to do with my boys?'

Aaron could have hugged her for that 'my'.

'It was a clever system – clever and unpleasant. Children were used to carry the stolen goods across the border into Chorlton. Who would suspect a child? They had no idea what they were carrying.'

'You mean – Layton and Cropper?'

'Amongst others. Young Layton fell foul of a thug-in-the-making called Shirley Henshaw, who is, incidentally, the nephew of Hobart Carstairs, also known as Bunny.'

'The hot-potato man?' asked Mrs Rostron.

'The Henshaw boy forced Jacob to carry packets on his way home from school.'

Mrs Rostron inhaled a small gasp. 'I thought it was the right thing to leave him at the Stretford school.'

'Shirley Henshaw had a tried and trusted way of keeping children in his gang. The first time they made a delivery for him, they'd be attacked and the packet would be "stolen". Then Henshaw would tell them they had to carry on working in order to pay back what they'd lost. In due course, Layton recruited Cropper – and before you say anything, he was forced to do it. The lads were paid sixpence each time they did a job. Apparently, Cropper wanted money so he could save up to run away.'

'He doesn't need to run away any more,' said Aaron.

'If the boys have money,' said Mrs Rostron, 'they can donate it to the police widows' fund.'

'Thank you, madam.'

'I'll make it clear to them that both the police and I are aware they received money, just in case they feel tempted to leave it where they've hidden it.'

'How did the boys pass on the things they brought to Chorlton?' Aaron asked.

'They sat on a bench on Chorlton Green and waited for a man to sit next to them—'

'That's it!' Aaron exclaimed. 'I knew I'd seen him before. That fellow at the police station, the one who was taken away in the police van – he collected the packets, didn't he?'

'Bill Thompson, aye, but it's his word against the boys' at present.'

'And against mine.' Aaron described seeing Thompson twice on the Green when first Danny was there, then Jacob.

'It's circumstantial, not hard evidence,' said the inspector. 'Will you give a statement?'

'I would have done so last week had I known what was going on.'

'At that time, we had reason to believe you might be involved.'

'What was I supposed to have done?'

'I'll come to that in due course. Without disclosing details of the investigation, I can tell you that Thompson has been under observation in Cheshire for selling what were presumed to be stolen goods, though they didn't match anything on Cheshire's stolen goods list. The Cheshire police wanted to find out where he was getting these things.'

'And you started comparing notes,' said Mrs Rostron.

'We were sure Carstairs – Bunny – was involved, but we couldn't find out how the items were being moved around.'

'Until Jacob Layton collapsed in a sobbing heap in the police station, thinking he was about to be carted off in the police van,' said Aaron. 'Poor kid.'

'He was most helpful once he calmed down sufficiently to make any sense. It's thanks to him we found out about the children. The reason the other lad toppled into the over-flow was because they saw a bobby on the beat and their guilty consciences did the rest. I take it the Cropper boy is recovered now?'

'Fully,' said Mrs Rostron. 'I'll hand him over in good health to the uncle who is to adopt him.'

Yes, and where was the damn uncle? Aaron shifted irritably. It was more than time Uncle Angus came to claim Danny. He had a poor sense of priorities not to have come rushing here the moment he was informed of Mr Cropper's death. How wanted must Danny feel right now?

'You still haven't explained my so-called part in this,' said Aaron. He sounded more annoyed than he meant to, but of course he was annoyed, and it was ruddy Uncle Angus's fault.

'You and Carstairs were friends, so we thought perhaps you were the one passing things to Thompson.'

The disbelief he still hadn't come to terms with washed over him again. 'I thought Bunny was my friend.'

'He was a friend to all the world,' the inspector said drily.

'He was a friend to St Anthony's,' observed Mrs Rostron. 'Look how he provided hot potatoes for the children on May Day, and he wouldn't take a penny for them. Everyone said he had a heart of gold.'

'Something was gold, but not his heart,' said the inspector. 'Possibly the contents of his strong-box.'

'Have you found him?' asked Aaron.

Woods shook his head. 'Vanished, taking goodness knows what with him. He lodged in a cottage on Sandy Lane and it's clear from the state of his room that he made a hasty getaway. We're sure he had about his person the stolen item or items the two boys were supposed to take to Thompson. Young Jacob said he put the packet on the ground when he tried to make a rope out of his coat, but when he searched for it later, it was gone. He was scared witless about what this Shirl character would do to him. He kept babbling about being shoved under a tram, would you believe.'

There was a brief burst of knocking and the door burst open. Michael Layton practically fell into the room, followed by Nurse Carmel.

'I'm sorry, Mrs Rostron. I tried to stop him.'

'It's our Jacob,' said Michael. 'He says you're going to send him to the reformatory. Are you? Only, if you do, you'll have to send me an' all. Jacob's my brother and it's my job to look after him.'

The sound of children's voices floated over the hedge surrounding the rec. Molly peeped through the gate to see if Aaron was inside, perhaps playing rounders, but he wasn't. Good. That increased the chances of finding him at St Anthony's, preferably on his own.

She walked down Church Road and through the gates into the girls' playground, where some girls were sitting in the shade and others were skipping.

Queen, Queen Ca-ro-line
Washed her hair in tur-pen-time
Tur-pen-tine will make it shine
Queen, Queen Ca-ro-line.

The familiar skipping rhyme bounced around inside her head, threatening to take up residence. Smiling at the girls as she passed, she headed towards Aaron's workshop, only to be wrenched out of her single-minded purpose as Jacob came tearing up to her, followed by his brother.

'Miss! Miss!' yelled Jacob. 'Do you want to hear my news? I'm staying. I'm really staying.'

'Calm down,' said Michael. 'Miss doesn't know what you're talking about.' His face shone with pride as he addressed Molly.

'Mrs Rostron says it wasn't our Jacob's fault that he ended up delivering stolen goods, so he's allowed to stay.'

'And that Shirl is going to be sent away to a reformatory,' Jacob added. 'Not the same one as our Thad, in case they get together, which would be murder.' His grin almost split his face in two. 'I'll never see him again – Shirl, I mean. I'll never ever see him again.'

He dashed away, whooping for joy. Michael shrugged at Molly and ran after him. What was all that about? Whatever it was, her heart lifted at the sight of Jacob's happiness. It must be to do with what had happened by the brook, but she would save her questions for later. The mission that had brought her here was more important than anything.

As she approached the workshop, Aaron's figure appeared in the doorway and he stepped outside. His shirt-sleeves were rolled up and the top two buttons on his collarless shirt were open, just like on her first day here as secretary. He stopped at the sight of her and she felt a flutter of uncertainty, but then he came towards her, smiling in welcome.

She spoke first. She couldn't have him looking so pleased. Not until he knew and had made up his mind about her.

'I want to tell you what happened to me in the war,' she said.

'You don't have to. Your old fiancé had no business saying what he did and I socked him one to make sure he knew it.'

'You gave him that black eye?'

'Turned into a proper shiner, did it? Good. Incidentally, when I referred to what he said, I meant only what he blurted out in front of you. I don't mean I listened while he poured out your story.'

'You were too busy punching him.' She shouldn't laugh, she really shouldn't, but she did.

Aaron laughed too. 'You've got to defend a lady's honour.'

That sobered her. 'You might think differently when I've told you my story.'

'Might I? I doubt it somehow. But I want to get to know you better, Miss Molly Watson. I want to know you a lot better and if you choose to tell me your story, I'll be honoured to listen.'

'I don't know about that. You might think it grubby.'

'I can't imagine you did anything so bad.'

'It isn't a question of good or bad – or I don't think it is.' Or was that her way of skating over her shame?

'I've got a couple of folding chairs,' said Aaron. 'If we sit over there in the shade, we shouldn't be disturbed.'

He disappeared inside, returning to set up the chairs by the wall, in the shade of a tree that overhung from next door. He waited for her to sit down before he too sat. Her heart beat slow and hard as her mouth dried.

'It won't take long to tell you. It's the same old story, I'm afraid…'

Aaron listened closely while she spoke. She made herself look at him when she had finished.

'So now you know.' She shrugged, then wished she hadn't. It might look as if she didn't care, when really it was nerves.

'You have just convinced me,' Aaron said slowly, 'that you're the right girl for me. I've wanted to tell my own story, to give you the chance to make up your mind about me.'

'Your story?'

'When I was a soldier, I came back on leave. I didn't come home. I stayed on the south coast and while I was there, I had a fling with a girl called Lily. She was the most beautiful girl I'd ever seen…until now. I never saw her again, but I sometimes wonder about her. I went back to find her after the war. I didn't like to barge in on her, so I called at the village shop and asked after her. I said I was an old friend. The shopkeeper said she wasn't Lily Hopkins any more, she was Lily Rogers.'

'Married?'

'With two children. I didn't feel I could ask anything else. What I wanted to know was when the older child had been born, but I couldn't ask that, especially not with other folk in the shop, all listening.'

'Did you go and see her?' Molly asked.

'I would have liked to, but it might have caused trouble for her. I hope with all my heart that I didn't leave her in trouble; I hope she wasn't obliged to marry a man she wouldn't otherwise have chosen; but I'll never know.' Aaron leaned forward, capturing Molly's hands in his and holding them tenderly, rubbing them with the pads of his thumbs. 'I might have fathered a baby out of wedlock and that helps me understand what happened to you and the unbearable choice you had to make. I hope your baby was adopted by a loving couple with the means to provide a comfortable background. I hope your child is loved and appreciated every single day. And I hope the same thing for my child, if I have one.'

'Oh, Aaron.' Tears thickened her voice. 'When I told Norris, he *forgave* me.'

'Forgave you?'

Aaron's indignation healed something inside Molly that had long been raw. Forgiveness from one man, understanding from another. Her body felt lighter as a burden was removed.

Aaron slid from the chair onto one knee, his face close to hers. 'I can't wait any longer to ask. Will you let me take care of you, Molly? Will you do me the honour of becoming my wife and having a family with me?'

'Mr Abrams! Mr Abrams!'

With a gusty sigh, Aaron rose to his feet, but he kept hold of Molly's hand.

'Over here,' he called.

A couple of lads skidded into view. 'Daniel Cropper's uncle has come to take him away. Mrs Rostron says do you want to say goodbye?'

There was a dazed look in Aaron's eyes. Molly squeezed his hand.

'We'll both go.'

They made their way to the office, where Mrs Rostron was speaking to a man whose plumpness and ruddy colour made him a shocking contrast to the brother he had lost. Danny stood to one side, his fidgety hands making him appear unsettled and downcast.

'Mr Abrams,' said Mrs Rostron, 'and Miss Watson: I wasn't expecting you. May I introduce Mr Angus Cropper? Mr Cropper, Mr Abrams and Miss Watson.'

'How do you do?' Molly was aware of Aaron's tension. It wasn't like him at all. He was normally good-natured and calm.

'How do?' Mr Cropper turned to his nephew. 'Say goodbye, Daniel.'

'His name is Danny,' Aaron said quietly.

'I beg your pardon?' said Mr Cropper.

'His name is Danny. That's what he prefers to be called. It's what his parents called him.'

Mr Cropper gave Danny a smile. 'Danny it is, then.'

'Mr Abrams saved me the night of the accident,' Danny piped up. 'So did Miss Watson.'

'We were in the right place at the right time.' Molly didn't know what was happening, but she felt she had to step in and protect Aaron during this situation.

'Thank you for what you did.' Mr Cropper slanted an uncertain look at Aaron before saying heartily, 'Time to go, Daniel – Danny.' He laughed. 'That'll take a bit of getting used to. I've always thought of you as Daniel.'

'Where have you been?' Aaron asked quietly. 'All this time, since Danny's dad died, where have you been?'

'Mr Abrams,' said Mrs Rostron, 'that is not your concern.'

'I've been working. What do you think I've been doing?'

'I wouldn't know,' said Aaron. 'I only know what you should have done. You should have got here as fast as you could to take charge of a boy who needs a new parent.'

'Now see here—' began Mr Cropper.

'No, you see here,' Aaron retorted. 'You're supposed to be the one taking care of Danny. You've had over a week to get yourself down here and you haven't bothered.'

'I've been busy—'

'So have I. I've been at work, and I've spent time with the kids here, and I've had young Danny sleeping round at my house because he was too upset to sleep in a dormitory. I've paid attention to him. I've tried to help him. I even saved his life. What have you done for him? Other than carry on working because you couldn't be bothered to fetch him. You? You didn't even know his proper name.' Aaron pushed back his shoulders, standing taller than Mr Cropper. 'One of us, sir, has behaved as a father should – and it isn't you.'

Chapter Thirty-Six

'YOU DON'T MIND my getting married first, do you, Dora?' Molly asked as they strolled arm in arm to Tilda's to help finish the bridesmaids' dresses. 'Back in May, we all thought you were getting married quickly by setting a date in September. Now here I am, going to get wed in August. I hope you don't think I'm stealing your thunder.'

'Course not – well, maybe for a minute.' Dora squeezed her arm. 'But let's face it. Your wedding won't be a patch on mine. How special can it be when you've given yourself only three weeks to build up to it? Besides, after your mad moment when you dumped Norris, you were jolly lucky to find another man. I don't blame you for wanting to rush him up the aisle.'

About to protest, Molly stopped herself. Nothing would ever change Dora's view.

'I'm glad you've got an engagement ring at last,' said Dora, 'though I'm surprised you didn't opt for something showier. If I'd been kept waiting all those years, I'd have wanted something the size of an egg.'

Molly laughed. 'Strictly speaking, I haven't been kept waiting at all. Norris never wanted an engagement ring, and that was something I agreed to at the time; and Aaron certainly didn't keep me waiting.'

Even so, there was some truth in what Dora said. Taken to the jeweller's by Aaron, she had half expected to choose something – well, showy, for want of a better word. A ring that would make up for the years of pretending not to want one, when she was engaged to Norris. Instead, she had fallen for a simple ring with a row of five dainty sapphires. It was perfect and in due course her wedding band would snuggle nicely alongside it.

She had moved back home to her parents', so she could spend her final days as a spinster under her father's roof.

'Eh, my lass,' said Gran. 'I'm pleased and proud you've got your happy ending.'

'I'm not going to say I'm sorry I left Norris,' Molly told her, 'but I am sorry it caused you such worry.'

'You've ended up with a better man and that's what counts.'

'Better? I thought you liked Norris.'

'I did. We all did. So did you for a long time. There's nowt wrong with Norris, but your Aaron has a bigger heart. Norris would never have opened heart and home to yon lad.'

Yon lad: Danny. Molly and Aaron were united in their wish for a family and their first child was going to be Danny Cropper, who was already calling himself Danny Cropper Abrams, bless him.

'I'm the first to admit,' said Aaron, 'that when I let rip at Angus Cropper, I never imagined I would have a son by the end of the conversation, but I couldn't be happier or more proud.'

Uncle Angus hadn't put up much of a fight, but he had promised to keep in touch, a promise Molly and Aaron intended to keep him to.

Danny had wanted to move into Soapsuds Cottage immediately, but Aaron laughingly refused.

'Not until Molly and I are married. That way, the three of us begin our new life together. It's not fair if you and I have a head start, Danny.'

Molly was well aware of the special relationship between Aaron and Danny and, to start with, she wondered whether Danny would feel less close to her; but she needn't have worried.

'I miss my mum,' Danny confided in a whisper. 'I can't wait to have you as my new mum.'

When she hugged him, he hugged her back, sending a burst of love coursing through her. Her child. Her son. Not her first child, but the first she would have with Aaron.

And then came the possibility of a second.

She had called round to Wilton Close and they were all in the sitting room, when Lucy asked if she might have a word.

'Of course.' Molly smiled. She was fond of Lucy.

'In private.' Lucy glanced down, avoiding the looks that came her way.

'What's this about?' asked Miss Hesketh.

'If it's private...' Miss Patience murmured.

'Very well,' Miss Hesketh conceded.

'Shall we go upstairs?' said Molly. That seemed cosier than suggesting the dining room.

At the top of the stairs, Lucy led the way into Molly's old room. 'This is my room now, though Vivienne still lets me use her wardrobe.'

Lucy sat on the bed, indicating to Molly to join her. Lucy twisted her delicate silver bracelet around on her wrist, her gaze fixed on it.

'There's something I'd like to ask you, but I'm not sure how to.'

Molly understood. 'You want to ask about the birth.'

Lucy's head swung up and she met Molly's eyes. 'No, it's not that. It is to do with the baby, though.' She stopped.

'Tell me.' Molly spoke gently, but her mind was racing. If not the birth, then what?

'It's about you adopting that boy – Danny.'

'Yes?'

'Would you – would you consider having my baby too? You've been good to me and – well…' Lucy's voice trailed away. 'It feels like the right thing to do. Will you think about it?'

Before Molly could finish speaking, Aaron gave her his answer.

'Yes. You of all people understand how a mother longs for her child to be part of a loving family. If Lucy hands over her baby to us, she'll do it in the knowledge that that is guaranteed.'

Molly had never loved Aaron more than she did in that moment. This was the man she wanted. A man who put family first, above all else; and a man whose notion of family was broad and generous. She couldn't wait to be his wife.

She was ready to burst with pride when he accompanied her to Wilton Close to tell Lucy they would be honoured to adopt her child.

'If you're sure that's what you want,' he told Lucy.

'I'm sure,' said Lucy.

But a few days later, while Aaron was helping her measure for new curtains, Mr Hesketh himself descended on Soapsuds Cottage, with steam pouring forth from his ears.

'Do you imagine I'll permit my daughter's child to grow up in a poky cottage like this, with a lowly caretaker for a father?'

'I may not have your money or social standing, sir,' Aaron replied, calm and civil, 'but my fiancée and I are decent people with a lot of love to give, and we're more than happy to give it to Lucy's child.'

After Mr Hesketh had stormed off, Aaron turned to Molly, his brows furrowing in concern.

'Do you think he'll talk Lucy out of it?'

Molly sighed. 'Who knows? I hope she'll stand firm, but it's a long time until December.'

'Imagine calling Soapsuds Cottage poky.' Aaron pretended to be indignant. 'Just let him come back in a few weeks and see Soapsuds House.'

Old Mrs Mulvey from next door had gone to live with her daughter. Mr Dawson, the landlord, who was a regular employer of Perkins and Watson, had agreed to let the two cottages be knocked into one.

'We won't have a two-up two-down,' said Danny. 'We'll have a four-up four-down.'

Dad and Tom and their crew had already started work and intended to get it finished in time for Molly and Aaron to come home to after their honeymoon. While they were away, Danny was going to stay with Mum and Dad and get to know his new family.

Molly was back in everyone's good books now that she was getting married. It was vexing to think she had to get wed to gain approval, but that was the way of the world.

'One thing is certain,' she told Aaron. 'If we have daughters, I won't measure their worth or success by whether they bag suitable husbands. Having said that,' she added with a cheeky smile, 'I'm glad I bagged you.'

Molly was enjoying being back at home with her family. Mum, Dad and Tom appreciated it too. Her confession about her lost child had created a new closeness between them and being together gave it a chance to flourish.

'I know nothing will make up for the one you gave up,' said Mum, 'but I hope you have a houseful to keep you busy.'

Molly quite liked the idea of her own houseful, but at the same time she fancied being more than a wife and mother. Her stints at the Board of Health and St Anthony's had given her a taste for that kind of work, so when she received an invitation to meet with Mrs Rostron, her heart bumped in anticipation. Might she be offered her old job back?

When she made her way up the stairs, she found Carmel at the desk in the alcove. Carmel came round to give her a hug.

'Do you know why I'm here?' Molly asked.

'No, but Miss Hesketh is in the office with Mrs Rostron.'

'I'll chat with you till she comes out.'

'No. You're here to see both of them,' said Carmel. 'Word of warning – Mrs Wardle has pushed her way in as well.'

Molly walked along the landing. She knocked and Mrs Rostron's voice called, 'Come.'

As she walked in, Mrs Wardle was saying, 'I am the Orphanage Committee's official visitor and if you're holding a meeting that includes a former member of staff whose outrageous behaviour led to her being sacked, it is imperative that I am included.'

'Very well.' If Mrs Rostron was displeased, she did a good job of hiding it; a far better job than Molly could have managed. 'I'll ask for another chair to be brought.'

'I'll do that,' Molly offered at once.

'It isn't your place to do any such thing,' cut in Mrs Wardle. 'You have no authority here now.'

'Mrs Wardle is correct, Miss Watson,' said Mrs Rostron, 'though perhaps not for the right reason. It isn't the place of an invited guest to do such things.'

Opening the door, Mrs Rostron called down the landing to Carmel to ask for another chair. Soon the four of them were settled, though it was a squeeze. It would have been more comfortable had Molly pushed her chair backwards and allowed the others more room, but when she attempted to do this, Mrs Rostron asked her to stay put.

'You need to be in the centre of this discussion, Miss Watson. Miss Hesketh has suggested that our more able girls could be taught basic office skills in the hope that one or two of them might become office juniors.'

'Office juniors?' Mrs Wardle exclaimed. 'That is ridiculous for so many reasons, I hardly know where to begin.'

'It is my understanding that the girls who leave here are placed in service or into shop work,' said Miss Hesketh. 'This will give the cleverer ones another option.'

'And what about the need for jobs that provide somewhere for them to live?' Mrs Wardle demanded.

'That's a problem, I grant you,' said Miss Rostron, 'but it's no reason not to try. The girls who go to work for the big department stores can sleep in the shop dormitories. Maybe a girl who works in the shop's offices would be permitted to sleep there too.'

'You'll over-educate them and give them unrealistic expectations,' said Mrs Wardle.

'We're going to give them another string to their bows,' Miss Hesketh replied.

'And what has this to do with Miss Watson?'

Mrs Rostron turned to Molly. 'Would you be prepared to teach the girls? It would take just a few hours a week. The pay would be very little, but I hope you'll agree that it would be worthwhile.'

'Me?' Molly looked at Miss Hesketh. 'But I'm only a pupil myself. I'm not even that any more.'

'You would be providing the girls with the most basic tuition,' said Miss Hesketh, 'and you're more than capable of that. I'll prepare a scheme of work for you to teach and give you guidance in how to conduct lessons.'

Mrs Wardle snorted. 'I don't know what makes you think that the Orphanage Committee will employ anyone to undertake such an unpromising scheme.'

'Miss Hesketh has a sponsor in mind to pay the bill,' said Mrs Rostron.

'My dear brother, I am sure, will be glad to put his hand in his pocket. Far from being unpromising, this undertaking will fit in nicely with his commitment to the business school. He'll pay a small wage to Miss Watson; or to Mrs Abrams, as she soon will be.' Miss Hesketh gave Molly a brief smile.

'You can't get round it that easily.' Complacency oozed out of Mrs Wardle's every pore and the miniature wisteria on her hat shimmered. 'We don't employ married women. In common with all right-minded employers, we believe their place is in the home.'

'But the orphanage won't be employing Miss Watson,' said Mrs Rostron. 'The business school will employ her and she'll be here as a volunteer.'

'She might not be on the payroll,' retorted Mrs Wardle, 'but she'll be here working. You can't wriggle out of it that way. I will not have this person,' and she shuddered as she glanced at Molly, 'on these premises after the way she behaved. She isn't fit to work here. She's a bad example and I'll make sure the Orphanage Committee thinks so too.'

'A bad example?' said Mrs Rostron. 'Miss Watson is a heroine, who helped to save the life of one of our children. I think she's a splendid example and I'm sure the Committee will agree.'

Mrs Wardle bounced to her feet. 'We'll see about that.' She marched from the room – or she would have marched, but there wasn't space. She bumbled her way round Molly's chair and made a grab for the door.

'Well!' Mrs Rostron let out a gusty sigh as the door closed behind Mrs Wardle.

'Shall you be able to sway the Committee?' Molly asked anxiously.

'I've taken the precaution of talking privately to a couple of the members already and I'm confident that you'll shortly be asked to take up this new role. I suggest that you make ready by seeking Mr Abrams's permission for you to do the work.'

'Permission?' Molly exclaimed.

'If you're a married woman, the Committee will require it.'

Outrage flushed through Molly's frame. She forced herself to speak softly. 'Did you need permission from your husband to work here?'

'Mine is a courtesy title, bestowed upon me by the Orphanage Committee,' Mrs Rostron said drily. 'Apparently, having Mrs in front of my name gives me more authority.'

Miss Hesketh made no attempt to disguise a *huh* sound. 'Miss has served me perfectly well all these years.'

'What do you say, Miss Watson?' asked Mrs Rostron. 'St Anthony's would be pleased to have you back. Are you interested?'

'...so I need a letter of permission from you.' Molly sat in Aaron's workshop, trying not to look as if she was fuming. There had been a moment back in Mrs Rostron's office when she had felt like turning down the opportunity out of sheer annoyance, but that would have been cutting off her nose to spite her face. She didn't want to do that – but, oh, it was galling having to ask for permission, even from the man she loved.

Aaron held out his arms. 'Can I have a hug?'

'What for?'

'I think I'm going to need one. You look as if you're about to explode.'

She shook her head, trying not to smile. 'I'd like to explode, but not all over you. I'm trying not to take it out on you.'

'Good. Give me a hug.'

She walked into his arms. 'If this is intended to take my mind off the – the...'

'Insult? Inappropriateness?'

'...the matter of needing my husband's permission, it isn't going to work.'

'I know; but I hope it reminds you that I love you, Molly Watson, and I'm proud to think that Mrs Rostron wants you back. Do you feel a little less inclined to explode now?'

'A little. Keep talking.'

'What's this? Fishing for compliments?' Laughing, Aaron gently put her from him, though he kept her hands in his. 'The best compliment I can pay you in this situation is to tell you what I'll say in my letter. I'm not going to use the words "permission" or "I agree to". I'll say, "I am proud to be married to the teacher who is going to help some orphan-girls make something of themselves." Will that be all right?'

She pretended to consider. 'Not bad. Could have been a lot worse.'

'Could have made you explode.'

'You'd never do that.'

'Never on purpose, I promise.'

'And never through thoughtlessness,' she said. 'I know you, Aaron Abrams. You've got a big heart.'

'Full of love for you, and plenty left over for the family we'll have.' Letting go of her hands, he delved in his pocket. 'I was saving this for later, but this seems like the right time.' He produced a long, flat box. 'For you.'

With a flutter of excitement, Molly took the box and lifted the lid. Inside lay a necklace. On a simple silver chain hung a pair of flat silver hearts, one a complete heart, the other just a silver outline.

'I designed it myself,' said Aaron, 'and the silversmith made it. The complete heart is for the son you had to give up. The heart-outline is for the open-hearted attitude we share about the family we're going to build.'

'It's perfect,' Molly breathed. Her fingertip brushed the heart-outline. To anyone else, it might look like an empty heart, but to her it was as filled with meaning as the solid heart that was in memory of the son she had had to give up.

'Let me fasten it,' Aaron offered.

She turned her back to him, bending her head and brushing her hair away from her neck. The necklace was light and cool against her skin.

Aaron turned her round to face him. 'Perfect,' he said, but it was her face he was looking at. 'Let's go and tell our son about your new job, shall we?'

With fingers warmly intertwined, they went to find Danny.

Acknowledgements

I am grateful to my agent, Laura Longrigg, and my editor, Susannah Hamilton, whose guidance helped make this a better book.

Thanks to all at Corvus, including Poppy Mostyn-Owen and Karen Duffy; and to Nicky Lovick, the copy editor.

Several chapters of this book was written during a wonderful week in Bath with fellow writers Jane Cable, Cass Grafton, Kirsten Hesketh and Kitty Wilson. Thanks, ladies, for all your support.

I should also mention NaNoWriMo. Every November, writers all over the world join in with the annual madness of aiming to write 50,000 words in a month. *The Surplus Girls' Orphans* was my NaNo project in 2018 and I managed to write 66,000 words that month, though, if I'm honest, I have to say that by the time December came round, I could barely scrape together enough brain cells to finish the book.

Love and thanks to Jennie across the Pond and Gayle down under. Also to Beverley and Sandra, who were first off the mark with their reviews and helped get *The Surplus Girls* off to a flying start.